THE
ANGEL
OF
WATERLOO

THE ANGEL OF WATERLOO

JACKIE FRENCH

Angus&Robertson
An imprint of HarperCollins*Publishers*

Angus&Robertson
An imprint of HarperCollins*Publishers*, Australia

HarperCollins*Publishers*
Australia • Brazil • Canada • France • Germany • Holland •India
Italy • Japan • Mexico • New Zealand • Poland • Spain • Sweden
Switzerland • United Kingdom • United States of America

First published in Australia in 2020
This edition published in Australia in 2021
by HarperCollins*Publishers* Australia Pty Limited
ABN 36 009 913 517
harpercollins.com.au

A catalogue record for this book is available from the National Library of Australia

ISBN 978 1 4607 5936 3 (paperback)
ISBN 978 1 4607 1161 3 (ebook)
ISBN 978 1 4607 8613 0 (international audio book)

Cover design by Mark Campbell, HarperCollins Design Studio
Cover image © Mary Jane Ansell
Author photograph by Kelly Sturgiss
Typeset in Sabon LT Std by Kirby Jones
Printed and bound by CPI Group (UK) Ltd, Croydon, CR0 4YY

*To all those who love the Matilda Saga —
and to the hundreds of generations of women
whose stories have become part of it.*

Chapter 1

WATERLOO

18 JUNE 1815

She'd been born on a battlefield; she'd lost her mother on another. Perhaps this would be the battlefield she died on.

Death crawled around her outside this small fort made of the piled bodies of French and English soldiers. A dozen living men perched their muskets on those who had once been their comrades to ward off attack.

Beyond the safety of her square, a thousand men, or ten thousand men, lay around her wounded or dead. Horsemen slashed at their enemies, though the main battlefront had moved hours before. The grey and yellow smoke made it impossible to see more than a few yards ahead.

The luckiest lay still. Other shattered bodies scrambled, struggled, men with legs blown off, some dragging their intestines as they vainly, briefly searched for aid.

Hen could not help them all.

She kept her eyes on the more superficial stomach wound she was stitching, glad her patient was unconscious, for she had neither the strength nor an orderly to keep him still. He was fifteen, perhaps, the same age as her, a smoke-black face seeping red from yet another wound, a scrape of shrapnel, perhaps, or a sword cut. Her father had ceased stitching altogether, taping wounds while their supplies held out. He and Hen had arrived in Brussels the day before, too late to acquire the horses, mules and panniers to which he was entitled. They had only the equipment they could carry.

Surgeon Gilbert's orders had been to proceed immediately to the Mont-Saint-Jean farm house. He, Hen and Assistant Surgeon Thompson had set out on the Waterloo road at first light, Hen wrapped in an old greatcoat, for the dawn was chill, even in midsummer. They'd trudged through mud and mist, and then green fields, and finally a wheat field sloping gently to a ridge. Larks sang, the wheat rustled. A few carts trundled past. Now and then horses passed them at a gallop, the only sign of war.

And then the thunder, ripping the air, the ground vibrating. Hen instinctively looked at the sky, but the noise didn't stop.

This storm was cannon. Somewhere beyond the ridge ahead of them the battle had finally begun. Within a few heartbeats white horses erupted through the wheat, their blue-coated French riders with sabres drawn.

Surgeon Gilbert flung Hen down into the mud. Men in red coats scrambled past, panting from a drift of gunpowder fog. British soldiers fleeing towards Brussels, thought Hen, holding her breath. They must be early deserters from what General Wellington called his 'infamous army', hastily assembled to fight the returning Napoleon.

She froze as the French cavalry pursued the men through the field, slashing at necks, shoulders, the horses rearing, their hooves striking down any man who tried to protect himself with bayonet or sword.

Minutes passed, or hours. Hen tried to peer towards the ridge, but already the battle smoke was too thick to make out what was happening. Even as she looked the haze spread towards them. More redcoats ran past, screaming, dying under the hooves of the cavalry horses or from sabre cuts. So many men, trying vainly to escape ...

Surely the battle had not been lost so soon? Napoleon had won the skirmishes at Ligny and Quatre Bras, but even he could not have defeated all the Allied armies within an hour, Hen assured herself. More men and horses appeared like apparitions in the smoke, then vanished, then surged forwards once more.

At last the French cavalry retreated, a waving mass of red feathers and the glint of steel. There was no need for her father to tell her that it was impossible to head to Mont-Saint-Jean now. Instead Surgeon Gilbert managed to grab the sleeve of one of the fleeing redcoats. He and his friends hesitated, staring at Hen, then her father, then back to Hen again, unmistakably female despite her army coat, her gold plaits shining under her cap.

'We need to form a square,' ordered Surgeon Gilbert. 'Hurry, you louts, if you want to live!'

The first man stared at him. 'Ain't got enough men to form a square ...'

'Use the dead to build the walls,' said Surgeon Gilbert shortly.

The man blinked, then gestured to his companions. Assisting a surgeon in a defended square suddenly seemed safer than retreat harried by French cavalry — especially if, by some miracle and the inspired leadership of the Duke of Wellington, the Allied side won.

Slowly other soldiers joined them, packing the bodies three or four deep at the base till the walls of dead were chest high — tall enough to shelter the living as the tides of battle swept back and forth, low enough to let them fire at the enemy, leaving a small gap that would let in a man, but not a horse. A square was impregnable, if each man held his position and kept his firearms loaded. Even cavalry could not penetrate an infantry square as long as the men who made up each side held their nerve. This square was doubly impregnable. The dead who made its walls could not retreat.

Hen and her father kept their bodies low, binding, stitching, amputating, Assistant Surgeon Thompson placing those too badly injured to survive in rows at the back of the square, where they could die gazing at the sky, not under the hooves of cavalry horses.

That had been hours back. The wheat was now a swamp of blood and mud. The sun drooped halfway to the horizon, spreading an orange glow through black and yellow smoke. Horses shrieked in challenge or died, their cries guttural among the shouts and moans of men. Somewhere across the ridge Napoleon and Wellington must still be urging on their troops. The ground trembled from cannon fire and horses' hooves.

Hen's bonnet sat on the muck-soaked soil, holding surgical instruments. Her cap had become a cover for an amputated thigh. She still wore the coat, despite the heat, for she had mislaid her apron. Even her plaits had come loose: a nuisance, as she had to keep pushing the hair from her eyes as she worked, gold now streaked with blood.

She bit off the final piece of thread from the stomach wound and began to stitch the boy's face, three quick stitches merely to hold the cut together, rather than the sixteen that would have meant less scarring.

There was no time at Waterloo for neatness.

Hen moved to the next man lined up against the wall of bodies. A veteran, for his red uniform had faded to pink, thirty perhaps.

And dead. She laid a blood-stiff coat over his face so her father would not waste time on a soldier beyond man's aid, and wiped the tears from her cheeks. The dead man deserved tears, even if she didn't know his name. The man lying beside him — a captain by his uniform — opened eyes as blue as the sky above the smoke and cloud. He stared at Hen and raised a trembling hand to touch her hair. 'I am in Heaven then.'

'Not yet I warrant, sir.' Hen sliced open his trousers to try to find the source of the blood still pooling on the ground. If the blood flowed, they were still alive. 'How goes the battle, Captain?'

'Lost,' said the captain, still smiling at her vaguely. He yawned, as men did as they died from loss of blood. 'The French killed Ponsonby, you know. They've routed the Scots Greys. The Household Cavalry are all broken up.'

He didn't seem to notice Hen staring at his thigh. His femoral artery had been sliced through. It was a miracle he had lived even a few minutes. Already his eyes were closing. 'The French waited till we were sixty feet away,' he murmured, almost happily. 'They opened fire. The whole rank of us mowed down like grass before a scythe ...'

The words faded. Hen gently shut his eyes.

'Don't you listen to 'im, Miss. The French cavalry is spent. The Iron Duke 'as us forming squares.' The speaker might have been thirty or eighty, with the leathery skin of a lifetime soldier. 'Don't you worry about me, neither,' he added. 'Just got me arm broke. Got it set right now. I'll be up and at 'em.'

Hen glanced at his arm. It had indeed been set, strapped to what looked like a French bayonet, though she doubted the man would be able to walk, much less fight ...

Which soldier was correct? Wellington had never lost a battle yet, but nor had he ever faced Napoleon, the master strategist of Europe. But Hen had seen enough warfare to know that those in the midst of battle might know least, for all they could see was their small corner.

'Hen! I need you!' Impossible to hear her father's words from across the square, but she guessed what he was saying as he nodded at a bloodstained sergeant the volunteers had placed on the ground before him.

She grabbed her bonnet of instruments and ducked over to him, keeping her head down, for shots still rang out around them, even if the main forces were deployed elsewhere, then crouched beside him. Surgeon Gilbert's arms were red to the elbow, and his leather apron black and dripping.

Their patient on the blood-damp ground was young to be a sergeant, short and wiry. A cut bled freely on his cheek, but pumped strongly from his lower leg, cloth and flesh mangled together.

And she knew him. Had she met him after the battle of Vimeiro? Or was it Corunna, Talavera, Lisbon, Ciudad Rodrigo, Salamanca? Perhaps it had been the Battle of Toulouse. Toulouse was where Mama had died, a cut turned septic so even her remedies couldn't cure her. Hen and her father's grief remained private among the public triumph as General Wellesley — now the Duke of Wellington — defeated Marshal Soult, ending Napoleon's rule over most of Europe.

Until ninety days ago, when Napoleon returned.

'Papa, it's Sergeant Drivers,' she said urgently. 'Remember? We met him and his wife just after the Battle of Salamanca. Sergeant Drivers.'

Surgeon Gilbert stared wearily at the crumpled body in front of him. 'That was a good night,' he said slowly.

Hen nodded. Sergeant Drivers had just been promoted on the field for bravery. He'd stolen a chicken to celebrate, breaking Wellesley's orders not to loot. He'd asked Mama to hide it. The best place to hide a chicken, of course, was in a stew pot.

She remembered the sergeant's mischievous face as he opened his coat to show Mama his feathered plunder. Sergeant Drivers and his wife had dined with them that night, on Spanish chicken stewed with orange juice and almonds, and Mama's soda bread. The sergeant's wife was Spanish, like Mama. She and Mama had danced after dinner, clicking their fingers instead of castanets, while one of the carters played a guitar, a crowd gathering to clap the beat.

And then the sergeant had danced with Hen, showing her the steps and laughing at her mistakes. So many women to choose from, but he had asked a twelve-year-old girl to dance with him ...

'His leg will have to go,' said Surgeon Gilbert abruptly.

Not his leg, thought Hen desperately. How could he dance with only one leg?

Sergeant Drivers stared up at them, echoing her thoughts. 'A man's no use without a leg.'

But there was no choice. Or rather there was a choice, but little time in which to make it. The sergeant had lost too much blood already. She took a breath, steadying herself, and bent down close to him. 'Sergeant Drivers,' she said clearly.

The sergeant tried to focus on her face. 'Little Miss Hen,' he muttered.

'Not so little now. Do you trust me, Sergeant?'

'Little Miss Hen,' he repeated, still gazing at her, as if wondering what she was doing among the bayonets and cannon.

'My father is a surgeon, remember? I'm helping him. If we don't take off your leg you'll lose your life. Do you understand? Please. Your leg or your life?'

Sergeant Drivers's gaze met hers. 'Life,' he said at last. He managed to smile. 'Little Miss Hen! Best chicken I ever ate.'

'Remember it now,' said Hen, automatically smiling back at him. *Sometimes we can give nothing but a smile*. After which battle had Mama said that? Hen had smiled at every patient since.

'Just keep thinking of that chicken and how you'll be eating more, and just as good. Is Mrs Drivers with you?' Hen grabbed the iron clamp.

'Aye, Isobel's waiting for me in Brussels ...' The words became a gasp as Hen twisted the clamp around his thigh, cutting off the blood supply as Thompson held the man down.

Surgeon Gilbert's bone saw began to cut through flesh, muscle and both bones in the man's leg. The amputation took less than a minute — the time that it took for Sergeant Drivers to scream eight times, gripping the ground with white fingers, holding himself with such iron control that the assistant surgeon didn't need to hold him down. Few surgeons could cut as fast or as neatly as Surgeon Gilbert. His patients mostly survived.

Hen took up the wooden-handled surgical iron, red hot in its bed of coals. Sergeant Drivers screamed again as she pressed the iron to the living stump.

Sergeant Drivers fainted, which meant Hen did not have to spare him some of her small supply of laudanum till he was conscious again. The wound was now sealed cleanly, with no further bleeding, and so unlikely to become infected, especially with his wife to care for him. Assuming the French allowed those in this square to live …

She blinked away tears. Useless tears. Stupid tears. But she had never seen a man take his surgery so bravely.

'Don't want to be tripping over this.' Thompson hauled the sergeant's shattered leg over to the wall of bodies. Hen forced herself not to look at it. It had been such a happy night …

Surgeon Gilbert wearily moved to the next man in line — a Frenchman, but Thompson had checked he was unarmed and Surgeon Gilbert did not refuse to tend the enemy. Hen picked one of the last clean rags from the surgery bag and dipped it in rose oil. She tied it carefully over Sergeant Drivers's stump, then removed the clamp. She took his hand as she studied his face, noting the darkness of blood loss under his eyes, but his pulse was strong. What had he and his wife been doing since Salamanca? Serving in the Americas perhaps …

Something moved behind her. She turned in time to see a young man — an officer in the fine uniform of the Hussars — quickly dismount from his horse, then haul the bloody body draped over it across his shoulder. He stepped through the narrow passage in their protecting wall of dead and laid the body down.

He beckoned to Hen. 'Surgeon! Attend this man. Now!'

'He'll have to wait his turn.' Hen moved towards the next patient. Back in their Peninsular days her father had adopted the new French system of triage — the most urgent cases attended first, no matter what their rank. Those he knew he could not help were not treated at all.

'How dare you?' The officer grabbed the collar of her coat and hauled her up to face him. 'Egad, sir, I'll have you cashiered for this. This man is a lieutenant in the Household Cavalry ...'

'I don't care if he's the Prince of Wales. Let go, you fool, or you'll get us both shot.' She pulled away from him, ducking down behind the cover of the walls again.

The officer squatted automatically and stared at her. Hen knew the moment he actually saw her face above the bulk of her army greatcoat, the tangle of her blonde hair.

'You're a girl!' The officer stared around the square. 'Someone said there was a surgeon here.' He hesitated. 'They've burned the chateau. I'd better try to get him to the hospital at Mont-Saint-Jean. But my horse is blown and there's Frenchies on either side. I don't know that he'll make it.'

The body on the ground groaned, becoming a young man, twenty perhaps. Hen kneeled, quickly assessing him. A pale face, with the sunken eyes of massive blood loss; his left arm shattered just below the elbow, a rough tourniquet above. No other wound visible.

The young man opened his eyes and stared at her. Brown eyes, the clearest she had ever seen. A small eddy of clean air and sunlight drifted over them. 'An angel come to hell,' the young man whispered, then closed his eyes again.

'Where is the surgeon?' demanded the other officer urgently, peering through the smoke.

'Busy.' She did not bother to call the man 'sir'. Surgeon Gilbert would operate on at least another six men before he would attend this lieutenant. 'Threatening him won't help,' she added, with pride.

Her father had been on a half-pay pension when he had taken up his commission again only a week earlier. If Wellington won — *when* Wellington won, Hen told herself — her father would probably be put back on half pay once more: there would be little need for army surgeons once the war was over. But there'd be the prize money from this battle. It might even be enough to have the cottage by the sea he had promised her mother, and which her mother had not lived to see.

And if Napoleon won?

Hen closed her mind to that.

'It will have to be Mont-Saint-Jean then. The surgeons there will obey orders!' The officer hesitated, peering out into the smoke as if he had lost all sense of direction.

The young man on the ground opened his eyes again. 'Get yourself killed trying,' he muttered.

He was right. Hen realised she had seen more battles than either of these men. This was almost certainly their first. A lone rider had no protection, with enemies on every side ...

'I'll see to him,' she said.

'You! You're a girl. A child!'

'That arm has to come off. You can either help me amputate it, or get back to your regiment.' She reached for the clamp.

'Don't be ridiculous, girl.' The officer bent, obviously intending to carry his friend away.

Hen grabbed his arm in fury. 'I am the best chance this man has, sir. No, I'm not an army surgeon, but you'll be lucky today to find one with more experience, or better training. Now either get out of the way or help me.'

'I'll see you damned before I'll let —'

Hen reached for the pistol under her coat. For some reason it seemed essential that this man, among the tens of thousands dying, should have a chance to live, just like Sergeant Drivers.

'Tim ...' The officer bent to hear the whisper. Hen left her pistol in her sash.

'Never argue with an angel.' The young guardsman managed to hold up his shattered forearm. 'It seems my arm is now surplus to requirements. I would be most grateful, miss, if you would ...' His voice clenched to a stop from screaming in another spasm of pain.

'Here.' Hen reached into her bag. She still had some laudanum, home-made and strong, though nowhere near enough of it. She put the bottle to the man's lips, waited till he'd sipped, then recorked it. She tightened the clamp, removed the rag, then handed the officer the scissors. 'Cut away as much of his sleeve as you can.'

'Why?'

'Infection. Any foreign matter in the wound could kill him. Be quiet, don't distract me, and do what you are told.'

The officer blinked at her. Probably no woman had spoken to him like that since his nanny in the nursery. But he did begin to cut the cloth, and carefully.

The young lieutenant's breathing slowed with the dose of laudanum. Hen reached for the bone saw as his eyes shut, hesitated, then took up a scalpel instead. A saw cut through bone and so was faster, and speed was necessary if a patient was not to die of shock. But the laudanum would give her time to cut back flaps of muscle and skin that could be sewn more neatly round the stump. It might even ... Hen wiped the smoke from her eyes, and looked at the arm more closely. The bone was broken, but bone mended. 'I can save his arm. I think.'

'You think?'

'Go and find a splint. A length of wood. A bayonet will do. Hurry!' She poured brandy onto the wound, splashed a little more on her implements, then used the tweezers to probe for splinters of bone. Scalpel next, to cut the shattered flesh, then needle and waxed silk thread. She had just begun to sew when the officer returned. He'd found a rifle stock.

'Thank you. That's perfect.'

'Are you sure you know what you're doing?'

'No,' said Hen bluntly, still sewing. 'If I amputated and sealed the wound now he'd have less chance of infection.' She snipped off the thread, and began another stitch. 'But if the wound goes putrid his arm can still be amputated. Once it's off it can't be put back.'

The sounds behind them changed. A trumpet called. Other trumpets replied.

'I need to go.' The officer hesitated. 'You'll look after him?'

'Yes,' said Hen. She did not say that she had possibly condemned two or three others to death while she spent time trying to save a young man's arm. She pushed the thought from her mind. The first lesson her father taught his assistants — and his family — was to focus on what you could do and what you were doing. If you thought of what you could not do you would go mad.

She glanced up. The officer had vanished in the smoke. She couldn't even see the white smudge of his horse. Would he survive this day? Would any of them? Was anything — even control of Europe — worth all this?

Perhaps the world was mad. She bent to her stitching again.

Chapter 2

A Dry Wash for the Hair When on Campaign

Take Florentine Orris Root. Grate finely. Dry then grind to
Powder. Leave unsealed in a dry position for six Months for
the Perfume to strengthen. Dust towards the Scalp and brush
outwards. The Scent lingers for a Week or more and is most
pleasant.

From the Notebooks of Henrietta Bartley

Two hours later, judging by the red smudge where the sun sat
on the horizon, the young man was still alive, still sleeping, his
breathing deep and, to Hen's relief, his pulse steady and strong.
It was impossible to judge a dose of laudanum. Some seasons
the poppy seemed stronger than others. A little as needed was
best — impossible on a battlefield.

Was this still a battlefield? The air nearby no longer sang with
mortar fire, but cannon still thundered in the distance. Hen could
still faintly hear the far-off clash of metal above the groans and
cries for help. But other figures moved among the wounded now,
not fighting, but carrying the wounded to her and her father or
to the small French ambulance carts.

Did the French ambulances mean Napoleon had won? Or
was their square just in a small backwater of the ground, not
strategically important to either side?

A corporal who had lost an eye and part of his cheek had managed to tell Hen that the French had taken La Haye Sainte, almost the centre of the Allied army, before the pain of his wound and her padding and stitching had finally given him the blessing of unconsciousness. The little laudanum she had left needed to be kept for an emergency, though she did not care to think of emergencies worse than this.

Time enough to face them when they came.

Victory seemed impossible now. Around her, French, Belgian and English soldiers bled together. No Prussian or Dutch allies had been brought to their aid post, though a Hanoverian, twelve years old at most, had been brought in with both legs crushed at the knee. Were the vital Prussian and Dutch troops fighting elsewhere? Or had they retreated, believing the cause unwinnable, and never joined Wellington's forces?

If this battle was lost she would be dead by nightfall, used, abused, then killed by the rampaging enemy, who would take loot and women as their due. She had the pistol under her soldier's greatcoat in case of that. Wellington kept control of his men, except for the occasional stolen chicken or pig. But Hen believed he was the only general who did so. His forces fought for their country and, yes, for the prize money, but also with honour. Other generals' soldiers' reward for risking lives or limbs was the freedom to loot, to rape, to ransack, to do anything and everything they wished in a few days of vicious, victorious freedom. Hen had seen the bodies of women with their ears cut off for their earrings, their skirts ripped and bundled, clearly showing the use that had been made of their bodies.

There was nothing Hen could do to change the battle's outcome. Nor, just now, was there any urgent work at her station. Sergeant Drivers was still unconscious, but his pulse was steady, despite the loss of blood. All the men within the square of defenders alive and dead had been treated. Some men would live and some would die, but just now there was no more she could do for them. Even her water bottle was almost empty. Outside ...

No. This was not the time to consider the uncounted wounded beyond the square. Hen allowed herself to sit, and then to lean against the wall of bodies, already cold. Apart from the time spent hiding in the wheat field she had not rested since dawn.

Eat, she told herself. There was bread and sausage in her bag, and a bottle of cold chicory coffee from the elderly woman they had been billeted with.

'Hen?' Her father stood grey faced, his eyes red rimmed, Thompson at his side. 'I don't think the fighting is going to head back this way, at least not for a while. We're going to see what we can do outside. Don't leave till I get back.'

She nodded. She did not ask if she could go with him, knowing the answer.

'You've done good work, girl. Now eat.'

She managed a smile. Always smile when you say goodbye, Mama had said, in case you do not get the chance again. Was this the last time she would see her father?

She watched as Surgeon Gilbert vanished in the smoke beyond the wall. Hen ate and drank, and felt her hands steady. She stood and peered out of the square, trying to ignore that the wall that had protected her had faces, unblinking eyes, blood already dried to black. But her father and Thompson were lost in the swirls of grey and yellow.

An English rider neared, his horse foam flecked, limping. The man seemed whole, till Hen saw he gripped the rein in his teeth. 'Do you need help, sir?' she called.

The horse slowed. 'Broke me arms, but they've been set.' His voice was hoarse from smoke and shouting. 'Looking for me younger brother. You've wounded in there?'

'Yes.'

The rider nudged his horse over to the wall of bodies. He gazed at their faces, then down at the men on the ground, and shook his head.

'I hope you find him,' said Hen. 'Sir,' she added urgently, 'how goes the battle? Is it still being fought?'

'We've maybe got the Frenchies on the run, but it's too close to call. Lost most of our men, but maybe Boney's lost more. It'll come down to who can hold their forces together long enough to claim the field. No man will dare run from a square around by the Iron Duke.' He nudged his weary horse onwards, as it slowly picked its way among the bodies.

Victory, thought Hen, desperately hoping his assessment was true. Possibly. And at a massive price. She pushed her hair out of her eyes again, and turned to see that the young man whose arm she had so carefully repaired was conscious, gazing at her. His lips moved. She moved closer, kneeled next to him to hear his voice.

'We've won?' His voice too was hoarse.

She hesitated. 'Yes,' she lied. Let him have what comfort he could.

'I knew we would.' He shut his eyes again.

He is possibly the only person in the world who was so sure, she thought. If the Iron Duke won today every man who'd survived would be a hero.

Though not girls, she thought. Even Mrs Fletcher and Mrs Marsh, who stood beside their men to load their muskets, and who took the muskets up to fire when their husbands fell, had never been mentioned in the broadsheets or the dispatches. Mrs Fletcher and Mrs Marsh had been friends of Mama, but both were dead now, like their husbands, one at Salamanca, one at Lisbon.

'What are you doing here?' The young man's voice was steady, despite his pallor. A good sign.

'Eating bread and sausage. Here.' Hen reached for the bottle of cold coffee. 'You need to drink. You've lost a lot of blood.' She glanced again at his bandages, but the wound was no longer even seeping. Her mother would have been proud of her.

She supported the young man's shoulders and held the bottle to his lips while he sipped, then took it away when he shook his head to say he'd had enough. She laid him down again, this time with a rifleman's coat folded to make a pillow. The rifleman did not need it now.

His lips twitched in the beginning of a smile. '*Why* are you here?'

'My father's a surgeon,' she said.

'And he brought you to a battle?' He sounded indignant.

'Yes,' said Hen shortly. This young man was definitely a green 'un. Anyone who'd been in the Peninsular campaigns would know a girl on her own in a strange town that would be looted if the French won here today was in more danger from retreating or rampaging soldiers than one working in a defended area on the battlefield.

He managed a full smile this time. 'I apologise for not being able to find anyone to introduce us properly.'

She smiled back, pushing her hair out of her eyes. 'My name is Hen.'

The smile became a grin. 'Hen as in cluck, cluck, cluck?'

'Hen as in "definitely not Henrietta". Hen means love where my father's family come from. Papa's Aunt Henrietta was supposed to be rich but all she left us was a mourning ring and a potted aspidistra.'

'What happened to the aspidistra?'

'Mama gave it to a family we were billeted with. Can't carry much when you are with the army. Aspidistras aren't any use. And we already had a chamberpot.'

Another smile. 'Your mother sounds … capable.'

'More than that. My father called her his miracle,' said Hen. She wanted to *talk*. Had to talk. She had spent the whole day murmuring reassurances and the last week had been too occupied by travel for conversation.

It would not be dark till near midnight this midsummer night, another two hours, at least, judging from the sword-like gleams of sun still perched on the horizon. By midnight she might be fighting off French soldiers, or trying to hide among the mountains of dead. She needed to remember the world beyond this battlefield, the good days between the battles when she and Mama and Papa had been a family, and had laughed.

'My mother taught me everything. How to deliver a baby or make a potion for the gout, or cook bread on a campfire, or catch pigeons for a stew. We mostly sold my father's rations and lived on what we could trap or shoot or forage. There are women who wait. My mother wasn't one of them. She went where my father went, and so did I. I still do.'

'Where's your mother now? Back in Brussels?'

'Dead. Not here,' she added quickly. 'A year ago.'

'I'm sorry.' It sounded like he really meant it. 'Another battle?'

'Yes,' said Hen shortly, though Mama's cut had gone septic two weeks after the battle itself was over. She checked her own hands again automatically, but they were unscratched.

'How long have you been following the army?'

'All my life.' For every man in the Peninsular army there'd been at least two women — wives, daughters, women of easy virtue — a massive train that followed the army wherever it went, halting briefly while the soldiers fought, then swarming onto the battlefield to retrieve the men, or bury them. Friendships forged in brief alliances to help and protect each other.

The young man gave the faintest grin that became a grimace of pain.

'Here.' Hen pulled the laudanum flask from her bag and held it to his lips. 'Just a sip.'

He did, wrinkling his nose at its bitterness. 'What's in it?'

'Laudanum. I made it myself. Tincture of poppy, a little monkshood, honey and brandy.'

'Waste of a decent brandy.'

'It wasn't that decent,' she admitted. 'Is the pain easing?'

'You know, it is. I can hardly feel it now.'

She didn't believe him: enough of the elixir to deaden the agony would kill him. But the dose she'd given him should be enough to make the pain bearable and, in a little while, she'd give him more, so he could sleep until his friend arrived — assuming he had survived — or other transport turned up to carry the officer back to his billet back in Brussels.

Or till the French arrived, and killed them all or — as he was an officer — took him as a prisoner for ransom. They would not bother to ransom her. But she would not think of that …

'Brussels,' she said wistfully. 'Did you go to the duchess's ball last night?'

'I did.'

She had thought from his accent that he was the kind of man a duchess would ask to her ball.

'Was it magnificent? I … I watched the guests enter on the way to our billet. The women in their jewels and dresses, and the Highlanders — I could hear them playing from outside.'

He laughed, then winced. 'It wasn't magnificent at all. No ballroom, a scrap of a place really. Everyone was crowded like ants in a nest.'

'I'd still have liked to see it.'

'You've never been to a ball?'

She shook her head.

'When you're older, maybe.'

She said nothing. Her family was respectable, but a poor army surgeon's daughter was unlikely to be invited to a ball. And even if the duke offered a personal invitation to a surgeon under his command, Hen no longer had a suitable chaperone for such an occasion. But she would not tell this young man that, this obviously very well bred young man.

'What are they like? Balls I mean.'

'Hot. Crowded. Filled with eagle-eyed mamas and simpering daughters.'

'But they must be beautiful. The dresses, and the music … are there flowers?'

'What? Yes, hot-houses full of them. I prefer my flowers in fields,' he added.

'And banquets?' The thought reminded her to offer him the coffee again.

He hesitated. 'There'll be none for you.'

'I haven't had my arm half torn off.'

'Only half?' He managed to hold the bottle in his good hand now, sipping slowly.

'It's whole now. And it'll stay that way if it's cared for. Don't you like dancing?' she added longingly.

'I like dancing well enough. It's the partners who are boring. Do you like dancing?'

'Oh yes!' Often there'd been music and dancing around the campfire, or in houses where they'd been billeted.

'So you can dance, and cook pigeons and make potions.'

He was joking, but the thought of the ball she had not been invited to — all the balls and opera parties and routs she would never be invited to even when she was old enough to officially 'come out' in society — still hurt. 'I can hit an ace at a hundred yards, but I'll never be a lady — not the kind who were at the ball last night.' She tried to make a joke of it. 'I … I am afraid I lack all sensibility. I cannot play the piano, or embroider or … or perform any of the womanly arts.'

He looked at her consideringly. 'Yet you sewed my arm back on. How many languages can you speak?'

Hen blinked. 'Spanish, Portuguese, French, a little Dutch and Prussian, some Flemish and Russian.' Alliances were made by kings. Friendships were made when their armies mingled.

'I think you are amazing, Hen who isn't Henrietta. I don't give a rush for embroidery and pianos. I think you are the most beautiful young woman I have ever seen. Even in an army greatcoat.'

She flushed. Men had told her that before. This was the first time she had cared.

'Your hair looks like sunlight. Your face is an angel's …'

He'd said that when he first saw her. Her blush grew deeper. 'That's the laudanum speaking. And you're ill. Men often think the women who nurse them are beautiful. But then they get better.'

Mama had warned her about that. Her father had just laughed, and kissed them both, and said they would always be beautiful.

'What do your relatives say about you following the army?'

'None left on my father's side. I've never known any of my mother's relations. We've been too much on the move.' And they were Spanish and in Gibraltar, a wealthy merchant family who had cast off their youngest daughter when she married an English naval surgeon with no prospects except one possibly wealthy aunt — but no need to tell this young man that either.

'What if something happens to your father?'

Hen shrugged. 'Then it's just me.'

He looked at her quietly for a moment. 'They don't give army pensions to daughters.'

He knew that much about the army then, even as a newly commissioned officer. She shrugged again. Her father had saved a little and, unlike most young women, Hen knew she could arrange a life alone. She did not have the skills to be a governess, but she could teach languages or be employed as a nurse, and survive in genteel poverty.

A man moaned a little way away: one of the amputees. Hen scrambled up. It was Sergeant Drivers. She checked his pulse again. Thready, but still strong, though he was still deeply unconscious. Trying to give him fluids now might choke him. There was nothing more that she could do till she was sure that he could swallow. If she managed to return to Brussels she must make sure Mrs Drivers knew her husband had survived, and where he was, so he could be taken to their billet — he would receive better care from her than in a field hospital.

She turned and found the lieutenant still watching her. She sat beside him again, glad that her promise to her father meant she had this time free to talk, to sit, to imagine what it might have been like to walk inside that house last night, dressed in silk with pearls, on the arm of this young man. To waltz with him …

'How old are you, Hen not Henrietta?'

'Fifteen.'

He said softly, 'It's not easy for a fifteen-year-old girl to manage alone.'

She gave him a reassuring smile. 'I can look after myself.'

'You shouldn't have to.' He grimaced again. She lifted the flask once more, glad she still had laudanum to offer him, and let him sip, saw his eyes lose their focus slightly as the pain eased too. 'That's good.'

She smiled, changing the subject. 'My mother knew herbs. Everywhere she camped we had a garden, and she had supplies sent by apothecaries in Lisbon and London. She and my father worked as a partnership. She used to say, "He cuts and I cure." One day we were going to have a cottage by the sea, and a garden of our own.'

'Is that what you want now, Hen?'

She looked out into the smoke, as if she might see the future. 'Oh, yes. I love watching things grow. But it doesn't have to be a cottage by the sea. Just somewhere with peace, but some adventure too, the kind that doesn't involve cannons.' Hen looked back at him and grinned. 'My father and I lived in lodgings till we came here. Do you know how boring it is, living in lodgings? I even learned to knit, though I'm no good at it. But my sewing is excellent.'

'I know.' He carefully didn't look at his arm. 'Am I going to die? Or lose my arm?'

'Neither,' said Hen, with only slightly more certainty than she felt. 'The wound is clean. All it needs now is rose and lavender oil applied morning and night, with hot fomentations to ease the swelling.' She gave him another grin, pushing her hair out of her eyes again. 'Unless the battle moves this way again and we both get hit by a cannonball.'

And unless the French had already won. She could still hear gunfire, though no battle ended cleanly. Whichever army won would be chasing stragglers for days.

He reached for her hand and kissed it. She was startled. She had never been kissed, except by her parents. But she did not draw her hand away.

He met her eyes. 'I can think of no one I'd rather die with. I've never seen a grin on a battlefield before.'

She flushed. 'I'd rather live.'

'I can think of no one I'd rather live with, either. Hen, definitely not Henrietta, will you marry me?'

'What?'

'That is not the correct way to answer a proposal,' he chided. 'You should say, "La, sir, this is so sudden! You do me a great honour, but I have not ever thought of marriage." And then you pause significantly for the count of three, then say, "Yes."'

'You don't know me.' She found her voice was trembling.

'Don't I? A friend of mine, Captain Smith, met his wife on a battlefield too. Love at first sight for both of them. They were married that day and haven't been a night apart since.' He squinted through the smoke. 'Juana will be on the battlefield as soon as this is over, to make sure he's not wounded.'

Hen had met Captain Smith, though never spoken to him. Mama had helped his young wife several times. Juana had the heart of a lion, but no experience of living in an army camp. What was she doing now? She was not one to wait quietly with her embroidery. 'I hope ...' Hen could not say, 'that he's not dead.'

The lieutenant laughed. 'Smithie? They say he's the only officer who's been through the entire campaign without a scratch. Got a charmed life. And a charming wife. Well, will you be mine?'

'I ... I ...'

'Hen, my darling, if I die you'll get my pension, plus my share of the prize money, now we've won. Not much else, I'm afraid. I'm a younger son. But you'll have the protection of my name.'

'No,' she said flatly. 'I'm not marrying anyone for their name and a pension.'

'How about for love then? Marry me and if we both live we'll ... well, I don't know what we'll do, but I'll promise you a garden, as well as happiness and adventure and a partnership, just like your parents had, and Smithie and his Juana.'

'Love?'

He nodded.

He couldn't be serious. He was serious. He was grateful because she had saved his arm ...

He'd said she looked like an angel. And he offered love. She looked at him, found him watching her. Papa said one day on a battlefield was like a thousand. An hour with this man today meant she had known him months.

She found she so very much wanted to say yes.

'If you marry me you can make sure I get those, what were they, fermentations on my arm? What is a fermentation anyway? Something to do with brandy?'

'Fomentations. Hot poultices. Bran is best, it holds the heat, but any hot cloth ...' Hen stopped, as he grinned at her.

'Marry me and you can teach me all about hot fomentations. And how to cook pigeons. And I will take you to a ball,' he added, suddenly serious. 'That is a solemn promise, Henrietta. You and I will dance and we will have adventures.'

She should say no. She should say, 'Ask me again, when you are well.' But no matter who won this battle, after this one day he and she would be in different worlds and she might never see him again.

'Say yes,' he said softly. 'Hen, I need you in my life. I never knew what I needed till I met you. After today I will never meet another girl who can shoot a pistol and sew up an arm. Marry me now.'

'Yes,' she said, before she'd even known she was going to say it.

He lay back, suddenly relaxed, smiling despite the pain.

'There are three problems though,' Hen added cautiously.

He weakly waved his good hand. 'Name them, my love, and they shall be solved.'

'We need a priest, and my father's permission. And I don't know your name.'

Chapter 3

An Excellent Fomentation for Dressed Wounds
or Rheumatism

Take Bran of Oats, or Peas, dried and split, or Rice. Sew in
a Linen square the size and thickness of a Man's Hand. Heat
by the Hearth. If the Linen scorches it is too hot. Apply each
Hour.

From the Notebooks of Henrietta Bartley

His name, it seemed, was Leowine Maxwelton Bartlett, known
as Max, with a family home in Sussex. Surgeon Gilbert, grey
faced with tiredness, gave his permission, to Hen's complete
surprise.

'He's right,' Surgeon Gilbert said shortly, nodding to the young
man he had just agreed to make his son-in-law. The surgeon's
skin was dark with smoke now, making his eyes seem bright. 'If
anything happens to me you'll have no protection. I don't want
you to be alone, Hen.'

Hen ducked as a shell whizzed over them, as if to counterpoint
his words.

'Marriage will give you a family, not just a husband. I've heard
of the Bartletts of Sussex. It's a good name, and you, sir,' he
nodded at Max, 'you've taken your surgery with courage. You
could go further, Hen, and do far worse.' Surgeon Gilbert shut

his eyes in weariness for a moment, then looked at her again. 'You are sure about this?'

'Yes, sir,' said Hen.

'And you, Lieutenant Bartlett?'

Max Bartlett was paler than he had been before, but his voice was still firm. 'I am, sir. I thank you. I did not think you would give permission so easily.'

Surgeon Gilbert gave a snort that might have been laughter. 'I married my daughter's mother three days after we met because I had been ordered to accompany the wounded back to England. Three hours, three days or three years would have made no difference to our choice. Life can be strangely clear on a battlefield, no matter how thick the smoke.'

'I saw a man giving the last rites near the Waterloo Road, sir,' offered Thompson. 'I'll warrant he's a priest.'

A French army chaplain, wondered Hen, or perhaps a local one, come to help? Just now it did not matter.

Surgeon Gilbert nodded. 'Could you find him again?'

'I think so, sir,' said Thompson. He vanished once more into the smoke-laden air.

Hen's fiance shut his eyes in what she hoped was painless sleep to wait for his arrival.

The priest arrived with Thompson just as the shadows thickened the gloom of smoke into the long midsummer dusk. Thompson clambered up over the bodies, then helped the small man in his black robes to do the same.

'Père Flambeaux,' said Thompson shortly. 'He says he's Flemish, not French. Seems the Frenchies burned his village, or maybe it was us.'

Père Flambeaux examined Hen and Lieutenant Max Bartlett without expression. Was he really a local priest? If he was attached to the French army they were technically his enemies. He nodded: it seemed Père Flambeaux was truly more priest than soldier.

Père Flambeaux spoke French. Hen and Surgeon Gilbert knew French. So, it seemed, did Max Bartlett.

Père Flambeaux did not seem startled by a request to marry a couple surrounded by small hills of the dead. Yes, he informed them tiredly, it would be a legal wedding, if they paid the licence fee. He did not even seem shocked by Hen's obvious youth. A girl on a battlefield needed whatever protection was available.

A man easily shocked would not have ventured here, thought Hen. Whatever reserves of emotion Père Flambeaux had seemed to have leached out of him. How many men had he, too, tended today? How many murmured confessions had he heard, how many last rites given?

The cannon fire still rumbled as war continued elsewhere, though the fighting had almost ceased around them. The earth had become a single song of groans and cries of pain. But there was love in one small square of this battlefield.

Quietly, efficiently, they gave their names, promised their offspring would be brought up in the Roman Catholic faith, which might prove difficult, but was the least of their concerns now. They clasped hands, her right one in his only available hand, the left. And in the distance guns still snarled, and men nearby screamed in terror or in agony. Soon, thought Hen. We will tend to you soon. Just a few minutes more of happiness ...

'Rings?' queried Père Flambeaux.

'We don't have —' began Hen, just as Max removed his signet ring, and, panting slightly from the pain, pushed it onto the fourth finger of her left hand. Surgeon Gilbert removed his own wedding ring and handed it to Max.

It fitted.

They were married.

Surgeon Gilbert offered Belgian francs to Père Flambeaux, who scribbled two small notes in return. Surgeon Gilbert produced the pen and ink he kept in his bag for urgent notes, then signed the forms as a witness. Thompson signed them too — he was probably the only other man present who was both conscious and able to write his name — and Hen and Max signed as well.

Hen read her copy of the note before her father placed it in his jacket pocket. Their wedding certificate. Her name and Max's would be entered tomorrow or next week perhaps in his church's register, Père Flambeaux assured them, as he pocketed the second note. Or, if his church was completely gone, the first register he could find ...

'Hen,' said Max softly, propped up on his good elbow.

'You may kiss him, my daughter,' said Père Flambeaux, and smiled for the first time, wiping away tears he had not shed before.

Her husband's lips were warm. A good sign after blood loss, thought Hen clinically, until suddenly there was only Max, the taste of him, the smell of him beyond the blood and gunpowder, the feeling that despite the haste this was the most right act of her life ...

Noise. The world ended.

Chapter 4

To Make Camp Water Safe to Drink

Strain Water twice through Cloth. Add Mint, two Sprigs for
every Pint. Boil and Cool.

From the Notebooks of Henrietta Bartley

BRUSSELS

1815

She was on a bed and the bed had soft linen sheets that smelled
of midsummer sunlight, unlike most beds in the billets she had
known, and her head hurt and the world whirled when she tried
to lift it.

She stopped trying to move and tried to think instead.
The room was a bedroom. One narrow bed, one wardrobe,
presumably one chamberpot, which she did not need, but she
did need water and it must be boiled. *Never drink unboiled
water*, Mama said. Perhaps Mama would come soon, with
some broth.

And suddenly the last two years of her life slid back to her,
like liver down the sides of a bucket. Mama was gone …

'Ma chérie?' The old woman's face was familiar. Madame …
she could not remember, but they had been billeted there before.
She must have been brought there from the … the … from
where? Madame Caroline, that was the name the woman had

29

given, though Hen did not know if Caroline was her first name or surname.

'Max!' she said. 'Madame Caroline, where is Max? My ... mon mari. My husband.'

Madame Caroline shook her head. 'A husband?' She spoke French, but with a strong Flemish accent. 'I did not know you had a husband. A soldier? I have not seen him. Your bon papa though, he is at the hospital. His arm was injured in the explosion, but no, ma petite, do not fret yourself. He is not a patient there. He supervises. He said when you woke I was to tell you he is well and you are not to worry.'

'I ... I was hurt?'

'A cannonball, your papa said. An accident. The men who tried to move it did not know that it was loaded.'

That doesn't make sense, thought Hen. Cannons did not just explode. They had fuses. But fuses might be too damp to burn quickly or evenly, and a movement might mean a spark flared and the fuse burned again ...

'All around you it exploded,' said Madame Caroline sympathetically. 'You were blown away by it and hurt your head. It was a gift of the good Lord God that you were not hurt more.'

Hen checked her body automatically. Feet: present. Hands too. No pain, except for the headache.

'Madame,' she said urgently. 'Who won the battle?'

All emotion drained from Madame Caroline's face. 'Those who could walk away once the fighting was done won the battle. It is always so. They say there are mountains of dead, and the wounded still in the fields, thousands dying of wounds, of thirst, of hunger. I would have gone to them, like the other women, but I had to care for you.'

'I ... thank you, Madame. But ... but Napoleon?'

'Napoleon, he is a monster, and he has fled.'

'Then the English won?'

Madame Caroline shrugged. 'I think perhaps the Dutch won the battle for you, or the Prussians. But, yes, all Brussels hails your Duke as the victor of Waterloo.'

Hen lay back. They were safe. She should be glad, she who had seen so many battles, skirmishes, as well as their aftermath, the wounded who might live or die, or live only crippled and in pain; the women left with hungry, wide-eyed children. She had seen it before, and still managed to rejoice in every victory.

But the battle around the Waterloo Road had been different, and not just because it had been the largest she had known. She could not feel any joy this time, only relief that it was over.

Madame Caroline looked at her with total understanding. 'I will fetch broth.'

Hen shut her eyes, trying not to remember the protective wall of corpses that must have been shattered by the cannon blast. Those dead soldiers had saved her life, and her father's and Max's and Sergeant Drivers's and all the others she and her father had treated on that endless day, a day that still seemed to ring in her ears, to pound with every heartbeat. Perhaps would always do so.

She should rest now. She should drink broth. She must do both so she would be strong enough to walk, and see that Max was taken care of at the hospital. If he was doing well she could take a cart or mule to the battlefield to help those left there. But she must be sure there was no infection, that the hot fomentations were renewed ...

Hot fomentations. She smiled, despite the pain. Her husband. Despite all the horror one thread shone gold.

Did Max have a home that he would take her to? He had said he was a younger son. Did he still live with his family, or did he have his own house? Would her father live with them? How bad was her father's injury? A surgeon must have two good arms. But there would be his half-pay pension again and prize money. Surely the prize money would be good after so large a battle — so many enemies ransomed, weapons seized, and so much else won.

Perhaps Max would live with them in the cottage by the sea. Surely Max would sell his commission now that Napoleon was gone, for without Napoleon there would be no wars to fight nor prize money to win ...

But Madame said Napoleon had escaped. Surely he could not raise another army now. And the Iron Duke must have survived, to be called the victor, and what was the name of Max's friend? Tim?

Her thoughts escaped back to the centre of her world. She had a husband. His name was Max, and they would have a future that would leave all war behind.

Madame Caroline returned, bowl in hand, and commenced to feed her, despite Hen's shaky attempt to take the spoon. It was good to be tended. Good to be on a feather mattress, between clean sheets, to be treated with such kindness. Hen was used to kindness from camp followers, but she and her father had been thrust upon Madame Caroline. She found herself crying at the kindness.

'Ma petite, do not weep. The monster Napoleon is gone, your generale triumphant. Your papa will be back soon.'

'How long have I been here?'

Madame Caroline smiled. 'You do not remember waking before? Your papa said you might forget. You have been here two days and have drunk my broth four times then slept again after your papa gave you medicine. But this time, I think you will remember.'

Two days! Her father must have given her laudanum, to make her sleep. Too much perhaps, for he was a surgeon not a physician, nor did he know the strength of the potion she had made. No wonder her memory had faded for a while. But rest was good after concussion, and so was broth.

She drank the whole bowlful, then used the chamberpot as Madame Caroline steadied her. But she was glad to lie down again.

'I will bring tisane,' said Madame.

'Chamomile,' said Hen. It would help ease any swelling.

'Chamomile I do not have. But there is linden flower.'

There was a packet of chamomile flowers in her bag, and a tincture of it too. But linden was almost as good; nor, now her mind was clearing, did she think her concussion serious. It had been the drug, not the injury, that had kept her unconscious so long.

A husband. Suddenly Hen was aware of all she did not know. Men's anatomy, yes, she was well acquainted with that, but under ... different ... circumstances. She even knew what men and women did together, and with what, and what might happen then, from pregnancy to the clap, and what to do with either. But a husband ...

She tried to remember the weddings she had known, laughter and dancing and the couple glancing at each other and then vanishing to the man's tent or billet. But what exactly happened then? Was there an ... an etiquette Mama had not explained? Perhaps she should ask Madame Caroline.

But Madame Caroline was a stranger, no matter how kind. And Max, her husband, her husband, her *husband*, would surely know what to do and how to do it, and not mind if he had to explain parts of the procedure to her.

Hot fomentations. She must check he had hot fomentations, changed regularly, and the wound checked for any redness, and his pulse and forehead for fever ...

Two days. Even if he hadn't had good nursing the dressing she had put on him, soaked in rose oil, would be enough, as long as she could find him soon, before a congestion of the lungs or other complications set in.

A life in England. Their lodgings had been pleasant enough, but almost as temporary as a billet. Now there would be prize money, and a *husband*.

A bed that was truly hers. A wardrobe where she could keep more dresses than would fit in two saddlebags. A proper garden, not just the few plants that might give leaves, roots or flowers in months, but ones that needed years to put down roots. She would grow medicinal roots too. Roots needed time to mature. And buy crockery, china, instead of using pewter that could survive being lugged in saddlebags or on a cart. The sum of her possessions back in England was three dresses, four petticoats, two boxes of pewter or iron cookware — and the chamberpot — and one chest of dried herbs and seeds. Her father had little more.

She dozed again. She dreamed of roses, waltzing among roses. She couldn't quite see the face of the man she danced with, as he was hidden by smoke, the grey-yellow smoke of the battlefield. And yet she could smell roses ...

Voices woke her.

'Papa? Papa!' She sat up. The world lurched twice, once in what she saw, the second in what she understood. The surgeon leaned against the doorway, his face sagging with weariness, his right arm in a sling.

'I'm all right,' he said abruptly, although he clearly was not. 'Broken collarbone, some torn ligaments. They'll heal.'

He'd been at the hospital. Why? He could not operate with only his left arm. 'Max?' she asked urgently.

'I can't find him. The cannonball knocked me out too. When I came to he was gone. I've been to every hospital I can find, asking for a Lieutenant Max Bartlett, but there are hundreds of hospitals, Hen — every place that had room for pallets has become a hospital. There are tens of thousands of wounded, many still out on the field. I've found Max's billet, too. He's not there, and they don't know where he is. Hen, don't look like that — he's not on the casualty list either.'

The unspoken 'yet' lingered. Tens of thousands, thought Hen. So easy to get lost among tens of thousands. The mountains of men Madame had said were still out on the battlefield after two days, cold, starving, dying of thirst or being harried by rats or crows.

She hated rats and crows.

The men were lying out there in the night, the cold, the rain, she thought. How many who might have been saved would die of exposure, or infection from their wounds or loss of blood?

'Sergeant Drivers?' she remembered.

'He's been brought in. His wife is with him. No fever, and the stump looks clean. Hen, I'm going to sleep and eat, and then I'll look for Max again. Half the men or more in the hospitals still haven't been formally identified.'

'I'll come with you.'

'No, Hen, that is a direct order. I don't want you with me now.'

'Why?'

'Because I don't want you to see ...' He broke off. 'I'm going to sleep. Rest well, Hen.' He left.

See what? she wondered. Limbs turning gangrenous, the swollen bellies of the dead exploding in the heat ... She had seen that, and more, during the Peninsular Wars, though not on the scale of the devastation here. The farmers might be digging bones from their fields for hundreds of years ...

She swung her legs over the edge of the bed and found that the world held still. Her legs carried her, too, with no trembling. Her sleep had been healing.

She found her dress, coat and boots in the wardrobe, and her medical bag too, then walked quite steadily out the door. The house comprised only the two bedrooms upstairs and the single room below. She found Madame Caroline downstairs, scraping the lint from freshly washed bandages at the table. A pallet by the hearth showed where she presumably slept now her house was occupied. Two lines of drying bandages hung from the ceiling. The room smelled of damp cloth and turnip.

'Madame, there are wounded still on the battlefield. I am going to help them.'

'Not alone,' said Madame Caroline sternly.

'My father is asleep. He needs his rest.'

Madame Caroline stood. She removed her clean white apron, then donned another, grey and stained, and a cloak. 'I will fetch my friends. We will go together. You roll bandages till I get back.'

'Yes,' said Hen. It seemed that even women who lived in houses in towns knew what to do after a battle.

Four women: one so old she seemed ageless, sexless, but who was slow and methodical; Madame Caroline and a woman who seemed to be her sister; and Hen, the only one of the four not wearing black and a shawl. Each morning before dawn they rose and gathered what they needed as Hen harnessed the mules to the cart Surgeon Gilbert had finally been assigned. Each morning they rode to the battlefield, a weary two-hour journey or more, the roads too cluttered with dead horses, scattered baggage and broken carts to take a larger carriage.

Bodies lay in mountains, as Madame had said. They lay in trenches, too. But there were still uncounted thousands lying as if felled by the scythes that would have cut the grain that had grown there only a few days before.

But even on Hen's first day, the third day after the battle, it was easy to see who lived among the carnage. The dead had swollen, even sometimes exploded, the gas within them built up and then released when a rat bit too deeply or a crow pecked.

The four women did not work together, but also they were never out of sight of each other, for many of the men who walked this battlefield too were not helping or gathering the wounded, but looting, cutting fingers even from the living for their rings. Twice Hen had to threaten the scavengers with her pistol, and Madame carried a firearm almost as old as herself. But most of those who walked on the battlefield were other women, directing the carts to the living and other carts to collect the dead, bandaging, giving water and sometimes a prayer. Priests knelt to give the last rites.

Had Père Flambeaux survived? Hen wondered.

She did not attempt surgery. In the chaos of battle a girl could get away with it. Now an ambitious or malicious surgeon might recognise her, and report her. Her father might suffer for it, even to demotion or dismissal, assuming his shoulder healed so he could work again. If he could not ... She closed her mind to that.

She bound wounds and sometimes stitched ones that might still heal without infection, though that grew less likely with every hour; applied or offered brandy or the soup that a small army of black-clad women lugged out to the field. If a man could walk to a cart, helped by two women, or was not too large for two women to lift, they could ferry him back to a hospital or a billet in Brussels. Their cart could carry eight men, if they could survive being draped over each other.

Many men, in fact, revived when fed soup and a little brandy, for like Hen they had suffered only concussion or minor injuries. It would have been neglect that killed them, not the enemy. Now they would live.

Mostly, Hen searched; she searched faces, pulled aside bodies in the trenches, some loose limbed, some like strange statues in rigor mortis, looking for familiar ones, till finally she was sure that no officer lay in those communal graves.

Max — alive or dead — must be elsewhere.

She had been sure he was alive. Still, somewhere, a stubborn knot said that he must live. But the reality of death all around her pummelled her belief.

The rats arrived on Hen's second day of searching. Somehow all the rats in the Low Countries must have heard there was a feast of flesh. There were too many to shoot. She armed herself with a bayonet to stab any that came close.

Three days searching, retreating with the women at dusk, the mules' way home lit by a single lantern, walking by the cart now so her place could be taken by a wounded man, fifty women or more clustered for safety in the darkness, coming back each morning with more bandages, boiled and dried by fires overnight, more stewpots, endless kindness for damaged strangers far from home. None of the women she worked with knew any soldier, beyond the brief acquaintance of those billeted with them. It did not matter.

'I had sons,' explained Madame Caroline wearily, as they shared barley bread and cheese sitting between two piles of corpses waiting to be buried. Food was hard to find with most supplies taken for the armies and their followers and so much of this year's harvest had been destroyed by battle or looting. 'My sons had sons. Each man here is some woman's son.'

Had sons, thought Hen. But Madame Caroline did not seem to want to say more.

'Au secours ...' The words were not quite a whisper, the wind perhaps, snickering around their ankles.

'Au secours ...' It came from the pile of bodies. Hen swallowed the last of her bread, grabbed her bag and ran to them.

But no one moved. Eyes stared at the grey sky, though some had already been pecked out by crows. A rat ran across her foot ...

'Au secours ...'

There — the boy's legs were trapped by rubble beside the corpses, mistaken for one himself. His eyes were shut, his hand limp when she picked it up. But she could feel the beat of a faint pulse at his neck. He did not speak again. Possibly it had taken the last of his strength to call to them when he heard her and Madame talking.

Hen reached for her flask of cold linden tea and held it to his lips. He swallowed. A good sign. Nor could she see any injury, beyond superficial cuts and a lump to the side of his head. Another who had been knocked unconscious, as she had, but instead of being tended left in the cold and damp? She shrugged herself out of her old army greatcoat, wrapped it around the boy and held him to her for warmth.

'Madame, can you find a French ambulance?' Napoleon had instituted an efficient way to remove the wounded from the battlefield, with many light swift carts rather than the larger, cumbersome ones used by the British — and of which there were far too few. Most of the French wounded had been collected now, taken to Antwerp or Brussels. Hen did not want this boy taken to Gens d'Armerie, the allied hospital for French prisoners. With medical services desperately overloaded she suspected there would be little help spared for the enemy.

'Ambulance!' 'Ambulance!' The cry went up from woman to woman across the battlefield, and at last one appeared as the air turned greyer and became neither fog nor rain. The boy gave a faint groan as the French orderly picked him up and laid him gently between two Frenchmen, one stoically gazing at nothing, especially the dried blood from one hip to ankle, the other clasping his stomach with hands black with dried blood, his eyes shut, though his wound must not have pierced a vital organ if he had survived this long.

'I think the boy mostly needs warmth,' said Hen urgently, in French.

'He will be kept as warm as possible, in the coach between the others,' said the orderly, not unkindly. Hen watched them depart, wishing desperately that the winning forces had their own ambulance service and the superior French medical organisation.

'It is time to go home, ma cherie,' said Madame Caroline quietly. Hen nodded. The surgeons might work for three days and nights without ceasing, but she could not; nor was it safe to be on battlefield by lamplight. The women must get back so the wounded in their cart could be unloaded at the hospital, the one her father would not let her visit, so the mules could eat and gather their strength, so they could sleep for a few hours, then come out again ...

Hen walked wearily next to the cart as the mules trod through the debris on the road. She chewed stale bread and even harder sausage, the kind that hung smoking in Madame's fireplace. Other women would be making the broth for tomorrow, baking bread, if any wheat or cornmeal or barley could be found for their grinding stones. The women would be boiling bandages to use again, scraping the lint from them and rolling them, ladies of the English gentry or Flemish peasants.

'Two more days,' said the woman who might be Madame Caroline's sister. The women all nodded, no explanation needed. In two more days any man not found and tended would have died, or at least the living would be so few that the army carts could collect them. Already as many wounded as possible had been shipped to other ports, even to England, where there was food and clean linen and hands that were not so weary that they trembled even after a few hours' sleep.

Each time the mules stopped, unsure which way to go around a broken carriage or the swollen bodies of dead horses, Hen or one of the other women climbed back into the cart to give more broth to the men in the cart and to check that they were still alive, for they did not have the space to waste upon the dead.

This time Madame Caroline gave the broth, and checked to see if each man lived. Hen held out her hand to help the older woman back down.

'The men were disappointed it was not you, ma petite,' said Madame Caroline, as her sister clicked the reins for the mules to walk again. 'Do you know they call you the angel?'

'What? I am sorry, I don't understand.' She must be too weary to remember her Flemish French.

'It is your hair, I think,' said Madame Caroline, taking another small loaf from her baskets. She tore off a hunk for Hen. 'Your hair glows like a halo in the sun.'

Hen touched her hair automatically. Her surgeon's tools had been returned with her, but the bonnet had been ruined and she did not have another. She had not thought to ask Madame for a cap, nor had she even had time to plait her hair properly, pulling it back instead into a knot at the nape of her neck, the tendrils escaping and wisping around her face.

'I'm not an angel.'

'Perhaps not. But it helps the men to think you are. They say a man touched by the angel of Waterloo will live, and perhaps they do live.'

'Because of my hair?'

Madame shrugged. 'It is as good a reason as any. They decide to live and that is all that matters.'

Max had said she looked like an angel. If only she truly was, then that would mean he must be safe. If other men could live because they believed in angels, then the man who had married one must be alive.

But she was not an angel. And she had not found Max among either the living or the dead.

It had now been four days since she had seen her father, though his bed had been slept in. Surgeon Gilbert, too, was out as long as the midsummer light continued. He was gone before she rose each morning and returned when she was asleep.

He might even have been on the battlefield. Despite the flatness of the fields the devastation was so vast, and there were so many aid posts, that he and Hen might have both worked there for weeks, yet missed each other every day.

Hen thought it more likely that he was working at the hospitals, advising others even if he could not operate himself. The only sign he had been at their billet at all was a growing number of hessian sacks in his bedroom. The house began to fill with the stench of them. But the sacks were sewn shut, and then sealed with his stamp as well; and Hen and Madame did not have the energy to care to open them.

If her father had found Max he would have told her. He had not told her, so he had not.

On the fifth day of searching — seven days after the battle — she returned early with Madame and the others, knowing this would be her last journey from Waterloo. The fields were almost empty of all but the dead. Even an angel could do little now, for any man left alive would be unconscious and unlikely to wake again. Their cart had only two men that afternoon, both likely to die before they reached Brussels. The clouds said rain and the

41

four women were weary beyond tiredness, with a hunger that hard bread and sausage could not quell.

As one they clustered, wordlessly, and turned the mules to the track that led to the road to Brussels, letting the cart carry them too this time. A carter offered them some of his ale. They stopped to drink with him, offering him bread in exchange. The carter's passengers did not object, for they were dead. Hen looked briefly at their faces, then looked away, at trees, at clouds, at anything but death ...

'Is she the angel?' she heard the carter ask. She was too tired, an exhaustion that went far beyond the physical, to even listen to Madame Caroline's reply.

It was dark by the time they reached Madame's cottage. Hen followed Madame Caroline in, then stopped.

Someone had lit the lamp. A strange man stood and bowed to them as they entered, his hussar helmet under his arm. Suddenly Hen recognised him. He was the one who had brought Max to their square, the friend who risked his life for him. 'Tim?' she asked, managing to curtsey.

'Miss Gilbert?'

'Yes. No. I ... I am married now. Max?' she breathed.

'I'm sorry,' he said quietly, in English. 'He's dead.'

Life stopped, and then began again.

'No!'

Madame Caroline, who understood no English, removed her pattens then her shawl, which she hung to dry, then added wood to the coals under her cooking pot with the look of a woman who had energy enough only to heat soup, and not for bothering with English strangers.

'His arm — it would heal! Even if it became infected ...' Hen couldn't continue.

'He died on the battlefield. A stray cannonball.'

Hen nodded dumbly, sat on one of the hard chairs at the table. 'I was knocked out by it,' she managed at last. 'I ... I have been trying to find him. My father has too.'

'I brought a copy of the lists to show you.'

Hen took it, read the names. Max's name was halfway down. Lieutenant *the Honourable Leowine Maxwelton Bartlett. Dead on the battlefield of wounds received.*

'I want to see him.' Hen would not believe this, could not believe it, till she had seen him.

'I told you, he's dead.' There was a touch of impatience in Tim's voice. Was that his way of showing grief? But perhaps Tim had lost too many friends that week to grieve.

'I am his wife. We married on the battlefield. I have the right to bury my husband.'

Tim hesitated. Hen realised he had not yet given his surname. 'I heard that Surgeon Gilbert was asking about a man he called his son-in-law. That's why I've come here.'

'Then take me to Max!'

Madame Caroline passed her a steaming cup of broth made of bones and vegetable peelings, then sat on the chair next to Hen. Hen took the cup absentmindedly, as Madame Caroline held her other hand tight in her own bony one. Madame Caroline did not ask the officer to sit.

The silence grew heavy. 'His body has been returned to his family in England,' Tim said at last.

'I am his family!' Hen heard the anguish in her voice and realised, for the first time, that she had accepted on some level that Max was gone.

'Miss Gilbert ...'

'Mrs Bartlett.'

'You cannot be Mrs Bartlett. Who witnessed this marriage? Where is it recorded?'

'My father and his assistant were witnesses. I do not know where it was recorded. But I have the priest's signature ...'

'No church? No banns, no licence, no independent witnesses to say that it was done? I am Max's friend. I've been to see the commander on his behalf. To put it briefly, the army doesn't recognise your marriage. Even if such a harum scarum affair was

43

valid, which I am sure it was not, Max could not marry without the permission of his commanding officer. If Max had lived, I am sure our commander would have given it. But as he did not, I'm afraid you are not entitled to a pension, nor of course to any share of prize money.'

'A pension!' Hen had not thought of such a thing, though Max had spoken of it, she remembered. If he died she would have a pension and a family …

She had been a wife for perhaps a minute. She could not ask for a minute's worth of pension. She had loved him …

Or had I? she thought tiredly. There had been so much passion on that battlefield, so much longing for every second of life. Calf love? And they'd had only seconds … would she have loved him today? Would he have loved her in ten years' time?

Yes, she thought. I loved him. I still love him. I knew him, too, and probably better than this very proper young man who was his friend. And she and Max had been married in the sight of God, even if the army did not recognise it. Père Flambeaux would surely not have performed the ceremony if it was not legal. But she did not want a pension, nor to presume upon a family who would have their own grief. They should not have to deal with hers as well.

'The commander has offered you this, though, as compensation.' Tim lifted a small bag, opened it, and began to pile gold coins on the table with the precision of a clerk. 'Twenty-five pounds …'

Madame Caroline stared. Hen blinked. Twelve pounds would buy a cottage. If her father was unable to work they could live on ten shillings a year, if Hen took in sewing, and grew vegetables as well as herbs …

'Take the money away,' Hen said flatly.

'I've heard your father has been injured. You may need the money. The army has no place for injured surgeons.'

'That is irrelevant, sir.' Hen stood. This time she decided not to curtsey. 'I thank you for your good wishes, for your care of my husband, for your efforts on my behalf now. But I wish only for Max. Money from his death would simply remind me of what I cannot have.'

'You will take nothing?'

'I have a memory and a ring. And his name.'

'You cannot use his ...' The man stopped at the expression on Hen's face.

Madame Caroline stood next to her now, uncomprehending but in solidarity.

Hen took a deep breath. 'Our marriage was valid, witnessed and documented, even if it is not recognised by the army. My father has our marriage certificate. My name is Mrs Max Bartlett. You will honour me, and his memory, sir, by using it.'

Tim replaced the coins in the bag slowly, as if giving her time to change her mind, then took up his helmet, which he'd put on the table while counting out the coins. He hesitated yet again. 'They say you worked all the day of the battle, just like a man. You have been out on the field every day this week.'

'So have many women tended the wounded, including Madame Caroline.' She said this in French, so Madame might understand it.

'My country thanks you, Madame.' Tim bowed, paused, then added, 'And you, Mrs Bartlett.'

'Thank you,' said Hen. His gift of her name — her true name now — meant he deserved the curtsey she gave him as he left.

She would need to get used to curtseying again. She would need to get used to many things.

Chapter 5

A Powder of Eglantine

Chop and dry Briar Heps to a Powder. It is most Efficacious
on small Wounds, and will banish The Whites.

From the Notebooks of Henrietta Bartley

'He's dead,' said Hen, still curled up on the bed. She had changed
her dress so she did not get muck on Madame Caroline's bed
coverings.

'I know, love.' Her father limped slowly into the room and sat
on the bed beside her, leaning against the wall for support.

She sat upright. 'Your leg?' she asked anxiously.

'Only a blister.'

'Take your boot off,' Hen ordered. Even a blister might go
septic and kill a man in conditions like these.

Surgeon Gilbert sighed and obeyed.

Lavender oil, undiluted, on the clean pad against the blister,
then a poultice of garlic on top of the pad, with another bandage
to keep it all in place. The garlic would be better at killing
infection, but would delay healing too. Best not to put it straight
on the blister unless it became puffed or red.

Surgeon Gilbert did not object. He, too, had seen many die
from wounds as small as this, including the wife he loved.

'Leave your boot off till it heals,' ordered Hen.

'Yes, Hen.'

She looked at him in shock. 'You agree?'

'There is no need to go out again,' Surgeon Gilbert said gently. Out in the hall she glimpsed Thompson lugging three more hessian sacks up the stairs. 'Tomorrow I will try to arrange passage to England, Hen. Home.'

She had dreamed of a home. She would never have that now. Back to lodgings, a landlady's watery stews and boiled vegetables ...

'You've had orders?'

Surgeon Gilbert managed a smile. 'To recover from my wound, and then become Superintendent of Hospitals.'

'Truly? That ... that is truly wondrous.' She had expected that at best he would be put back on half pay. Superintendent of Hospitals was the second highest rank a surgeon could achieve. It might even lead to a knighthood. And it would not be arduous in peacetime.

'I had an audience with His Excellency himself. Only two minutes, and with a dozen others, but the position is confirmed. His Excellency said, "You held your square through the entire battle, Surgeon. If only such steadfastness had been shown by all our forces."'

'It really is all over?'

'Yes. No more war, Hen. Not in our lifetimes. They are calling it "The Battle of Waterloo".'

It was as good a name as any.

'It was a close-run thing, Hen. By mid-afternoon it seemed all was lost. But then the Prussians finally advanced, and the Dutch. It wasn't till eleven, with dusk falling, that the French lines suddenly broke, except for the Guards, and they were surrounded by fleeing Frenchmen crying, "Save yourselves" even as the Guards yelled, "Save our eagles!" They say the Duke stood up in Copenhagen's stirrups and waved his hat in the air, ordering our men to advance again. And every man there followed him, harrying the French till almost midnight.'

So that was victory, thought Hen. One side triumphant because they had stood firm until enough of the other side began to run. 'How many lost?' she asked quietly.

'No one knows yet. Maybe fifteen thousand of our troops dead or badly wounded ...'

'Fifteen thousand!' And yet even from their small square she had seen hundreds dead. She had seen the carpet of wounded on the churned black mud all that week, the piles of bodies, the trenches, already stinking. Somewhere, dimly, she had known.

'Blücher and his Prussians lost about seven thousand. No one seems to know the Dutch and Russian casualties. But Napoleon lost more, twenty-five thousand men perhaps. We've taken at least seven thousand prisoners to ransom, and thousands more are still offering their surrender to anyone who will take it. It is a horror and a mess, Hen, but you and I will be out of it.'

'Where will we go, sir?' she asked numbly.

'I'm being given a posting at Chelsea. There'll be a good house to go with the position. It's a healthy area, clean air, small farms.' The smile again. 'There have been commendations for both my "assistant surgeons", too. I think they refer to you. Unfortunately no one could find your name or rank, so don't expect a promotion.'

Hen tried to smile for him. 'This is ... is wonderful.'

'But you would rather have your husband.'

'Yes, sir. I would. Papa, Max's friend told me our marriage wasn't valid.'

'A marriage would have needed banns or a licence in England, which is probably the only kind of marriage he is familiar with. His opinion doesn't matter now,' he added gently.

'No,' she said numbly.

'Hen, if it is any comfort ... and it probably will be no comfort ...' Her father seemed to look for words. 'I promised your mother I would care for you.'

'You have!'

'I am not sure that many would think taking my daughter to the deadliest battle in history would qualify.'

'It was my choice.'

'No. The life you led gave you too few choices. But I hope it will be different now. You have no need to persuade the army to give you a pension for a battlefield marriage.' Surgeon Gilbert took a deep breath. 'Hen, I have served under Wellington almost since you were born. I believed that he would win. Believed it so strongly I took one of the greatest risks imaginable when we came here. I don't mean just risking our lives.'

'Then what ...?'

'The day we left England I invested all I had and all I could borrow in Consuls. Their price had crashed. Consuls are now ten times higher than they were last week, and rising. I have also heard that the prize money for every officer is going to be the largest ever.'

Hen nodded, still trying to understand what this meant. Prize money was made from ransoms and the sale of the weapons and other effects of the enemy. This had been the largest battle ever, and with so many Allies killed there were now fewer to share the proceeds ...

'I am saying we are rich, Hen. That you will want for nothing again. I also have a confession.' Surgeon Gilbert looked at Hen intently. 'I have spent the last week supervising surgery, but the three men I employed have not. They have been taking the teeth of the dead on the battlefield. They will keep removing them until all the dead are buried. I'm paying them well for the task.'

Hen stared. 'Teeth?'

'They are your security, Hen. Tens of thousands of teeth, to be sold over the next ten years or more for dental plates for the wealthy. I won't try to sell them now, for the price will be low. Others have taken teeth, too. I will have them preserved and stored. In a few years' time they will make us wealthy indeed, Hen.'

For a moment all Hen felt was horror. The teeth of dead men. Though the dead had no use for teeth. And her father had done this for her, because he had spent his life caring for others and not his family. Perhaps death owed him some teeth.

Surgeon Gilbert looked at her steadily. 'Hen, it has been only just over a year since your mother died. My love for her is as strong as ever. The grief, too. Don't think I don't understand a little of what you feel now.'

'I ... I'm sorry. I didn't realise ...'

'What is worse, eh? To lose your love after an afternoon together, or after twenty years?'

Hen didn't know. She felt neither loss nor happiness. She was not sure when she would ever feel anything again.

Chapter 6

A Most Excellent Biscuit to take with Tea After Dinner

Take beaten Eggwhite, two, with two tablespoons fine sugar.
Mix gently one cup ground Almonds and six drops of bitter
almond oil. Roll in small Balls and bake in a cooling enclosed
Oven after the bread has been baked till touched with brown.

From the Notebooks of Henrietta Bartley

ROSALY HOUSE, CHELSEA

12 JULY 1819

Chère Madame Caroline,
Translated from Flemish French
I hope that You are well, & Winter's touch of Ague has passed. I
enclose another Bottle of Oil of Wintergreen with Tincture of Red
Pepper. Rub it on your Hands each Morn & Night, & keep taking
the Tisane six times a day, & the Pain in your Fingers should not
trouble You again.

Life goes well for Us here. I have attended a Dinner with His
Excellency the Duke of Wellington himself! Admittedly there
were 600 others, & my dear Father and I were seated well below
the Salt, but afterwards his Lordship came up to me & said he
remembered the Night that I was born, & that my Father drank an
entire Bottle of Sherry Wine & danced a Jig on the Mess Table,

*which I had never known. His Lordship then asked Mrs Colonel
Jadestone who accompanied me if he could have the Honour of
the next Country Dance! I was most grateful for his Lordship's
Attention.*

*I wore yellow Silk, with a silver Gauze Overlay, and the Pearl
Necklace & Earrings my Father gave me on the first Anniversary of
the Battle. My Skin remains too brown for me to wear white, though
I have now passed the three Years of Mourning & put my Blacks
and Mauves away. I have suddenly a love of strong Colours, &
yesterday bought a bolt of blue Silk that I wish I could show to you.*

*All my best wishes, my dear Madame, and Remembrances of
your great kindness to my Father and myself in your Home.*

I remain,

Yours truly,

Mrs Maxwelton Bartlett

The roses were blooming in the gardens of the substantial
dwelling of His Majesty's Superintendent of Hospitals, which
was not the simple cottage they had imagined for themselves.
Hen's herb garden bloomed as well: yellow chamomile, red
bergamot, white blooms on the comfrey leaves, the pink poppy
that was best for laudanum and the spires of monkshood, all
sheltered by hedges of lavender and rosemary. The Greek oregano
thrived in summer, but could only be grown in pots and placed
into the hot-house each winter. The hot-house also sheltered the
potted peach trees, almonds, olives, lemons and oranges, and
was kept warm by charcoal braziers each night as well as beds of
fermenting manure.

That morning Hen had arranged tonight's dinner with
Mrs March, the cook: a leg of lamb, forced with lemon and sage
stuffing; a dish of buttered spinach; one of macaroni; a capon.
Hen did not trust fish or oysters in this heat unless she'd seen
them caught, but there would be a relish of anchovy toast that
her father had a fondness for, placed near his hand with a bowl
of fresh buttered peas; and an apple pie, the fruit of their own

orchards within his reach too; as well as cherries preserved in cider in an ornamental glass centrepiece rimmed with gold. Henderson would see to the wines.

The previous week she had been her father's hostess at a dinner party for two surgeon colleagues and their wives, a colonel visiting a hospitalised friend and a local silk merchant with his wife, son and daughter.

There had been two full courses that, with the women leaving the men to talk over port and nuts afterwards, and tea served in the drawing room, was all as etiquette required. Hen had learned to keep house now, helped by the wives of her father's colleagues. She had even given a dinner for Sir James McGrigor, head of His Majesty's Medical Services, and knighted for his work. Sir James had made it plain that her father, too, might soon have that honour, for his administration was much admired.

It was a long way from stolen chicken on pewter plates around a campfire. But that, thought Hen wistfully as she placed yet another bunch of roses on the bench in her distillery, had been more fun.

The distillery took up the entire attic area above the floor where the servants slept, but her rose oil and its other products would mostly be used by others. It was not considered suitable for the widowed daughter of the Superintendent of Hospitals to treat patients herself, beyond the cut finger of a kitchenmaid that had at least required a little stitchery.

She was bored.

She had not been bored the first year, buying all she'd never had, from a dining table to a sideboard carved with pineapples, and the morning dresses, dinner dresses, walking dresses, the innumerable hats, pelisses, muffs, shoes, silk stockings suitable for a young woman who was also a widow. It was ... useful ... to be a widow — for a widow even at her age could dispense with a chaperone, except of course a maid to walk with her to shop, or the company of the wives of her father's colleagues at the few select dinners or balls she attended.

There had been no invitations, of course, the first year, not to a widow in mourning. But when she had put on lilac and mauve instead of black, slowly the number of letters by her breakfast plate grew.

Some invitations were pure kindness, offering an entry into society to a girl who had known none. Others were from the mothers of unmarried sons, for her father had let it be known that he had settled five thousand pounds on her. He had done this kindly, too. Other invitations were at the request of junior surgeons who hoped for patronage from her father for his future son-in-law, as well as for her own attractions: youth, beauty and the experience of running the household of an important man.

She found she still enjoyed dancing. She enjoyed balls, too. But what had Max said about the stupidity of partners? After half an hour of inanities about weather or breeding dogs, she would slip, and mention the time she had bathed in the river in Portugal when suddenly a whole platoon marched by, or said, 'Ah, Armstrongs — they make the best bone saws in the country.'

Men did not like to be perplexed; nor did they wish to marry a woman who might be *unexpected*, even with five thousand pounds to her name. Hen's partners rarely danced or escorted her in to dinner twice.

Nor did she want them to. They bored her. Young women her own age bored her as well, for they had seen nothing but the schoolroom, could talk of nothing but young men and silks and flounces.

Somewhere, she knew, there were salons where intelligent women met, to talk of mathematics or the sciences, politics or poetry, but she had no way of knowing how to find them, nor how she might gain admittance to their circle. She did not even have access to the hospital her father oversaw; no gently reared girl would be a nurse and nor did it occur to anyone — even her father — that she had not been gently reared. Surgery and apothecary had been Hen's life for eight years, and a life of flower arranging and writing menus was not sufficient exchange for that.

Ever since she was ten years old she had added almost daily entries into the notebooks her parents encouraged her to keep: observations, scraps of knowledge, receipts for meals that might be made on a wet trek through the Pyrenees from a hare unwise enough to break from cover as their wagon passed.

These days the receipts were for elegant dishes suitable for the Superintendent of Hospitals: useful, but adding little to the large repertoire of any well-trained cook they might employ.

She looked at the roses, already wilting. Why bother with distillation, when she could send James to buy a bottle of rose oil? Three years in England and her closest friend was still the Belgian woman who had sheltered them for a mere fortnight, though they had been the most vivid days of her life.

They were likely to stay the most vivid, too. She did not want to paint. What was the use, except to identify a herb? She did not want to embroider, she who had stitched legs and arms. She did not enjoy going into the coal fug of London to shop, wearing silk while the legless beggars, who might well have been on the same battlefield as her, starved and pleaded, and urchins scrambled among the horse dung and rubbish or swept a path along the cobbles for her in exchange for a penny.

At least out here, among the market gardens of Chelsea, the air was clean and children did not starve. Mrs Maxwelton Bartlett, the widowed daughter of a Superintendent of Hospitals, who was wealthy in his own right too, did not need to search for a husband to provide her with a home, the normal occupation for a young woman her age. She was mistress, financially independent, and her father showed no inclination to marry again.

Her one longing was to take a medical degree. She suspected Papa might even have agreed, despite his obvious wish that she remarry, for happiness and children and protection after he was gone. But no medical college in Britain, nor any that she knew of overseas, would take a woman.

It was time to change for dinner, or rather, to be changed, standing while Ethel dressed her, sitting while Ethel did her hair. She left the roses, wilting, and made a note to ask Norah to clean them out tomorrow.

A pale green silk, high-waisted, matching silk slippers, her pearls. As a widow she *could* wear diamonds, but not, perhaps, at nineteen.

'Papa!' She lifted her cheek to be kissed. Surgeon Gilbert took her arm as they progressed along the hall to the dining room. He too had changed for dinner into the hessians and long-tailed coat of a gentleman.

'You have had a good day?' he asked her. He smelled of the bay rum he applied after John had shaved him, and faintly still of hospital lye soap.

She seated herself, checked the dishes on the table. 'Most pleasant, thank you, Papa.' She tried to think of something she had done that might interest him and failed. 'And you?'

'An argument. Capon or lamb?'

'Lamb please, Papa.'

Her father began to carve the lamb. 'That cursed idiot, Surgeon Johnson, has no concept of quarantine. Two cases of smallpox last week and he didn't isolate them, just ordered the windows kept open to dispel miasmas. There were fourteen cases today and who knows how many more by next week. I ordered the patients isolated, and quarantine for all who had been with them, including Johnson. He may while away the time reading my copy of *Opera Medico-Physica*.'

'You think that will convince him that contagion is spread through animalcules?' Her mother had taught her that disease spread from person to person — she had seen it happen in families — and had convinced her husband, too. Most surgeons, however, still clung to the theory of bad air.

Surgeon Gilbert placed the slices of lamb on her plate. 'I hope so. Don't worry. I washed and changed before I came home.'

Hen helped herself to spinach. 'I'm not worried. Do you remember the smallpox epidemic back in Portugal? I didn't sicken then, and doubt I ever will.'

'I'm more concerned for the servants. I vaccinated you myself.'

'Did you? I don't remember.'

'You were only three years old.'

She leaned forwards eagerly. 'I did not know you had been interested in vaccination.'

Surgeon Gilbert laughed. 'The need never arose again. But I have a paper on it in my study. I'll hunt it out for you.'

'Thank you, Papa!'

Her father helped himself to buttered peas with mint. 'Did you know that General Washington had the entire rebel army inoculated if they hadn't had smallpox as a child? The fleet to Botany Bay took variolous matter with them too, in case inoculations were needed. But one must be sure of the source of the vaccine: one supplier, at least, accidentally caused an outbreak of smallpox.'

'Should we vaccinate the servants?' Hen asked eagerly. She knew of several titled women who had had their staff inoculated, though she doubted they had performed the task themselves. Most of the market gardeners of Chelsea kept a cow, or shared one with their neighbours, so would have had cowpox, making them immune to the more deadly disease, but their servants would likely have no such immunity.

'It might be wise. Smallpox is the most contagious of all diseases. Johnson truly is an idiot. I believe he thought the first was nothing but chickenpox.'

'If you could provide me with the variolous matter, I could do it.'

'There is no need. I'll send one of the junior surgeons. There is a new one, a Surgeon Turner, who you have not met yet.'

And Surgeon Turner is undoubtedly unmarried, thought Hen resignedly.

'This pie is delicious, my dear. Perhaps we should ask Mr Turner to dine with us after the inoculations.'

'Mrs March makes excellent pastry. I will pass on your compliments to her.' Hen thought wistfully of the last pie she had made herself, cooked in a camp oven from fallen apples scavenged over a fence and flavoured with rose heps. 'They are our own apples, too. It is an excellent crop this year.'

He smiled. 'It is a delight to see you so happy, my dear. To see you dressed as you should be, comfortable and safe.'

Hen reached for his hand. 'I am entirely comfortable, Papa.'

'Hen, you should marry,' he said quietly.

'To give you grandchildren to comfort you in your old age?'

'To give you love. Hen, you were so very young. If I had been sure we'd survive that day I'd never have given permission. You can't live with only memory.'

You do, she thought. There had been several eligible widows who had flirted with her father — or tried to, for he never seemed to notice their efforts. 'When I find a man I love, I'll marry him. Please, tell me more about the vaccination. What method do you advise?'

They were still discussing vaccination methods and the hazards of inoculation after the table had been cleared and the port placed on the cloth with a dish of nuts and candied plums. It was the happiest and most interesting night she'd had for years.

By the next evening her father was dead.

Chapter 7

To Keep Away Mice and Ants

Take Salt Sand from the Beach and mix with Equal Parts Talcum Power. This may be strewn along Skirting Boards, or Larder Shelves or when planting Peas. A few Drops of Peppermint Oil increases Efficacy.

From the Notebooks of Henrietta Bartley

'One would never have thought that his heart would give out, and so suddenly. Not a man of his age, and after all he had gone through. To think of him dropping suddenly like that.' Mr Gates, lawyer and general man of business, shook his head.

'Quite,' said Hen, dressed in black silk again. 'Will you have another sherry, Mr Gates?'

'Thank you. Most excellent sherry. This house, of course, must pass to the next incumbent, but I am assured by the authorities that you may stay as many months as you need.'

'That is kind of them. But I have no wish to stay.'

Perhaps, if the house had been truly theirs, she would have wished to, for there at least she had memories. But she had no real desire to rattle round such a large establishment with no need even to order dinner, not for a single person.

Gates peered at her over his glasses, sympathy for her loss obviously warring with his pleasure in informing her that she was indeed a wealthy woman. 'And as a widow, you are entirely free to use your father's estate.' He coughed politely. 'Though of course I shall be delighted to carry on managing the affairs your father entrusted to me.'

'Thank you,' said Hen briefly.

'You will need a house. Can you think of a companion, perhaps?'

'No.'

'You might advertise,' he offered. 'You cannot wish to live alone.'

Wanted: impoverished, amiable woman with an interest in anatomy, botany and surgery. 'Thank you, Mr Gates. I will consider that.'

'Or you might travel. A holiday in Italy perhaps. Some more … adventurous … ladies even venture to Greece, to see the ruins.'

'Thank you. But I have already travelled. I am not interested in ruins.'

She thought perhaps Mr Gates wanted to ask what she was interested in, but good manners constrained him. Which was a pity, Hen thought, for she might, just possibly, have given an interesting answer back.

'What will you do then?' He smiled at her benignly. 'You have only to pass your orders to me and I will see they are carried out.'

'Thank you. You are very good. But Mr Gates, I have managed my father's affairs since we came to England. If you examine your correspondence you will see from the handwriting that I wrote the letters instructing you, even though my father signed them. We will continue on that basis.'

He blinked at her. 'Of … of course, Mrs Bartlett. I did not realise —'

'Quite so. I would like the furniture and all household items put in storage, to begin with. Annuities for all the servants.'

'Annuities! That is too … I mean, most generous.'

'I have enough,' said Hen. Indeed, her fortune was more than enough, even if sometimes the teeth it was based on haunted her nightmares, an army of the dead come to reclaim their teeth. Her fortune must be used well, not frivolously. If only she could find a way to make her own life of use.

'There are no items of furniture you wish to keep with you at present?'

'No, thank you. My father's clothes — if you would offer them to the servants.'

'And his ...' Mr Gates struggled to find a refined term '... surgical, ah, equipment. You will want that sold?'

'No. Thank you,' said Hen. 'That does not need to be put into storage. I will also reserve the books I wish to keep with me.'

Mr Gates waited, but Hen did not add anything further to her answer. 'Letters of credit ...' he offered.

'Yes, please. All of our affairs must be put in my name now. You will find I am fully aware of our investments.'

'Ah.' Mr Gates seemed to hunt for something he could offer this young woman who looked exactly as a young widow should, but who knew a most unseemly amount about the world. 'And a house perhaps?'

'I would like lodgings for a short period, but would like you to enquire where a woman such as myself might attend lectures of a scientific nature, whether that be in London or ... or I don't know where.'

'I do not think —'

'You offered your services,' said Hen. 'That is what I wish.'

'I ... yes, of course. My most sincere condolences ...' Mr Gates seemed distressed at his inability to suitably support her in her bereavement.

'Thank you,' said Hen again.

She sat alone in the drawing room after the lawyer left. She had answered all the letters of condolence and kept only one of them, a brief note from the old Iron Duke himself, offering not just sympathy but describing himself as *Your servant always*. It was the only letter that seemed real. His Lordship was the only person of their present acquaintance who knew who she really was, if that was known by anyone.

She was not entirely sure who she was herself.

There would be other letters. Her father's previous friends had moved to other posts, as those in the army always did, or back to their home towns or estates. Even more letters would come, undoubtedly, after the next Waterloo dinner, as more of her father's friends and old colleagues learned of the loss.

But now? She had nothing in the world to do, and no one to do it with. Nor had she any place she wished to be. London was the obvious place to find the company of women with an interest in the sciences. But her few visits to London had shown her that she could not live there — the coal fogs thicker than the smoke of Waterloo, an even denser mix of yellow grey; the yells of carters, pot boys, men who sold brick dust, oysters, rags, hot potatoes, all at the tops of their voices; the only birds the sparrows or pigeons hunting for food among the horse droppings.

She rubbed her eyes again, probably reddening them still more after her weeping. And she saw it.

Her wedding ring. Max's signet ring. She, who had called herself a widow for four years, who still grieved for the man she had known so briefly — an extraordinary man who would marry a woman not in spite of her ability to amputate a limb, but because of it — she had never thought of her husband's family, beyond the grief they must feel at Max's death.

Perhaps there *was* a place in the world for her. Perhaps there even was a family. Perhaps Max's mother might be lonely; she might have longed for a daughter-in-law but now believed she'd never have one. Perhaps even her fortune, built on a gamble and the teeth of dead men — which Mr Gates would still sell in small numbers from those in storage, enriching her still further — would be of help to Max's family. Gentle birth did not necessarily mean riches, and many gentlemen had lost their fortunes in the long unsettled years of war.

And, if not, Hen would at least have accomplished the single duty she had inherited from her husband, that she had been too shocked at first to perform it, and then too unwilling to remember the pain.

She moved to the writing desk, took out pen and ink, blotting paper, pen wiper, paper, the sealing wax. She did not want a conversation with Mr Gates so soon again, but he could be of use to her, in finding the Bartlett family of Sussex.

She said goodbye to the house with no tears, for it had never been truly hers. She regretted the garden more, but Mr Gates had found her four acres and a cottage to buy, and a tenant farmer who would transplant whatever was possible from the Chelsea garden, take cuttings of what was not, and grow fields of whatever she required in return for a secure home and fifteen pounds a year.

Her hopefully temporary lodgings, in the meantime, were with a widow who could no longer afford to keep her home on her own. Hen hoped to buy her own house, if not by the sea, at least in an area where a widow might find congenial company. It was a smoke-stained red brick London house in a back-to-back street of houses, but with the luxury of looking out onto a small gated park, where a few trees loomed through the ever-present smoke and vanished entirely when the smoke met fog. But the house itself smelled of lavender furniture polish and toasting teacakes. Hen would have the front bedroom, the drawing room and whatever meals she requested.

Mr Gates seemed shocked that Hen did not want more. It seemed he had not yet been able to find an area where a woman might participate in intellectual discussion. Perhaps there was none to be found. Possibly he, too, did not know even how to begin the task, when the Royal Society and similar organisations were open only to men, and Oxford and Cambridge allowed male students only, as did Edinburgh and all the medical schools he had approached.

He had, however, found a family of Bartletts in Sussex, a well-respected name there, it seemed, just as her father had remembered.

She asked her maid, Ethel — shocked and delighted at the annuity that would allow her to move to her home village and have her choice of husband — to stay in her employ a few weeks longer. Ladies did not travel unaccompanied. Her father's carriage would be sold and the horses retired to the farmer who kept her herb garden, but the horses, and the grooms, too, would provide a final service: taking her to Sussex to the family she did not know.

She also realised they might not know anything at all about her, including that she existed. The only person she had met who'd known her husband was the man she only knew as 'Tim'. It seemed 'Tim' had not told Max's family of Max's marriage. He had not even believed it was a true marriage. It was also an alliance of which he had obviously not approved. If he had told them that Max's last living act was to marry — even if it was not recognised by the army — surely, after the edge of grief had gone, someone in the family would have searched for her, if only to hear what Max's last moment had been like. Any man who had attended the many Waterloo commemorations could have easily found Superintendent of Hospitals Gilbert and his daughter.

Hen had looked for Tim at the dinners and ball for Waterloo veterans the previous year, but had not seen him. This was not unusual, of course, for there were many dinners given across the country in honour of those at Waterloo. If Tim had stayed in the army he might even be with the force strengthening fortifications in Flanders, or even in the colonies, the Americas, South Africa, Jamaica, even that far-off prison colony of Botany Bay, for all of them needed the soldiers of the king.

Tim knew Hen's family name. She did not know his. Her few queries about a 'Tim' had given her so many varied results that she sometimes thought that half the Iron Duke's army must have been Timothys.

Bartlett Manor was a day's journey from London, but she could not arrive in the evening. Mr Gates booked rooms at an establishment he vouched for. Its sheets smelled of sunlight, welcome after the London air. Hen ate in her room with Ethel, while the two grooms ate in the public rooms below: a chicken stewed with leeks and buttered cabbage, and an apple pie, which made Hen remember the last dinner with her father. It probably always would.

Ethel talked: of her home, her mother, her six sisters, and of a young farmhand called Jacob. Hen listened, and even smiled, glad that her sorrow had at least hatched Ethel's happiness. She offered Ethel the advice she had heard her mother give on how best to limit the number of children. She had not been meant to hear it. But the advice had been detailed. Ethel received it with blushes but deep interest.

Hen knew she would not sleep, but did.

She dressed with care the next morning: the dull-sheened black silk mourning dress of the recently bereaved; a widow's jet-embroidered cape; the widow's cap she had dispensed with after a year; the jet earrings her father had given her when they had first returned to England; and black lace gloves. She had a year in mourning clothes ahead of her once again.

She looked at herself in the mirror: pale and too thin. She'd always had to think of meals for others. It was difficult to remember to eat just for herself. The reflected image did not seem to be her. Who was Henrietta Bartlett?

Four years back she had been a wife, a widow, and a daughter. By tonight she might be something else. A daughter-in-law, companion, comfort ...

The carriage rolled through the Bartlett manor gates at ten minutes to eleven exactly, not the time to make social calls, but this was not a social call. It was a time when a woman would be consulting her housekeeper or cook, writing letters or compiling guest lists.

A neat, freshly gravelled driveway, rhododendron hedges that must be a glory in spring and which also indicated that those in residence would be at home in spring, rather than taking a fashionable London residence for the season. The house was a gentleman's residence of red brick in a horseshoe shape, garlanded by shrubbery.

It was — ordinary. Hen had not expected that. Max had not been ordinary. She felt a sudden panic. Had Mr Gates been mistaken, and this was entirely the wrong family? But if it was, they must surely know of any other families of their name nearby.

The carriage stopped. She waited for Elkins to open the carriage door for her. She let him precede her up the steps and to pull the bell, too, Ethel behind her.

The door opened on a butler, stout and grey haired and with a nose made for looking down on undesirable visitors. Hen's heart clenched. She had hoped for a house with not quite the estate for a butler, despite the 'Honourable'.

'Mrs Maxwelton Bartlett to see Mrs Bartlett.'

'I beg your pardon, madam?'

Hen handed him her card.

He stared at the card for a moment, then more searchingly at her. 'One moment, madam. I will see if Mrs Bartlett is at home. If you would come this way?'

The butler hesitated in a hallway that was the size of a reception room, walnut panelled, portrait daubed, with small uncomfortable chairs, as if wondering whether Hen and Ethel should wait there, then opened the door of what was evidently a morning room with a fire lit, for its scent of apple wood, perhaps, not to heat the sunlit room, with an embroidery frame and a sewing box left on a low table between a pair of sofas.

Three portraits hung above the mantelpiece, two of them of young boys, and one of a girl with brown ringlets. One boy stared arrogantly at the painter; the other seemed to be gazing impatiently out the window. Max, unmistakable even at perhaps ten years old.

'Would you mind waiting in the carriage, Ethel?' asked Hen, attempting to breathe normally.

The butler seemed reassured by Hen's accent. 'If the young person would care to wait, I will show her to the kitchen.'

'Thank you,' said Hen. She sat on the sofa furthest from the embroidery, which was thus not the favourite seat of her hostess. Was the Mrs Bartlett she was about to see Max's mother? Sister-in-law? Cousin?

The door closed. Hen waited. The door opened. A woman stood there, tall, with grey-streaked hair, in a buttercup yellow dress that sang of summer. Hen stood and curtseyed. The other woman did not.

His mother, Hen thought. She had known his face for only a few hours, but this woman had his chin and eyes below her lace cap.

'Mrs Bartlett?' the woman enquired.

'Yes. Please excuse my appearing like this. I should have written first, I know. I should have written to you four years ago ...'

'I'm sorry, but I am afraid I have no idea what you are talking about. Are you claiming acquaintance or a relationship?'

The coldness could have frozen a bear. Hen stopped, startled. Her life had been irregular; she had known hostility and wariness, but mostly friendship, camaraderie, gratitude and kindness. She wasn't sure how to deal with ice.

Except with the truth.

'My name is Mrs Maxwelton Bartlett. I married my husband on the field of Waterloo.'

The woman's expression cleared, but she came no nearer. 'Ah, so you are the pretender. Gilmore, isn't it? Or Gilkins? I was warned that one day you might appear.'

'I pretend nothing. I have my marriage papers with me.'

'A piece of paper can be scratched by anyone.'

'The Church of St Thérèse has a record of our marriage.' Hen had seen it written in the register there, when she farewelled Père

Flambeaux the day she and her father left for England. Surgeon Gilbert had sent a substantial contribution to the welfare of Père Flambeaux's flock each year. 'The priest there will vouch for me.'

'A Frenchman —'

'Flemish. Mrs Bartlett, I apologise for disturbing you. My presence is obviously unwelcome. I merely wished to meet ...' Hen could not speak. Nor would she cry in front of this woman.

'I suppose you want money,' said Mrs Bartlett flatly.

Her words evaporated Hen's tears. 'On the contrary, I wished to make sure that you did not.'

'I ... I beg your pardon?' For the first time Mrs Bartlett seemed to look at Hen as a person, not an object.

'I am ... comfortably situated. My father, who died two months ago, left me with an independence ...'

'My condolences ...' the other woman murmured. She still had not asked Hen to sit, much less rung for tea.

'I also wondered if you would like to know your son's wife, or if you needed ...' Hen noted the rheumatism that bent the older woman's fingers, and which must ache '... a balm for your fingers, which look painful. Did you know I was the daughter of an army surgeon?'

'The friend who warned me to expect a Miss Gilbreth, claiming a form of marriage to my son, did mention that. But my son did not.'

'I am sure he would have, had he lived.'

'What do you mean?' The shock on the woman's face was genuine. 'Max is dead? How?'

Hen blinked. Did this woman overindulge in laudanum and sherry, as so many ladies did? She *seemed* quite sane. 'At Waterloo, Mrs Bartlett,' she said gently.

The woman sat quickly, her twisted hand pressed to her heart. 'You should not have shocked me so. Max returned quite unharmed from the continent, apart from a small injury to his arm.'

'Small! I stitched it myself. The arm was almost shattered ...' The words suddenly sank in. 'Max is ... alive?'

'Yes.'

The room vanished into shadows, then burst into colour more vivid than she had ever seen, as though a dishcloth had been shading the world for the last four years. Hen found her breath at last. 'Where? Mrs Bartlett, please ...'

She should never have believed Tim; she would not have believed him if she had not hunted for Max through shattered corpses for a week, if she hadn't been so tired and beginning to despair. She had searched, but obviously not in the right places.

It would have been so easy, Hen realised, for him to secrete Max in his billet, or a house rented by the many English families who had come to support relatives in the army. Of course Max would have been taken somewhere like that if possible, rather than to the overcrowded hospitals or even his own billet. He might even have been taken directly to Antwerp or to England ...

'I think that you should leave, Miss Galmont.' Mrs Bartlett rang the bell. The butler appeared with the promptness of a man who had been waiting outside the door, but not in any way with his ear pressed to the keyhole. 'Please show this person out.'

'No ...' began Hen, then stopped. This woman — Max's mother, impossible that she should be his mother — would not tell her where Max was, no matter how much she entreated. But now she knew he was alive she would be able to find him ...

... if he wanted to be found. Hen saw the other woman see her make the deduction. Max Bartlett lived, but he had never contacted the woman he had married on the field of Waterloo. He had never even mentioned her to his mother.

A hasty marriage. A rash marriage. A marriage he did not repudiate, but just ignored, not even telling his parents a wife might appear. It would have been so easy to find her, in Brussels or in England.

He did not want her.

Hen curtseyed, her back straight, her head unbowed. 'Good morning, Mrs Bartlett. I apologise again for interrupting you. I will not bother your family again.'

For the first time what might be sympathy appeared on the woman's face, mixed with relief. The pretender had arrived, but would take herself away with no demands and no persuasions. The pretender was — despite her attempts to keep tears away — also clearly distressed. But to offer her tea would be a false encouragement. Hen could almost read the woman's thoughts.

She allowed the butler to show her to the hall just as a young man emerged from the door opposite. 'I say, Lamson, would you take a note to old Weatherby and tell him we'll be shooting ...'

He stopped and smiled appreciatively at her. 'Good morning,' he began. 'I do apologise —' His words stopped. He recognised her.

Tim.

'What are you doing here?' demanded Hen.

'I think that is a question for you. I live here.'

'Your surname is Bartlett?'

'My wife's maiden name was Bartlett, not that it is any business of yours. Miss Gilbert, I believe.'

'You know it isn't.'

'I know nothing of the kind. Max denied any marriage had taken place.'

It wasn't true. Could not be true. Or was it Max who had sent Tim with money for her? For pity? The concern for her welfare that had prompted his proposal?

Suddenly one fact floated above all others.

Max had returned here, but it had been a 'friend' who had warned his mother that a woman claiming to be a wife might appear. Surely if Max feared that he would have been the one to tell his parents.

He had not.

'If you will excuse me, Miss Gilbert.' Tim moved towards the door.

'No, I will not excuse you. Look at me, if you please.'

He turned, stared at the pistols in her hands. Hen directed one at him, one at the astonished butler. 'I am an excellent shot, though in truth I haven't practised for the last four years. But I am sure I won't miss at this distance. Tell me where Max is.'

'Don't be ridiculous.' Tim turned.

Hen fired. The panel just above his head exploded. A scream erupted from the next room. The door opened. Mrs Bartlett stared into the hallway.

'I have one shot left. This time I will aim at your knee,' Hen said to Tim calmly. 'You will probably survive the wound,' she added. 'But you will be a cripple and in pain all your life. Or you can tell me why Max did not tell his mother about our marriage.'

Tim looked around for the butler, but the man stood next to Max's mother, her light touch on his arm restraining him from intervening.

'The truth please,' said Hen. 'I am extremely good at discerning the truth.' Which was a lie — she was no better or worse than anyone else she knew — but he did not know that.

Tim cast her a poisonous look. 'Because I told him you were dead.'

Mrs Bartlett gave a faint moan. Was she realising a pistol-whirling mad woman was indeed her daughter-in-law, or bewailing the destruction of her panelling? Hen didn't care. 'Where is Max now?'

Mrs Bartlett spoke, slightly breathlessly. 'In New South Wales.'

Hen turned to her, but kept the pistol pointed at Tim. 'He is commissioned there?'

'Max sold his commission when he returned from the continent. He never intended the army to be his profession.' Mrs Bartlett seemed to regain her composure. 'Miss ... my dear ... please put the pistol away.'

'While you call to have me removed?'

'No.' The woman spoke sincerely. 'I do not know if you are truly married to my son. He would never speak of the battle, nor its aftermath. He hardly spoke at all. He spent most days walking in the woods with only the dogs for company, and left as soon as he could organise his affairs. I put his anguish down to the losses there. I never thought …'

'The battlefield is not a usual place to find a wife,' admitted Hen. 'Though he said a friend of his had done so.'

'Nor do you seem the usual kind of wife.' Was that the beginning of a smile? The smile vanished. 'Tim, go away. We will talk of this later. I suspect there will be quite a lot to say. Lamson, would you please fetch tea? And tell Cook the two of us will have a luncheon, here in the morning room. Miss … Mrs … I am afraid I do not know your name.'

'Mrs Bartlett,' said Hen dryly. 'Henrietta Bartlett. They call me Hen.'

Mrs Bartlett seemed to start at the name. 'Did my son call you Hen?'

'Yes.' Hen ignored the tears suddenly running down her face. Why should the news that Max lived make her cry? But the tears would not stop. She placed the pistols back under her belt below the cape, found a handkerchief and blew her nose. 'I told him Hen was a northern word for love. He liked that.'

'My dear, I would very much like to have tea with you, and talk about my son. I miss him. I believe I would like to know you too.' The smile lingered again. 'I am regarded as quite a shot myself, though my targets have more generally been pheasants.'

'I apologise for ruining your panelling.'

'It's far too sombre. High time it was replaced. Please, come back into the morning room. That chair is the most comfortable. Do you mind if I call you Hen?'

'Of course you can, Mrs Bartlett.'

Mrs Bartlett looked at her consideringly. 'It seems you have the right to call me Mama. But I do not think you would enjoy staying here to do so. My older son is as dull and small minded as my son-in-law, and my husband is a bore. I think you would frighten the remaining males of this household into rudeness. Indeed, you have already begun. Please excuse my frankness, but

I did not choose any of them — including my husband — so I believe I'm not at fault.'

'You ... you sound like Max.'

'I'm glad there was one good pup in the litter. So will you go to New South Wales?'

'Of course.'

'You know even the voyage is dangerous? The colony is a place of criminals, with few free settlers, such as my son.' Mrs Bartlett looked amused. 'But then you carry pistols in your reticule.'

'I will set out as soon as possible. Unless ...' Hen hesitated, a sudden doubt bayoneting her joy '... unless Max ... he didn't ... he hasn't ...?'

Mrs Bartlett leaned over to her and patted her hand. 'Remarried, thinking himself a widower? No. I think it will take Max far longer than four years to recover from the loss of you, and even if he had a mind to marriage, which I am sure he has not, I gather there are few unmarried women in the colony, and even fewer eligible gentlewomen.'

She sat back and shook her head. 'The poor boy. Why didn't I see what was wrong? No wonder he never spoke of his time in Belgium. I should have guessed it was more than just the battle. Yes, from all accounts it was horrific, but Max is the strongest man I know. He asked for a land grant, you see, as far away as possible from all he knew.'

'How is he now?' Hen asked tentatively.

'Enjoying the colony and all its challenges. I think he is finally happy. I had a letter from him just last week. He does talk to me now, thank goodness, even if it is only by letter, and with such long gaps between them. The voyage takes so long, six months, twelve, or even longer, depending on the route. This one is dated almost a year ago. Will you take a letter to him?'

'Of course,' Hen repeated.

Mrs Bartlett smiled. 'You are possibly the only young woman in the world who would agree so easily to undertaking a long voyage with so much peril.'

'I am sure there are many more like me.' If only she could find them. She longed for friendship almost as much as she longed for Max. 'What else should I do but go to New South Wales?'

'What else indeed. I'll tell Max I approve of his choice, but that his father will probably be glad that a pistol-wielding surgeon's daughter is across the world away from polite society. I presume you will sail as soon as you can? And you truly do not need money?'

'Yes to both. Before I leave I must give you a receipt for an ointment for your hands. You will find it most efficacious for the pain and stiffness.'

Mrs Bartlett looked pleased. 'Thank you.'

'May I read the letter he wrote you?'

'You have every right to read it,' said the other woman softly. She reached into the space between dress and petticoat. She had kept it next to her heart.

Dear Mama,

It is hot as Hades, and every time I sit down I seem to meet another snake, but I have seen the Land I've been assigned and it's good. It is the furthest grant made so far in New South Wales. I am indeed on the frontier here, with wilderness about me. There is a River, which is navigable, which is lucky as it will take a Month at least to get Stock here overland. I will build my House up beyond Flood level — if the Logs washed up upon the River Bank are anything to go by the Land floods high. There is a Creek that I've called 'Gilbert's' and I think Gilbert's Creek may be the best Name for the Property too. I called the River The Hen — and it does have an amazing Number of native Poultry — then discovered back in Sydney Town that some wretched explorer had named it already, having crossed it only once, while I am to live Here. The Natives may have some word for it, but I cannot tell which of their Words is the name of the River or just 'Water' or even 'What are those odd Garments?' They do find my Breeches hilarious, and more than once I have been afraid that if I took them off my trousers might vanish for further Inspection.

Please tell my estimable Sister that the Natives here are not Cannibals, and thank her for her concern for my Carcase. The Natives have indeed proved most friendly, helping me roof my first Hut with great swathes of bark they peel off the local trees, and which we now use for the Huts of my Workmen. They do however have an unfortunate Habit of going stark Naked, unlike the Indians of the Americas, but possibly do not tell her that, in case it overpowers her delicate Sensibilities.

I hope this finds you as well as it leaves me. I am giving it to Simpson, my foreman — a Convict, but a Waterloo man, who came Home to find his family starving. A shilling Pension did not go far. Simpson will take the mail to Sydney Town then bring back supplies, but I will return there myself next month, to arrange to buy Stock and much else. I have a Cottage just down from the Brickworks, small, but sufficient for when I am in Sydney.

Please give my best to the Pater, and Donald and Tim. I doubt they'd like it here, but I find I do.

Your loving son,
Max

Chapter 8

Portable Lemonade

Most efficacious against Scurvy and the Pantings and also
quite Delicious. Thinly slice fifty Lemons or Limes and cover
with fine Sugar. Leave for one Day, strain off all Liquid. Boil
it with six tablespoons Cream Tartar, stirring to thick Syrup.
Bottle with a Wax Seal. A tablespoon to be taken twice a
Day mixed well in boiled Water or added to the Ration of
Rum for members of a Ship's Crew.

From the Notebooks of Henrietta Bartley

Mr Gates stared at his client. He looked as nervous as if Hen
had wielded a pistol at him too. But there was no need for him
to ever know of the weapons now back in her reticule. Mr Gates
was competent, and honest, even if he had never experienced a
young female client who knew exactly what she wished.

'A journey to Sydney Town is not as simple as crossing the
Channel, Mrs Bartlett. We are talking about the other side of the
world. The few ships that venture so far are convict transports,
which I do not recommend …'

'I would prefer not to travel on a convict transport,' agreed
Hen. Desperate as she was to see Max, she would like to reach
Australia alive. Most convict ships carried typhoid or worse,
often reaching port with not even enough crew to bring them

in to harbour safely. The loss of a third or more of their human cargo was considered reasonable. One of her father's assistant surgeons had served on the squalid hulks that held prisoners on the Thames. While the passengers' accommodations would of course be separate, the diseases and infectious miasmas rising from the filth below would hazard everyone on board.

Mr Gates took off his glasses and polished them. At last he said hesitantly, 'Your letter stated you also wished me to advertise for a companion for you on the voyage.'

Hen nodded. 'It does not seem advisable to sail so far, stopping at several ports, by myself. A single woman might be ... misunderstood, even with a maid, and nor do I know a maid who wants to travel across the world.'

'Perhaps the problem has been solved. No, I have not been able to find you a companion,' he added hurriedly. 'But another client, a Mrs Angus McDougal, has asked me to advertise for a companion for *her*. She is the widow of a Glasgow merchant, and her son is established in the colony as a ship's chandler. One of his customers, who captains his own ship and is bound for New South Wales, has agreed to take Mrs McDougal even though he does not usually take passengers. His ship is undoubtedly the fastest and safest way for you to reach the colony.'

'Mrs McDougal and I might companion each other?' Hen smiled. The sky was suddenly blue, even though it rained, and the larks were singing even if all she could hear were the cries of street vendors offering hot potatoes, dubious pies or elderly lavender drenched in scent. Max was alive and there was a life she'd like to live on a hill above a river that had once been called The Hen.

Mr Gates looked nervous. 'I doubt Mrs McDougal would accept ... a joint companionship. She is advanced in age, and set in her ideas. By companion she means someone who will fetch her knitting and make her tea.'

'What else should I do on board a ship? I enjoy caring for people.'

'You might find her … difficult.'

'Mrs McDougal may find me difficult too, Mr Gates. But it is a long voyage. At some stage we will learn to accommodate each other. I remember at one camp —' Hen stopped, memories of her parents still too poignant to share. 'When do we sail?'

'The *Ivy* sails for Ceylon in three weeks' time, and from there to New South Wales. You will find it … rough.'

'Probably not as rough as the camp in Spain when it rained for three weeks and the supply train was bogged and the oxen got the squits —' Hen stopped at Mr Gates's expression. She carefully resumed the role of English lady. 'I will write to you about which of my stored possessions I wish sent out. Where do I go on board?'

'Here in London, if you wish. Mrs McDougal intends to board at Plymouth the day the ship sails. Her letter states that she does not enjoy travel.'

And yet she was about to cross the world. 'I look forward to meeting her,' said Hen.

An expression passed over Mr Gates's stout features. It might almost have been relief that he would never need to deal in person with either lady again.

Chapter 9

Soup For a Voyage

Boil the Flesh & Bones of ten Chickens, forty carrots, ten
apples chopped, ten leeks, twenty prunes, one tablespoon
salt for four hours in Water sufficient to cover. Strain. Boil
the liquid till it has reduced to four cupfuls. Leave to set on
a Tray then store portions in calico, layered with dry Rice.

From the Notebooks of Henrietta Bartley

Dear Mr Timson,
I hope you and Mrs Timson are as well as this leaves me, and that
the cottage has proved to be comfortable, and the well Water sweet.
I intend to set sail for Sydney Town in the colony of New South
Wales shortly and will probably take Residence there. This means
I will need you to pick and package Herbs to be sent to me in the
colony.

Please dry the herbs in list one and send them to me at the
above address with all haste. A similar package should be sent to
me care of the Governor of New South Wales on each available
convict ship travelling to the colony. Please do not send any plants
or seeds on a merchant ship as it may for many reasons be diverted
to a more profitable enterprise on the way and so never reach New
South Wales.

Mr Gates will provide you with the dates when the Packages
will be needed. Please ensure all herbs are well dried and in
packages weighing no more than one-ounce each, sewed into oilcloth

*and packed into a tin-lined wooden Trunk with dry rice between
each layer. Mr Gates will provide the funds to do this.*

*As Governors change I cannot tell you the name of the
Incumbent when I am there, but it is likely to be Governor
Macquarie. None the less, it will be more secure not to add his
name, in case any mail directed to him is forwarded to his next
posting.*

*Would you also please pot cuttings or rootings of the
plants in the second list, and seeds of those in list three. There
should be at least six pots of each. Mr Gates will arrange to have
them transported by a passenger who can tend them during the
voyage.*

I remain, yours most sincerely,
Mrs M Bartlett

Mrs McDougal stared at the two bunks, the single porthole, the
hinged tray in place of a table, and two of Hen's trunks taking
up a quarter of the cabin space. Mrs McDougal was sixty, a face
of chin, nose and bright black eyes, bony as a clothes peg under
what were surely three layers of flannel petticoat beneath her
black bombazine dress, with white hair under her widow's cap
and her arm around a small Highland Terrier that seemed to be
mostly teeth, all of which it bared at Hen.

Mrs McDougal fixed Hen with an accusing glare. 'Two
cabin trunks? They must be placed in the hold immediately. If
you knew how to pack properly, girl, you would not worry that
your frills and furbelows would be damaged by bilge water.' Her
accent was carefully not Scots.

Hen decided to give another curtsey. 'They don't contain
clothes, Mrs McDougal. Or only in small part. I hope their
contents may prove useful to you as well.'

'Then what do they contain, madam?'

That was an improvement on 'girl'. 'Plum puddings wrapped
in brandy-soaked calico, a dry lemonade I made with zest and
sugar, flasks of lemon syrup, portable soup ...'

'How can soup be portable?' The dog gave a bark, as if it didn't want to be left out of the proceedings. 'Be quiet, Waddles.' Mrs McDougal placed the dog on the floor.

'I boiled the stock to the thickest jelly, sliced it when cold and solid, then wrapped each portion in oiled calico. I used a beef and vegetable base for one, and a chicken and prune base for the other ...'

'Cock-a-leekie? Do ye mean to say you have brought cock-a-leekie soup?'

'Yes, Mrs McDougal.' Hen could have mentioned the dried rose heps and chamomile flowers for tisanes, the calomel and quinine and laudanum, the apricots she had bought at vast expense and dried above the fire in her lodgings, the strings of dried apple she had purchased, being short of time ...

'Then the trunks may stay,' allowed Mrs McDougal. 'But we will have little room with my trunk as well.' She looked again at the two narrow beds, the single porthole, the hinged table flat against the cabin wall. 'I expect that a fine lady such as yourself expected better lodgings than this?'

'Mr Gates told me what to expect, ma'am.' Hen did not add that she had known far worse.

'I hope you are not too fine to help me into my night attire when we have dined.'

'Not at all, Mrs McDougal.' Hen could have said she was more used to undoing male attire, but there had been female patients too, when Mama had been alive. She twitched her skirts to try to discourage the sniffing dog. 'I am here to be of assistance always.' She hoped that assistance did not include walking the dog. Nor cleaning up its droppings.

Mrs McDougal sniffed. 'I informed the captain that we would dine in our cabin, as we are the only women on the ship. Stop it, Waddles. There is no need to bite the young lady.' Her tone seemed to add 'yet'.

A dinner of boiled mutton and potatoes, which Hen suspected would be their daily ration, with ship's biscuit, salt butter and hard cheese. At least the mutton was fresh tonight, not salted as it would be on the voyage except when one of the sheep on board was slaughtered. They ate sitting on their beds, the fold-down table between them. Mrs McDougal gazed with dismay at the grease around the meat, more hacked than carved. 'My William assured me we would be provided with every comfort.'

'Mutton and boiled potatoes may be the captain's idea of comfort, Mrs McDougal. The sailors likely get much poorer fare. William is your son?'

'He is. A fine lad, a regular attendee at the kirk and with a prosperous business in the colony. But he needs me to keep house for him. I doubt there is a servant you can trust, much less one properly trained, in all of New South Wales, not with most of the poor wretches criminals.'

'You may be correct, Mrs McDougal.'

Mrs McDougal pursed her mouth, as if to say she was not paying Hen to have opinions. But then she was not paying Hen at all.

Beyond the airless cabin the wharf creaked. Hen could hear men haul at ropes and the shudder of sails above the hammering, the shouts and thumps of every port. 'It seems we are finally setting sail.'

Mrs McDougal stood, shifting Waddles from her lap. 'I have no appetite. I will go up onto the deck for a while.'

'Would you like me to accompany you, Mrs McDougal?'

'Thank you. I will go alone.' Mrs McDougal took one of the lamps. Waddles trotted at her skirts as she left the cabin.

Hen ate the potatoes, a slice of mutton, and nibbled a biscuit, which seemed reasonably fresh — 'reasonably' meaning baked within the last six months and free of weevils.

She could read by the light of the remaining lamp, or she could take a final look at the dark land to which, quite possibly, she would never return.

Nor did she feel any wish to. 'A cottage by the sea in England' had been a dream while on campaign, but the reality of English society had been stifling. Somewhere, somehow, women must lead good fulfilled lives on this island, but she did not know them, nor how to find their society.

But she would still like to say farewell. She wound a shawl around her head and shoulders and took the remaining lamp.

The cabin — the captain's own — opened out onto the deck. She checked she was out of the way of the business of sailing, then sought Mrs McDougal's lamp, shining by the rail. Beyond her a pen of damp sheep looked as miserable as if they knew their fate was to be eaten on the voyage. Pigs grunted somewhere beyond the lamplight, their smell unmistakable.

Hen walked a few yards past Mrs McDougal before moving to the rail herself, making it clear she was not offering the unwanted companionship.

The *Ivy* had made good use of tide and wind, for the land was already a black smudge against the stars. At least her final look at England would be free of rain or fog. One look was enough. The air was as chill as a new-minted penny. Nor did she feel even a hint of wistfulness.

She had spent most of her life with men who offered their lives for this country, had never questioned their duty to do so, nor the nobility of the cause. But in the past four years, England had been like the corsets of last century, attempting to confine her into a shape that could never naturally be hers.

She moved back to the cabin, glancing at Mrs McDougal. The old woman's face was firmly expressionless, but her cheeks gleamed wet in the lamplight.

Mrs McDougal might be eager to housekeep for 'My William' but it seemed she loved her homeland too.

Hen slipped back into the cabin.

It was perhaps hours later when Mrs McDougal returned. Hen had undressed but kept a gown on over her nightdress. She slid out of bed and wordlessly began to undo the buttons on the back of Mrs McDougal's dress. Even after four years with the services of a maid, Hen still preferred dresses with buttons down the side that she could manage herself.

'That will be all,' said Mrs McDougal shortly, once the buttons were undone. Hen slid into bed and turned away to give the older woman privacy while she slipped off her dress and replaced it with a much-ruffled white nightdress, and her widow's cap with one of white linen. Waddles had already made himself comfortable at the foot of the other bunk. Mrs McDougal put a cloth over the lamp. The bunk creaked as she lowered herself into it.

Hen slept.

She woke to small feet across her face, the scratch of whiskers.

Rats! She reached under her pillow for her pistol with one hand while pulling the cloth off the lamp with the other. The rat stared at her from the end of her bunk now. She aimed ...

Then stopped, as with a flying leap Waddles grabbed the rat by the throat, dispatched it neatly, then grabbed another over by the door, breaking its neck too. He managed to kill a third before the others fled.

'Guid laddie,' said Mrs McDougal softly.

Waddles allowed himself to be patted, arranged the rats neatly in a line, then sat by the first. Hen turned away at the first crunch of bone to see Mrs McDougal staring at her. 'Ye weren't going to fire that, ye daft hennie!' The Scots accent was strong now.

'Yes,' said Hen.

'And put a hole in the side! We're on a ship, ye know!'

'I'd have made sure the bedclothes stopped the bullet from going further.'

'And have us covered in shreds of rat into the bargain ...' Mrs McDougal shook her head. 'Put that pistol away now and gie me yer word ye will not use it again, unless we're boarded by pirates. Waddles will see tae any rats,' she added. 'And I have always found a guid hatpin sufficient to discourage any man who might nay be a gentleman.'

Hen unloaded the pistol then put it in her trunk.

Mrs McDougal regarded her. She might have disapproved of the pistol, but she seemed impressed by Hen's enterprise in carrying it. 'Ye said ye have cock-a-leekie in that trunk?'

'Yes.'

'I packed porridge oats. Enough for two, if ye would care to share them.'

'Very much so, Mrs McDougal.'

'Do ye knit?'

'Only poorly,' admitted Hen.

'Well, we shall see how guid ye can become by the end of the voyage. It is lucky I packed spare needles. A lassie's hands should always be occupied. Tomorrow we might perhaps pay a visit to the galley in the morning and offer our services, unless we are to eat tough mutton all the way to New South Wales. Wales! Why couldn't they name it for Scotland, I'd like to know? What has Wales to do with the colony?' Her accent receded with the shock. 'But at least Governor Macquarie is a good God-fearin' Scot.'

'You will miss your home?' asked Hen quietly, sitting on the bed, trying to ignore the slurp as Waddles began on the innards of the second rat.

'My Angus is buried there and my William was born there, and his sisters born and buried there too. And that is where my heart will be, forever more. But my William needs me.' Mrs McDougal blew her nose, no longer trying to hide her tears. 'And ye, lassie?'

'I don't have a home. Or perhaps I do.' And, haltingly, Hen began the tale of the marriage on the battlefield, the river that had been called The Hen, and the hope of what might wait for her at the other end of the world.

Chapter 10

A Stale Biscuit Pie of Great Use Aboard Ship

Take four cups stale biscuit, broken to Crumb. Add to half
a cup Salt Butter, melted with a quarter cup Cocoa powder
and fine Sugar, half a cup. Currants and Raisins of the Sun
may also be added for good Effect. Press into a Tray to set. If
powdered sugar available, one cup mixed with one teaspoon
ground ginger and water, sufficient, may glaze the Whole.

From the Notebooks of Henrietta Bartley

A line appeared on the horizon that might be cloud or land,
but as Hen and Mrs McDougal sat on the deck, bonneted and
veiled ('Ye must guard your complexion, lassie. Luckily, I have
brought sufficient cucumber water for us both!') the line became
firmer.

But they did not venture nearer. The western coast of New
Holland was treacherous, the graveyard of too many ships
sailing up its coast to reach the rich trading port of Batavia in
the Spice Islands. Instead winds that tasted of ice filled the *Ivy*'s
sails to take her south, then east once more, into lashing waves
and on a wary look-out for icebergs.

By then Hen had discovered that even a routine voyage
such as theirs could be more dangerous than Waterloo. She
did not wish to remember rounding the Cape of Good Hope:

three weeks, each crash of the vast waves threatening to turn the *Ivy* into matchsticks, then, at last, a lull. The two days utterly becalmed on a flat ocean had been almost as terrifying, suddenly realising that until the wind rose they were stranded between sea and sky.

But, on the whole, the voyage had been most interesting. She had even managed to knit a pair of stockings, though Mrs McDougal had turned the heels for her, and expressed her relief that the knots and slipped stitches would not be seen under Hen's skirts.

Other enterprises had been more successful. Hen had asked Captain Jansen's permission to administer portable lemonade to the sailors sickening with scurvy. The captain seemed to regard tending to ill sailors as a harmless female foible, and was glad that the female passengers he had been persuaded to take on board kept themselves occupied.

He had been slightly more startled when Hen set a fractured leg bone after his First Mate slipped on the icy deck past Cape Hope, and wary but not interfering when she amputated or repaired fingers mangled in the rigging.

Three days out from Ceylon — intense heat and a thousand scents and colour and the chance to replenish her supplies and also observe elephants (Hen would have loved to buy an elephant) — Captain Jansen asked tentatively if she had any experience pulling a tooth.

Once he had recovered from the extraction the ladies were regularly asked to the bridge. He thereafter offered port or madeira with dinner, as well as his conversation: fascinating stories of thirty years at sea, rivalling the First Mate, who claimed to have been a pirate, and the Third Mate, who had lived three years with a mermaid, while Waddles crunched the remnants of yet another rat under the table. Captain Jansen took it for granted now that Hen would be tending toes turning black from frostbite on the icy decks while sailing across the Southern Ocean. Whales sported in the waves, leaping up and crashing down as if performing for the crew. Birds soared and screamed, including the almost familiar cry of seagulls, following them to dive for the ship's rubbish.

The freezing waves were to their south now, and the new land was to their north. Their journey had nearly reached its end, just as Mrs McDougal completed her twentieth pair of woollen stockings and she and Hen had finished reading *The Complete Works of Robert Burns* — Mrs McDougal's most prized possession — to each other in turn for the eighteenth time, or possibly the five hundredth.

Hen gazed at the coast every day through the captain's eyeglass. Vast cliffs; even vaster red or yellow plains, with no trees nor grass nor, according to Captain Jansen, any streams or rivers either. But she had glimpsed distant green as they rounded the continent and soon more of the colour appeared again — a faded, sun-drenched green, reminding Hen slightly of the light in Spain. Sunsets shone pink as a baby's toenail, but late at night the sky to the south shimmered green and silver.

At last the *Ivy* turned northwards, the coast of New South Wales finally to their left. The sheep, pigs, goats, poultry and even Mrs McDougal's oats had been consumed. Most of the crew subsisted on salt pork, rum and ship's biscuit, regarding Hen's offerings of Ceylon spinach in vinegar and dried pineapple or mango with suspicion. Of course they lost three teeth for every voyage. What sailor didn't? But they would not touch fruit without the captain's order.

Despite it being winter the morning sun was so warm the ladies left off the calico petticoats that had been needed in the Southern Ocean, though Mrs McDougal still wore two of cotton. They changed their woollen stockings, shawls and mittens for cotton too, and their thick wool dresses for lighter ones, retrieved from trunks brought up from the hold and dreadfully creased. Hen managed to smooth them with the surgical iron, but she, too, longed for a maid's services again. And a washerwoman, and fresh water to bathe in. And an apple ...

The coast was close enough to watch without the eyeglass now. Beaches of white sand or gold; blue mountains and green; spires of smoke each day; but mostly ... space.

She had not realised how cramped and confined she had found England, she who'd known the French and Spanish mountains. Each parcel of England was carefully corralled into fields or woodland by hedges, fences, stone walls and conventions.

Here there was room to carve out a different life. An estate where she would be free to be herself, for on that battlefield Max had seen the heart of her.

Max. She was sailing to Max.

She had not expected beauty. The ship passed between narrow cliffs where the waves foamed and spluttered, into a harbour of sudden calm that might have been painted blue. There were a hundred inlets, tiny peninsulas, mostly uninhabited, except for a distant beach where dark-skinned natives seemed to watch the ship, too far away for her to see their features.

Hen had known many lands, but this was the first where so much lay untouched by man. Birds flew overhead that she labelled parrots and macaws, but she had no name for the smaller ones, the size of a sparrow but brilliant green, that soared in a mob across the inlets. A cloud of yellow butterflies flickered through the trees.

This was the southern winter, yet the day was warm enough for a light dress, a bonnet and a pelisse, though Mrs McDougal wore a tartan shawl, carefully wrapped in her trunk to wear for her meeting with 'My William'.

The ship's cannon boomed to signal their arrival to the pilot boat that would guide them past rocks and islands to shore. Chain jangled as Captain Jansen ordered the anchor dropped.

Waddles barked. A fishing boat approached. Hen was startled to see two dark-skinned women rowing it, dressed in stained chemises and petticoats. Their hair was long, and only slightly wavy. Their muscles flowed back and forth as they pulled at the oars.

But it was the man at the helm who drew the most attention. Tall, and dressed in a tattered soldier's red coat and sagging hessian trousers, he doffed his hat politely, grinning up at the ladies.

'It's just old Bungaree,' said Captain Jansen, coming up behind them. 'Governor Macquarie made him king of the natives. He comes out to welcome every ship in return for a drink of rum or brandy, and a bag of whatever provisions are still in the pantry.' He called for the ladder to be let down.

The man in the red coat climbed nimbly up it. He removed his hat again, bowed deeply to the ladies, and then to Captain Jansen. 'Ladies, Captain,' he enunciated in a strong Scottish bur, 'I bid you welcome to this fair land. We will not spare any pains to encourage you to useful industry, nor to dress any grievance you might have.'

Captain Jansen gave a snort of laughter. 'You've got the governor down pat, you rascal. He can imitate anyone,' he added to Hen and Mrs McDougal. 'Give him a shot of rum and a sack of meat and biscuit, lads. Show the ladies the Reverend Marsden, Bungaree.'

Hen met the native's dark eyes. For a moment she saw pain and wisdom, and then Bungaree smiled again. He drew his hands together, as if in prayer. 'A hundred lashes!' he yelled, in the English accent of a gentleman. 'Give the wretch a hundred lashes. No, three hundred. Whip him till his back is pulp, for he deserves it!'

Hen blinked at the unthinking savagery in the voice. Could there really be a clergyman who urged such violence. Bungaree met her eyes again, with a twist of a smile. Hen had no doubt he had imitated faithfully. The old man bowed once more, took the tankard offered to him, drained it, then accepted a sack of provisions from another sailor. He turned his back and made his way towards the ladder again, his posture suddenly sagging, no longer the comic king who had come aboard. He threw the sack down to the women, and clambered into the boat. He did not look back as the women rowed him away.

'That's today's entertainment, ladies,' said Captain Jansen.

'I do not see the humour in mocking a man of God,' said Mrs McDougal coldly.

'There's no harm in old Bungaree,' said the captain. 'I should have asked him for Governor Bligh instead. Bungaree can imitate them all. Yes, I should have asked for Bligh. "Clap them in irons! Dance, you wretches, I order you to dance!"'

'The natives are fully tamed then?' enquired Mrs McDougal, as Hen gazed after the fishing boat, still wondering at the glimpse of tragedy she had seen on the old man's face.

'Tame?' Captain Jansen chuckled. 'Not a bit of it. They've got spears longer than a man, and can throw them further than a musket ball can reach. They're all wild beyond the settlements, and in them too, sometimes. But they won't worry you in Sydney Town. Governor Macquarie has set up a school for the children out at Parramatta, and a big feast with roast beef and plum pudding once a year to tempt them to be civilised. He gives farms to the best of them, or fishing boats. Ah, and here's the pilot now.' The captain left them.

The anchor was hauled back on board. Men yelled from the rigging as wind filled the sails.

The ship began to move again, following the small pilot's boat, twisting into another arm of the harbour. Hen saw farms carved from the landscape, strangely neat, as if trying to impose England's order on such a wild land.

'I'll see my William soon,' said Mrs McDougal, her voice shaking, her face white. Suddenly Hen realised why. It had been two years now since 'My William' sent the last letter his mother had received. So much might happen in two years — typhoid, consumption, a wound in battle, though there were no battles here. Or hadn't been, two years back. Life was slithery and slippery, love sliding away without notice.

And Max?

No, Max was alive. Max had survived Waterloo, the journey here. Hen would not believe him dead again. He was …

A wisp, said a small voice, that you have created from a few hours on a battlefield. A man you do not know.

No. She did know him; she had seen the echo of the man she loved in his mother and in his letter. She was here at last, and life — real life — would soon begin again.

Chapter 11

THE COLONY OF AUSTRALIA

JUNE 1820

'That's my William! Oh lass, that be my William!'

Tears streaked the older woman's cheeks as she gazed at someone in the crowd on the wharf. Hen realised that many in the colony probably watched the waves for the next ship from home. Anyone with a telescope might have made out the *Ivy* as she sat at anchor, and sent a message to merchants like William McDougal.

Hen too scanned the crowd on the wharf. But Max would be far away, by the river he had called The Hen. There would be few reasons for him to be in Sydney Town, and even fewer that might bring him to the dock today. She looked instead at Mrs McDougal's son.

'My William' was as tall as his mother had described, and as handsome, neither of which Hen had expected. But neither she nor his mother was prepared for the young woman holding William's arm: small, dark haired and capable looking, elegantly gowned and bonneted. Nor had his mother expected the baby William held in his other arm.

Two years indeed.

Mrs McDougal's look of joy froze.

Hen squeezed her hand as the young man waved. 'Look at the joy on his face.'

Mrs McDougal forced a smile. She waved back, then turned to wipe her eyes. 'William will hae nay use for me.'

'Except to love you.'

'But I must be of use! I hae always ...' Mrs McDougal stopped, and forced another smile as Captain Jansen approached.

'Ladies, may I have the honour to escort you to Sydney Town?'

'We would be delighted, Captain,' said Hen, taking his arm.

Sailors still yelled up in the rigging. Half the crowds on the wharf had vanished. The *Ivy* was evidently not the ship they had been hoping for. The gangplank shivered under their feet. The wharf seemed to sway, till Hen realised that her body expected swaying after so long at sea.

'Mother!'

'William!' The embrace was long and 'My William' shed tears too.

'Mother, may I introduce my wife?' William spoke with pride and open happiness. 'Gwendolyn, this is my mother.'

The two women faced each other. The younger curtseyed, the baby, now in her arms, sleeping in its white shawl.

'And this,' said William, 'is little Jean. She will be four months old tomorrow.'

'You ... you named her for me?'

'But who else?' William looked genuinely surprised.

'We have so longed for your arrival, Mother McDougal,' said Gwendolyn shyly. 'We would have waited to marry, but thought it might be another year or more before you could get safe passage.'

The baby opened her eyes. Mrs McDougal stared, then stroked the pink cheek with her crooked finger. The baby smiled, blinked, then cried.

'She is hungry,' apologised Gwendolyn. 'We have been down here all morning watching the ship come in. She has missed her feed.'

'Routine is important,' said Mrs McDougal. 'And is she feeding well?'

'I ... I think so.'

'A bonny bairn,' said Mrs McDougal softly, as Waddles sniffed ecstatically at the smells of city boots. 'Bonny indeed.' She remembered Hen. 'This is my companion, Mrs Bartlett.'

Hen and Gwendolyn curtseyed to each other as William took his screaming child higher on his shoulder and extended his arm to his mother.

They had arrived.

She had not expected the beauty. She had not expected the squalor, either.

Carters yelled. Coopers hammered. Ladies — whose virtue was not questionable at all, so obviously were their charms displayed — waved invitingly to sailors. Small boys and wizened men with the innocent gaze of pickpockets, all in an ever present stench of humanity, sweat and chamberpots, leather and salt, horse droppings, fish heads, fermenting garbage, with the scent of rum and unfamiliar wood smoke over it all.

No carriage awaited them once they'd left the wharf. It seemed William McDougal esquire lived in a house next to his warehouse near the docks, instead of a more refined quarter. 'But we will be moving soon, Mother,' he assured her. 'I have the site already, and the plans drawn up.'

He held his mother's arm as they walked past rope makers, wheelwrights, water sellers, a blacksmith's forge, men mending barrels or making new ones, oyster sellers, the shouts of fishwives: the familiar sounds of every port Hen had known.

Up on the hill to their left Hen could see what seemed to be impressive public buildings, even a small castle and a fort. But William led the way into a narrow lane to their right, each side crammed with wooden or wattle and daub shanties with sagging thatch or shingle roofs, and gutters that smelled of filth and faeces, the cobbled road piled ankle deep in muck, as bad as any in London. The stench of rum grew stronger. Urchins, so ragged it was impossible to tell from their clothing if they were girl or boy, squatted begging. Men collapsed in their drunken vomit on the cobblestones, even so early in the day. It was as if a giant had taken up a slice of the English slums and placed it here. All that differed was the strong harbour light.

Hen carried Waddles, to keep him clean, though he looked yearningly at the muck heaps and greasy lumps that might be rags or human. Women with dresses open down to the waist leered from doorways, smelling of sweat and rum.

'Look away, hinnie,' whispered Mrs McDougal, scandalised. Hen immediately gazed where she was not supposed to.

On the rocky slope above the shanties four Indian men sat stark naked, watching the hubbub below, their faces impassive. Hen tried not to stare at them. She had seen all portions of the male body, but never all at once …

'I'm sorry. You must be disturbed by the sight of such primitive rudeness. We are to some extent used to it,' apologised Gwendolyn.

'How can they be allowed?' demanded Mrs McDougal.

William smiled. 'I am afraid, Mother, there is naught to stop them. His Excellency has done all he can to civilise the natives, and others have attempted it, but they remain stubborn and ungrateful. Judge Barron Field believes the occupants of this continent are incapable of reflection, judgement or foresight.'

Hen thought of the joker on the *Ivy*, playing his farce for rum and rations. Was his mimicry a parrot's, merely a repetition of what he had heard? She had not thought so.

'At least there are fewer natives in town now,' continued William. 'The influenza this winter hit them badly. It is said most have moved further down the coast to escape the contagion.'

'Influenza!' Hen looked at William in alarm, and then the baby. 'But that is most infectious, especially for children and —' She tactfully stopped herself from adding 'the elderly.'

'Do not worry, Mrs Bartlett,' said Gwendolyn, 'it seemed only to infect the natives this year. They say that —' She stopped as a man in drab trousers and shirt erupted from a hovel and urinated against its wall. William and Gwendolyn merely averted their faces and stepped to one side. Hen and Mrs McDougal followed them. On the other side of the alley a muck pile of cabbage leaves and manure — some of it animal — burped as it fermented.

Is all of Sydney Town like this? wondered Hen. But William had said his new house site was superior, and the London docklands had been as bad; worse, the air smoke soiled, the street filth knee-deep except for the paths swept through it. Nor did she want to intrude a critical query on the McDougals' joy.

The family and Hen turned a corner into a short lane. Here, at least, the cobblestones were not just swept but freshly washed. The buildings on either side were of brick, and looked like warehouses, well built with slate roofs. At the end of the lane stood a commodious two-storey residence, made of a pale yellow sandstone. 'I know the area is not salubrious,' said Gwendolyn, as William opened the front door, letting out a welcome scent of lavender furniture polish and fresh-baked bread. 'But it has been convenient. I do the firm's accounts.' She looked embarrassed admitting to such an unfeminine activity. 'I do hope you like your rooms, Mother McDougal.'

'Rooms?'

'The front bedroom has a view over the harbour that we thought you would like, and I have furnished a sitting room next to it, for when you and Mrs Bartlett might be tired of our company. Your companion's room is next to yours.'

'Mrs Bartlett is not a hired companion, as I planned, but my friend. She will soon have her own establishment.'

'Oh, that's wonderful!' Gwendolyn flushed, her hand over her mouth.

Hen laughed. 'Am I so very bad?'

'I meant only ...' Gwendolyn stopped, unable to find the words.

That you will welcome your husband's mother, but are relieved that you won't be outnumbered in your own home, thought Hen.

She settled with strange relief into her room. It was well proportioned — a silk counterpane on the bed and velvet curtains and an Indian carpet on the floor. She was introduced to Denise the chambermaid, a convict as it seemed nearly all servants were in the colony, but correctly clad in cap and apron, though she swore like a sailor when she spilled some of the hot water for Hen's first freshwater bath in months.

But the girl knew her job well enough to unpack, dividing clothes into those that must be cleaned or those which merely required pressing, and chose blue sprigged muslin for Hen to change into once her hair had dried by the fire. Perhaps she assumed Hen's choice of black clothes on board the *Ivy* was practicality, not mourning.

Hen's father had been dead for nearly a year, so her blacks could be packed away. Colours seemed to suit this land. Light streamed through the windows, as though the harbour took the sun and magnified it.

'Mrs McDougal asked if you will have tea with her when you've bathed,' said Denise, carefully confining Hen's hair into a French plait, then expertly twisting the shorter edges into ringlets. 'That's Mrs McDougal the old biddie, not —'

'Mrs McDougal senior, not Mrs McDougal the younger,' suggested Hen tactfully.

The maid grinned. Hen had never known a maid to grin. Even a smile was presumptuous. 'Thanks, Mrs B,' she said.

Mrs McDougal had changed into black silk instead of black bombazine, her grey hair silky too, her knitting now of fine white wool. A tiny matinee jacket was already taking shape. Waddles lay on the carpet, looking well washed too, and as if he had never dreamed of catching a rat.

Mrs McDougal looked at Hen approvingly. 'Blue suits you more than black, my dear. Will ye have tea? And a scone or teacake? A good scone is hard to find south of the border.' She raised her chin. 'But my William has chosen a strong lassie to stand at his side who knows how to train her staff. The cook may be a villainess, guilty o' crimes we canna ken, but her scones are excellent, and the teacakes too.'

Mrs McDougal's voice almost hid the bleakness she felt at the prospect of a life of idle comfort, without the purpose that had brought her across the world. 'Will you take milk, my dear, now that we have a supply?'

'Black, thank you, Mrs McDougal.' The milk for sale in London was contaminated by filth and adulterated with chalk, unless you sent a servant to see it taken from the cow. Hen did not trust any milk unless she knew its source.

Mrs McDougal eyed the china teapot. 'I will be glad when my trunks are unloaded. This house should have a proper silver tea service.'

'Mrs McDougal, could you ask your son if I may stay here until I can find a boat to take me to Gilbert's Creek? There is much I need to arrange first, and much I need to take with me. Perhaps Mr McDougal can find me a good agent?'

'I will ask Gwendolyn if you may stay. I will be tactful. But my William always expected me to bring a companion. Instead I brought a friend.'

'I ... thank you.' Hen suddenly realised that for the first time in her life she had a true friend, a friendship that could last their lifetimes. Their backgrounds might differ in every possible respect, but Mrs McDougal, too, was not a woman to be content with gossip and frivolity.

Mrs McDougal coughed. 'My dear, there is a reason we drink tea here, and not in the drawing room downstairs. I ... I have some news for you.'

'Yes?'

'Gwendolyn's late father was at Waterloo. Gwendolyn and William are naturally invited to the Governor's Waterloo dinner each June ...'

Hen drew in her breath. 'And Max was there last year?'

'He attends each Waterloo anniversary. William says he believes he may be in town already to attend the dinner next week.'

'William knows him?'

Mrs McDougal shook her head. 'Only an acquaintance. It is not such a coincidence in a colony as small as this.'

'How ... how is he?'

'Flourishing, it seems, or he was a year ago. But my dear, he keeps a Sydney house, a small one. And next week Governor and Mrs Macquarie are giving a ball to commemorate the battle. William says ...'

Hen closed her eyes. Max had promised they would dance together at a ball. She found her voice shook. 'Did you tell William that Max Bartlett is my husband?'

'No. He asked if you were related to him. I said that he must ask you, implying that I didn't know.'

'Thank you. I ... I would like to tell Max myself.'

'You would like to see his face when he discovers you are alive?'

'Yes.' Because in that moment Hen would know if he still welcomed her as his wife. Not that she had doubts. Except a thousand of them.

'Tomorrow,' said Mrs McDougal firmly. 'A night's sleep on a bed that doesn't roll and a decent breakfast too, with an egg to it. I had a look at the kitchen earlier. They have a good yeast plant so there'll be proper bread, and porridge with no weevils in it.'

'Yes.' Because the ground beneath her still felt like waves. Because she had planned the dress she'd wear when she met Max at last, and Denise would need to sponge and iron it when the trunks from the hold of the ship were delivered. Because Mrs McDougal was her friend, and even though she had found a family waiting for her, it was not the road she had expected, and you didn't abandon a friend who was trying to map out her future afresh.

'And he will love ye true, my dear, till all the seas gang dry,' said Mrs McDougal softly. 'If I were you, and he was my Angus, I'd hae nae worry, child. He will love you.' She paused and added, 'I ken ye are an easy lass tae love.'

Chapter 12

A Sweet Salve for Chapped Lips

Take Beeswax, two teaspoons fresh from the Hive. Melt in two tablespoons Almond Oil. Remove from the fire and add one teaspoon Oil of Lavender. Apply twice Daily. Sovereign for Cold winds and Sea Voyages.

From the Notebooks of Henrietta Bartley

The dawn woke her, spilling pink and gold over the unexpected glory of the harbour, for Denise had not pulled the curtains last night. How could a port of such squalor crouch against a sea of blue and gold like this? A bird called, a coarse laugh rather than a song, but then another answered, more lovely than a lark. Suddenly the air was sweet with birdsong, despite the chaos around them.

She couldn't stay in bed. Nor wait for breakfast nor for the maid who Mrs McDougal would insist accompany her in this land of thieves and vagabonds.

Her dress had waited in her trunk all through the voyage, wrapped in tissue paper with dried lavender flowers, and now hung in the wardrobe, freshly pressed by Denise while Hen and the family had been at dinner. That had been a splendid affair of roast turkey and excellent vegetables, all from William's land elsewhere in the colony.

The dress was blue silk with a pink sash at its high waist, her light wool cloak a matching blue, embroidered at the hem. Her bonnet's ribbon matched as well, and she tied it daringly at the side of her neck.

She gazed at herself in the mirror. Thanks to Mrs McDougal's insistence on hats, veils and cucumber water, Hen's skin had not been browned by the voyage, and her healthy provisions had meant that she did not look gaunt and shadowed like other travellers. She looked …

Hen smiled. Happy. Excited. Beautiful, even to her own eyes. She hoped Max thought so too. If he had loved her in an army greatcoat, surely he must approve of her appearance now.

She brushed her hair, delighting in its cleanliness after the salt baths at sea, scattered it with drops of lavender oil to give it shine, fastened it in a loose knot, twisted her ringlets into place again, then tiptoed down the stairs, carrying her bonnet. Sounds came from the kitchen out the back, but no one noticed as she slipped outside.

And now to find 'the house by the brickworks'. Back in England Hen would have called for a chair so she would arrive with a smut-free face and clean hem. She had seen no chairs for hire on the way from the docks, nor did William keep a footman she could ask to procure one. But the wind blew fresh from the south, strong enough to remove the smoke from a thousand chimneys. She lifted her skirts well above the muck in the streets beyond the warehouse lane — mud, straw, horse and goat droppings, and rotting cabbage leaves as well as the contents of the night's chamberpots: the same as back home, though here there seemed to be a higher proportion of goats.

Her heart beat like a regiment of Highlanders drumming. In less than an hour, perhaps, she'd see Max again. Should she have worn the green sprigged muslin instead of silk? She wanted to show him she was suitable for his world.

Stupid. Idiot. He had loved her in the middle of a battlefield, wearing an old army greatcoat, stained with blood and worse. Would he even recognise her now?

She hoped he would think her beautiful.

She glanced back at the harbour. Two navy ships flew proud pennants. There was the *Ivy*, still at the wharf, and further out small canoes with native women fishing, despite the early hour, as naked as the men of yesterday. The harbour seemed to smile at her, giving her courage.

'Sweep your way for a penny, lady?'

'Thank you.' She held a penny out to the urchin, grime the only thing holding his rags together. He held an implement that was more rake than broom. 'Can you tell me where the brickworks are?' she asked, as the boy began to clear away the rubbish in front of her.

He grabbed the penny. 'Up thar!' He pointed. 'I can take you there for another penny.'

'Threepence,' said Hen.

The boy grinned at her, his teeth already blackening. He swept a path for her up an alley so narrow she wondered if he was taking her instead to his gang leader. But once through a handful of lanes they emerged on a wide and cobbled street, heading uphill.

Miraculously the cobbles were clean here, and the air too, blowing chilly from the south. The boy tucked his broom under his arm. Unlike the lower settlement each house along the street had a large garden, well fenced or guarded by thorny hedges of citronelle or hawthorn, the latter leafless now. A goat trotted down the road towards them. The boy threw a cobble at it. 'Garn out of it!' he yelled, then looked at Hen for approbation.

Even so early two men in drab shirts and trousers wheeled barrows of manure into one of the orchards. Further along the road a gang of men in rags and chains ambled slowly up the hill, each carrying a rock hammer. They looked at their feet, or perhaps at the cobbles they had helped to break.

'Brickworks is just up there, lady,' said the urchin.

Hen gazed around, suddenly realising there were several dwellings that might be described as 'near the brickworks'.

And then she saw it. Max's home. Unmistakable, for he had named it Waterloo, the sign nailed to the garden gate.

'Thank you.' Hen held out a silver threepenny piece to the boy.

He bit it, then nodded. 'I can take yez back agin. I don' mind waiting.'

'I don't know how long I'll be.' Five minutes? A lifetime? She handed him another threepence. The urchin's eyes widened. He glanced around to make sure no one had witnessed his sudden unexpected wealth, then ran off.

Hen looked at the house. A cottage, as he'd written to his mother, but substantial, made of stone, looking down onto another section of the harbour. And a garden, just as she might have planted, roses growing with thyme and rosemary, gravelled paths, chickens clucking in the orchard out the back, with a goat, tethered, for milk. Smoke sifted from the chimney. Either Max was at home or a servant caretaker.

She forced herself to walk up the path, to knock upon the front door. A wife didn't knock at her husband's home, but nor did a wife returning from the dead walk straight in.

The door opened with a gust of warm air, smelling of the strange wood of this country and of toast. A maid wiped her hands on her apron, which was made of the print fabric many of the convict women seemed to have been issued, rather than the black uniform at the McDougals', with a soft cap instead of a starched headdress.

'Is Mr Bartlett at home?'

'Just gone out to get a pail of milk. The goat be drying up.' The woman looked at her curiously.

'Agnes, who is it?' A pretty woman appeared, in her thirties perhaps, a good muslin dress, no apron. She smiled at Hen, obviously curious about a well-dressed stranger knocking on the door so early. 'You have just missed my husband. He has gone on an urgent errand to find milk — he enjoys an early walk as much as you — but he will be back shortly. Will you join us? We are just having breakfast.'

The world around her seemed to fade. Hen managed to say the words: 'You are Mrs Bartlett?'

'Yes, of course.' She waited for Hen to give her own name.

A wife. But not a wife, for Hen was Max's wife.

Impossible to call herself Gilbert, for she had been introduced as Mrs Bartlett to William, Gwendolyn and their servants. Even Captain Jansen knew her as Mrs Bartlett. Hen forced herself to smile. 'My name is Mrs Bartlett too.'

'You are related to Leo? How wonderful. Please, do come this way. Martha, please take Mrs Bartlett's cloak. Your husband is not with you?'

Leo. Not Max. Did Max have a brother in the colony then? A cousin? Hen closed her eyes in gratitude, then found Mrs Bartlett looking at her strangely. 'I am seeking Maxwelton Bartlett,' Hen explained.

The other woman laughed. 'You have found him. His family call him Max, as his father's name is Leonwine too. Leonwine Maxwelton Bartlett. Such a mouthful, is it not? I just call him Leo.'

Impossible to keep the heart stab from her face. 'I ... I see. No. My ... my husband has not come with me. I was widowed.' Not a lie.

Mrs Bartlett touched her arm in sympathy, obviously assuming Hen's look of shock and grief was from a reminder of the loss of her husband. She seemed a woman of warmth and easy manners, so like the women Hen had known in her years on the Peninsular campaigns. 'I'm so sorry. I lost my husband too, my first husband, Steven.' It was — not easy. But Leo was Steven's friend, and because of Leo my children and I have, well, a miracle. A home and happiness and a family. I will pray that there is a miracle for you, as well.' She opened the door to a dining room, small but well proportioned, with a comfortable fire glowing in the hearth. 'Children, say good morning to Mrs Bartlett.'

Three. A boy of twelve, a girl of ten perhaps. They could not be Max's children. But the baby, perhaps a month old, cuddled on her sister's lap …

Mrs Bartlett scooped the baby up and pressed a kiss to the top of her still bald head. 'This is Henrietta,' she informed Hen. 'She was named for my husband's first wife. That's her portrait over the mantelpiece.'

Hen looked. An angel with a halo of gold hair stared back, the smoke of battle grey behind her. Apart from the hair the portrait was nothing like her. But the artist could only have painted what Max described.

Mrs Bartlett smiled. 'I know my Henrietta is not nearly as beautiful yet, but I hope she will be when her hair has grown a little and she stops drooling and grows some teeth.'

'I … I am sure she will be lovely,' Hen managed, as the baby let out a fretful cry, and grabbed her mother's curls.

The mother disengaged the baby's hands. 'And these are Andrew and Juana.'

The girl stood and curtseyed. The boy stood and bowed. Both children took their place at the table again.

'Mrs Bartlett, please do take a seat. Henrietta, stop that! You will have your breakfast soon. Martha, fresh tea please, another cup and more toast. Would you like an omelette or a boiled egg? The hens are still laying excellently.'

Hen glanced at the table, polished wood and plain, presumably colonial made, and set with thick pottery plates that looked amateurish as well, though the cutlery and breakfast service were silver. A well-filled toast rack sat next to a crock of butter, a bowl of marmalade and one of what looked like strawberry jam and three egg cups, each with a brown egg sitting in it.

'The tea and toast. Thank you.' But she could not eat. Could not even swallow. And she had to find a reason for a call so early. 'I must apologise for appearing so suddenly on your doorstep. I … I enjoy early morning walks. A friend mentioned your name and your direction. I wondered if our husbands might be related, so when I passed your house this morning I ventured to call in.'

The baby made a determined pull at her mother's dress. Mrs Bartlett gave her a spoon in an attempt to distract her, obviously enjoying the chance to talk with someone new. 'Visitors are welcome at any time! Especially when we may be related. Colonial society is thin of women who might become friends. Nor are we in town often — if you had come in two days' time you would have missed us.'

'You don't live in Sydney Town then?'

'No. Our property is a two- or three-day voyage from here, and far longer overland.'

'We have sheep,' said the boy proudly. 'Over a thousand of them. They are ours now too since Papa married Mama.'

'And I have a horse of my own now too,' said Juana, helping herself to more jam. 'Her name is Butterfly. But she couldn't come to Sydney.'

'She's a pony, not a horse!'

'Children! What will our guest think of us, with you rattling like a pair of peahens.' She stood, and began to walk the baby around the room. The child continued to grizzle for her breakfast. No nursemaid, thought Hen, with a slash of anguished envy. The child's mother must feed the baby herself.

'Have you been here long, Mrs Bartlett?'

'We only arrived yesterday.' Hen forced a smile. 'I am trying to settle my sea legs but the land still keeps jumping up and down.'

'I sailed from England too,' said the boy proudly. 'But Juana didn't. She was just born here.'

'I don't want to go on a ship for months and months,' said Juana scornfully. 'Have you seen a kanguroo yet? We have lots of them and emus too.'

'No, I haven't seen a kanguroo, only illustrations of them.'

'They bounce up and down,' Juana informed her. 'Like this.' She left the table to demonstrate.

'Positively rag mannered,' apologised her mother, looking down at her daughter indulgently. 'Which ship did you come in on?'

'The *Ivy*, a merchant vessel. They will head to China from here. My friend and I were the only passengers on board.'

'What news is there of England? How goes our poor king?'

'Not well at all, madam.' Hen was glad to move onto matters less personal. William and Gwendolyn too had pressed her and Mrs McDougal for all news from Home, though her 'news' was now more than six months out of date. 'He is said to be declining, and still in seclusion from all.'

Both women had carefully refrained from using the word 'mad'. Hen had discussed His Majesty's case several times with her father. Most surgeons believed that nothing could be done for those with mental afflictions, beyond confining them for their own good and so they could do no harm to others.

Hen would have liked to try the remedies she had seen soothe troubled patients — not laudanum, which merely made the patient sleepy, rather than calm, nor the gentian and arsenic with which the king had already been treated with no success, but motherwort, currently used only by midwives. But it was impossible that a woman, or anyone not already an eminent surgeon, could treat the king.

The other woman shifted the complaining baby to her hip. 'I am so sorry there has been no improvement. Hush, Henrietta! And the Prince Regent?'

'Fatter than ever, especially as his doctors have now forbidden him to wear his corset, as it constricted his bowels sadly and made him quite dyspeptic.' Hen blinked as she realised her preoccupation had made her careless. That was not how a gentlewoman should speak of royalty, nor was constriction of the bowels a proper topic for breakfast conversation. The children were already giggling, but their mother just laughed too. 'You have met his Royal Highness?'

'I haven't been presented to him, but attended a gala he gave. His Highness wore several acres of gold cloth and a waistcoat that might have been embroidered with diamond dragons, though I was not close enough to see. He spoke to us all for several hours on the subject of military uniforms.'

'We heard about the death of Princess Charlotte only last year. Such a tragedy.'

Hen nodded, carefully not adding the details that had been described to her father, and which he had passed on to her. The heir to the throne had died in childbirth, attended by male doctors who had repeatedly bled her, starved her, and then wondered why she did not have the strength to expel her babe. Neither forceps nor spoons had been used. The child, a large boy, was born dead. His mother died soon after. It was a needless tragedy, but Hen dared not give the details, in case Max had told his ... wife ... that his first wife had been a surgeon. The coincidence of her name, her hair, her accomplishments would be too great ...

The maid entered with a fresh pot of tea and toast rack. 'Thank you, Agnes.' The other woman approached the table again, and poured Hen a cup of tea with her free hand. 'Sugar? I am afraid there is no milk till my husband returns.'

And Hen must get away before that. Whatever must be done about this could not be started with children looking on. She had to think ...

Inspiration flashed. 'No sugar, thank you, Mrs Bartley.' She slightly emphasised the final syllable.

'Bartlett,' corrected the other.

Hen feigned befuddlement, then spread out her hands. 'Bartlett, you say? What must you think of me? I have misheard the name. My husband was a Bartley. There can be no connection.'

'I am so sorry!' The woman looked genuinely disappointed. Hen's accent and dress had proclaimed her respectable, she had fascinating gossip, and she had been invited to a royal gala, even if she was an eccentric who wandered around the town at breakfast time without a maid or footman. 'But none the less, will you perhaps dine with us tonight?' The baby let out a yell, then kept on yelling.

Hen raised her voice. 'I ... I have passed my year of mourning, but still do not care to mix much in society.'

'Henrietta, hush! My dear, you must not give up your life for mourning. It is true, perhaps, that one's first love can never be replaced. But as my husband and I have found, there can be friendship between a man and wife that grows to love as well. Please, do come to dine.' She looked at her screaming daughter with happy exasperation. 'I assure you the dinner will be more peaceful. Our household is not always so harum scarum.'

'That sounds delightful, but the friend who I accompanied to the colony has already made plans for tonight.' Hen stood. 'She will be wondering where I am. I am so sorry to have kept Henrietta from her breakfast. No, please, do see to her. I can see myself out.'

'It will do her no harm to wait another minute!'

Henrietta's mother accompanied Hen to the front door as Hen managed to smile at the children, managed not to weep at the sight of the baby already nuzzling in a position to be fed as soon as the visitor left.

'Perhaps you and your friend might care to dine tomorrow night? After that I am afraid we head back to Gilbert's Creek. It is quite in the wilderness!'

'We are already engaged tomorrow, too, I'm afraid.'

'Then it must be when we return to Sydney! Though that will be a year, at least.'

Hen dragged up yet another smile. She had to leave, and quickly, before Max returned, before she betrayed herself with sobs, too. 'Thank you, you have been so kind. But I must hurry now. My friend will be worried at my absence.' Hen carefully did not give the friend's name or direction, in case Max and his ... wife ... followed up the brief acquaintance. The baby's fretfulness had distracted her mother this morning. She might be far more curious the next time.

'You could come to breakfast again tomorrow,' offered Juana hopefully. 'Then maybe Mama will make pancakes. Did you know we have lemon trees? We can have pancakes with lemon and sugar.' She curtseyed again. 'Mama says I have to curtsey when I meet people but when we know them well I can hug them.'

Hen gazed at the child. She did indeed look huggable. 'Thank you. All of you. I ... I would love to dine with you, or have pancakes for breakfast, but I suspect that the next few days will be taken up with my friend's family.'

She found a final smile, turned and waved to the children from the front gate — Henrietta's mother had already vanished to feed her — and walked quite steadily down the street despite her thumping heart as mother and children went inside again. At last she found a clump of thorny citronelle bushes, somewhat nibbled by goats, to hide her from the street.

She waited. She tried to think. Max would be coming soon. She must waylay him before he reached home, explain the matter to him in private. And then?

Hen had liked the woman who thought she was Max's wife. But that kind woman was not his wife. Hen had liked the children, too, and the wonderfully determined baby who must be Max's — quite enchanting children, like their mother, who had offered a stranger breakfast and friendship, so like the women she had known from her army days. To claim Max now would be to proclaim his baby illegitimate, to deprive those children of a father yet again ...

He came striding by, not noticing her, carrying a pail of milk. She stared at him. She had not guessed he was so tall. She realised she had never seen him even stand.

The children must have seen him through the window.

'Papa, I caught a spider!'

'It's a big horrible one. You have to make her let it go.'

'We had a lady visitor, Papa, but now she's gone but she might come again.'

'A visitor at breakfast!' Max laughed down at the children. 'Another spider? Or an emu this time?'

'She was a person!' said Juana scornfully. 'She was pretty, too. Her bonnet had blue ribbons.'

'We can have pancakes if she comes again,' added Andrew.

'Milk at last! You wondrous man.' The woman who believed herself to be Mrs Bartlett appeared in the door, holding the now contented baby and adjusting her dress.

Mrs Bartlett took the milk pail then held her cheek up for a kiss. Max delivered the kiss, then swung the baby high into the air. 'How is my little Hen then? Ugh!' The baby deposited a small milky splodge on his shoulder. Max expertly wiped it with his handkerchief, then used it to clean the baby's face. He arranged the child on his shoulder, patting her back to burp her. 'Now, about that spider ...' He led his family into the house.

His family. His happy family.

All Hen had to do was walk down that path again, knock on the front door. Max would recognise her, and then ...

And what had she to offer him, except herself? And a charge of bigamy, even if he would almost certainly escape a sentence as he had married in ignorance. Even if he and Hen had their marriage annulled as unconsummated, his present marriage would still not be valid, nor could it be for all the time spent with courts and lawyers till finally he was free to marry again.

No matter what the outcome, it would be tragedy for the woman who had welcomed her, a stranger, and further loss and confusion for her children too. Baby Henrietta would have the stigma of illegitimacy all her life. The colony would swallow the scandal like a sugar plum. The gossip would eventually reach England, too, to shame his mother.

A life with Max, if that was what Max chose, or even felt it was his duty to choose, could only be based on the breaking of other lives, a family.

Max was happy. That mattered, deeply. Max had loved her. She found that mattered, as well. Max still loved the memory of her, and his wife — for that kind woman was his wife, Hen realised, whatever the law might say — knew of Max's lost love and honoured it, her portrait hanging on the wall, the child named for her.

There was no choice to make, really. No choice at all.

No life, either. No reason to stay here in the colony. No reason to go back to the fog of England either.

She was nothing. Not a wife, and yet she was a wife. Not a widow, though she had worn a widow's black. She could not remarry, as Max had done, for he had done it innocently, thinking her dead, while she knew the man she had married was alive.

I am nothing, she thought again, her feet moving even though all will had fled, down the street and then automatically down the first road she came to, to make sure Max would not see her if he came out of the house again. I am nothing now and will be nothing and ...

She would need to find a passage from the colony as soon as possible. Perhaps she could even travel on the *Ivy* again, though she would have to think of some reason why one who had crossed the world would leave without even taking a few months to recover from the voyage, and see a little of this new land. Maybe ...

'Lady!' The urchin from earlier leaped up from hunting through a pile of garbage, probably hoping for another threepence if he delivered her back home. He ran towards her ...

'No!' The cart driver didn't see him, pulled at the reins only when his wheel lurched over the child. The man leaped from the cart, then stopped, gazing at the blood. The wheel had almost cut the boy's lower leg in half. Red pooled around the tiny body. The fall had knocked him senseless, too.

How much blood could so small a body have?

Hen ran, kneeled, tore the lace from her throat, the frill from her dress, wrapped them as tourniquets around his leg. Impossible to save it. The bone itself was severed.

'You!' she yelled at a woman peering from a doorway. 'Do you have your fire hot?'

'Yes'm.' The woman looked bewildered.

'Heat your iron, please. As hot as it can be.'

'Ain't got an iron.'

'What can you heat? It must be metal!'

'Got a kettle on the boil,' she offered.

'Bring it now!' She looked around. 'Anyone please who has an iron they can heat. I'll give a guinea for a red-hot iron!'

The blood still seeped, too much despite the tourniquets. She fumbled in her reticule, found the small scissors, needle and thread she always kept there — women's tools, not a surgeon's, but all she had. She began to snip at the flesh, trying to make a flap to fold over the stump.

'What's she doin? Murderin' 'im?' The enquirer showed nothing but curiosity.

'Nah, the carter did that.' Again no sympathy. 'He's gone and legged it now.'

The woman thrust the kettle at Hen.

Was there enough undamaged skin? There had to be!

'Stand back!' Hen upended the kettle, pressing the base to the boy's wound. Flesh sizzled. The water spilled onto the cobbles, diluting the blood. She pulled the kettle back.

Not enough. Not nearly enough, she thought, just as someone passed her a pair of tongs holding a sheet of metal. She grabbed the tongs, pressed quickly, lifted it.

The wound sealed with a hideous sizzle. She felt the boy's pulse. Weak, thready, but he was still alive. 'We have to get him to a hospital.'

'What about my guinea?'

'And mine?'

'I will pay you as soon as we have seen this boy to hospital. Another guinea to whoever can carry him there,' she added desperately. 'The colony does have a hospital, doesn't it?'

'Aye. The Rum Hospital that old Wentworth and his chums built. Fallin' down already. Don't think they'd take the boy, but.'

'Why not?'

'Well, he ain't a convict, and he ain't a soldier. Ain't nobody, I reckon.'

Nor would the child live long enough for Hen to argue for his admittance. 'Another guinea then for a door, and two men to carry him on it down to the house next to McDougal's warehouse.'

'You gunna sell him off to be a cabin boy like that?' The growing crowd sniggered.

Was there no pity in this place? 'I'm trying to save his life!'

'Not worth much to save.'

'You shut your trap, Joe Higgins, or there'll be rat in your stew for supper and not mutton.' It was the woman who'd brought her the kettle. 'You and Long Bill take our door now, and make sure you wash the blood off it afore you brings it back. And our two guineas.'

Was the offer kindness, or greed? Both, Hen thought, as the woman brought out a cushion for the boy's head. The two men lifted him gently enough, too. The small bloody foot lay on the cobbles, a reminder that this child had once been whole.

He had to live! Of all the people she had tended, of all the days she'd tended them, this boy and this day mattered most. Because if he lived this day had been worth something, and if he died it was worth nothing, for it had been because of her he'd crossed the road, eager for another threepence.

Hen lifted her skirts, running in front of the men carrying the child, through the front door of William McDougal's house.

'Hen, lass, what is it?' Mrs McDougal stared at her from the stairway, evidently on her way down to breakfast. How could a day hold so much and it still be so early ...

'A boy. Injured. Yes, please bring him in, down the hallway to the scullery. Mrs McDougal, I have promised these men two guineas.'

'Two guineas!'

For the first time Hen remembered this was not her house, nor a surgeon's home nor a billet, a place that would automatically take in an injured child. Then suddenly Gwendolyn was there, leading the men to the scullery, calling to Denise to bring fresh towels and bandages. Hen followed, just as Mrs McDougal called to the men, 'I will bring your coin down. Two guineas to carry that scrap of a lad. The hide of you!'

'She was the one who promised it us,' said Long Bill as Hen made her way to the scullery. 'We'd a done it for sixpence.'

Please, Hen prayed, please let the boy be alive.

Chapter 13

To Prepare a Surgeon's Thread

Heat best quality Thread with Beeswax. Rub your Fingers
over so that the Thread may be fine but not stick to Flesh.
In hot Climates make new Thread each Month.

From the Notebooks of Henrietta Bartley

The boy still lived an hour later, laid on the well-scrubbed
scullery table. He'd been sponged clean by Gwendolyn and
Mrs McDougal, his rags cut off him ('Burn them,' ordered
Gwendolyn), his hair shaved off and disposed of, as well as the
creatures that lived in it, dressed in a clean old shirt of William's,
while Hen stitched a wound on his arm she hadn't previously
noticed. It had stopped bleeding, but it might begin again, and
the child could spare no more.

Now Mrs McDougal spooned broth into him, sweetened with
a little honey and, miraculously, the boy swallowed, though
still deeply unconscious. Hen would have liked to add drops of
laudanum, but that would depress his breathing even further.

She had dressed the sealed stump and stitched the wound with
rose oil and lavender. Should she add a few drops of hawthorn
tincture to his broth, to strengthen his pulse?

'Mrs Bartlett?' It was William, his top hat in hand, an elderly
stranger behind him.

'Bartley,' she corrected, automatically standing and curtseying. Mrs McDougal looked at her curiously, but said nothing.

'I have brought Dr Wentworth to see the lad. He is the colony's foremost surgeon.'

'Thank you. That was good of you.'

'Retired surgeon.' The old man stumped forwards. Despite his age he was tall, handsome, with a well-tailored coat. He raked Hen with an appreciative gaze before lowering himself onto the cushioned stool Gwendolyn had placed for him. He felt the boy's pulse first, lifted his eyelids, inspected the wound, then felt carefully over the body, pinching here and there to judge the reflexes. He stood.

'A drop of brandy, sir?' offered William.

'That would be good. Mrs Bartley, would you mind if we discuss this somewhere with more comfort for my old bones?'

'Certainly, sir.' This man knew his business. He also seemed kind — was kind, for she saw the marks of many years of compassion in the wrinkles of his face. Hen hoped desperately he approved of her work.

William led the way to the parlour, a well-proportioned room with a polished wooden floor under more Indian carpets, and well-upholstered chairs and sofas, the scent of pot pourri overwhelming the faint stench from the streets beyond. Mr Wentworth waited politely for Hen to sit, then sank into an armchair. Hen shook her head as William offered the first glass of brandy to her. 'How do you find him, sir?'

'It may go either way, but I am surprised the little chap is still alive. That work is yours?'

'Yes, sir. I was there when the accident happened.'

'A few more seconds' delay and there'd have been no hope. Excellent brandy, Mr McDougal. No, you did good work, Mrs Bartley. Surprising work. I have never known a woman capable of surgery before.' He smiled reminiscently. 'Much else, in my years, but not surgery.'

'My father was an army surgeon, sir. My mother and I assisted him as needed.'

'And doing surgery yourself?'

Hen hesitated. 'I have never set myself up as a surgeon, sir.'

The old eyes crinkled with laughter. 'That was not what I asked, Mrs Bartley.'

'If the need was great, and no one else could do it, then, yes, sir, I have done surgery on the battlefield and after it. But not since Waterloo.'

'Waterloo, eh? You were there?'

'Yes, sir.'

'As a surgeon?'

'As my father's daughter. My mother had died by then. But the need ... there was such terrible need that day, and the days after it. I ... I have seen many battles, sir, but none like that.'

'Let us hope the world never sees a battle of that size and cost again. And with Boney gone I think we may be optimistic. Now, as to your patient ...'

'My patient, sir? You will not take him on?'

Mr Wentworth glanced at William, quietly listening to this exchange. 'Mrs Bartley, I am old and tired but I will not turn away from a child in need. The boy, however, has you, and I judge you to be as capable as myself. And you have excellent assistants! Is this agreeable to you, McDougal?'

'It is, sir,' said William.

Mr Wentworth took an appreciative sip of the brandy again. 'I will come if you call me, or send a message if you need my advice. But for now, keep on with the broth and keep him still, for there is likely a head injury.'

'I think so too, sir. He was unconscious even before the loss of blood.'

'I thought so. You may need restraints if he begins to thrash around.'

'Should he be taken to the hospital? Someone in the street said there was what he called the Rum Hospital but they did not think they'd take the boy.'

Mr Wentworth laughed. 'That wretched name! A group of us had the hospital built in exchange for a sole licence to import rum. I think the colony had a bargain.' He grew serious again. 'But as for the hospital admitting the boy — this is a colony of convicts, ticket-of-leave men or soldiers and their families. The few free settlers nurse their families at home, with a surgeon such as myself or Redfern called in. There is less chance of infection and better food and nursing. And it is the nursing that will mean life or death for this small chap.'

Hen looked at William. 'You truly do not mind if the boy stays here, Mr McDougal?'

William looked shocked. 'Of course, Mrs Bartlett, I mean Bartley. I too would not turn a child in need away.'

And yet there are hundreds outside your door each day, thought Hen, homeless, hungry ...

'The colony has many urchins who need care, Mrs Bartley,' said William quietly, as if he read her thoughts. 'My wife and I cannot feed them all. But any child who comes to our back door knows they will be given bread and cheese or a helping of stew, and those who creep into our warehouses to sleep will not be turned out by my watchmen, but be kept safe for the night.'

It was not enough; but it was also a lot.

'I am glad,' said Hen. 'Your mother is rightly proud to have such a son.'

William flushed.

'We're a colony of villains,' admitted Mr Wentworth cheerfully. 'But we can aspire to be better.'

'You could never have been a villain, sir,' said Hen.

Mr Wentworth grinned again, his faded eyes lighting up. 'And it's lucky the jury believed that too, or I'd have been hanged as a highwayman. And you'll not hear from me whether they were right or wrong.' He winked at Hen. 'An after-dinner tale, perhaps one day. You'll find everyone in this colony was sent here or is escaping from their past.' He nodded at William. 'Or escaping the Glasgow fog.'

'And being found drunk in the office of the solicitor to whom you were articled,' said William. He raised his eyebrows at Hen. 'But never mention that disgrace to Mother.'

Hen blinked at this revelation about the saintly 'My William'. 'And Gwendolyn?'

'Her father came here after Waterloo. There're many here who travelled to the end of the world to forget that battle,' said William more soberly, just as Gwendolyn appeared at the door.

'Mrs Bartlett —'

'Bartley,' corrected William.

'The boy — he's opened his eyes, but will not stay still ...'

Hen ran out the door, forgetting courtesy or curtsey. The urchin was trying to sit up, muttering wildly, and Mrs McDougal and a wiry monkey of a woman in the cap and apron of a cook were trying to hold him down. This must be the 'villainess, guilty o' crimes we canna ken' that Mrs McDougal had spoken of, who could nonetheless make an excellent scone.

Hen bent down to the boy. 'Threepence,' she said quietly. 'Remember me? I said I'd give you threepence.'

The boy blinked at her. 'Hurts,' he muttered. 'Black John 'as been at me again, an' it hurts, hurts bad ...'

'Shh.' Hen put her arms around him, partly to comfort him, partly so he did not see his missing foot. 'Black John is never going to hurt you again. You are safe here and you will have threepences and bread and good mutton broth ...'

'And jam tarts and syrup dumplings,' added the cook, obviously thinking that mutton broth was no incentive to recovery.

'Here.' Mr Wentworth handed Hen a spoon with what smelled like laudanum on it. Hen would have preferred her own mix — she knew the strength of that — but she respected this man too. She slipped it into the boy's mouth. He made a face at the bitterness, but clung to her when she tried to move away.

'You'll really keep me safe?'

'You're truly safe now,' promised Hen. 'What is your name?'

'You won't let Black John find me?'

'Never.'

'He allus finds me,' muttered the boy.

'If Black John puts one foot inside me kitchen I'll brain him with me skillet,' said the cook. 'There's many in the colony who will tell him to watch out for me skillet.'

The boy seemed to accept this, quietening.

'Do you have a mother? A family?' asked Hen urgently, before he drifted into sleep.

His eyes grew unfocused from the laudanum. 'I had a ma. She called me Jem.'

'Where is she?' Hen did not want the complications of a mother — not one who let her son go filthy and starving.

But the boy just said, 'Gone.'

Did Jem mean she had died? Or left him? Or perhaps had been taken as a doxy on one of the ships. Nice girls did not know about ship's doxies, but Hen had never been a nice girl. The boy's eyes closed again, but his breathing was steady and his pulse stronger.

'Well, girl?' asked Mr Wentworth, observing all this with interest. 'What do you plan to do with him?'

'More broth, with laudanum drops six times a day at first, then easing the dose after the fourth day if all goes well, hot fomentations on his leg but we'll bathe his head with cool cloths and peppermint. Porridge if he will take it tomorrow ...'

'Naught better for an invalid's bowels,' agreed Mrs McDougal, eyeing the cook in case she offered other items unsuitable for an invalid. The cook grinned at Hen and winked, as if to say she would tempt the boy with tarts as soon as he was well enough to chew them.

Mr Wentworth smiled. 'I meant what will you do with him when he recovers. I suspect he *will* recover now with such excellent care.' He bowed towards Mrs McDougal. 'Not to mention the porridge.'

'I'll go put more broth on,' said the cook. 'My mutton bone broth would tempt the angels down from heaven. Lemon barley water won't go amiss neither.' She vanished back to the kitchen.

Hen glanced at the boy, so thin and pale faced on the table. 'We'll have to get a wooden foot made for him and show him how to wear it. Teach him his letters. His only chance at work now will be as a clerk, or possibly a cabinet-maker, if he has no hand for writing. We will have to see. I think he is intelligent and a good boy, despite where he has come from ...'

Where so many others dwelled, too. It seemed the urchins she had seen yesterday had no help if they sickened. How many children like Jem might die if Hen sailed from the colony?

Suddenly it seemed as if the rudderless ship that was her life was in full sail again.

Why shouldn't she stay in New South Wales? It would be a year at least before Max and his family would visit the colony again. Sometime before that she would find some way to inform Max discreetly what had happened, and that they must apply for an annulment, while making it clear that 'Mrs Bartley' did not expect to be acknowledged as his wife.

Because somehow, it seemed, in these few hours, Hen had found a life. Not the one that she expected, but one where she might at last use her surgeon's skills again.

She looked at Mrs McDougal, wiping the boy's face with lavender vinegar; at Mr Wentworth, who so easily accepted a woman's competence. Out in the kitchen she could hear the cook ordering one of the boys to find her mutton bones, and William instructing a gardener to clean out a storeroom so the lad could sleep near the warmth and oversight of the kitchen. All of them, it seemed, had come here for a new life. Now Hen would have one too.

Chapter 14

A Wash for a Midwiffe's Hands

Take Rosemary leaves, one handful, Flowers of the English
Lavender or Spanish but not the French, boil for the Count of
Five Hundred. Wash while still hot. Instruments may be boiled
with the Wash with good Effect, for Both are Women's Herbs.

From the Notebooks of Henrietta Bartley

She ate the breakfast she had missed, and a nuncheon too, up in
Mrs McDougal's sitting room: eggs baked with herbs and cream,
and extremely good toast with sweet butter and raspberry jam,
and a fruit compote of stewed apple and quince from William's
garden and orchards. The convicts who tended them must know
their job, just as the villainess cook seemed a genius in the
kitchen. A maid sat with Jem with orders to bathe his head with
lavender vinegar and fetch Hen when he woke again, or if he
seemed in pain.

'Well, lass?' asked Mrs McDougal.

Hen stared out the window, unsure what to say. The harbour
stared back at her, blue and silver now, the most beauty she had
ever seen, and she had known the Pyrenees at dawn and the
golden orange groves of Granada.

'Ye left the house this mornin' in search of a husband and
came back with a crippled bairn. Ye hae nae seen your Max yet?'

'I've seen him,' said Hen shortly. 'He did not see me.' She explained as briefly as she could.

Mrs McDougal sat quietly till she had finished and then simply said, 'Ah, well, that's the way of it then.'

'He is happy,' said Hen simply. 'They all are happier.'

'Do ye no' think ye should give the man a choice, then?'

'It wouldn't be a choice. If I am known as his legal wife, then his daughter is illegitimate, and that good woman is just his mistress, and it all results in pain and confusion. And if Max chose me now I would never know if it were love or duty.'

'I ken it would be love,' said Mrs McDougal quietly, her knitting unheeded on her lap.

'Then maybe that would be the worst of all, to give him two wives to love, when the law allows only one. No. I will not burden him with choice. The family will go back to Gilbert's Creek in two days' time. I need only avoid them till then. I ... I will write to him, in six months perhaps, to ask for an annulment.' She flushed. 'Any investigation would ... would find reason for the annulment. Max can then determine the most discreet way to handle the matter, as well as another quiet wedding with the woman who believes she is his wife.'

'Ye won't tell him now?'

'If he knew I had recently arrived in the colony he would feel responsible for me. I need to have my own life, and my own house to prove I do not need his care.'

'But what of his love?' asked Mrs McDougal quietly. 'Did ye no' love him when ye saw him again?'

'Of course,' said Hen quietly. 'If I did not love him so much, I do not think that I could part from him. I want him to be happy.' She raised her chin. 'I can be useful here. And God has granted me the best of friends.'

Mrs McDougal grasped Hen's hand with her aged spotted fingers. 'He has indeed, hinnie. I think ye're wrong, child. What God has joined together let nae man put asunder. But in this case, and with a priest from foreign parts at that ... well, I will bide by your decision. You are Mrs Bartley from now on. I ... I am glad you are staying, hinnie. I think ye can be happy here.'

'And you? Will you be happy?'

'Aye. I have my William, and bonny Jean. Gwendolyn is a fine lass, even if she does burn wax candles when tallow burns as bright. But then, my William can afford wax candles,' said William's mother proudly. 'I am sure I will find occupation. The devil finds work for idle hands, so I must seek a way to keep mine busy. Both of us, perhaps. My William says your home is here, and the lad's too.'

'I think ...' Hen's gaze was drawn out to the harbour again. It struck her fully that for the first time in her life she could truly choose the life she wanted, here in this colony where each person was given or had taken a chance for a new life. A small chance for some, but more than they would have had in England.

What did she want?

'I think I want a house,' she said slowly. 'A house by the sea, beyond the town, in one of the coves perhaps, where only a boat can reach me.' Where a woman could live her life without being continually inspected by her neighbours. 'I want a garden and an orchard. And two, no, six cows, and a bull, so I will need a dairy too. And sheep and chickens and pigs enough to feed the household, and maybe geese, if they have them here.'

The plan suddenly seemed as brightly obvious as the light upon the water. 'I will build two dormitories, one for girls and one for boys, for children like Jem who the hospitals won't take in.'

Mrs McDougal stared. 'You're setting up a hospital, chick?'

'No. A woman cannot run a hospital; nor can a woman call herself a surgeon or physician. My home will just be ... a home ... but for children who are ill or hurt, who have nowhere they can be nursed.'

'Then they must be taught, too,' said Mrs McDougal, a joyous fire lighting her eyes. 'The lassies taught how to cook and clean and be a wife or cook or parlourmaid. There is no shortage of work or husbands here for a lass who's been well trained. And the boys given their letters and then apprenticed to good men. They must know poetry, and the beauty of words, and God's word too.'

'Will William help me find a place to build my house and dormitories? I don't know how to buy land here, nor how to hire workers. It seems land is mostly given to people, and convicts assigned to them. Will the authorities allow a woman to have land and convicts?' Once again she was glad of her status as a widow, even if she now knew it to be false. A young single woman would never be granted land, but widows were deemed to be a trifle more capable.

'My William will see to that,' said William's mother.

And William would, thought Hen. A kind man and a kind wife who would soon see, if they hadn't already, how in a well-run house and with no old friends to share her memories, Mrs McDougal needed to make new memories, and keep her hours filled with more than tea and knitting.

With Mrs Henry Bartley, who her friends called Hen …

The footman at Government House took Hen's card with his thumb and little finger. The rest of his hand was scar.

'His Excellency is expecting me,' said Hen. 'Mrs Henry Bartley.'

'If you will take a seat, I will ascertain if His Excellency is free.' The accent was cultivated — carefully cultivated — and recently by the sound of it.

'Waterloo?' asked Hen. Governor Macquarie was said to give ex-military men preferment.

The footman nodded.

'I was there too, helping my father. Surgeon Gilbert.'

'Ah, I've heard men speak of him. Wish I'd had Surgeon Gilbert instead of the butcher that did me. This hurts something awful.' The accent changed to that of London's East End.

'Let me see. Does this hurt?'

The man winced. 'Yes.'

'I wish you'd had my father for your surgeon, too. The one who tended you should have stretched your hand out further when he sealed it. The only remedy will hurt, I'm afraid, but it will mean you have more use of your hand.'

'I ain't havin' the knife again!'

'No need. Your scar has shrunk, that's all. Get yourself an India rubber ball and squeeze it whenever your duties permit. Your hand will ache by the end of the day for a while, but I'll warrant within a year it won't hurt at all, except when there's rain on the way. But keep holding the ball for an hour each day after that, or the scar may shrink again.'

The butler grinned, showing a few long yellow teeth. 'You're your father's daughter and no mistake. No need to sit, Mrs Bartley. I will announce you to His Excellency now.'

The hall was unimpressive. Major-General Macquarie rose from his desk as Hen entered. Tall, hatchet faced, with short grey hair, he looked kind, preoccupied and deeply tired. 'Mrs Bartley, welcome to Australia.' His accent was almost as Scots as Mrs McDougal's. 'My sympathies on the loss of your husband and father.'

Hen curtseyed. 'Thank you, Your Excellency.'

'Forgive my mentioning it, but you are younger than I expected.'

Hen flushed. 'Time will remedy that, sir. But I assure you I am capable of managing both land and men.'

'Very well. Make your wishes known to my secretary, Mr Campbell, and he will see them carried out. Good morning, Mrs Bartley.'

Hen blinked. 'That's all?'

'I beg your pardon?' The Governor seemed surprised to have his words questioned.

'Sir, I am both young and female, and yet you will give me land and men to work it.'

Governor Macquarie seemed to see her for the first time. He laughed. 'Mrs Bartley, you see in me the last of the autocrats.

I need only say "Do it" and it must be done. Even His Majesty the King, and his Regent, must answer to parliament. I have no such parliamentary gnats that bother me here.'

Hen wondered if the governor also had the power to annul marriages. 'That must be a great challenge to live up to, sir.'

'Aye, you speak the truth, Mrs Bartley. The first officers in this land abused the power for their own enrichment and enjoyment. To me it has been a burden I will most willingly relinquish. I return to England soon.'

'I am sorry to hear it, sir.'

'I must answer for my work here and defend it. I resigned two and a half years ago, and am awaiting my replacement. I came to a colony of mud and corruption. I leave it thriving, a place of law, where none starve except by their own want of industry, with roads across the mountains, and to the rivers to the north and west that let men tame the wilderness with goodly farms and pasture. Yet the authorities in England still wish this colony to be a mere dumping ground of human refuse, disposed of as cheaply as possible.'

He paused, obviously waiting for Hen to comment. 'That seems a most mistaken policy, sir.'

'Exactly, Mrs Bartley. I am glad to meet a woman of sense. I see this country as a land of infinite potential, and every man and woman who has served their time has potential too that would be unrealised in the poverty of England. I doubt my successor will be as free with land grants and the assigning of convicts as I have been. But I am building a city here, Mrs Bartley, and a nation ...'

Was he rehearsing the speeches defending himself and his expenditure that he must deliver back in England?

'Mr McDougal, who I respect, has assured me you will contribute to the building of civilisation here in the south. We have endless land to grant, and more convicts than I can employ on the projects this colony so badly needs, the roads, the hospital ...'

'You need a hospital for children, sir.'

He blinked at her forthrightness, then smiled. 'Undoubtedly you are correct, Mrs Bartley. But I have given Australia all I have strength for — including an orphanage, and a hospital where children may be admitted.'

'But —' Hen stopped. For the Rum Hospital had not refused to take Jem. There had merely been uncertainty that a boy of the streets, neither convict nor soldier's child, would be admitted. The comments in the street had been made in ignorance and perhaps prejudice, too.

'And now my superiors have sent Mr Bigge to restrain my work,' continued Governor Macquarie. 'A hospital dedicated to children must be for my successor, or for the citizens of Australia, such as yourself, to see done.'

'Australia, sir?' Hen had not heard the term before.

Governor Macquarie looked at her thoughtfully. 'Will you take a glass of wine and a biscuit, Mrs Bartley?'

'Thank you, sir, though I would regret wasting what little time you have.'

'I suspect it will not be wasted. Please be seated. And I apologise for my curtness before.' The governor rang the bell.

'No apology is needed. You have far too much to occupy yourself with to be hearing my requests, sir.'

'No, Mrs Bartley, I have too little. Too little time here to effect more building and reform, and no support at all from England for doing it. Two glasses of claret,' he added, as a footman opened the door. 'Or would you prefer tea, Mrs Bartley?'

'The wine would be welcome, sir.' In fact she didn't like it. But tea must be brewed, which took time, and she was determined to keep him as little as possible from his work. The footman was already moving to the decanter on the sideboard. Hen took the glass of claret and the oatmeal biscuit, sipped once, then put the glass down.

'This land has had many names, Mrs Bartley. New Holland, and then this eastern portion named New South Wales. But we need a name for the entire continent, for one day our small colony will spread across the empty spaces, filling it with farms and enterprise. The name Cook gave this land must stay, of course, but that name is now tarnished as a prison. Australia is a new name for a new land, one that will outgrow its convict beginnings. And so I believe with all my heart, Mrs Bartley.'

'I do not doubt you, sir, not in your hope nor that it will happen. I have seen already a ... a freedom to make life anew here. Good lives, for those who had none before.'

'My sentiments exactly, Mrs Bartley, and those of my wife. No doubt she will call on you, and Mrs McDougal. I hope when we meet next it may be at our dinner table.' Governor Macquarie raised his glass. 'To the nation of Australia.'

Hen raised her glass too. 'To the nation of Australia.' And for a moment the man's weariness seemed to vanish, and his tired eyes looked to a future decades away.

Chapter 15

Fricassee of Orange Chicken with Tomatas & Almonds

A Spanishe Receipt

    Roast one chicken not six months olde on the Spit. Take ten tomatas peeled and chopped, add to a pan of four Onions chopped & Garlic cloves, ten, seethed in Olive oil, but they must be soft before the tomatas are added, with six cups good chicken broth, one cup fresh orange juice & one cup Almonds, fine ground. Chop the chicken into the sauce & simmer till it thickens. This is the best of dishes & good hot or cold.

From the Notebooks of Henrietta Bartley

Dear Mrs Bartlett,

I write to You with great urgency. This Letter will be carried to England by the Captain of The Ivy *and I hope will reach You before You send any further Letter to your Son. Indeed, I hope that You have not already, or if so, have not referred to Me.*

Max is well, thriving and happy. However a Year ago he wed the Widow of a fellow former Officer. He has undoubtedly written to tell You. I expect the Letter informing you of his Marriage would have reached You soon after I left England. I hope that You have not been distressed, imagining what might befall when I appeared. I have not, of course, given Max the Letter you sent with Me.

It has been a difficult Choice, but I believe it is in the best Interests of Max and his new Family that He does not suddenly

discover that I survived the battle of Waterloo. I have met his Wife,
a capable, loving and eminently suitable Wife for your Son, far
more suitable in his Family's eyes than I must be. His step Son
and step Daughter are a Delight, as is your new Granddaughter.
They met me as 'Mrs Bartley', the Name by which I am known
in the Colony. There is little Chance of their meeting me again for
at least a year, as they come to Sydney Town seldom.

In a few months, when I am established here and Max need
not feel duty bound to one who has sailed to His Majesty's
furthermost reaches of Empire, I will write to him, explaining that
our Marriage can be quietly annulled. His Excellency Governor
Macquarie and his wife have been most Kind to me. I dined with
them last night, and by coincidence Mrs Macquarie mentioned that
His Excellency has annulled many marriages here where there is
no hope of a spouse in England joining their convict husband or
wife across the world, so that they may be joined in lawful and
Christian wedlock. If His Excellency accords such Charity to the
most Humble in this Land, I am sure he will look Kindly and
Discreetly on a Request from a man who served at Waterloo.

Please do not grieve for Me. I am staying in the Colony. It is
beautiful, and there is Scope for a far wider Life than I might hope
for in England. I already have Friends who I may depend upon if
I need Help or Comfort. It is enough to know that Max is happy,
or, if I am honest, almost enough, but I can see the Day when my
Life and Heart will be full. I am glad, too, that my Search for him
carried me across the world, for I can think of no better Place to
carve out a Life than 'Australia', the new name for this Land.

Thank You for your great Kindness to me.
Yours most sincerely,
Mrs Henry Bartley (Hen)

Hen had been in Australia for two weeks: she had renounced a
husband; found welcome and good friends; had dined on wild
duck, excellent roast mutton and Rhenish Cream at Government
House. She also had a ward already able to hobble around the

kitchen on a crutch, eating as much as three men together, Cook complained, but with a smile on her narrow face, as if Jem's appetite was a compliment to her cooking and not his life of hunger and deprivation.

Jem's small bedroom was now furnished not just with a narrow bed but also a chest to hold the clothes Hen had procured for him. Neither she nor Gwendolyn thought it suitable that such a young boy — even one taken from the streets — share the convict men's quarters across the courtyard from the main house. Cook kept him occupied, sitting up in bed to pod peas or string beans or peel potatoes, with a well washed sack spread over his lap to keep the sheets clean.

Hen had also acquired an account at the new Bank of New South Wales and four hundred acres of land, a size that startled her, even in a colony where parcels of thousands of acres were given out, as well as the right to choose convicts to clear them, plant her gardens and do the rough building. The government would even provide clothes, boots and rations for her workmen for six months, though Hen suspected that the rations would need to be a good deal supplemented to keep her workforce in good health.

The land she had chosen from the titles map had in fact already been granted, but to a member of the New South Wales Corps returning to England, who was happy to surrender his grant for ten pounds. It was only one of the many properties he had acquired in the days when the Corps ran the colony and granted vast estates to its members.

The land encompassed a small promontory and two coves on the north side of the harbour, hidden from Sydney Town and not on the route through the Heads. Two men in a rowing boat could reach it in half an hour, but with no neighbouring properties it would be invisible to the colony's thieves and vagabonds.

Best of all, the map showed a small stream running down one of the gullies, though William warned her that many streams marked on the map dried up in summer. Like many householders, William relied on water pulled up from a backyard well for household needs, and even that was boiled. The colony's main water source, the Tank Stream, was referred to as 'The Stench' and, although its water had to be bought from the water carriers for garden use, any vegetables watered with it must be eaten with caution.

William organised a small expedition to inspect the land: himself, Gwendolyn, baby Jean and Mrs McDougal accompanied by Waddles, as well as Hen, two workmen to row, and an ample supply of picnic baskets.

They landed at the sandiest of the coves, the men removing their boots to jump out to pull the boat up onto the shore before helping the women out.

William gazed around, clearly assessing the cove for danger: escaped convicts, insane ticket-of-leave hermits, natives bearing spears (though Hen had been assured that Governor Macquarie's troops had overcome any rebels who might attack the colonists and that those Indians who remained in the colony were tame), or the many snakes Hen had been told were deadly in this land, though she had yet to see one.

But all seemed peaceful. Sunlight shimmered from the rocks above and waves small as the frills on a lace curtain shivered back and forth on the sand. 'No sign of the stream,' William announced.

Hen merely nodded. She had seen the vast household cisterns of Spain, storing water through the summer heat, refreshed by stormwater from tiled roofs. If necessary she would do that here, though it might mean reducing the size of the garden and limiting the orchard to fruits that could survive both heat and drought.

Gwendolyn retired to a cushion placed under the scanty shade of a tree to feed Jean for, despite the season, the day was warm, while Mrs McDougal fanned the flies away from them and Waddles investigated a dead seagull. William and his workmen gathered driftwood for a fire while Hen climbed the rocky slope, pushing away branches on a twisting path that might have been made by animals, for it was clear only to knee height.

Then there was a rock pool, two yards wide and just as deep perhaps — it was hard to tell as its base was dark with decayed leaves. Its smooth sides seemed to have been carved by the water. A small stream trickled into it and an even smaller stream trickled out, vanishing in the soil below.

Water then, and perhaps enough, even in summer. She climbed further, finding a wide flattish rock at the summit. She made to climb onto it then hesitated as a snake regarded her from its surface, an unblinking gaze from a black head, a hint of a red belly.

Her boots were sturdy and her skirts thick, but a snake at eye height might strike at a less protected limb.

Instead it slithered off. Hen clambered up to the wide rock ledge where it had been and surveyed her territory.

She could see why its previous owner had not used it. The soil on this part of the promontory seemed almost non-existent, with thin tussocks scattered on the clay and shale, but further back must be good enough to support the trees, though there would be much labour to cut them down and grub out the roots. But labour was free in the colony.

Something flickered on the edge of her line of sight. Hen turned, but all was still. Surely that had been a person? Dark skinned. She waited, but nothing moved but shadows.

Her house would sit on the point of the promontory, she decided, the dairy and storerooms to one side of it and the dormitories to the other, with the back of the men's quarters marking the far end of a courtyard that could not be entered except by a high gate that could be locked and bolted. The doors and windows of all the buildings except her own house would face outwards, leaving her courtyard and home secure, a design she knew well from her years in Spain. The herb gardens would go to the north, and then the vegetables, the orchards, the cow paddocks. Perhaps some sheep, for wool and mutton ...

'Well, Hen, my dearie? What d'ye make of it?' Mrs McDougal puffed up beside her, back in black bombazine for the row across, with a black bonnet and, Hen suspected, the two petticoats she had worn even when the *Ivy* crossed the equator. Waddles panted, a few white feathers about his mouth.

'It's beautiful,' Hen said simply.

'Aye. And needs a lot o' work and a guid bit of gilt to see it right.'

'I have the money.' Teeth, she thought. The teeth of Waterloo. Part of her still shied away from the source of her fortune — she had not shared that information even with Mrs McDougal. But here her teeth money could do good, wresting civilisation from the wilderness as Governor Macquarie had said. Just as Max was doing at Gilbert's Creek ...

Part of her wished she had not seen him. That way she could remember him only as the wounded man on the battlefield, his eyes shadowed with pain and blood loss. The man she had seen, only a fortnight back, had been sun-browned and healthy, striding up the hill, the pail of milk held in the hand whose arm she had so painstakingly saved. He had been entirely different and entirely the same.

She could more easily imagine life with the man he was now. Indeed, the life she would lead here — ordering her land cleared and ploughed, her house built, her sheep guarded — would be similar to the one she would have led as his wife.

Would she and Max have come to New South Wales if they had been reunited after the battle? Most probably, she thought. As a younger son Max needed land; he would still have been offered the land grant here in return for his service. Her father might even have accompanied them, either to a surgeon's post or even to leisure in the sunlight. Her father might even have still been alive if they had come here ...

'What are ye thinking, lass? What might hae been?'

She turned to Mrs McDougal's penetrating glance. 'How did you know?'

Mrs McDougal looked down at the small beach without answering. William and the men had the fire burning now, and a pot of water waiting to boil to make tea. Jean lay kicking her legs on the blanket while Gwendolyn laid out their nuncheon.

'There are always might hae beens,' Mrs McDougal said at last. 'But it has tae be enough to say this is good, and say farewell tae what didnae come tae be.'

'You are happy here?' urged Hen.

'Och aye, I am that. But if you were tae ask me hae my dreams come true, my dearie, I'd say that none o' them hae, for I never dreamed of this.'

'But your son is happy in his work and marriage and you have a thriving grandchild.' She looked around. 'And this will be a good place for sick children to grow strong, and for you to teach them.'

'True enough. We will do well here, even if it is in a barbarous land of Sassenachs and savages. There has to come a time, Hen my dearie, when grief steps back and ye let happiness fill the world again. And who knows? What comes next might be better than any might hae beens. Did ye know that William's grand new house will be three storeys high with attics as well? He will be setting up a carriage and stables too. He's doing right well,' said his mother proudly.

It is an easy colony to do well in, thought Hen, where land is free and so is labour. Each day brought new ships to the harbour, mostly American whalers and sealers, but often navy ships or convict transports. At least five ships sat at the wharves each day, and each of them needed resupplying with everything from food to ropes, candles, sails or new-made barrels, all grown or made in the colony and sold by William or his friend and rival Mr Campbell, or one of the smaller suppliers.

'I'm glad they'll move away from the docks,' said Hen. 'Every ship might bring your family business, but it may also bring in a new illness.'

'Aye, and it will be quieter,' agreed Mrs McDougal. 'And no foul language from the street for wee Jean to hear.'

Waddles snapped at a lizard, fat, gold and sun sleepy. It ran off, leaving its tail behind. Waddles crunched.

'A cup of tea,' said Mrs McDougal firmly. 'My William is grilling mutton steaks. I made us guid Selkirk bannock to be eating with them. Can ye credit that Cook had ne'er heard o' Selkirk Bannock, nor Bridies neither? There's fresh butter too, none of that salt, and Cook made an apple pie, which will be a test of her pastry. It canna be easy to make a tender flake in a kitchen as big as hers, feeding the warehouse men as well as the household.' Hen helped her down the track, with Waddles leading.

Behind her, dark shadows flickered among the trees.

Chapter 16

**Sweete Hearth Cakes or Fattie Cutties as I am Informed
They Call Them in Scotland**

Mix flour, two cups, Currants of the sunne half cup, fine
Sugar half cup, sweet Butter or good Lard half cup, add
ground Vanilla if it can be procured. Roll flat and cut to thin
Cakes. Fry each in butter till brown on each Side, or they can
be cooked on a hot Hearth. They keep most Well in the Heat.

From the Notebooks of Henrietta Bartley

Dear Père Flambeaux,
Translated from Flemish
*I hope you and your Congregation prosper and that the Harvest
has been good, of both Wheat and Souls. I hope, too, that your
Church has received the annual Gift from my Agent in England.
As you will see, I am now in the Colony of New South Wales.*

*It is a strange Place, a colony of Criminals but also Men and
Women of great Vision or great Desperation, and sometimes Both.
It is also beautiful, even if much that man has made here is not.
I will not be at the above Address by this time next year, I think,
but any letter sent to me care of McDougal's Chandlery will always
find me, for it is a small Colony and I now have Friends. Please, if
you or your Flock need my help, do not hesitate to write, though for
reasons too complicated to explain letters should be sent to the Name
with which I now sign myself, as yours with sincere affection,*
Mrs Henrietta Bartley

This land seemed to have discarded spring, for suddenly sunlight boiled between blue sky and harbour. The colony smelled of faeces and the strange tang of native trees. The air was filled with the shrill cry of the beetles that infested the native trees, as well as the familiar cries of 'Rag and bones! Bring your rag and bones!' 'Mutton Pies', 'Hot Potatoes', 'Clean water for sale!', 'Oysters, fresh from the harbour!' — the last two claims rarely true.

Mrs McDougal accompanied Hen to the barracks to choose the convicts allotted to her. On William's advice she would hire the experienced stonemasons and the ship's carpenter he himself used, instead of relying on the free labour allotted to her to build her house. Any convicts with a trade were soon put to government work, but their hours were from dawn till two in the afternoon, and any time after that the men were allowed to take paid work. There were now enough skilled ticket-of-leave men to hire, as well, who were experienced at building with the local stone.

The men she would be assigned today would almost certainly be unskilled but, hopefully, able to fell trees and even shape them with an adze if shown how. They would grub up roots, make fences for the stock and dig her gardens.

The convict barracks had been finished only a short time before she arrived. Mrs Macquarie had described how previously the convicts in government employ, and even those newly arrived, had been able to live where they wished, and discipline had been reduced accordingly. Now all unassigned convicts must dwell within the stone walls, sleeping in canvas hammocks, beyond a few who were married and given passes to live elsewhere. Government convict rations were given at the barracks daily instead of weekly, with their clothes exchanged for clean ones twice a week, with an arrow and their barrack number painted on them, instead of the featureless drabs the men had been issued before.

Hen was used to filth, but even she hesitated at the barrack gates. The buildings might be new, but were already squalid, the stench from inside almost impossible to bear even in the courtyard, where a stout pole was ringed with dried and fresh blood. The tinny scent of that added to the smells of ulcerated bodies and bad meat.

The work parties were already out on building sites or breaking rock for the roads. The hundred or so men lined up for her choice, shepherded by two guards with whips, were evidently newly arrived, semi-blind after months of poor diet and no sunlight down in the filthy holds, their blinking eyes sunken but their skin swollen with scurvy. Some were manacled. Hen eyed them warily. None looked more than half a man, nor to be trusted.

'Would any man with building experience come forwards?'

At least half the men shuffled out of line.

'How many of you can farm?'

Again, the same number moved towards her. But of course these men were criminals, and probably liars. They'd guess that working for her would be easier than breaking rock for cobbles.

She pointed to the first. 'What were you transported for?'

'Wasn't guilty,' he mumbled, from a toothless mouth.

Mrs McDougal snorted. Hen met the man's red-rimmed eyes. 'That wasn't what I asked.'

'Forgery.' And he had the accent of a Londoner, a man who'd never seen a carrot grow.

'And you?'

'Dab hander. Pickpocket.' The man looked more like a rat than human.

'And you?'

'Stole fourteen sacks of turnip seed so we might get a crop of summat after two summers when the wheat rotted in the field.' The voice had no expression, nor the face. The man might be stocky if given the right food, and time to recover, though his skin was covered in small ulcerated sores. But he had a countryman's accent.

'And you?' she asked a younger man, who stared only at the ground.

'He's me son,' said the ex-farmer. 'Don't talk much.'

'What's your name?'

'I'm Big Lon. He's Young Lon.'

'Very well, Mr Lon. You and your son please choose another eighteen men to work with you. We will be clearing and fencing land, preparing ground for gardens and livestock. You'll be their overseer. They will return here each evening at first.' She hated consigning men back to this dank hole, but she had no alternative yet. 'I'll provide lodging for you as soon as possible, though it will be tents to begin with.'

'A tent will be fine, lady.'

'I'm Mrs Bartley. I will return this afternoon to see who you have chosen.' The sooner we get you cleaned, fed and those sores attended to the better, she thought.

'Thank ye, Mrs Bartley.' For the first time there was a faint look on his face of what might be hope.

She turned to go. A man's face caught her eye; he was familiar but she couldn't place him. He had not put himself forwards. If anything, he lurked behind the others, but it was impossible to hide in the harsh light of the courtyard.

'You, step forwards,' she ordered.

The man shuffled a short way towards her, so that she saw his manacled arms. Only prisoners who had reoffended wore chains, but he must be available or the foremen wouldn't have brought him out, so it must have been a minor crime. His face was skeletal, his hair thin, lank and to his shoulders, his shoulders hunched, his whiskers like a wild man's. But she was sure she knew him. She stepped around the other men, and saw the stump of his leg, a peg bound to it.

'Sergeant Drivers!'

The man said nothing. The foreman flicked him with the whip, not hard, but enough to make him flinch. 'Answer the lady.'

'My name is Drivers,' he mumbled.

'Sergeant Drivers! What … how …?' But she could not ask what had brought him there in such a condition now. She stared at him, trying to find more of the man she remembered, but he looked only at the filthy cobbles, his face expressionless.

'Sergeant, don't you remember me? I was Hen Gilbert before I married, though I am widowed now.'

The man gazed at the muck on the cobbles, as if he hadn't heard.

The guard stepped between him and Hen. 'That one won't be no use to you, lady. Only one leg, and a trouble-maker at that.'

'He's not,' said Big Lon unexpectedly. 'He only dropped the pick cause he couldn't manage it one legged.'

'You shut your trap.' The guard advanced on him, whip raised.

'Stop,' ordered Hen. 'Mr Lon works for me now. I will have no one whip him.' She turned back to the sergeant. 'Will you work for me, Sergeant Drivers? Indeed, you are exactly who I need.'

He made a hoarse sound that might have been laughter.

'Lass, are ye sure?' asked Mrs McDougal quietly. 'Perhaps the puir man's wits hae gone.'

'Then good food, clean air and sunlight will restore them. Sergeant Drivers, you know how to set up a camp, and probably better than anyone in the colony. As soon as you can set up tents on my land the men can stay there, instead of coming back here each night.'

He glanced up at that. So he did understand, thought Hen. 'I'll warrant conditions will be better on my land than here, or on the ship or prison. The food will be as good as I can make it. I will also pay each man threepence for every hour he works beyond the allotted time, if you and Mr Lon will keep a record of it. Paid at the end of the first year,' she added. William had warned her that otherwise the men would vanish on the first pay day to drink away their wages.

Sergeant Drivers met her eyes. 'Make camp with what?' His voice lacked all emotion, but his gaze was watchful now.

Not for the first time, Hen thanked providence that 'My William' was a chandler, able to provide whatever was needed for her estate. 'I have eight tents with ropes and tent pegs, sixty blankets, twenty-five pannikins, twenty-five water bags, eight cooking pots, eight ladles and wooden spoons, five kits of flint and tinder, ten spades. There is water on the site, and ample firewood from fallen branches. If I have the men ferried across at eight tomorrow can you have the tents erected and the latrine dug by nightfall?'

She also had six muskets, lead shot and powder, for fresh meat was healthier than salt, and while she had yet to see a kanguroo or emu William said they should be plentiful, and that the o'possums made good eating too. But she would not give the muskets out till she knew the temper of the men — and they knew her.

'It would be best to put the fires on the beach till the site has been cleared,' she added. 'Can you do that?'

'Yes.'

She hesitated at the blankness in his tone. 'Sergeant Drivers, do you remember me?'

'I do. Surgeon Gilbert's daughter.' Something flashed in his eyes, gone too fast for her to interpret it.

'I am Mrs Bartley now. A widow, as I mentioned.' Had the sergeant seen Max that day of battle, or witnessed their wedding? No, he had been unconscious when Max was brought in and, even if he had not been, she doubted he could have made out much in the smoke.

The sergeant made no answer. The arms that had once been muscular looked as thin as a cat's under the manacles.

'I will make sure fresh provisions are brought over to you each day. For the first week I will expect no work, apart from setting up your camp, as you recover from ...' from months of hell in the hold of a ship, from prisons where rats outnumbered prisoners and nibbled their feet as they slept, from whatever lives of squalor they had led before their jailing '... from your ordeal. This afternoon I wish every man's hair to be shaved, and then each man to be scrubbed down on the beach when you arrive tomorrow. I will provide new clothes and boots while the ones you have on now are boiled. I will hold a clinic tomorrow noon for any illnesses, skin conditions or other problems you may have.'

She looked at the men and raised her voice. 'Please do not be squeamish about admitting them to me — whatever your ailments I will see them treated, and will not expect you to work until you are well enough, nor send you back here if you need more time for recovery. Will you unchain the men when Mr Lon chooses them?' she asked the guard. She handed him a shilling. 'Then please lead them down to McDougal's Warehouse tomorrow.'

The guard looked at the shilling — Hen had already discovered that coinage was rare in the colony and most goods were exchanged for their value in rum. He bit it, to ensure that it was silver, then nodded.

It seemed she had her men.

Twelve cases of scrofula, a ringworm, one of the clap — she was glad she had enough mercury, but the man would not be able to work while he was dosed with it — varied skin infections that should clear with fresh food and sunlight, as would the scurvy that afflicted them all in various degrees. There was also one possible consumption of the lungs that might improve, though she would not send the man back to the barracks even if it did not.

On the whole she was pleased. Big Lon, it seemed, was a good judge of men, and had had time enough to know the ones he'd chosen.

Sergeant Drivers also retained the skills he'd had back in Wellington's campaigns.

By the following afternoon the tents were in four straight lines up on the peninsula, well behind the area pegged out for her house and outbuildings, their entrances facing east, away from the coldest of the winds but catching the cool breezes. The latrine was deep, with stout branches across it to sit on, and placed on the slope away from the stream. It already had a wattle and bark fence to spare her blushes.

Two fireplaces were marked out with rocks on the sand of the cove. Young Lon had skinned an o'possum for the pot, as well as snared four of the small hopping creatures that almost might be rabbits, but were not. Hen mentally added 'poaching' to the theft of turnip seed. The animal skins lay curing over a branch. William had informed her that native animals' hides, especially the o'possum, fetched an excellent price in London, though they were despised as local in the colony.

She found Sergeant Drivers down at the cove. He had not been there when she arrived; she suspected he had seen her boat and limped off to collect driftwood. But now he sat by one of the fires, his wooden leg outstretched, mixing up soda bread as they'd done at countless camps. His skin was slightly reddened from sunlight after so long belowdecks, and his hair and beard had been shaved off, the one sure remedy for lice. Hen made a mental note to bring hats for the men tomorrow morning. She watched as he poured the water drained through wood ash for leavening into the flour sack, pulled out the lump, and trusted its dusting of flour to insulate the loaf from the ash. Already more than a dozen small loaves sat baking at the edges of the coals. He added another as she watched, the slight trembling of his hands the only sign that he needed more time for recovery.

'You have done miracles with the camp. Thank you, Sergeant.'

He nodded without looking at her.

'Please assure the men that I don't expect work till they are stronger, but as their first task is to prepare the ground for planting, they will reap the benefit of vegetables, and eventually fruit.'

'I'll tell them,' he said shortly. 'Likely they'll see grubbing out tree roots as better than breaking rocks for cobblestones.'

'Would you make a loaf for me?'

He still stared at the loaves, not at her. 'You don't have bread where you're lodged?'

'Extremely good bread. But your loaves bring back memories.' Good ones. Those who travelled with the army were soon inured to tragedy. You learned the art of happiness, of living for the day.

It seemed Sergeant Drivers had forgotten.

'There is a sack of scrubbed potatoes in the boat, and a side of mutton already chopped, and bunches of leeks. They'd be best all stewed together now, eaten tonight and for breakfast. Perhaps a store shed should go up first, netted to keep out the flies.'

The sergeant said nothing, punching up another loaf, then turning the others slightly so they'd brown evenly.

'I've a lotion for your wrists too.' Hen had seen where the manacles had rubbed them raw.

She waited for a word. He didn't give it.

'May I see your leg?' she added quietly. 'If the peg leg is chafing you can use the same ointment, but if you need to have another fitted I will arrange it.'

'It's good enough. Were given to me afore I were discharged.' The words seemed pulled from him, but he must have given efficient orders for the camp to be in such good order so soon, and with the men still weak, though it had been their own comfort they'd been arranging.

'Is there anything I have forgotten? It is so many years since I have had to think of these things, and I was never in charge of a camp, as you were.'

'We have what we need.'

'Sergeant, have you left family in England? I remember your wife. She was lovely. I will willingly pay for her passage to the colony.'

'She's dead, and the child with her.' Both his voice and face were still devoid of expression.

'I'm sorry. My father died too.'

Another glimpse of emotion, quickly suppressed, and silence, broken only by seagulls and a coarse phrase of appreciation of her femininity from above and another voice hushing the first speaker. Working for her was as soft a billet as any were likely to get in the colony, and she suspected the men Lon had chosen knew it. The threat of being returned to the barracks, as well as the promise of money at the end of a year or more working for her — enough perhaps to set up their own small holdings — would do more for discipline, she hoped, than any whips or threat of the lash.

'Oh, I nearly forgot. There are apple turnovers as well, two for each man.'

Sergeant Drivers looked at her face for the first time. 'You brought turnovers for cons?' he asked incredulously.

'Yes,' said Hen, glad to have provoked some reaction from him. 'Fig tarts tomorrow.' The McDougals provided meals to his workmen too, and his skinny Cook had help aplenty in the kitchen. She'd proudly assured Hen that pastries for another twenty men were little trouble. The pastries would also be a way to ensure that the men ate the fruit necessary to cure their scurvy, for fruit in its raw form would be foreign to many of them, even those who had eaten fruit before would find chewing difficult with their swollen mouths and loose teeth.

'They'll think you're a soft touch.' The sergeant's tone was almost the familiar one.

'I am. But I expect hard work, too. I hope you will make that known.'

'Aye, I will.' He seemed slightly dazed by the supply of pastry, as if she'd shocked him deeply, though she couldn't think how. Surely he remembered her parents' kindness, and would assume she would act with a good heart too. He handed her a small loaf, the size of her hand. It was too hot to hold long. But she broke it open anyway, to inhale the steam.

'We need knives, one for each man. Not one set of decent teeth among us.' It was the first request he had volunteered.

'I'm sorry. I'll see to it today. I knew I would forget things. Spoons?'

The sergeant shrugged. 'We can drink from the pannikins. A barrel of small beer wouldn't go amiss, if you're treating us.'

'A barrel a day. The cook where I am living now makes an excellent brew. I won't have spirits on my property though.'

He gave her a glance as if to say, 'Good luck with that.' But the men would need a boat to buy rum or gin, and money or something to trade for it. Like knives and axes. She would put the men's initials on any tools they used personally, and perhaps take from their wages the cost of any necessary replacements.

'It is beautiful here,' she said impulsively. 'I don't know what you've come from, Sergeant, only that it must have seemed like hell. But there are good lives to be made here. A man can rise from convict to magistrate in twenty years, with his own estate far grander than this will be.'

He did not look at the harbour but at her when he asked, 'Aren't you scared of being alone among so many men?'

'Of course not.' She had been an army brat. Armies were made of criminals escaping from the law or debtor's prison, as well as heroes.

'You should be.'

'Should I be scared of any man in particular?'

He stood, pushing himself up with a branch he must have appropriated as a walking stick. 'I hope you enjoy your loaf, Mrs Bartley. I need to collect more wood.' He limped off around the promontory without looking back at her.

Chapter 17

Fritters of Sage

Sage tea is efficacious for the Palsy. It strengthens the Sinews
and clears the Mind. Oil of Sage is Sovereign for all Infections
but Difficult to Distil. Mix half a cup of Water with One of
Flour. Beat two Egg Whites till Stiff. Mix. Dip in young Sage
Leaves and fry in hot Oil. Leaves of Rocquette are also most
Healthful and Delicious in this Manner.

From the Notebooks of Henrietta Bartley

The first summons was unexpected.

Hen was supervising the kitchenmaids pack the daily hamper
for her still unnamed property.

'... a keg of butter, a cheddar cheese and five rhubarb puddings,'
concluded Cook, who was also in charge of marketing for the
household, warehouse and now Hen's stores as well. 'I'll warrant
none o' them cons has tasted anything near as good as one o' my
puddings. It's my experience, Mrs Bartley, that men will work
harder for a bit o' good cooking than they will for sixpence.'

'You may well be right, Cook. And I must apologise, for I
have been calling you Cook for nigh on a month now, and have
not learned your name.'

The little woman before her, more bones than flesh, grinned,
showing four gaps in her teeth. She was mouse coloured, from

skin to hair, and probably only a few years older than Hen. 'It's Cook, Mrs Bartley.'

'You mean Mrs Cook?' Cooks usually were given the title 'Mrs' no matter their marital position.

'Just Cook. I never married. Not I,' averred Cook.

'So Cook was your father's name?' persisted Hen.

'It was not.' Cook peered around, but two kitchenmaids were lugging the provisions out to the cart to take down to the harbour and another two were flirting with the butcher's boy, while a fifth scrubbed out the scullery. Jem left his room by the kitchen each day now for the counting house in the warehouse, where he had discovered the astounding fact that the world contained more money than threepences. He sat next to one of the clerks now, his leg up on a cushioned chair, absorbing the wonder of numbers.

'I mean I was cook at ... let's just say an establishment,' said Cook softly.

'Of bad repute?'

Cook laughed. 'Of extremely good repute to them as liked such things, and interesting things they were, to be sure. The things I could tell you ... but I won't, because discretion would be my middle name, if my name weren't just "Cook". I were just the cook, ye understand,' she added hurriedly, 'not having the, ah, attributes for more.'

'But how did you come here?' asked Hen. As far as she knew such establishments were illegal, but not a transportable offence.

'Well, let's just say there were a difference of opinion about how much certain, ah, services should cost. And let's say too that certain ... items ...'

'Snuffboxes? Handkerchiefs? Fobs or watches?'

'Well, them too. They might go missin', an' who's to say they weren't dropped under the bed — nor would a respectable gentleman make a fuss calling the Runners to look for 'em.'

'Except one did.'

'Aye,' said Cook gloomily. 'And there was me all helpful like takin' the night's haul to a certain gentleman in the East End.'

'And you were nabbed?'

'I was nabbed as a swag carrier. But I never blabbed me trumpet sayin' who I was taking the haul too, nor who I might'a a seen at that particular establishment. And for not blabbin' I got a soft berth cookin' for the captain and officers on the ship that brought us here, and this job with Mr McDougal which is as downy a pallet as you might want, with all the butter and fresh fruits I could wish for, an' milk which comes out of the right bit o' a cow, an' it got even better when Master got spliced, 'cause the mistress with her kind heart will let the men have dainties, just like I used to cook.'

'But your name?'

'Well, it's like this. If certain gentlemen, even back in England, thought I knew about their habits, they might want me trap shut fer good in case I should be tellin' someone here and they'd tell their ma or pa in a letter and the gossip would get round. So back in the House I were called Auntie.'

'Auntie what?'

'Just Auntie, and here in the colony me name is Cook, and will be till I die. And ain't no use lookin' at me like that, my girl, 'cause I ain't goin' to tell you no more of their 'abits, not bein' suitable for a young girl like you to know.'

'I bet I can guess.'

'And nice girls don't go bettin', neither,' said Cook, whose accent had deteriorated through the conversation. 'Now, 'oo 'av we 'ere?'

It was a boy, dressed in the good clothing of a household servant, not convict drab, though even so young it was likely he had been a convict, like most servants in this land. 'What is it?' demanded Cook.

'Got a message for Mrs Bartley.'

Hen stood up from the stool on which she'd perched. 'I'm Mrs Bartley.'

'Nah, I needs the other one. The midwife what lives here what stitched up young Jem, and some of the *Ivy*'s sailors too.'

'I've done some midwifery,' said Hen cautiously. She had helped her mother deliver babies, and learned much of the theory in the years before she had been allowed to help. But she did not think herself experienced enough to be called a midwife. But she supposed it was natural to assume that any woman with medical knowledge must be a midwife too.

'Well, my mistress needs one bad. Forty hours she's been screamin' and Mr Redfern's out at the Macarthurs' and not back till tomorrow and Mr Wentworth has an ague and the mistress won't let Surgeon Bowman touch her after last time when he bled her half to death an' the babe was born dead, an' won't you come, missus, I mean ma'am?'

'Of course I'll come. Mrs Cook, would you mind asking Mr McDougal if he could get the men to take out the provisions without me? Tell Mrs McDougal and Mrs McDougal senior where I've gone.'

She ran upstairs and shoved the needed implements into a carpet bag, glad she had kept her father's instruments to hand — a starched and ironed apron, boiled bandages, dried lavender, rosemary, motherwort, styptic, laudanum, the birthing spoons, string, scissors, knife, needles and thread, trying all the time to remember what might be needed.

She questioned the boy as they hurried through the streets. 'Who has been attending her so far?' Hen desperately hoped it wasn't some filthy hag from the streets. Her mother had been sure that no woman would die of fever as long as the midwife's hands and all else that touched her had been cleaned in a strong solution of lavender and rosemary tea, as Culpeper directed in his *Complete Herbal & English Physician*, though few surgeons — or city midwives — gave any credence to the theory, or even knew about it.

'Dunno,' said the boy.

Hen saved her breath for running.

The house was further than she had thought, high on the eastern side of the colony, an imposing, two-storey mansion with ornate Grecian columns, made from subtly striped sandstone blocks, each colour melting into the other. A circular carriage drive led up to the front door. The boy began to lead the way to the servants' entrance around the back. Hen ignored him, hurrying up the wide shallow steps to the front door and banging the bronze knocker.

The door opened.

'Mrs Bartley to see Mrs …?'

'Mrs Salisbury? Please come in, Mrs Bartley,' the butler — with a proper butler's accent, too — did not comment on a midwife's use of the front door. 'Colonel, this is Mrs Bartley.'

'What?' A man of red-faced middle age stared at her, holding what looked like a full glass of brandy. 'You're just a gel!'

'True,' said Hen. 'And it has been years since I delivered a baby. But it appears I may be all you've got.'

'We should wait for Mr Redfern.'

'You may wait,' said Hen, as a scream rent the air from upstairs, 'but I do not think your wife would thank you for it. Babies do not wait for surgeons.'

She made her way up the staircase at the end of the hall without giving him an opportunity to answer. Indian carpet, bronze statues, crossed swords decorating one wall and an antique pair of muskets on another. The screams led her to the correct room.

An elderly abigail looked up as Hen came in, her face ashen. 'You're the midwife?'

'Yes,' said Hen. Whatever her deficiencies, it was important the woman on the bed had confidence in her. That confidence might just be enough to help her, and her babe, through this alive.

Her patient appeared to be in her early twenties, much younger than the man Hen presumed to be her husband. In other circumstances she might be pretty. Now her face was white except where it was flushed red and her eyes were darkly shadowed. She screamed again, holding on to the bed posts, straining.

'Quickly,' said Hen, handing the abigail the lavender and rosemary. 'I want these boiled.'

'The kettle's on the hob, miss.'

'Two cups of herb to six cups of water, boiled for two minutes. Leave the herbs in and bring the pot they boiled in, don't pour the liquid into another. Fast as you can then. And these,' she handed over the motherwort leaves, 'must be steeped in a cup of boiling water.' She turned to the woman on the bed. 'Mrs Salisbury, I'm not going to examine you till I have washed. You have been forty hours like this?'

'Not ... not so bad till the last two hours —' Mrs Salisbury's words broke as she shrieked again. Hen took hold of the woman's hands and held them till the contraction had passed, and Mrs Salisbury had enough panting breath to answer again.

'Has anyone attended you?'

'No. My husband will have none but Mr Wentworth or Mr Redfern, but they —' Words vanished as another contraction hit.

Hen wondered where Colonel Salisbury had heard of her experience, just as the woman managed to gasp, 'Mr Wentworth could not come, but said he knew of a competent midwife he might recommend.'

Which made sense. Mr Wentworth too would have assumed Hen knew more of women's needs than surgery, instead of it being the other way around. 'This is your first?'

'Second.' Her anguish filled the room. 'The first died at birth. A girl. I nearly did as well. It was not ... I think it was not well done. The surgeon had little experience of —' Another scream.

The door burst open, with the abigail and a maid carrying the pot.

And it was steaming, and the leaves well stewed. Hen put in the two birthing spoons, washed her hands, bearing the heat as long as she could, then thrust in the towels and bandages. They would have been better soaked and freshly dried by a fire, but there was no time. At least she hoped there was no time ...

'Mrs Salisbury, I am going to examine you. Please could I take the sheet down? That's right. Now I am going to put a wet towel here. It will feel warm. I am going to bathe your parts too. More towels,' she added to the abigail. 'Now, what shall we see?' She peered, using the spoons to help her see.

The cervix was fully dilated. But that was not a baby's head ...

This would not be easy. It might not even be possible to save both child and mother, or even either one of them.

She leaned back and took a breath. She had seen her mother do this. Just once, but she had talked Hen through it later. 'Mrs Salisbury, your baby is coming out legs and buttocks first. That means you have to strain more.'

And there was also the danger of the baby strangling on its cord, but she did not mention that, nor was this the time to try to turn the baby, as she might have if called the day before. 'You two, lay clean towels on the floor. Now a pillow ... Mrs Salisbury, I want you to crouch on the floor. Here, I'll help you ...'

'Like a dog!'

'Dogs have easier births than women,' said Hen.

Either the woman saw the sense in that or, more likely, she was desperate. She staggered two steps, crouched, her head down, kneeling legs apart.

'Now the baby can fall down, while you push and I pull. These are just spoons, Mrs Salisbury, now this is my hand.' Thank God for her small-boned hands, inherited from her mother. Mrs Salisbury shrieked again and Hen managed to grasp, twist slowly, slowly, gently ...

And the baby moved. Suddenly there was enough leg to hold it firmly, and a second foot through the cervix too.

'Another push, Mrs Salisbury. As soon as you feel the contraction ...'

A scream. Hen pulled both legs downwards, gently, gently, steadily.

The baby fell into her hands, red and wrinkled, the cord about its neck.

'Please ... please ... may I see it ...'

'In a minute.'

She removed the cord swiftly, tied it twice and cut between the knots, then opened the baby's mouth and breathed, a shallow breath of air only, once, twice, three times ...

The tiny body shuddered, gasped, then at last gave a cry.

Hen shut her eyes, muttered a prayer of gratitude, then wrapped the baby without cleaning him. 'A boy,' she remembered to say, as she put him in his mother's arms. 'Let him suck, if you will. There will be no milk yet but it will help you expel the afterbirth.'

She bent to this task. The door opened just as the afterbirth emerged.

An elderly man with the starched high shirt points of a dandy stared at her. 'It seems I am not needed,' he remarked.

Hen looked up from her careful assessment of the placenta, panting, aware her apron was bloody, and her hands, and her hair hanging over her face. 'I would be glad of your opinion, sir. You are Surgeon Redfern?'

'I am.'

'I apologise, but it seemed most urgent that ... that the baby ...'

'I understand, I think. A problem?'

'Breech,' said Hen, hoping Mrs Salisbury didn't realise how dangerous her position — and the baby's — had been. 'Cord about the neck.'

'I see.' It seemed he did, looking at the pot of implements, the baby, the mother lying back, eyes shut but clasping her child, the afterbirth. He peered at it with his eyeglass. 'It appears intact.'

'I think so too, sir. It came out quickly and cleanly and there is little effusion now. I do not want to stuff the uterus, as the cervix has been somewhat torn. But I will apply bandages soaked in lavender and rosemary externally and then a dry towel that should be changed every two hours. I will prepare more —'

'I think you have all well in hand.' He seemed almost amused. 'You are Mrs Bartley? Darcy Wentworth has spoken of you.'

'Kindly, I hope, sir.'

'Most kindly, and it seems you deserve his praise. A most accomplished midwife.'

She would need to correct his impression, but not now. And, just possibly, she might indeed have as much experience of childbirth as these surgeons, who mostly tended to wounds and infirmities.

An hour later she was sure that there would be no haemorrhage, and reasonably sure that, as no hands had touched her but Hen's own, Mrs Salisbury would not contract childbirth fever, either. The motherwort tea had not been needed.

She left orders that lavender and rosemary should be burned in the bedroom fireplace each morning for a fortnight to dispel injurious miasmas; and that the pads be boiled in lavender and rosemary tea before being dried by the fire, and touched by no hands that had not also been washed well in the hot tea. She left Mrs Salisbury drinking cocoa and eating oatmeal biscuits after her brief doze, with two drops only of laudanum to make sure the pain did not disturb her sleep, and orders to drink a glass of good sherry before each meal, and have liver and onions for breakfast each morning for a fortnight as well as mutton steaks for dinner, then descended the stairs.

Hen hesitated at the door of the library. She could hear men's voices in there. Should she interrupt them?

The question was answered for her. The door opened and Colonel Salisbury looked out.

'You have a son, Colonel, and a very fine one, as I am sure Mr Redfern has informed you. Your wife is doing well. You may see her now if you like. I should not expect any complications, but if you like I can visit her tomorrow.'

'If you would be so good, Mrs Bartley. Ahem, may I offer you a brandy?'

Hen hesitated. Her father would have accepted. 'Actually, sir, I would fancy a cup of tea.' She followed him into the well-lit room.

The colonel rang the bell. 'Tea for Mrs Bartley,' he ordered. 'Cakes too, that kind of thing.'

'Thank you, sir, but I would prefer bread and cheese. I have not eaten since breakfast.'

The colonel gave the order, then turned back to Hen. 'Won't you have a seat?' He gestured to the sofa. Mr Redfern had arranged himself by the mantelpiece.

Hen sat, wishing she'd worn a poplin morning dress under her apron, instead of the flannel walking dress and pelisse she'd donned as suitable for inspecting the work on her property.

'Now, if you will both excuse me.' Colonel Salisbury bowed to Hen and Mr Redfern, then headed hastily towards the stairs and his wife and son.

Mr Redfern smiled at Hen. 'Mr Wentworth tells me you are new to the colony. And His Excellency proclaims you are establishing a farm on the north shore.'

'That is correct, sir,' she said carefully.

'It is a trifle distant if you wish to set up as a midwife.'

'I have no such ambition, sir, though I will attend if called, and perhaps give shelter to unfortunate children who need my help.'

'By George, you're not building a hospital?' asked Mr Redfern, looking at her keenly.

Hen flushed. That was perilously close to what she was doing. But she could still say honestly, 'No, sir, simply a place where children can have good food and clean air, and perhaps learn their letters while they are there. I have no qualifications to run a hospital,' she added.

'That goes without saying,' said Mr Redfern. 'But your experience?'

'My first memory is holding my father's surgical instruments, sir. My father, Surgeon Gilbert, served in the Peninsular campaign, and then was recalled for Waterloo. He died as His Majesty's Superintendent of Hospitals at Chelsea, a little over a year ago.'

'My condolences, Mrs Bartley. And your husband? Will you pour?' he added, as a footman entered with the tea.

'My husband died at Waterloo, sir.' It was what she had claimed for four years, and only Mrs McDougal, Tim and Max's mother knew differently, and they would not contradict her.

'You must have been young!' exclaimed the surgeon.

'Yes, sir. There seemed ... an urgency. War does that.' She bit into the bread and cheese, the butter sweet, the cheese delicious and on good bread, home-made with an excellent yeast plant.

Colonel Salisbury returned, the smile so etched on his face Hen wondered if anything could remove it. 'They are both asleep. He is a fine lad. So big!'

'Indeed,' said Hen with feeling.

'Mrs Bartley's father served at Waterloo, sir. A Surgeon Gilbert.'

'Gilbert? Took off Colonel the Right Honourable Justin Farquhar's leg at the knee on the Peninsula, didn't he?'

'He did, sir.' She tried a slice of cold beef on bread next, piquant with mustard.

'And old Jolly Jo lived to tell the tale. They say he has a dress leg for dancing and dining, one for shooting, and one for walking out.'

Hen smiled. 'I hope so, sir.' She stood. 'What time would you like me to call tomorrow? Though I do not expect there to be problems.'

The colonel glanced at Mr Redfern, who nodded. 'Tomorrow afternoon if you would be so kind, Mrs Bartley. Ahem, the matter of the fee ...'

Hen was about to say that none was needed. But Mr Redfern would surely have charged a fee, and she had been called to this house. She had not volunteered. Which meant this was her first — and possibly only — professional consultation.

'Ten guineas, Colonel,' she said on impulse.

'Ten guineas? For a midwife!'

'Perhaps you should have asked my fee before you called me, sir,' said Hen demurely.

'Ten guineas! I never heard the like.'

'Pay it,' said Redfern, smiling. 'I warrant she has earned it. It was no easy birth.'

'Indeed. I apologise, Mrs Bartley. I will send the money around tomorrow morning, or pay it to you here, of course.'

'Tomorrow would be quite acceptable, sir.' Hen smiled. 'Or you might donate it directly to the Regimental Widows and Orphans Fund, to save me doing so.'

'Ah, I see. Shall we make it fifty guineas then?' Colonel Salisbury hesitated. 'My wife would probably enjoy it if you would stay to dine with us. We dine early, at four o'clock, so you would be home in daylight.'

A midwife would not be invited to dine at a home like this in England. Her father had been, but only at the peak of his career. But this was the colonies, and respectable gentlewomen were scarce, even one as eccentric as to be not quite a midwife. 'I should be honoured, sir.'

'And if … if we are ever blessed again …' The colonel flushed. He loved his wife deeply, Hen realised. He probably would have given his entire fortune to see her safe.

'Again, sir, I would be honoured.'

She glanced at Mr Redfern, the man who had founded the Rum Hospital with Mr Wentworth and who had been expected to be its chief surgeon, but had been passed over as an ex-convict. He had been a mutineer and was now a fierce advocate for the rights of emancipists to own land and hold government positions.

Perhaps, thought Hen, Mr Redfern did not feel as strongly as others that a woman's place was in the parlour, attending to flower arrangements. Hen was beginning to suspect that few women in the colony limited themselves this way, from Mrs Macarthur who seemed to run the family estates far more competently than her husband in his long absences, to Gwendolyn or even the barmaids tending the shanties by the wharves.

She did not think Mrs Salisbury would be well enough to sit at table the next day. Undoubtedly she would dine on a tray, and Hen with her. But the formal offer had been made.

It would be interesting to see who Mrs Salisbury was when not in desperate labour.

Chapter 18

Calendula Cheese

It is impossible to overstate the Healing Power of Calendula, being entirely efficacious with all Inflammations external and internal, expels Fevers, strengthens the Heart, and applied removes Scars. A Syrop or Tea may be supped through the day.

To make the cheese take four cups Milk. Curdle with one tablespoon Vinegar, Rennet, or Sorrel Juice. Hang curds in clean Cloth till the whey is drained and the Cheese soft, perhaps two days. Add three tablespoons Calendula Petals ground to paste in a Mortar, & Sugar to taste, & serve it forth. Rum or Whisky & grated Orange Peel may be added for Flavour.

From the Notebooks of Henrietta Bartley

Hen had walked half the way back to the McDougals' when a grimy hand grabbed her. 'You the flash cove what fixed young Jem?'

Her assailant was obviously female — her filthy gauze dress had no chemise under it — but she could have been anywhere from twenty to ninety. She put the age at the lower end of the range when the woman added, 'It's me daughter. She fell and her arm is all which way. You'll come?'

'Of course.' Though that sounded like a compound fracture and Hen had none of the right tools to either set a fracture nor, if it was truly bad, to amputate. But she could send someone for them.

She nodded to the footman who accompanied her. 'I will go alone from here.'

'But the colonel said —'

'Thank you,' said Hen. There was no need to lift her skirts as she hurried after the woman, for the cobbles there were almost clean.

The hut was set back behind a prosperous dwelling. Its darkness smelled of turnips and cabbage — a gardener's hut, perhaps, and this woman his doxy. But the child who gazed up at her from the bed of corn-husks and bracken was perhaps ten years old. Her arm, indeed, was 'all which way', but Hen saw with relief that it was dislocated, not broken.

The child shrank away. 'You cut people's feet off!'

This was true. 'But only if it has to be done, to make them better. Hardly ever. And I can make you better just by pulling at your arm a bit.'

'No!'

'Do as the nice lady tells you!' The sharpness did not hide the worry and the love.

'She ain't touchin' me!'

'You need doctorin'.'

'She ain't no doctor.'

'No, she's …' The woman looked at her, as uncertain as Hen about how to describe her.

Hen remembered Cook's words. 'I'm an auntie,' she offered.

The child looked at her suspiciously. 'Auntie what?'

'Auntie Hen.'

'Like cluck, cluck, cluck, cluck, cluck?'

'Squarrkkkk!' said Hen, making the girl laugh. 'Yes, I'm Auntie Hen. But I won't peck or scratch you. Hen means love where my papa came from.'

The girl looked at her thoughtfully. 'Auntie Love?'

It was a good, reassuring name. 'Yes, if you like.'

'You'll let Auntie Love make your arm better then?' asked the mother, her hope equally distributed between Hen and her daughter.

'You won't cut it off?' the child demanded.

'Certainly not. Here.' Hen took a small spoon from her bag, then poured out a little laudanum, mixed with honey. She needed the child's body to go limp so the pain would be reduced. 'Take this, like a good little chicken.'

The girl took it obediently, wrinkling her nose, unsure about the bitterness under the sweetness.

'Now I'm going to sing you a chicken song. Ready? Cluck, cluck, cluck, cluck-ark, cluckity cluck cluck ...' Hen waited till the girl's eyes began to close, then turned to the mother. 'I need you to hold her steady. You see where the arm goes into the shoulder?' Hen demonstrated with her own.

The woman nodded.

'The end of her arm has popped out of the socket. I can put it back in, which will relieve the pain, but she may have torn some of the ... the bits of the body that help hold the arm in place, so she'll need a sling till any soreness is gone.'

'She won't be maimed?'

'Not in the slightest.'

'She's ... she's all I've got. Pretty enough to catch the eye of an officer, even, in a few years' time.'

'Er, yes,' said Hen. This was not the time to discuss possible futures. 'Hold her steady, like this. Good. Now ...' She felt for the bone, the socket. 'One, two, three ... back and forth ...' She gave a sharp push '... and in!' The shoulder felt firm and everything in place too so, hopefully, minimal other damage had been done.

'You did it! Just like that!'

'Yes, well, there are few times it's as easy as that. I'm glad this was one of them.' Hen reached for a bandage to make a sling. 'See how I fold this? Let her arm rest in the sling as long as you can convince her to while her shoulder heals enough to keep it from popping out again.'

The mother smiled. 'She's stubborn.'

'And bright. If you could get her a place in a household ... like that of Colonel Salisbury perhaps, in a few years' time, she'd learn how to speak like a lady and cook and keep house. An officer would like a wife who knew how to care for a home.'

'A wife?' The thought had obviously not been among the mother's previous ambitions. It was now. 'How would I do that?'

'Ask for my help to get her a good position. And, till then, teach her not to swear and to be obedient and maybe teach her her letters, too.'

'Well, we'll see.' The mother's eyes drifted to the child, sleeping now, breathing deeply and evenly. 'When will she wake?'

'Whenever she's woken. It's not a deep sleep. But leave her quiet as long as you can, to let the shoulder settle.'

'I will.' The woman seemed to hesitate. 'She's getting older, Auntie. Master's got his eye on her already.'

'At her age! She's what, ten?'

'Twelve, thirteen come Christmas. Never had a chance to grow till we came here eight year ago. But she's why I got sent here. A bein' can stand hunger for herself, but not for her young. I don't ever want her to be as desperate as I were.' Another pause. The woman looked at the fruit trees behind the hut, not at Hen. 'You know any ways to get a girl outta trouble?'

'End a pregnancy, you mean? No,' said Hen quietly. 'Or rather, I know of them, but they are all as likely to end in the mother's death too. It is safer to carry a child to term.' She was not going to tell a woman who had once been desperate, and might be so again, about the uses of pennyroyal or Queen Anne's lace, quinine, motherwort or maiden's hair. More likely she would kill herself using them, or kill her daughter or anyone else to whom she passed the information.

For this was another kind of carnage Hen had seen too often while following the drum: women poisoned by herbal concoctions or dying of infection or haemorrhage because they'd tried to lose the child they carried.

'I can tell you ways not to conceive in the first place,' Hen added.

'What? Didn't know there was none!'

'You need a womb shield. Do you have a sponge, and olive oil?'

'None o' those.'

One of the other ways involved crocodile dung, which Hen supposed was as equally unobtainable as a French purse for the man. 'Do you have a lemon tree?'

'Aye. Master's got two o' they.'

'You take a lemon, then slice the end so it will fit ...' Hen described the manoeuvre, gesturing with her hands to make it clearer, as well as describing what was needed afterwards.

Even the concept of fertilising an egg seemed foreign to the woman in front of her, as Hen supposed it was to most women. 'Do you understand?' she asked at last.

'Aye. That stuff works true? Ma told me a blue ribbon round my leg would stop it happening, but happens she were wrong.'

'A blue ribbon will never stop a baby coming. If you don't have lemons, or if you find using them stings, you might try boiled cabbage leaf smeared with honey. Try to avoid the days between ten and fourteen after your bleeding begins as well if you can.' Hen had read that advice in an old Moorish book that had advised the days to get pregnant. If those were the best days to conceive a child then, for a woman like this, they must be the days to avoid — if she could. Hen doubted the choice would be hers.

Hen looked back at the sleeping girl. 'Call me if your daughter's in real pain again. I'm at the house next to McDougal's warehouse for a while yet.'

'I just ask for Auntie Love?'

Hen hesitated. If she was going to get a reputation for doctoring the poor, it was best not to use her own name, except where her patients might know her already. And she rather liked being Auntie Love.

I am not Miss Gilbert, she thought, nor Mrs Bartlett or Bartley. But Auntie Love was a name that fitted, and not one she'd ever need to give up either. 'Yes. Call for Auntie Love.'

But she was Mrs Bartley when she called on Mrs Colonel Salisbury the next afternoon at three, wearing green silk, suitable for dining, her pearls and a Norwich silk shawl, with her apron and instruments in a covered basket.

Hen found her patient propped up on pillows, feeding the baby. Hen smiled, put her finger to her lips and sat quietly till the baby had finished. He burped once, then slept.

'There is colour in your cheeks now, too. Now, if you don't mind ...' Hen took her pulse — firm and steady. The room smelled of her herbs, too.

'You're doing wonderfully. But I think perhaps you should dine on a tray tonight. Your husband kindly invited me to dinner. May I have a tray with you instead?'

'I'd love the company. I have the latest copy of *La Belle Assemblée* if it would interest you.' Mrs Salisbury laughed. 'Well, when I say the latest, the fashions are at least six months old. By now everyone in Paris may be wearing chicken-skin bonnets instead of satin. But it is at least the latest here. Do you enjoy fashion, Mrs Bartley?'

'I like a pretty dress,' admitted Hen. 'But I never have patience enough to follow whether it should be trimmed with gold lace or bunched ribbons.'

'Then you must let me help you! Of all things, I love to retrim a hat or a bonnet. I was a lady's maid once, you know.' The latter was admitted with a sharp eye to see how Hen took the news.

'Here in the colony?'

'In England.' Mrs Salisbury stroked her baby's downy head. 'We've called him Eric, after my husband's father. I was a lady's maid to a good woman, who was kind enough to see me well trained. But I had a mother and seven brothers and sisters still at home, and a maid's wage was not enough to feed them. I'd been stealing for three years before they realised. Just a silver spoon one month, a shilling from a reticule another.'

Mrs Salisbury kept her eyes on Hen as she told her tale. 'It was a visitor's quizzing glass that got me caught. I was stupid, but it was gold and the winter had been hard — days at a time when they'd had naught to eat while I'd eaten my fill down in that kitchen. But the house was searched when it went missing ...' Mrs Salisbury sighed. 'Even then, my mistress spoke up for me at the trial, so I was sent here, not to the gallows, and even with a letter of recommendation. But Colonel Salisbury chose me, right off the dock, and not as a lady's maid.' She still watched for Hen's expression. 'We were married six months later. Governor Macquarie insists his men marry. But Hubert says he would have wed me even so.'

'He'd been married before?'

'A widower for fourteen years. We're happy.'

'I can see that,' said Hen, realising that to be free of a criminal background made her an aristocrat in the colony. 'Thank you for the confidence.'

'If ... if we are to be friends, you have a right to know, and I'd rather it was from me than another.'

'I have nothing but admiration for a woman who cares for her family,' said Hen honestly. 'How are they now?'

'Ma died the year I was in prison, and Mary too. But Hubert arranged for the boys to go to Charterhouse for schooling, and then into the army. He bought them commissions — my brothers, lieutenants in red coats! And the girls are each married to farmers, for Hubert gave them good settlements. I am an aunt twice over, or I was when I last heard from them. Hubert paid for my sisters to learn their letters from our old parson so we can write to each other.'

'I'm glad.'

'You will soon find a good husband here, Mrs Bartley.' Mrs Salisbury smiled. 'Perhaps not as good as my Hubert, but there are ten men to every woman in the colony, and even fewer gentlewomen. Hubert knows he can never return to England now. Even when I have served my sentence and can legally return, the scandal of my past would touch our children.' The smile grew wry. 'Most in the colony have some secret to hide. Mine is not such an interesting one, and I hope will be forgotten.'

'I don't wish to remarry,' said Hen shortly.

'But ...' Mrs Salisbury stared at her. 'Are you perhaps put off by the thought of childbirth? You must have seen ...'

Hen smiled. 'I have luckily seen only happy births. My mother was skilled.'

'If it is the thought of ... marital relations ... you may have had a poor experience with your first husband, but I do assure you that if the man is kind they are truly quite pleasant, even extremely pleasurable at times.'

Hen laughed. 'It's not that either.'

'But what will you do?'

'Build a house, plant a garden, gaze at the harbour.' Hen did not think it advisable to mention her desire to care for injured children.

'Will that be enough, with neither husband nor children?' The question was a sincere one. This woman was no innocent; nor had she been brought up to think of herself as a flower to bloom for her husband and nothing more.

'I don't know,' said Hen frankly. 'But England seems so cribbed, cramped and confined. I think I am more likely to find ways to occupy me, and happily, here.'

'If we might help in any way ...'

'Could you recommend a lady's maid? I didn't bring one with me.'

Mrs Salisbury laughed. 'That shows how new you are to the colony. There is not a trained lady's maid to be had, unless you steal mine or Mrs Macarthur's or some other lady's and that, I may tell you, is a crime for which no one is forgiven. But I can undertake to find you a woman who will not drink herself into a stupor nor entertain her lovers in your parlour and who, quite possibly, will not help herself to your silver, either. I will have her work here with my Betty, who will instruct her, as I will. But I cannot guarantee that after training she won't catch the eye of an officer or farmer and be married just as she becomes useful.'

'That is enough. Thank you, Mrs Salisbury!'

'Will you call me Laura?'

'Thank you. And I am Hen. Not Henrietta.'

Laura held out her hand and Hen took it. They shook hands, exactly as men would do. Hen now had four friends, and ones who would not vanish when they moved camp.

By evening she had five friends. Hen liked Colonel Hubert Salisbury. He had given up his home, family and connections back in England for his wife, yet appeared extremely happy with his decision. She also approved of a man who kept his baby in the crook of his arm while he ate dinner instead of handing him to the nurse who kept hovering at the door.

The colonel had taken the most unusual step of requesting that a card table be brought to the bedroom so his wife might dine with him and Hen, and not from a tray. Two card tables were needed, spread with a white cloth, excellent silverware — Hen was glad the girl who had stolen spoons now had such grand cutlery of her own — and adorned with a first course of mutton steaks, as Hen had suggested, accompanied by a roast duck, green peas and spinach fritters. The second course was fish in sauce, cheese tarts, a buttered cauliflower, a steak and oyster pie, and mulberry jellies.

They talked of acquaintances they had in common in the army, or from her father's days as a student at Oxford. To Hen's surprise she and Colonel Salisbury knew many of the same officers, though she had been a child during the acquaintance, while he had known them as friends or colleagues.

At last he said, 'Mrs Bartley, will you excuse an observation from a man old enough to be your father?'

She smiled. 'Of course, sir.'

'The colony is a not a place for an unprotected woman. You have a safe berth with the McDougals — Mr McDougal has a fine reputation. But this scheme of living by yourself ...'

'I have followed the drum since I was born, sir. My father was posted to Gibraltar to support the fleet there.'

'The Algeciras campaign? Good man, Sir James.'

'My father met my mother in Gibraltar, sir.'

'Your mother was Spanish?' he asked in surprise. 'Your colouring is so fair.'

'You forget Gibraltar is English, sir! But yes, her ancestors were Spanish, except for a Dutch grandmother.' She did not add that her parents had met while her mother, too, tended the wounded; nor that her mother's knowledge of Spanish allowed her to study the Moorish medical treatises that described the human body so much more accurately than English theorists, as well as the book *Trotula*.

'You had the protection of your father in those days, and his fellow officers,' insisted Colonel Salisbury.

Hen thought of the men on her property across the harbour dining tonight on goat, onion and potato stew, fresh-made soda bread, fresh butter, cheese and quince tarts. Sergeant Drivers would have shown them how to make camp beds and even pillows by now. 'I'll have the protection of twenty men, sir, and a maid and other servants.'

'Convicts? Mrs Bartley, I am suggesting you may need protection from them.'

'By the time my house is built I will know them, sir, and whether they will be loyal to me or not. They will have every reason to protect me — they will have a more comfortable life than they might otherwise have been assigned, as well as pay for each year in my service.'

'I doubt that is enough to stop a drunken wretch attacking a lone woman,' he said frankly.

'Then I would need to defend myself, sir.'

He glanced at her reticule, as if he guessed the pistols it held, then laughed. 'I cannot say I like it, Mrs Bartley, but if any woman can defend herself, I believe it is you. But know that in this house you will always have friends who will shelter you.'

'Thank you, sir,' Hen said, much moved. For some reason it was deeply comforting to have a friend who understood so much of her life, that vanished world of the Peninsular campaigns.

Chapter 19

A Mulberrie or Cherrie Jelly

Take four cups juice of Cherries or Mulberries pressed from the Fruit. Add Sugar as Necessary. Dissolve one heaped tablespoon of prepared Gelatine in half a cup boiling Water. Mix with the juice. Leave to set. Serve with a sweetened whipped cream cheese. Fruit such as Peaches or Abricots, lightly cooked, may be added as the Jelly sets.

Ascorbic to a high degree and Sovereign for Aching Joints.

From the Notebooks of Henrietta Bartley

The conversation lingered long after the sun had dipped behind the mountains. The colonel sent two footmen with flaming torches to guide Hen on her way home by moonlight — one perhaps to guard her from the other. But another summons awaited her on the back doorstep.

'There's a cove says 'e's looking for Auntie Love,' said Denise, taking Hen's pelisse. 'Cook told 'im there ain't any such person 'ere, but 'e's still there, a-sittin' and waitin' for who knows who. Clutched in the noggin, I reckon.'

'I think he's waiting for me,' said Hen tiredly. 'Did he say someone was ill?'

'His chillun — didn't say how many 'e 'ad, just that they 'ad a fever.'

Typhus, measles, smallpox, influenza, scarlet fever ... it could be one of so many. If she was going to be called out to illnesses she would need to stay away from Gwendolyn and Laura in case the miasmas or organisms were carried on her clothes.

She should keep a change of clothes in the washhouse, perhaps, with instructions to boil whatever she had been wearing. Which should not be any of her silks or muslins. Hen sighed and began to climb the stairs to change into a cotton dress and fetch one of her long-sleeved aprons.

She did not want to become a physician to the colony. But neither could she ignore a summons from someone who needed help.

Another problem faced her the next day as she took hats for each of her workers, the government rations, as well as fresh food over to her property: five large boiled apple and treacle puddings, more fresh goat meat, potatoes and cornmeal, which the colony had more of than wheat. It grew well there, William said, but the colony still lacked enough storage to keep the price low.

Many convicts scorned it, and it was true that cornmeal loaves resembled cannon shot more than dinner. But Sergeant Drivers would know how cornmeal had been prepared at camp, soaked in water, then fried in lard. Hen had brought the lard, too, as well as two skillets, expensive, as was anything that must be brought from England.

I must remember to tell Sergeant Drivers to keep the skillets in the locked box for the tools, she thought, as the rowing boat rounded the corner of the harbour. She smiled at the sight of the promontory that already seemed more like home than any she had known, even in the last years with her father, for they would have had to move from that, too, once he retired on half pay or had been promoted again.

The blunt-toothed rocks, the clean rippled waves, the two big hearths on the shore already seemed home-like and familiar. Sergeant Drivers was again tending the fire as the boat approached. Hen thought he already looked stronger, his hands steadier. Another man sat beside him, hunched over with a red-stained shirt about his shoulders. The sergeant stood as the rowers helped her from the boat. 'We've had an injury, Mrs Bartley.' He gestured to the man still huddled on the sand.

She wished he would call her Miss Hen again. The sergeant was her last link to her old life, as well as to that day of battle that had changed her life. 'How did it happen?'

'Spear in the shoulder,' said Sergeant Drivers briefly.

'What?' Colonel Salisbury had assured her that while there had been battles in the past, his troops, under Governor Macquarie's orders, had entirely vanquished any rebel natives. Those Hen had seen seemed friendly, some sitting and observing the newcomers, the women fishing from their small canoes and young men selling fish by the seashore. Colonel Salisbury had also told her that the natives made excellent sailors, which seemed quite different from William's opinion of them, and indeed she had now seen natives dressed in the most civilised fashion drinking in the harbourside shanties that catered to seamen, their behaviour no more uncivilised than that of their companions in imbibing.

But this was no time for questions. Hen gestured to one of William's rowers to bring her medical bag while she undraped the man's shirt. Someone had cut the spear off, leaving a small protruding length of wood. She could see from the bruising that there'd already been attempts to pull it out. The spear must be barbed.

'Wiggins, isn't it?' she asked.

'Yes'm.'

'You know this will hurt? But I will be quick. Sergeant, do you have water boiling?'

The sergeant almost smiled. 'Yes.'

'Please put these into the pot.' Hen handed him a bunch of dried rosemary, her knife, a scalpel and a needle.

'Drink this, Mr Wiggins.' She handed him her flask of rum, then took it from him after he had drained half, and offered him a spoonful of her laudanum mix. The two together seemed to have at least five times the effect of either on its own, though Hen had seen no one else use the mix, including her father. Like many surgeons he had regarded medicines as an apothecary's trick, or tools only for a woman.

Hen waited till Wiggins's muscles began to relax under its influence, then nodded to the sergeant to hold him down.

The scalpel was almost too hot to hold, but she had been trained by a man who could remove and seal a leg within a minute. She splashed rum over Wiggins's shoulder while she tried to measure the size and shape of the barb by the bruising, then made one long, deep cut — poking around the wound would only increase the inflammation and chance of infection. Wiggins screamed and jerked away, but hard hands held him down.

Yes, that was the whole of the barb revealed, and it had not damaged anything but flesh and muscle. Hen pulled it away cleanly, poured more rum on liberally, sprinkled basilicum powder, then began her stitching, snipping off each stitch as she knotted it. Six were enough to hold the wound together, but she added another twelve, for close stitching also meant less risk of infection. Wiggins fainted on the sixth stitch, a combination of pain, shock and medication.

A final application of rum over the neat cut. Wiggins was still unconscious.

'Would you mind carrying him up to his tent?' she asked the boatmen, who had been watching with interest. 'I'm sure the other men will show you which it is. Place him on his side. Tell one of them to sit with him — if he vomits he may choke, so tell them to lift him to a sitting position if he begins to retch. He may have ale as he wants it. Leave an empty bucket with him, too, in case he needs it.'

She'd have liked to leave the patient rum, but there was little chance the other men would let him keep it.

She washed her instruments in the rosemary water while they shifted Wiggins onto a blanket then used it as a litter to carry the injured man up the track. It was well worn now, with stone steps where necessary.

Hen turned to Sergeant Drivers. 'Well?' she demanded. 'How did it happen? Was it a native, or did one of the men get hold of a native spear?'

'Native,' said Sergeant Drivers.

'How can you be sure?'

'Wiggins went off by himself. None o' the others followed him. Came back cryin' and yelpin'.' Sergeant Drivers still showed no sympathy or any other emotion.

'I didn't know there were wild natives here. Surely they are all in Governor Macquarie's reserve?' The governor hoped that the reserve might even become a native township, with their own farms to supply them as they learned civilisation.

'There's natives about. Can smell their smoke at night. Young Lon's found a few possum hides hung up to dry on branches when he's gone out to check his snares, and once a string bag with roots in it.'

Young Lon had presumably brought the hides back to add to his own collection to sell. 'I had no idea the area was dangerous,' Hen said slowly.

'I don't think it is.' The sergeant did not tell her why.

'But Wiggins has been injured!'

'Probably won't happen again.'

How could he know that? Did he simply not care if the men were injured? 'I think you had better begin work on the barracks at once. Make sure there are shutters for the windows, and bolts on them and the door, and musket flaps. I'll bring one over, with powder and shot, but for your use only. Keep it with you at all times.'

'You don't need to tell me that,' said Sergeant Drivers.

'You might begin to shoot game for the pot now, too.'

The sergeant looked down at his peg leg. 'Not a hunter these days, Mrs Bartley.'

'Nonsense. A good hunter waits not follows, as you know as well as I do. There are animal tracks all around the waterhole.'

He nodded agreement but said nothing more.

'Was Mr Wiggins setting snares?'

'Don't know.'

She gazed at him, but he didn't meet her eyes. 'Should I ask the governor for a party of men to hunt the natives away?'

'No,' said Sergeant Drivers. Once more he added no other comment. Hen thought with sudden anguish of the laughing man she had known so long ago. What had happened to him?

Waterloo, she thought. It took us, changed us. But I have friends, and hope, and money. The sergeant had hope, and a friend too, if he would only realise it.

'Very well, Sergeant. I won't request troops.' He knew his business far better than she did. If the sergeant thought there was no danger she'd accept it. Men quarrelled and were injured. It seemed this was just another quarrel, but with a native. Had Wiggins gone out to steal the native's furs or stores? Or to set traps, and they had suspected he was after more?

She would ask him when she inspected the wound the next day, but she suspected Wiggins would tell her he was strolling innocently through the woods, no matter what his real errand had been. And, for all she knew, he might be a secret nature lover and, like herself, enjoyed watching the light on the harbour with none to disturb her.

She stood. 'I'll check on him now. I've brought cornmeal today and two skillets to cook it with.'

'I'll keep 'em safe.'

'Thank you, Sergeant.' She began to climb up the path, but suddenly the shadows of the trees seemed to be watching her. She remembered the almost-glimpse of someone moving through the undergrowth on her first day there, how she had put it down to imagination.

Well, this was her land, granted and paid for, and improved by her money, from the teeth of Waterloo. The natives could look as much as they wanted, but if they hurt her men again, or encroached upon her acres, she would go straight to the governor, no matter what Sergeant Drivers said.

Chapter 20

A Rum and Roses Fruit Cake to Last Six Months

Steep fresh Roses in Rum each day till the rum is fragrant. Mix half a pound Butter with one cup sugar, two tablespoons of Treacle, then four eggs well beaten, five cups Sultanas, a quarter cup orange Marmalade, one cup currants, then flour, one cup, and rum enough to moisten the whole. Bake when the oven is cooling after Bread for four hrs or till firm to Touch. Fruits preserved in sugar may be added too. Pour over half cup rum or good Whisky as the cake leaves the oven. Wrap in double calico when cool. Men especially seem to like this Cake.

From the Notebooks of Henrietta Bartley

OCTOBER 1820

My Dear Hen, if I may call you that,

You undoubtedly know, as I was informed by Letter a mere week after you left England, that Max has married the widow of Captain Steven Blaine, an Acquaintance of his from his Army days, and no doubt a closer friend by the time of his death in the colony. Max it seems married his Mrs Blaine a bare six months after her husband's death, but I believe did so out of a Need to protect his Wife and two Children than a disrespect for his Friend.

My son did not tell me that he loves his Wife. He certainly likes, admires and respects Her, and possibly Love will ripen

*from their Friendship. Max must also have wished for the
Companionship of a wife on his Property and, if I know my son,
Captain Blaine's two Children would only add to his contentment.
Please do not blame him, for I am sure the Marriage was done in
Kindness and Chivalry.*

*My Dear, by now you will have seen Max. I do not know in
what Position You are now, his acknowledged Wife or not, nor
do I even know which I wish for, for it is possible — though I did
not mention it to You — that You both might find that Time and
Circumstance have changed your Affections.*

*I do know that I love and trust You both, and You may trust in
both my Love and my Discretion, whichever Path you have chosen.
As a seal of this, I enclose a Locket, with a portrait of my son as a
child. The Locket was my Mother's, and of all things I would like
Max's Wife to have it, which You have been, even if You have
decided it should be no more.*

*I greatly wish that You would write to tell me how You are
placed, and that if this is not at Max's Side, that You might
continue to write. I have met You but once, but like Max, that
once was enough to hold You very dear.*

*Yours who would claim you as a Daughter always,
Winifred Bartlett*

Hen read the letter for a second time, then laid it down, her hand
trembling. She almost wished she had never received it.

It had been four months since she had seen Max. She had not
walked past his house again, but in a society as narrow as Sydney
Town's she would have heard if he and his family — her throat
clenched at the word — had remained in residence for longer
than expected. Colonel Salisbury had even casually mentioned
'my friend Max Bartlett' when describing his fellow players at
piquet. 'A good man,' Colonel Salisbury had remarked. 'Joined
up for Waterloo but left straight after. Has a property far to the
south. Only comes to town for the Waterloo dinners, but that
may change now he is married.'

Hen had carefully betrayed no interest, turning the conversation back to King George's sad death. It had taken the colony so long to hear the news that few felt the need for full mourning, merely a few months of mauves or black ribbon, while waiting eagerly for news of his son's coronation. Mostly she was able to fall back into her familiar widow's state of mind — Max gone, mourned, irretrievable. But the moments when she was reminded that he might be sought, found, talked to, embraced ...

She shut her mind carefully on that thought, then shut the letter away in her jewellery box. She was building her own life now, and it was a good one. Soon she might even be able to bring herself to write to Max, thus relinquishing forever any hope they might be together.

There had been no more problems with the natives. Sergeant Drivers informed her that even the scent of their fires had vanished. Wiggins's shoulder had healed cleanly. He stated that he had not even seen who speared him. One moment he walked through the trees. The next he was in agony and on the ground.

Hen did not believe him, nor entirely trust him. But Big Lon said that Wiggins worked well, and had not even taken his wound as an excuse to avoid labouring for as long as possible. The men did not seem to fear native attacks, despite the spearing, though perhaps they relied on the knowledge that Sergeant Drivers was not just an excellent marksman, but could clean and load his musket in seconds. Hen had no need to bring fresh meat out now, other than as a change in diet, though she still delivered the salt beef and pork of their official rations. Now their scurvy had cleared, the men could eat the familiar food of home.

The knowledge that the colony had another doctor — one who would treat the poor free — soon spread. It was a rare day, or even night, when Auntie Love was not called out now to people in shanties or small cottages or to tend injuries in alleyways, for those the Rum Hospital would not admit, the free settlers and free-born of Sydney Town.

She cured sometimes. More often she did not, but that was a surgeon and physician's lot, for there was no physic for many illnesses, though Hen could ease the suffering of most. She had been taught to feel content with this, as long as she had done her best with no mistake.

And she was happy. Here, in the make-do spirit of the colony, she had found the camaraderie of military camps again. She had friends who would be her neighbours for all their lives. She had work that challenged her physically and mentally, as she had not been challenged since her last visit with Madame Caroline to the battlefield of Waterloo.

She also had gratitude. Hen had not realised before that she had been fed gratitude all her life, as those around her blessed her father's and mother's work, and hers as well as she assisted them. Now she had praise again. She was drunk on gratitude, which seemed to flow as easily there as rum.

Mr Wentworth took her on a tour of the Rum Hospital that he and his partners had paid for, when the surgeon in charge, Mr Bowman — no friend of either Mr Wentworth nor Mr Redfern — was absent.

Only the hospital's south wing was presently in use for the sick. The design was excellent but the execution had been so poor that the rubble walls were collapsing, leaving holes for the rats who scurried between the filthy pallets. The place smelled of mould and filth; nor in the hour Hen was there did she see a physician or nurse. Some of the men were tended by friends, or women who might be their wives — they did not wear the apron of nurses.

'Drunk, most like,' had been Mr Wentworth's comment when Hen asked after the nursing staff.

The most common complaint seemed to be congestion of the lungs, either influenza or one of the complications from it, like pneumonia, common in England, too, or consumption, which only clean air, good food and sunlight could cure, not rat droppings and salt beef. There was one surgical case, which she longed to inspect, a man with a broken leg and a long gash that seemed to have been neatly sewn. Soldiers inhabited a ward of their own, considerably cleaner, and with pillows, and chairs by their beds, but a far stronger stench of rum.

'They are all convicts or soldiers here, sir?' she asked Mr Wentworth.

'I think so. Redfern and I made no difference if a man was convict or free, but back then there were far fewer free settlers in the colony.'

'And women, sir?'

'They are treated here, but in a separate ward, and there are few patients.' Mr Wentworth added unemotionally, 'There is no way to guarantee a woman's safety here, Mrs Bartley. Most prefer to be seen by the surgeon then taken home by their friends or protectors.'

'I see.' Hen was glad there had been no time to send Jem there. This was not the place for a child.

'Well?' asked Mr Wentworth, as he offered his arm and they descended down the stairs to the relatively fresh air above the harbour. He shook his head. 'Do not hold back your views on my account. I had no oversight for its building, nor was it in this state when Redfern and I worked here.'

'Surely Governor Macquarie can have the walls repaired?'

'Our governor has his hands tied, having vastly exceeded his allocated funds. He is merely waiting for his replacement, who should have come a year back. The governor's made an enemy of Bigge, too — the man sent out to report back to England. I do believe His Excellency will be as careful as possible with expenditure now that Mr Bigge scrutinises all.'

Hen hesitated. The only hospitals she had seen had been organised by her father. The chief deficit here seemed not just sound walls, but supervision. 'What of Surgeon Bowman?'

They detoured around a cabbage-laden cart with a broken wheel while Mr Wentworth took his time formulating a response.

'Bowman knows his surgery, and I admit that he has organised the ration system well,' he said at last. 'Half the food and medicines would go missing under Redfern. Organisation is not his strong point. Bowman's furnished a dispensary, too, and a proper mortuary, and the medical equipment is now locked up.'

'But the filth, sir! And the lack of staff.'

'Probably no filthier than where most of the patients came from.' It was obvious that Mr Wentworth did not see cleanliness as necessary for good health.

'Where was Dr Bowman today?'

'He is out at Elizabeth Farm, I expect. Bowman is courting one of the Macarthur girls. He was supposed to lodge in the hospital, but it is not grand enough for a man of his ambitions, and he keeps a separate home. He believes his true bent is farming. Bowman came out on the same ship as Bigge and is Bigge's man to the hilt. I'll warrant the next governor makes him an excellent land grant, and that is the last the hospital will see of Dr Bowman. To put it bluntly, Mrs Bartley, there are fortunes to be made in the colony, but not from running a hospital.'

'You can do nothing to help, sir?' They had reached the McDougal residence.

'Bowman will have nothing to do with me, nor Redfern, nor anyone with the taint of convictry. I would not have taken you there if I hadn't known he'd be absent.'

'Will you come in, sir? Mr McDougal has a new shipment of tea, from China, extremely good.'

Mr Wentworth smiled. 'I would for your charming company, Mrs Bartley, if not for the dish of tea. But I admit I am tired. This southerly wind each afternoon is hard on the joints of the old.'

'I would advise an embrocation of warmed soap with oil of wintergreen and laudanum ... but I should not presume to advise you, sir.'

'I had not thought of an embrocation. Thank you. My dear, will you allow an old man to give you advice?' They moved aside as two workmen rolled a barrel up the hill to the warehouse. 'You have found favour with Governor Macquarie, and you are understood to enjoy the company of myself and Mr Redfern and Colonel Salisbury too, who is known to be one of Macquarie's men, not to mention that his wife still has two years of her sentence to serve.'

Hen blinked. She had assumed her friend was now a free woman. But the minimum sentence for transportation was seven years, and fourteen was common. If Hen had thought about the matter she must have known Laura was too young to have finished her time. This was a jail without walls.

'You may not appreciate how divided this colony is. The governor aspires to turn convicts into respectable citizens. Mr Macarthur wishes a colonial aristocracy of wealthy landowners, where convicts are slave labour effectively for life. Unwittingly you are now seen as part of the emancipist camp.'

'I ... I had no idea, sir. I do not follow politics.'

'So I assumed. I do not know who the next governor may be,' continued Mr Wentworth. 'But he'll be advised by Bigge, or at least Bigge's reports, and Bigge is said to favour the Macarthur camp, and not His Excellency's. Mrs Bartley, midwifery would be overlooked, but if Surgeon Bowman were to hear that a woman was performing surgery in the colony ...'

'I understand, sir, but I cannot refuse those in need.' One did not need a licence to perform surgery, here or in England. She had no wish to be a matter of gossip, though, especially not in a colony where one man's word could make a new law.

'Be discreet.' The grin that had charmed women for decades returned. 'Ah, if only I had been able to follow my own advice.' He lifted his hat to her. 'Good morning, Mrs Bartley. I will try that embrocation.'

An amputation of a man's crushed leg; four cases of typhus, after which she washed most carefully with lye soap before entering the McDougal residence; a case of cowpox she was pleased to diagnose as the mild disease, not smallpox; as well as setting limbs or sewing wounds for the patients who could not afford a surgeon's fee and who the Rum Hospital would not accept. The cottage farmers pressed pennies on her, which she took to save their pride, or cabbages, turnips and, once, an emu's egg, hollowed out and carved with a scene of natives fishing in the harbour, which Gwendolyn was glad to put on her mantelpiece. The poorest often gave no thanks at all, just watched her work in sullen anger, too worn down by fate to know the gift of gratitude.

Many of the callings-out were for childbirth. Hen discovered she knew far more than she had realised. Mr Redfern began asking her in to help him at the arrival of each convict ship to tend those who disembarked, though in most cases all she could do was advise sunlight, emollients for their skin, fresh food and rest, none of which they would get, though Mr Redfern and even the governor did their best. But the vice-regal funds would only stretch so far. Indeed, as Mr Wentworth had intimated, Governor Macquarie's grand buildings, road and other works *had* stretched them too far, and she had heard the exchequer was in debt.

She enjoyed working again. But she was uneasy working with Surgeon Redfern. She might be unable to cure many of her patients, but nor did she bleed three pints a day from them, nor tie a toad skin on their scrofula (one of Surgeon Redfern's favourite offerings). More of her patients survived because of what she refrained from doing to them, rather than what she did.

The calls for her help were increasing, especially as 'Auntie Love's' reputation grew, but one young woman could not manage the injuries and illnesses of all who had no other help in the colony. Her removal to a more remote home would mean she could not be so easily summoned, and would instead devote her care to the cases in her dormitories. Good nursing cured more patients than a single visit from a surgeon.

By mid-November the foundations of her house and outbuildings had been laid, and the stone ferried across so the stonemasons could begin work. The trees on four acres had been felled, the roots grubbed up and the timber used to make a storeroom, two huts for the Lons and Sergeant Drivers, who seemed to have worked out how to share the ordering of work details between them, and a barracks for the other men. The next project was to fell and dress the timber for the dormitories, with a promise that any man who married would have a cottage of his own once the other buildings were complete. The newly acquired wives, she hoped, might be useful in the house and garden.

She had also asked the men assigned to her if they would like part of their wages for extra hours sent to families back in England, or if they would like her to pay their family's passage to join their husbands. The government did not facilitate family reunions, but instead encouraged new marriages in New South Wales. Big Lon had declared his wife was dead. None of the others admitted to wives or families, though she overheard Wiggins muttering that his 'old lady' had abandoned him in prison for another man, and saw no reason for him to 'send me dosh' to her. She suspected that others had at least had a form of marriage. But all had spent at least two years imprisoned and on the voyage here, and the women of the colony's slums often needed to take up with a protector.

She had made the offer. It was all that she could do.

The fruit trees William had procured for her from the Cape had been planted. They had arrived far too quickly for him to have written an order for them. Hen suspected some less favoured customer would be told their trees had not arrived yet, and must wait another month or three till another ship made the trip. Plums, many varieties of apple, elderberry, quinces, pears, medlars, mulberries, oranges, lemons, citrons, cherries, a strange Chinese fruit called persimmon that William recommended she try, peaches and apricots …

Back in England an apricot could only be grown against a sheltered stone wall, and peaches were hot-house fruit. Even in Spain and Portugal citrus were grown in sheltered groves. Hen's well-fenced beds of asparagus were already showing their first spears, though it would be two years at least before the plants were big enough to harvest, but she had already picked the first stems of rhubarb — unnecessary, as William's garden provided all the rhubarb his household needed — but for the sheer pleasure of picking the first crop from land that was her own.

Each tree was given a bucket of water every second day, for the rain there was unreliable: weeks of dry followed by a thunderstorm that ripped the sky apart with light and noise. Once a week two men were given leave to row across the harbour to gather manure from the streets, with tuppence each for a shot of rum to discourage them from thieving to procure it. Once the latrines were full and covered well with soil she would plant them out with pear trees to make a wind break in the summer …

Today, as the men rowed her back over to the colony, Hen gazed back at the peninsula that would be her home, measuring its changes from the week before. It had already taken on an air of civilisation, its crown of trees removed, the spires of homely smoke, the scent of fresh-cut wood and, yes, a hint of the latrines too. She must remind Sergeant Drivers that wood ash should be sprinkled in them every day, and earth too once the days were warmer and the flies breeding. Should she plant the herbs yet? Her seedlings presently grew in pots in the McDougals' kitchen garden. No, they were better left where they were, for she might need their harvest, too, unless the new supplies from her tenants in England arrived soon.

The tide was out. Hen had to accept two hands about her wrists to haul her up as she clambered from boat to wharf. She gave the hands' owner threepence — she must ask Mr Gates to send her more coins from England, for she refused to pay in rum, as so many routinely did in the colony, for want of currency. The governor's new 'holey dollars' were held in suspicion, but a good English threepence was a most useful coin …

Voices greeted her now as she walked up from the wharf.

'Evening, Auntie!'

'Your health, Auntie Love.' An old man winked his remaining eye at her, raising his tankard to her. She'd treated his leg after a rat bite had become infected.

'Noddin' Sally says to tell you the young 'un's thrivin', Auntie Love.'

Hen had no idea who Noddin' Sally was, but she smiled and answered, 'Excellent.'

Waddles met her at the door, sniffing her feet to see if she had trod in anything interesting: an honour, as these days Waddles preferred the warehouse where he might find a rat. He preceded her into the parlour after she had handed her pelisse and bonnet to Denise. 'Gwendolyn, the men have moved into the barracks at last. I will have the tents delivered back to William —'

Hen stopped, as a young man stood as she entered, of middle height, not anything remarkable about him, except a nose reddening from rum or sunburn, and the starched high shirt collar under a too-tight coat with padded shoulders that advertised his pretensions as a dandy.

'Mrs Bartley?' The stranger gave the smallest skerrick of a bow.

Hen curtseyed politely, but also with the shallowest bob it was acceptable to give. 'Yes, I am Mrs Bartley. You have the advantage of me, sir.' Who was this man who did not have the manners to wait for his hostess to perform introductions?

'This is Surgeon Bowman,' said Gwendolyn uncomfortably. 'He wishes to speak to you —'

'On a private matter,' interrupted Surgeon Bowman. He looked meaningfully at Gwendolyn. She glanced at Hen. Hen nodded. Gwendolyn too gave the smallest possible curtsey, and left the room.

Hen looked at Surgeon Bowman, her anger rising. He had shown not just discourtesy, but rudeness. He now even sat on the sofa without asking permission, and not waiting for her to sit first.

Hen stayed standing by the door. 'Yes, sir?'

'It has come to my attention that you have been acting as a physician in the colony, Mrs Bartley.'

Ah. She raised her eyebrows. 'Hardly that, sir. But my father was a surgeon and Superintendent of His Majesty's Hospitals in England ...' and a far higher rank than you, sir '... and I have some experience at nursing, which I offer to unfortunates here.'

'You act as a midwife, Mrs Bartley?'

'I do not call myself a midwife, sir.'

'Nor apothecary? You may not know that it is now illegal to do so, under the Act of 1815.'

'Indeed, sir? That is of no interest to me. I have never called myself an apothecary, nor do I intend to.'

'But you dispense remedies.'

'As does any woman to her household, sir. That is not illegal.'

'But you have no household, Mrs Bartley, nor do I know of a housewife who would amputate a boy's foot.'

'The boy's foot was severed by a wagon wheel. I merely stopped the bleeding. Helping others is not illegal.'

'No,' Surgeon Bowman said slowly. 'But if you are not licensed as a surgeon and your patient dies, you could be hanged as a murderess, or at the least charged with grievous wounding, and receive a seven-year sentence.'

Hen managed to keep the shock from her face. She had never considered that. How could she, when her practice had been condoned and protected as her father's assistant? She lifted her chin. 'My work was approved by the Duke of Wellington himself. I was named in dispatches after the Battle of Waterloo, where every brave man in England fought Napoleon.'

'What is permissible in battle may not be suitable for civilised society, Mrs Bartley.'

That, too, she had not considered. Yet after all, her father had not invited her to help at an English hospital, despite his pride in her work in their army lives. Had he encouraged her to marry again partly because he knew that part of her life had ended at Waterloo? Meanwhile, she had this man to deal with.

Surely her work could not infringe on his? Nor would she let him bully her.

Hen raised her chin. 'I gather you were not at Waterloo, sir?'

'No,' Surgeon Bowman said shortly.

'I do not think Governor Macquarie would reproach me if someone died because I could not save them, especially those who are not admitted to your hospital. But if he should, I would appeal directly to the Duke himself.' Hen was sure the old Iron Duke would not just remember her, but would rebuke any who tried to limit her activities. His Lordship protected those he liked.

Surgeon Bowman clenched his fists, obviously unused to a woman who answered back. 'Macquarie will not always be governor, Mrs Bartley.'

'No, sir,' said Hen coolly. 'But I have a suspicion that any military man who fills His Excellency's position will be someone who knows His Lordship, and who also knows my father's reputation. The threads of Waterloo bind those of us who served there.'

'Even with the crime of contraception?'

Hen stared. Surgeon Bowman gazed at her with triumphant fury. 'I have a witness, in my own household, who will swear that you gave her advice — illegal advice — on how to avoid the natural woman's lot.'

'That is not illegal, sir.' Hen's voice was ice now.

'You are mistaken, madam. Under Lord Ellenborough's Law of 1803, it is most definitely illegal.'

'Surgeon Bowman, you are speaking to a woman who grew up in the household of one of England's foremost surgeons, and who spent three years keeping house for him as Superintendent of Hospitals in the company of other surgeons, all familiar with the Act of which you speak. The Act refers only to harming a living child, not a … potential one.'

'I do not agree. Contraception is wrong under the laws of England, and also under the natural law of man.'

Hen hesitated. She was sure her understanding of Lord Ellenborough's Law was correct. It had been much discussed among her father's acquaintances. Lord Ellenborough himself had stated that the reason for his law was the protection of bastard children. Any competent lawyer in England would surely say as much.

But this was not England. Hen had already seen that English law could be ignored here. Governor Macquarie was a man of high morality. If no law such as Surgeon Bowman claimed existed, the governor might very well proclaim one, if urged by the superintendent of his hospital. And if she broke the new law unwittingly and Surgeon Bowman demanded she be charged with illegal and immoral acts, the governor might have her sent back to England, not as a prisoner, but expelled none the less, to face the courts there.

The English courts would surely find her innocent, but only after what might be two years of scandal and disgrace, blackening her name forever as a supplier of immoral products. It would also bring 'Mrs Henry Bartley' to unwanted prominence, where her change of name must be discovered ...

Hen stared at the smirking man before her, aghast. For unknown to him she actually was guilty of a crime under British law. She was not a bigamist, but she had connived in the crime of bigamy by not immediately reporting Max's situation to the authorities. Even her change of name would be seen to be part of that ruse, which indeed it was. Max and his family would be caught up in the tangle ...

If only she had held her tongue in that filthy shed hidden by the respectability of the house in front of it. She had only offered it to protect the girl when her almost inevitable fate caught up with her ...

Suddenly she saw the only way Surgeon Bowman could have come by his information. Was he the master who had been looking thoughtfully at a twelve-year-old girl? Who presumably had the mother as mistress and noticed a slice of lemon ...

Hen was not the only one in the colony to have part of their life hidden.

'I gather you are courting Miss Macarthur, sir?'

'What is that to you, madam?'

Hen smiled at him with all the honey she could muster. 'Miss Macarthur might not like to hear your name in conjunction with such a case, sir. Not under the circumstances.'

He reddened further. 'Are you threatening me, Mrs Bartley?'

'Not in the least, sir,' she lied. 'I have committed no wrongdoing and I am sure the governor, any governor, would take my word over whoever you might have as a witness, especially as she might need to say how you came to suspect that any such advice had been given.'

Surgeon Bowman stood, furious. 'I have given you fair warning, Mrs Bartley.'

'I found nothing fair in your words. Good day, sir.' Hen did not curtsey as she left the room, nor call a servant to see Surgeon Bowman out. But someone stepped back as Hen entered the hall. Hen shepherded her down the hall and into the stairwell before Bowman could see and whispered, 'Cook! Were you listening at the keyhole?'

Cook grinned. 'O' course I were. How else would I know if you needed a bit o' help?'

Hen smiled, despite the scene she had just been part of. 'How could you have helped me?' She glanced around the corner at Surgeon Bowman, left finding his own hat and coat upon the rack and with no one to open the door for him, trying to imagine this scrawny woman evicting him.

'"Oh mistress," I would've yelled. "The dog has run off with the turkey and won't give it back." I might've tried, "The kitchen maid is 'aving 'er baby," but him being a surgeon, he might've felt fit to stick 'is nose into my kitchen.'

'He might indeed,' said Hen with feeling. 'Do you have tea on the brew, Cook? I could do with a cup.'

'Always.'

Hen followed her down the hallway, past the green baize door that led to the servants' area, and into the kitchen, empty for once of delivery boys, hopeful urchins and kitchenmaids. She sat as Cook handed her a cup of tea that looked like it had indeed been brewing on the side of the enclosed stove since breakfast and could now possibly dissolve cobblestones.

Cook regarded her, her skinny arms folded. 'You did right well with that prig back there, but now you know why I went by the name Auntie. If people don't know yer name they can't gossip about ye.'

And Hen was also 'Auntie' now. Surgeon Bowman had found her because she had helped his mistress as 'Mrs Bartley', dressed as a gentlewoman, not the cotton frock and all-covering apron worn by Auntie Love. Hopefully any of 'Auntie Love's' other doings in the slums of the Rocks would not be connected with Mrs Bartley.

Cook eyed her. 'What you goin' to do now?'

'I don't understand?'

'Goin' to keep building your house 'an' your hospital for strays?'

'Not a hospital,' said Hen automatically. Though that was what she'd planned, even though she had carefully called her potential buildings dormitories. 'No,' she said slowly, 'I think that would ... no longer be wise.'

She had already called enough attention to herself. 'Mrs Bartley's Children's Hospital', or even 'dormitory', would be talked about, even without the active enmity of the colony's chief surgeon. Mrs Macquarie took a great interest in the foundlings of the colony, as did other charitable women like Mrs Moore.

The widowed Mrs Bartlett might have taken on such a project, expanded her dormitories across her peninsula, spent her life helping the colony's children. Mrs Henry Bartley, with a scandal hidden like the lavender bags under her linen, could not.

Cook grinned at her, with both sympathy and understanding. 'Ain't one of us come here without something to hide, whether it's at His Majesty's pleasure or not.'

'Not Mrs McDougal.'

Cook raised a shaggy eyebrow. 'Her? She's running from more'n most.'

Hen could think of no one with fewer scandals to hide than Mrs McDougal. 'She came out here to keep house for her son.'

'A son what could afford a dozen housekeepers, including yours truly. Mr William did right well for himself afore he were married, not that he and the mistress ain't happy now, 'cause they are. But Mr William didn't need no ma crowdin' him while he found himself a wife.'

'But Mrs McDougal said ...' Hen hesitated. Exactly what had Mrs McDougal said? 'I must be of use ...'

'Perishing of loneliness she were, and Mr William knew it. "Cookie," he says to me — that's afore he met Miss Gwendolyn — "don't take it wrong," he says, "but I got to ask me ma to join me here and be me 'ousekeeper. Half crippled with the rheumatics she be, can't even toddle down to the kirk when the wind blows off the mountains, and talkin' about gettin' ready to meet her maker. No," Mr William said, "I got to get me ma here, into the warmth."'

Hen stared at her. Was Cook implying that she and William had enjoyed a ... a relationship? She had already discovered that the housekeepers of most unmarried men here became their mistresses, and an expert housekeeper like Cook, insignificant as a mouse until you saw her grin, and extraordinarily discreet, would be kept on even after marriage even though they moved out of their master's bed.

Cook grinned again. 'I know what yer thinkin'. No, me an' 'im were never like that. Like I said, I ain't got the attributes. Mr William had other company, but he valued me cookin' an' organisin', an' for company sometimes too. Many's the chat we had over the kitchen table, just like me and you is talking now.'

Hen nodded. Mrs McDougal must never know why her son had asked her to travel across the world, she thought. But Mrs McDougal, too, had looked forward to Hen's dormitories and assisting there, teaching the children to read tracts and even the Bible. Now she would have *that* plan taken from her, just as Gwendolyn had taken the housekeeping. And soon the McDougals would be in the new house, mixing with the highest society of the colony, most satisfying to William and Gwendolyn, but not for William's mother ...

'Lemon custard tarts for your men tomorrow, Mrs Bartley. I wish I could see their faces when they try them.'

Hen managed a smile. 'Thank you, Cook. I wish you could, too.'

'Word is you've got two foremen out there, an' neither has a wife,' said Cook, too casually.

'True,' Hen admitted.

'I imagine you'll be keeping them on, when the others leave? Foreman an' butler, maybe?'

Hen couldn't see Sergeant Drivers as a butler. But she did intend to keep him in her employ, if he so wished. 'Something like that, Cook.'

'I would be minded,' said Cook slowly, 'to manage a household like yours.'

'And leave the McDougals and the warehouse men unfed?'

'The McDougals will soon be moving up to the hills,' said Cook frankly. 'The warehouse men will need to fend for themselves. There's cook shops aplenty where they can eat these days, not like when we first came here. The men will do fine without my cookin'.'

'You don't wish to be cook at the fine new house?'

'The old biddy has me learning my letters already,' said Cook indignantly. 'I said to her, "Madam, I can sign me name" — well, one o' them, but she don't need to know that. "What more does a body want than that," I asked, "if she can make pastry that melts as soon as you look at it and a jam roll fit for the King's own kitchen?" An' now she wants me to serve mashed swede — bashed neeps she calls them — 'cause she thinks they're wholesome. Me, serve cattle food to the master? Cattle food is cattle food, no matter how much butter you mash it with.'

Cook wrinkled her nose. 'Besides, grand houses bore me,' she added frankly. 'It's going to be a footman in every passageway and curtseys all day long, yes ma'am, no ma'am, and a butler who measures the spoons on the dining table to make sure they are the right distance from the edge.' Cook winked at Hen. 'I reckon managing any establishment o' yours ain't goin' to be boring, beggin' your pardon.'

And Cook might also find a husband, if she wished, one who cared more for good cooking than 'attributes', or even a less formal relationship, which Hen might tolerate but the McDougals would not. Even respectable 'followers' were not permitted in the kitchens of most households and, with the dormitory plan abandoned, Mrs McDougal would have more time to spend supervising the moral and physical wholesomeness of the kitchen. Nor, out on the peninsula, would there be any danger of a gentleman, who had enjoyed the facilities in the London house where Cook had worked, recognising her.

Hen wondered suddenly what William intended to do with this house. Extend his adjoining warehouse and use the house for offices, perhaps. A whisper of a plan for her friend began to grow. If William had no need of the kitchen and the upstairs parlour, this house could become a school. A full-time teacher might even be housed in one of the bedrooms, with Mrs McDougal overseeing it all, arriving like a Scots queen each morning in her carriage, being handed down by a footman and imparting reading, poetry and porridge-making.

'Well, Mrs B?' demanded Cook, with a touch of impatience, giving Hen clear warning that she would be no subservient companion.

'I would be honoured if you would join us,' said Hen. 'On one condition.'

'And what may that be?'

'That I call you Mrs Cook. A woman needs a title to respect.'

'You got yourself a deal then.' Mrs Cook spat on her palm, and held it out for Hen to shake on the arrangement.

Chapter 21

A Most Interesting Ginger Peach Cake

Line your tin fully with sliced peaches, peeled. Strew some
butter & some brown Demerara Sugar over. Mix more
butter, half cup; Demerara Sugar half cup; then eggs, two;
then cinnamon and ground ginger, a teaspoon each; flour,
one cup. Spread across the peaches & bake after the bread
has been removed & the oven cooled a little till firm to touch.
The Peaches should show a most Pleaseing Pattern on the
top when inverted on a cake plate. Crystalised Ginger or
Sugared Violets may be Strewn before it is Served Forth.

From the Notebooks of Henrietta Bartley

Dear Mrs Bartlett,
I am getting Married this Saturday to Farmer John Burrows a
Gentleman of this Parish. Parson Wilson is writing this for Me. It
is Thanks to your Annuity because now John can drain the Lower
Field and I will bring three fat Sows to the Marriage and if the
Crop fails another Summer we need not be afraid our Children will
go hungry.

  Your grateful and obedient Servant,
  Ethel

Christmas, a strange hot Christmas that smelled of gum leaves
and the giant beetles whose cries whirred through the air and
emitted sprays of moisture when you walked under their trees.

Gwendolyn decorated the fireplaces with seasonal greenery that wilted almost immediately, and the dining table with a cornucopia of summer produce: cherries, peaches, apricots. Hen and the family attended church in the morning, sitting five rows behind the governor and his wife — a most Anglican service, which the kirk-going Mrs McDougal deplored, though she kept her usual mutterings to herself in honour of the day.

They dined at midday on green goose served with tangerines picked from William's orchard, as the geese they were eating had grazed beneath his trees; new potatoes from his vegetable gardens buttered with parsley; carrots glazed with honey; a saddle of lamb with Eglantine sauce; a spinach pie; a peach trifle; a honey syllabub from William's cows; a ginger peach cake (it was a most excellent year for peaches); mince pies that no one ate but which must be there for the tradition; no buttered swedes whatsoever (William had tactfully informed his mother that the crop had failed) and a vast jam tart with raspberry, mulberry and apple jelly creating the designs of St Andrew and the Scottish flag, as well as the Union Jack.

Tomorrow the family would consume the leftovers, leaving Mrs Cook and the kitchen staff free of toil, for as Mrs McDougal said, it was not as if she and Gwendolyn did not know how to boil a kettle or an egg, or cook the porridge she still insisted the household eat each morning, and she had a most excellent receipt for a hash of leftover roast lamb with potatoes and cabbage fried together in good dripping, and they would have yesterday's bread toasted.

The convicts assigned to Hen had been rowed over to the colony in the early morning, ostensibly to attend church, though she did not believe she had seen any of them there. She, Mrs McDougal and Gwendolyn had prepared the men's Christmas boxes, as well as those for the servants and William's employees, who now included Jem, still residing in the storeroom but spending his days in the magic world of figures that could always be relied upon, no matter which way you added them up, a degree of certainty he had never dreamed existed.

Each box contained good woollen stockings knitted for them by Mrs McDougal and Hen (though Mrs McDougal had turned the heels on all of them for her and picked up her dropped stitches); a new shirt and trousers each, far superior to government issue, made by a seamstress in The Rocks; a pamphlet on the virtues of sobriety and twice-daily prayer, contributed by Mrs McDougal, who had shipped a chestful of similar literature to improve the new world; a small jar of preserved Chinese ginger, which William had over-ordered and was happy to distribute before it spoiled; and a shilling, made up of whatever coins Hen was able to procure, unwilling as she was to use up her dwindling supplies of threepences.

Her men, as well as William's employees and their families if they had them, had their own feast at a long trestle table laid out in the main warehouse, with a hind of beef roasted on a spit in the courtyard outside, along with three sheep, a hill of buttered potatoes, fresh bread, and a mountain of boiled puddings that had been made throughout December so there might be banquets today.

The men would be drunk by tonight for, as well as kegs of ale, William had supplied rum, despite his mother's protestations about the evils of strong drink. William declared he would not have a man still working for him if he did not provide spirits for Christmas.

Those in Hen's employ who wished to would be rowed back to the peninsula that night, but if they wished otherwise they had permission to stay on makeshift pallets in the warehouse until New Year, when there would be another feast, including the haggis and vast clootie dumplings Mrs McDougal would make herself.

Hen, Mrs McDougal, William and Gwendolyn visited the warehouse feast after their own had finished with nuts and honeyed fruits (a heavy emphasis on peach). The men raised their tankards to toast each of them in turn, none of them showing signs of inebriation yet, to Hen's relief, for she feared Mrs McDougal might give them a lecture on sobriety if they did.

She looked at the faces, brown from the sun now, their shipboard pallor and subsequent sunburn vanished, each of them fleshed out from good feeding and hard work and, she must admit, distance from the demon rum. They seemed happy, Big Lon sitting at one head of the table and William's foreman at the other ...

Hen looked again. There was no sign of Sergeant Drivers, nor an empty seat where he might have been. She interrupted Big Lon as he attacked his plate of piled slices of beef, followed by more beef, and topped by beef again. 'The sergeant didn't come with you, Mr Lon? He's not ill, is he?'

Big Lon began to stand politely. She patted his shoulder to tell him to stay seated.

'No, Mrs Bartley,' he said, wiping his mouth on his sleeve. 'Said he didn't feel like the noise and would enjoy the quiet for a while.'

That was understandable, perhaps, after so long crammed with others on the ship and in prison, but for some reason Hen felt uneasy.

William lingered to chat to his foreman. Mrs McDougal retired to sleep away the heat of the afternoon, and Gwendolyn to feed baby Jean and change her napkin. On impulse, Hen grabbed her bonnet, filled a basket with leftovers and walked the short way down to the wharf, where William kept a small skiff for whenever he wished to make a quick journey to a ship at anchor. Her father had taught her to row, a useful skill in their journeying, and surely it wasn't far to her promontory ...

It was, in fact, both harder and further than she realised. But by now it would take as long to return as it would to reach her land. Perhaps Sergeant Drivers would row her back, then row himself to the peninsula. William would not need the skiff till after the New Year.

At last she neared the cove. The beach was empty, though a small spire of smoke rose from one of the firepits on the sand, no more than a clear eddy in the midsummer air. Hen felt the little boat rock beneath her as she tied her skirts about her waist, revealing a scandalous amount of stockings, garters, legs and much else to the seagulls, slipped off her shoes and jumped into the water.

It was waist deep, and the sandy bottom difficult to grip with stockinged feet, but she had the edge of the skiff to steady her, though she feared her blue silk would be stained past recovery. She slowly pulled the craft up onto the sand, panting, the salt stinging her blisters. She dressed them with lavender and mint from the medical basket she always carried with her now even before pulling her skirt down, in case they festered, then sat on a log by the firepit to get her breath back before setting out to wish Sergeant Drivers a merry Christmas.

The waves nibbled at the sand; the seagulls cried above her. The harbour was empty for once. Even the native women's fishing canoes had vanished, though Hen doubted the heathen natives observed Christmas. Reverend Marsden had declared during one of his services that it was useless even trying to convert them. More likely the summer fishing was better in the cool of the morning or the evening.

The strange beetles shrilled in the gum trees. The beach breathed out heat. Her dress would be dry soon, the thin fabric no longer revealing the shape of her body beneath it. She took off her bonnet, careless for once of the sun and wind on her complexion and sat on a rock to let the sweat dry from her hair.

She smelled him a second before she felt the edge of a knife at her throat.

Her body froze. Her mind did not. If Sergeant Drivers wished to kill her he would have done so by now.

She waited.

He moved now. The knife did not. He eventually crouched in front of her, only the knife tip touching her skin.

She forced herself to keep her voice steady. 'Sergeant Drivers? What are you doing?'

'Killing you.'

She must seem calm, as though this happened every day. 'Why? Has something happened? I thought you enjoyed the work.'

'Nothing to do with that.'

'What is it then?'

He thrust out the wooden leg. 'You stole my life.'

'I don't understand.'

'You know what they called you, back in the hospital? The Angel of Waterloo. That's who I saw that day, an angel telling me she'd give me a life if I gave up my leg. Instead you took it.'

'But you have a life now.' She tried to sound reasonable. 'A good life, with hope of even better.'

The sergeant gave a sound between a sob and a snarl, the knife steady at her throat. 'What do I want a life for? If I'd died that day Isobel would have lived. She'd have had a bit o' pension. She'd've found another man easy enough, a woman like her. But no, she stuck with me. She died an' our babe with her 'cause I had no food to give her, nor coin to pay a midwife. Not even any good at thieving, not with the thump of a peg leg to give me away, nor a good enough scar to be set up begging.'

'I ... I am so sorry ...'

'Sorry! I've dreamed of killing you ever since I saw you in silk and parasol, plump and pleased with yourself at the barracks. You'd come through the battle, and the years after, looking like Lady Muck. Isobel's hands were so thin you could almost see through them. Hardly had enough strength to walk, much less birth a baby. Three days I watched them die, heard her plead with me for help. The only help I could have given her was to have died back on that battlefield. You took that from me, and from her too ...'

Hen screamed inwardly, in pity and in horror. But neither must appear on her face, or in her voice. Nor could she ever let him know that her fortune had indeed been made from that battle, not just her father's position, but his investments on Wellington's success, not to mention the sacks of teeth, slowly being sold as the price rose again, making her wealthier still every year.

'I will remember that day all my life,' she said quietly. 'I gave you a choice. Life or death. You chose life.'

The hand that held the knife to her throat trembled. 'What use is that life to me now?'

Suddenly she knew what she should say. Because this man was a soldier, battle hardened. If he had truly wished to kill her it would have been done on the first day, here on the sand.

She kept her body as still as possible. 'If you truly don't want your life,' she said softly, 'I can give you something that will do the job quickly and painlessly.'

Sergeant Drivers stared at her. 'You'd take my life, too?'

'No,' Hen said calmly. 'But I'd help you to take it, if you think I owe you your death.' She hoped he believed her. She had never used her medicines for harm. Never considered that she might. 'Sergeant Drivers, you have a chance at a good life here,' she added, letting her urgency show. 'If you kill me you'll be sent to Van Diemen's Land if you're lucky. More likely they'll hang you.'

'Not if they don't know it was me.' He pulled his shirt open. An Indian axe, with its sharp stone edge, was held in place by his belt. 'This will hide the knife cut. It'll be the natives that killed you, not me.'

'Good plan. Hard tack for the natives though. Who knows how many will be slaughtered in retribution? Do you really wish men to die just so you can have revenge? Women and children too, perhaps.'

Sergeant Drivers stared at her. Hen very slowly moved her hand till it touched his, the one that did not hold the knife. 'Sergeant Drivers, I can't replace your leg; nor can I feel guilt because my father took it from you. We did our best at Waterloo and, no, not all our decisions were the right ones, or even good. How could they be, when we had only seconds to choose?' The shadow of the teeth from Waterloo seemed to lie on her as she added, 'But I will not spend my life regretting what cannot be undone, the thousands we did not have the time or skill to save, those perhaps we should not have tried to save. Nor do I believe your life is a waste.'

'Isobel died because of you.' But his voice wavered. So did the knife.

'Sergeant Drivers, the colony is full of convicts with two good legs who fought at Waterloo and starved for lack of work and bitter harvests. You have a good life now and it will get better. You have a cottage. Eventually you can have land of your own. You may end up a wealthy magistrate, like Mr Redfern. But that will be more likely if I am alive to help you.'

The sergeant gave a bark of laughter. 'I should have known you would try to argue your way out of it. I remember, back in Spain ...' The sergeant halted.

'You remember you were our friend, who ate Mama's chicken?'

'I had forgotten,' Sergeant Drivers said slowly.

Hen didn't doubt it. Pain and grief had led to gin, most likely. And then the dark grim horror of the hulks, the journey in the stinking hold to New South Wales, darkness and starvation, the lash as he tried vainly to break stone with a stump for a leg.

She watched him blink as in one moment the mindset of his last four years changed. Watched him look at the sand, the harbour, the sky, then finally at her.

He began to put the knife into his belt, stopped, then handed it to her. 'I'm sorry,' he said simply. 'I ... I've never hurt a woman.'

'You still haven't,' she said gently.

'I think somehow after Isobel died my mind went back to the battlefield. It's as if I still hear the guns in my sleep, and during the day too sometimes. Life and death, life and death.'

'And now you realise you are here, instead, where there are good things growing and birds singing. There are many whose bodies survived that day, but who could never leave Waterloo behind.' Hen did not add that many of them were in insane asylums, raving about the roar of cannons, or haunted by the shadow of Napoleon that fluttered around their bed. 'An injury of the mind can be more crippling than an injury to the body.'

'I thought you were an angel,' he repeated. 'That's what I thought sometimes in the darkness coming here. Waterloo was dark too, but the sunlight caught your hair. I hoped you'd survived the battle, that you weren't an orphan, struggling to earn a crust. I knew you had no one but your Pa. You'd been the Angel of Waterloo, but I knew that wouldn't be enough to save you.'

'And angels are supposed to work miracles? I'm just a woman.' Hen hoped he assumed that her wealth came from her lost husband, not from the battle's dead.

'Will you have me charged? Or just send me back to the barracks?' He sounded resigned: the first sane emotion she had heard in his voice.

'Are you going to try to kill me again?'

'No. Miss Hen, I can't swear that the darkness won't take me again, but I promise I'll never hurt you. I'm sorry. I'll forever be sorry.'

'So you bloody well ought to be.' She had never sworn before. 'No, I won't send you back to the barracks, nor have you charged.'

He replied incredulously, 'So we go on like before?'

'Why not? You're a damned good foreman.' Hen had now sworn twice, and discovered why men did it. It was ... emphatic. Women were not supposed to be emphatic and so they should not swear. She took a deep breath. 'I came to wish you merry Christmas. There is a basket of food in the skiff.' She hoped he didn't see her hands were trembling. 'Would you mind fetching it?'

'Miss Hen ...'

'Oh, go away so I can burst into tears and not be embarrassed. You scared me stiff.'

'You shouldn't cry alone.'

She looked at him in surprise. His eyes darkened with memory. 'Isobel taught me that. After every battle there'd be widows, and she would comfort them. But if you want to cry because I frightened you, I'd best be off.'

She shook her head. There was so much to cry for: her father; the loss of Max; her vanished dream of a sanctuary for children, for she loved children, but now might not even have any of her own; the agony of Waterloo that haunted her dreams, too; the owners of the teeth gazing at her from the yellow smoke of battle. She had not cried since her father's funeral because she'd had hope, had learned to see the joy around the pain. But the grief was there as well and suddenly it emerged, tears even hotter than the sand.

'Miss Hen ...' His hands were very gentle as he tentatively touched her hand, and then her shoulder. Suddenly she found she'd pressed her face to his shirt. She let the sobs come. Not elegant tears, but gulping cries and snot. When at last she moved back she saw that his face was wet as well. She reached into her basket, found a handkerchief, and blew her nose, then scrambled to her feet and crossed to a rock pool to wash her face. When she turned he was over at the skiff.

He returned bearing two mugs of ale with slices of the pudding and a leg of goose from the basket. He handed one of the mugs and a slice of pudding to her. 'For shock. I learned that from you.'

'Thank you.' He sat next to her on the sand as she sipped, ate and discovered that her tears were spent. Tears alone could not wash away the memory of Waterloo and its aftermath.

The sergeant finished the goose and pudding, then downed the rest of his ale. 'Thank you for the food. I'd have gone hungry else.'

Hen looked back at him, surprised. 'But there is plenty in the storeroom.'

'There's nothing in the storeroom,' he said calmly.

'But the sacks of potatoes, the dried corn, the flour ...'

'Sold the day after you brought it here, mostly.'

'But that's impossible! How, I mean, who ...?'

'The Lons, o' course,' he said patiently. 'Miss Hen, ain't you realised yet this is a land of felons? We walk around with no chains because the wild about us is prison-walls enough, but none of us is innocent, no matter what we claim. Nor was we caught the first time we broke the law, neither. Most of us are damned good at it.'

'But the Lons were farmers.'

'Aye. They robbed their own neighbours, who were starving, just like them. Bags o' turnip seed? That's what you steal from the poor, not from the rich.'

'But you are all stranded here ...'

The sergeant laughed. 'Didn't you hear what I said? We're cons, Miss Hen. Big Lon stole an Indian canoe the second day we were here. There's been just enough potatoes goin' to the pot to stop you getting suspicious and none of the meat — our meat comes from Young Lon's snares. They've got an arrangement with a shanty, don't know which one, but I'd bet a farthing to a farrow that's where they all are now, getting drunk and getting women with what they've made from you. Half the profits to the Lons, the rest shared among us all.'

Hen stared at him. 'I ... I didn't know. I never suspected.'

'You know less than you think you do, Miss Hen. Always did.' His voice held kindness now. 'You thought you saw the hard side of life. You didn't. Your ma and pa was good people, and so people around them did mostly good too. You never got to see what happened when you left.'

'Like you with your leg?'

'Like the little girl the Lons said you helped when her shoulder broke. They heard about her from her ma when she was drinking in that shanty.'

'What about the girl?' Hen asked in trepidation.

'Mended properly it did, and now she's washed and pretty and will be spending tonight in her master's bed, after he's fed and drunk his day with the gentry. Mebbe if you'd left her alone she'd have set crooked and he'd not have touched her. But an angel visited, then just walked away.'

'Would you have had me not help her?' Hen demanded.

The sergeant regarded her thoughtfully. 'I don't know. And that's an honest answer. I reckon I owe you honesty now. Should you have let me die instead of living as a cripple? I don't know the answer to that, neither.'

'We can only do our best,' repeated Hen shakily.

'Maybe what people need ain't an angel flying down to help them, then flyin' off again.'

'I am not an angel! I never claimed to be one. If people thought they saw one, then it was what they wanted to see. You want me to be a guardian angel, who stands behind you all your life, protecting you, just because I helped save your life? I will do good, Sergeant Drivers,' she said fiercely. 'But do not judge me by the standards of angels. I am a woman. No more, no less.'

A seagull dropped down and strutted towards them, hoping for pudding crumbs. Hen threw a handful of sand at it, so it flew away.

'Aye,' said Sergeant Drivers at last. 'You're a woman. And a good one.'

'So do I send the Lons and all the rest back to the barracks?'

'No. You'd just make them your enemies, and the men that you'd get instead are like enough to be worse, and know less about farming. Lock the storeroom and give me the key.'

'Should I trust you?'

'Well, I didn't kill you,' he pointed out reasonably.

'That is true. And, who knows? I might need a chicken stolen again.' She suddenly wondered exactly how many chickens or other goods this man had stolen, even while he'd been under the stern command of the old Iron Duke.

She raised an eyebrow at him. 'Should I keep Big Lon as foreman?'

'Aye. He doesn't do much work, nor his son neither, unless you're here to see it. But both o' them know what needs to be done and are good at ordering others to do it.'

'I ... see.' She gazed out at the harbour, absorbing the information. 'What else don't I know, Sergeant?'

He made a sound that was almost a laugh. 'Too much to tell you this afternoon.'

'What don't I know about you? You said you'd tried to be a thief.'

'The only thing I ever managed to steal was that chicken, and that was larking. I left a shilling for it. No, I got caught first time I tried to break a window, not by the Runners but by other cons, for poaching on their patch. They beat me up for it. That was when I tried begging, then Isobel died.' He shrugged. 'I don't remember much after that. I'll tell you one thing you don't know — my pa was a farmer. I don't know as much as the Lons, but I know more than they think I do.'

'Why did you join the army?' Suddenly she realised she had never thought of his life before the campaign.

'Six children. I was the youngest son, so when the wheat rotted the year England didn't have a summer I enlisted.'

'Your family couldn't help you after Waterloo?'

'They were dead,' he said flatly. 'Typhus. My two sisters had children by then, but they all died too. I was supposed to be the one in danger, but I was the only one who lived.'

'All we owe the dead is to live our lives well.' Hen tried to smile. 'I tell myself that every morning. Sometimes I even believe it.'

The waves crept closer, foam-edged ripples. One touched her foot, and then retreated, and none other came as close. The tide was on the turn.

'Will you still move out here?' he asked her, as her silence lengthened.

She considered. She had planned a paradise, one shared with sick children. Neither the paradise nor the children were going to eventuate.

But she still had the harbour, which she loved, and the land, which she was growing to love, too. She wanted a garden where she could see dead-looking sticks grow into trees, and shrivelled seeds blossom into healing herbs. She wanted her own home, as well.

Despite the kindness of the McDougals, her position there was slightly uncomfortable, neither companion nor relative. Hen had stayed quite long enough merely as their guest, and one who had brought embarrassment in offending Surgeon Bowman and also possibly his patrons the Macarthurs, so prominent in the colony.

Governor Macquarie had finally been sent the letter accepting his resignation. His replacement might not arrive for months, or even longer but, eventually, one would come, a man she possibly would have no influence with, though she hoped it might be another military man, one who might even have served at Waterloo, or known her father …

'I want to live here. But the Lons will do no more stealing.'

'Of course they will. They'll steal the radishes from your garden and the washing from your line. But they'll do it less once they know your eye is on them.'

'And if you tell me what I need to know.'

'Aye. I'll do that.' He hesitated. 'I can't ever make up for what I tried to do, Miss Hen, but I promise you this: you can trust me, forever and for anything. I'll begin by helping keep the Lons in line.'

'Thank you.' Hen suddenly thought of the diminutive Mrs Cook, who had a most excellent eye and far more experience of ruffians than Hen did, as well as probably unconventional ways they might be manipulated. The Lons were in for a surprise.

She stood. 'Will we share Christmas supper, Sergeant Drivers? I wouldn't mind another slice of goose and possibly a peach. Then you might be good enough to row me back to the wharf.'

'I will. And … and just I'm sorry, Miss Hen,' he repeated.

'For wanting to kill me, or spoiling my illusions?'

'For the first. I think I shut my eyes back at Waterloo and didn't quite open them till today.'

'Perhaps I did the same,' Hen said quietly, then went to set out the food, while the sergeant stoked up the fire.

Chapter 22

A Lime, Tangerine or Lemon Butter

An Excellent Ascorbic, most Strengthening and Delicious, especially Efficacious for Colds of the Head.

Heat gently the juice of six Lemons, or six Tangerines or twelve Limes, a half cup Butter, a cup Sugar, four beaten Eggs, fine Cornflour one tablespoon. Bottle as soon as it thickens. Seal & keep cool. It will last three Days in a stone Larder.

From the Notebooks of Henrietta Bartley

1821

Dear Mrs Higginbotham,
Thank You for your Christmas Wishes! They arrived on the
Celeste in late January, but were most Welcome. It is so kind
of You and Surgeon Higginbotham to remember me. I am afraid
there was some Confusion over the spelling of my Surname when
I arrived. It has been erroneously changed to Bartley, and it seems
easier to accept the Misspelling than attempt to change it.

Our Colony is still small, though growing rapidly, and
Governor Macquarie sees a great Future for it, even equal perhaps
to the Cape. I have enclosed a Watercolour of the Harbour. It is
magnificent, and could hold twenty Navies in its many Branches.

The work is not by my own Hand, which is as Clumsy with
the Paintbrush as always, but by a Friend of mine, Mrs William

McDougal. She and her Husband and Mother-in-law offered me
Hospitality until my new Home was completed. Mrs McDougal
is the former Miss Gwendolyn Lloyd, daughter of the late
Major Douglas Lloyd, who served at Coruna when Surgeon
Higginbotham was also posted there.

   May 1821 bring you and Surgeon Higginbotham Health and
Happiness, and may you receive this before the Year is out! Please
give my good Wishes to Elinor, Mary, Janet and Master Thomas,
   Yours most respectfully,
   Mrs M Bartley

'You must have a verandah,' declared Colonel Salisbury as
they sipped turtle soup in the stifling January heat of his most
splendid dining room. 'Couldn't do without a verandah back in
India. Perfect place to sit in the summer and catch the breeze.'

'An enclosed stove, Mrs B,' announced Mrs Cook, kneading
bread lightly salted with sweat. 'And no need to worrit your head
about it, 'cause I've given the order meself to the blacksmith and
the stove will be ready as soon as the flagstones are laid in the
kitchen.'

   'I planned an outdoor oven,' offered Hen. 'They have them in
Portuguese villages — big enough for twenty loaves of bread or
to roast a whole sheep without heating up the kitchen.'

   'I will look forward to that,' said Mrs Cook politely. 'You just
tell me when the floor has settled, and I'll have Jenkins install me
oven.'

'More manure, and you will soon have most excellent crops,'
enthused William, as he showed her his neat rows of orchard,
all enclosed in a thorny hedge of citronelle that (mostly) kept the
goats out. 'It is impossible to give the soil in this place too much
manure. Not just from your own stock, or with buckets as you
do now, but send your men over to the wharves with barrels
thrice each week to sweep the streets.'

'A water closet,' Sergeant Drivers advised, 'A private one for your own use. As well as convenience, it will mean greater security. If your gates need to be locked for some time you don't want to be locked in with full chamberpots. Now, if we dug the tunnel you could have an outlet above the smaller cove here, and put a tank to supply the water here ...'

'Prayers morning and night, for your household and all the men,' imparted Mrs McDougal as they sipped tea up in her sitting room, and Waddles lay on his back to cool his tummy. 'Not only is it an excellent example for the men, but you will be able to judge from their breath and steadiness if they have been imbibing. I like the colony more than I expected,' the old woman admitted. 'But it needs discipline! Christian instruction each evening on how to lead a sober and industrious life.'

By mid-February Hen's new rooms were whitewashed, her roof shingled with timber from her land, and both wooden and flagged stone floors had been laid. They were adorned with carpets William imported from India in blues and reds. The other furnishings had been purchased from local carpenters and joiners. She had her linen from England, along with blankets, quilts, crockery and silverware; her books, including her precious copy of *Trotula* by Trota of Salerno, copied by Trinity College, and Culpeper's *Complete Herbal & English Physician*. All the appurtenances of good living were unpacked.

Her home was waiting for her. England, recreated in the colonies: the cottage by the sea her mother had dreamed of and that Hen had imagined too in the carnage of Waterloo, and the herb garden as well.

Her house was of roughly dressed sandstone, a single storey, situated at the point of the peninsula so her drawing room looked out at the harbour, and her bedroom looked out on one inlet and the dining room that would be a breakfast room as well looked out upon the other.

Two guest bedrooms stood next to hers, as dinner guests might need to stay the night. The back of the house held a small kitchen and scullery, suitable for heating water or making a tisane; the servants' dining room; a private housekeeper's parlour for Mrs Cook; and bedrooms for her, Millie the housemaid and Sal No-Last-Name-Recorded, who had been hurriedly trained by Laura in the arts of caring for Hen's dresses and preparing her bath, as well as mending linen, refraining from speaking to any gentlemen visitors and the other rules of a civilised household.

The main kitchen, with its enclosed stove and a range for roasting meats or simmering a large pot, was connected to the house by a stone breezeway so that no kitchen fire could spread to the main building. Mrs Cook already spent each day there, to supervise the furnishings and to cook for the men. She had burned the first two batches of pies she had baked in the outdoor oven, using words Hen politely pretended she did not understand, but then suddenly had the knack of it. Perfect tarts, bread and cakes now emerged from it in the vast numbers Hen's employees consumed.

Wiggins had orders to light the oven at dawn each morning so that it might be hot enough to rake out the ashes and bake Hen's breakfast bread at seven am, with enough stored heat to cook the day's cakes and pies, though Mrs Cook's beloved enclosed stove, and the fireplace and turning spit next to it, would be used to cook their supper.

Mrs Cook had rapidly assessed the Lons ('Don't trust 'em as far as you can throw 'em, Mrs B, but don't worry, I'll keep me eye on 'em.') and the sergeant ('A good man. Needs feedin' up.').

The sergeant saw to the maintenance of a pile of well-dried firewood, surrounded by sand to show the tracks of any snake that decided to live in the wood heap. Already three had been killed, one brown, and two black with the red belly, like the one Hen had seen on her first day on the peninsula. 'The Peninsula' seemed to have become the name for her home, without her intending it, but it was not inappropriate, for so many of her formative and happiest years had been spent in the Peninsular campaigns.

She had her dairy, her still room ready for her work, with an adjoining chamber to hang dried herbs, an alehouse — Mrs Cook brewed an excellent small beer — and a new storeroom with a root cellar lined with stone for keeping fruits and vegetables over winter, which with the kitchen wings made up a gated courtyard at the back of the house, with bars on all the windows and locks on the high, sharp-topped gates.

She also had her orchard, an acre of herbs, four acres in vegetables and two acres more prepared for winter's cabbages, turnips, leeks and onions and thanks to Mrs Cook's insistence, no swedes whatsoever, enough vegetables for her and her employees — and instructions that if any man sold the produce, or traded produce for rum or the temporary affections of a barmaid, they would be sent back to the barracks. The sergeant let it be known he counted even the radishes each evening, and would no longer turn a blind eye to pilfering.

Hen could not in conscience order whipping, the common punishment for misdemeanours. Hopefully the loss of what was indeed a comfortable life, with the promise of more comfort still, would be the greatest punishment that could be inflicted.

The new orders seemed to work. By the end of February only two of the original twenty assigned convicts had been replaced, one for refusing to take Mrs Cook's orders, the other for stealing from his workmates. ('Lucky to be sent back afore one o' them cut his throat,' remarked Mrs Cook as the miscreant was rowed away.)

The sergeant rowed Hen, Millie, Sal and Mrs Cook to and from the Peninsula each day, for the women would not sleep there till the house and courtyard could be securely locked. The sergeant seemed to have thrown off the shell of bitterness he had worn since Isobel's death, though Hen suspected it would take years for the shadows to leave him entirely, if they ever did.

The sergeant had grown physically stronger, too. He even smiled, at the swallows already building a nest above Hen's back door, and at Mrs Cook's pungent comments about the need to get Millie to scrub the back steps to clean away their droppings. All the convicts assigned to her had regained their health, even showing enthusiasm now it was obvious that their work would make their own lives more comfortable.

Hen knew their names and some of their histories: Dan the Dip, who'd been a pickpocket, but could put up ten yards of picket fence in a day, though he said it had left his hands too calloused now to dab even a greenhorn. Samuel Picket had been an orphan, one of the few to survive the workhouse, taken by the Runners before he could learn the trade of housebreaking '... all proper like, Miss Hen. You should'a seen Slim Billy shin up a drainpipe.'

Samuel liked the sun on his face as he hoed between the rows of vegetables. He had seen little sun in East London, and none in jail or on the hulks or while coming here. He had tamed the red and green birds to sit on his hands or the plates of breadcrumbs he held out for them each day. Hen liked him, even though she could sense him evaluating how much he'd get for her copper bedpan or silver spoons every time he peered in at her windows.

She didn't like Small Luke much (over six feet tall and a bully with it) nor Matthew Obermann, who stank of rum although she had never caught him at it. Strong spirits were still forbidden on her property. Matthew Obermann smelled of sweat and grime and faeces too, and boasted he'd had only two washes in his entire life, the anti-lice dip on the ship that brought him to the colony, and the one Hen had insisted on when the men arrived on her beach.

No one had asked for her convicts back, though her home and farm were now established, and she did not have it in her to send any of them to breaking stone for the governor's new cobbled roads. Let them clear more land and grow vegetables here, milk her goat and eventually her precious cows in calf, keep the wild dogs and hawks from eating lambs or pens of chickens, plant more fruit trees, and build brush walls to keep out the wallabies — though most who ventured onto her land were likely to end up in a stewpot, the skin tanned for Young Lon to sell.

But Hen no longer made the mistake of trusting them. Nor did she assume that her seclusion from the colony kept her property safe. The courtyard gates and the doors to the house were locked at five each evening, unless she had guests. She kept her pistols in her reticule, and with her at all times, as well as one beneath her pillow, and muskets hidden behind various items of furniture. She had shown Mrs Cook and Sergeant Drivers where these were kept.

Mrs Cook, it seemed, was already familiar with both loading and firing a musket, though she did not vouchsafe what part of her early life had led to her acquiring these skills.

How far should she trust Mrs Cook? Hen suspected there'd been secrets in the woman's life even before her employment in that London house 'of extremely good repute'. But Mrs Cook was capable and intelligent and a survivor, and Hen's survival and comfort would undoubtedly also make her life more pleasant. Hen did have confidence in Mrs Cook's self-interest.

Hen had told the older woman about the thefts, wanting to gauge her reaction. Mrs Cook had shaken her head. 'Selling their rations ain't stealing, Mrs B. That's perks. But selling good meat and pies I made with my own two hands, or Millie's? Don't you let them get away with that. And don't you worry. I won't let them get away with it neither.'

Which left the question open: what did Mrs Cook expect her own perks to be? Candle ends to sell, perhaps, or a pie or two, and undoubtedly possession of any linen Hen deemed worn out, or cracked china someone else would pay a penny for. Hen had already accepted those transactions in her household back in Chelsea. But had Mrs Cook transferred her services to Hen to have more chances to fleece her employer away from the eagle eyes of two Mrs McDougals?

Hen had also mentioned the thefts to Laura Salisbury and Gwendolyn, and received only a sigh and a not quite hidden smile at her naivety from each of them. She realised she was in the possibly unique position of coming to the colony with no real understanding that its prime purpose was to be a prison, even if one carefully positioned to also be a provisioning port for the growing Pacific trade and years of war with the now defeated French empire.

The colony did have free settlers, others free only once their sentences had been served, and ex-soldiers who had been posted here and stayed to farm, like Mr Macarthur. There were the children of government officials, like Mr Wentworth's offspring from his various liaisons, ship's carpenters like Mr Moore or supercargoes like William who had seen opportunity and let their ships sail away without them.

But though she had heard of others who had come deliberately, not by accident, she had not met any. Just herself, and Max ...

Every time she used the name that was not his, nor rightly hers, she remembered him. Every market day she glanced at faces, hoping she might glimpse him while hunting through the stalls with Mrs McDougal, who loved to disparage the growth of others' rhubarb compared to her William's even more than finding a set of kitchen knives, genuine Sheffield ware, or eels from Parramatta (William loved eel pie, and luckily their new cook could made an excellent one, so Hen was forgiven the theft of Mrs Cook).

But Max was at Gilbert's Creek, undoubtedly each day growing deeper into his new family, just as every day Hen changed from the fifteen-year-old girl men had called the Angel of Waterloo.

Sergeant Drivers had been right. There, in the bloodiest battle of history, she had still been innocent; she had remained innocent until he held a knife to her throat and showed her that mending skin and bone was not enough to mend a life.

Her parents were dead. Her husband was not her husband, nor could she marry while he was alive, or at least until the tangle that bound them was laboriously unwound. Her dreams of a life with him had vanished, as had her plans for a small hospital of her own.

A woman of true sensibility should be sobbing again every night.

And yet she walked out of the McDougals' home to move to the Peninsula with a feeling that her life was beginning its true path.

Gwendolyn embraced her at the door. 'You'll always be welcome in any home we have.'

'A true friend.' Mrs McDougal pressed a gift into her hand. Hen blinked back tears. It was *The Complete Works of Robert Burns*, the ploughman poet of Scotland. Hen had seen the volume many times and had seen its inscription, too — *To my dear wife from her loving husband, Angus*.

'I will only be across the harbour,' said Hen, wiping away a stray tear.

'I dinna like to think of you on your ownsome,' said Mrs McDougal, who had been prepared to cross the world on her ownsome to care for her son.

Hen managed a smile. 'I won't be.'

Mrs Cook had been rowed over at dawn, with Millie and Sal. Mrs Cook's role now was again 'Cook Housekeeper'. Sergeant Drivers waited for Hen in the sailboat, one of a pair that would ferry her or her friends and household back and forth across the water.

And yet Hen knew — as did Mrs McDougal — that this venture was more revolutionary than any of her other friends realised. Many women ran a household without a man at its head while they waited for father or husband or brother to come home from war or sea, or where the master had died, but his spirit would linger.

Let Laura and Gwendolyn think that Hen built this home like a nest, waiting for the next ship, or the new governor's staff to bring her a man to marry and to command her acres properly. If her marriage could not be annulled — which could not even be begun until she had worked out how to tell Max his marriage was not legal — Hen could not smile at an unattached man, nor dance with one more than once in an evening. She would grow old with no family but ample friendship.

Yet on the first afternoon, sitting on her verandah, on a chair that only wobbled slightly (the colony's best joiners were employed on government work, or on the vast estates like the Macarthurs') she had no regrets, including taking 'Auntie Love' away from easy summoning. She minded her father's motto: do not weep for what you cannot help, but keep your strength for what you can.

She could smell the sea salt mixed with the apple cakes Mrs Cook was baking, the roast chicken for her dinner, the hot tang of ancient rocks. Behind her, men worked to make her land productive. On either side she had sun-gilded trees on quiet peninsulas, where the only guns shot would be to bring down dinner.

She had her own life to make now. And here, where there was space and where rules could bend and twist, she would construct it.

Chapter 23

Rumbledethumps — a most Delicious & Economical
Scottish Dish, contributed by a Dear Friend

To two cups potato, mashed, add two cups cooked fine
chopped cabbage, and two chopped onions, sauteed in
butter. Place in an oven dish & strew with grated sharp
Cheese. Bake till hot in any Temperature of Oven. If fried
in a Skillet, strew Cheese after each Cake is cooked, or place
Cheese in the Middle as the Cake is formed. Chives may be
added with good Effect, or wild Garlic, watercress, or young
Nettles, well boiled.

From the Notebooks of Henrietta Bartley

5 MARCH 1821

Dear Madame Caroline,
Translated from Flemish
I hope this finds You as well as it leaves Me, and that the Ulcer on
your leg has healed with the Spanish Honey Poultice. I have found
some of the darker Honeys here to be most efficacious on Ulcers or
Abrasions, but the Climate of your Country is too Mild, I think,
for the Plants the Bees need to make a Honey for Application and
not just for Toast.

Yesterday His Excellency the Governor's Wife came here
to dine again. We keep early Hours in the Colony, and Four

O'Clock is still an acceptable time for dinner. I like Mrs Macquarie very much. She was a Campbell before her Marriage, but even Mrs McDougal admits that She is most agreeable and able, even if She also warned me to, 'Ne'er trust a Campbell', as the Clan betrayed their guests before the Battle of Culloden, a Scottish Battle more than a hundred years ago, and not forgotten.

I am sorry Mrs Macquarie and His Excellency will leave the Colony when his Replacement arrives, for they have established a most fine Orphanage and a School for Native Children at Parramatta, and Mrs Macquarie is most interested in my desire for a Hospital for those who are neither Military nor Convict, especially the Children born here in freedom, but who live with such Neglect and in dire Poverty.

My friend Mrs McDougal has begun a School for the Unfortunates, with Porridge and stewed Prunes each morning, too, for all who ask for it, but though People tell of Years of great Food Shortage in the colony twenty Years ago and more, this Land is so Productive, and the Convict Rations so accessible, that there is none of the Starvation you see in every other City I have known.

The colony Children may be Ragged, with crumbling Teeth, and beg in the Street for Farthings to buy Rum, to which they are as addicted as the Adults, but if they have the Strength to beg also at the back doors of those well off, they are not hungry, for every well-founded Household has its own Vegetable Gardens and Orchards, and as for Goats, so many roam the Streets that anyone who can catch a nanny may have Milk.

Our lives have fallen into a most pleasant Pattern here. Each Morning I meet with Mrs Cook and Sergeant Drivers, to give the Orders for the Meals and the day's work for the Men, though both are so efficient the time is more truly spent with them telling me what should be done. I tend my Herb Garden and Distillery, or am sailed across the Harbour to give medical help to those Cases recommended by my Friends for my Assistance, or to meet with friends and of course to attend Church on Sunday, followed by Sunday dinner with the McDougals in their fine new house.

I entertain here, too, and our Dinner yesterday was almost all from
my own Estate, though only one course, as we were all Women.
My Friend Mrs Colonel Salisbury sailed over in the same boat that
carried Mrs Macquarie, as did Mrs McDougal. We had two wild
Ducks roasted, stuffed with Abricots that I had purchased dried
& soaked; a dish of the first of the season's Peas; Potatoes in your
Flemish manner, fried till crisp, which Mrs Macquarie had not
seen before and greatly liked; & a fish baked upon a bed of sliced
lemons, served with a sorrel sauce. Mrs Cook also made a raspberry
flummery & a Rhubarb Tart, and another with a Custard
sweetened with Pumpkin, which is here eaten as a Vegetable, as
well as grown for Fodder. The Pumpkin grown here are most hard
Skinned but extremely Good for cooking. We also ate a lemon
Syllabub, a baked fresh Cheese, a Honey Bread and small hot
Rolls with sweet Butter. It all looked very fine, and we enjoyed
much Laughter at the doings of some of the Convicts. I wish You
could have been with us.

I enclose a small Gift that I hope You will make use of, as well
as a Receipt for a Tisane to help the Swelling. I would make it for
you, but it might turn sour on the long Voyage in the damp.

I remain, yours most truly,
Henrietta Bartley

Hen heard the screams on a Sunday afternoon as Sergeant
Drivers pulled the skiff up onto the sand of the cove and gave
her his hand to step out, for she had worn her new blue muslin to
church, with blue-dyed kid slippers that she did not want to get
wet. Mrs Cook, Millie and Sal had new dresses too, and were
presumably still parading them over on the main shore, for her
staff were given the entire Sabbath day for their own.

Hen gazed at the house above her. 'That is a woman's cry!'

'Aye,' said Sergeant Drivers. But he did not immediately leave
her to rescue whoever was in so much trouble.

'There should be no woman here!' Hen began to run, lifting
her skirts. The scream came again.

'Miss Hen! Stop a moment!'

She whirled round. 'Why?'

The sergeant hesitated. 'The men expected you to stay and dine at the McDougals' this afternoon, as you did last week.'

'What has that to do with anything?' Gwendolyn was in the most nauseous stage of pregnancy and feeling the heat too, so Hen had refused the polite invitation.

'The men will have a woman here with you away,' the sergeant said flatly. Which he had obviously decided was something a nice woman did not need to know. 'They might be drunk by now. Miss Hen, I'm not sure I could protect you against a mob of them,' he added honestly. 'Best you stay here, and let me see what's happening.'

'That woman is in pain, or terror!' Hen scrambled up the path. The sergeant pounded after her, his wooden leg clumping on the summer-hard soil, so close she almost expected him to grab her arm, to try to send her back down to the boat. Instead he kept pace behind her.

She checked the lock on the courtyard gate. Still locked, so the screams had not come from there.

'Miss Hen, wait a moment, will you? I need to get my musket!' Sergeant Drivers pulled out his key, and vanished into the courtyard.

Another scream. Hen could not wait. She lifted her skirts for greater speed as she ran down to the barracks. The screaming had stopped, but that seemed the most likely source ...

She flung the door open. The barracks were empty, apart from Matthew Obermann, hurriedly hiding what was almost certainly a brown jug of rum.

She'd checked the storeroom and dairy doors were locked before she had left for church. That left the two cottages. Not the sergeant's, for he had been with her. She ran to the Lons', turned the handle and pushed. The door refused to open, evidently barred. Hen pounded on it. 'Let me in!'

No answer.

'I order you! Open this door.' She pulled a pistol from her reticule and cocked it.

'Miss Hen! Wait!' The sergeant limped towards her, musket in hand.

She ignored him, and fired at where the bar would meet the wall. The wood splintered. A man yelled inside.

She pushed again. The door still wouldn't open. She flung her body at it. The remnants of the bar shattered, so she stumbled into the room, still holding the smoking pistol.

Big Lon stared at her. So did Small Luke, his trousers around his ankles. The native girl tied to the bed stared at her too.

She was young, fifteen perhaps, and naked, though the string still around her waist with a small basket attached indicated that this might be her choice. The ropes that bound her upper body, however, had been tied cruelly tight. Her legs had been left free.

The men stared at Hen. The girl took the opportunity to kick Small Luke between the legs. He howled, clutching himself, as the girl kicked him again, in the kidneys this time. Small Luke collapsed gasping on the floor, swearing at the girl, at Hen.

Hen found herself shaking, with anger, not fear. 'Untie her,' she said to Sergeant Drivers.

He obeyed wordlessly, meeting neither her eyes nor those of Big Lon or Luke. The girl stayed panting on the bed, even with the ropes removed.

'Pack,' Hen ordered Big Lon. 'And you too,' to Small Luke. 'You will be off my property within the hour and you will not return.'

'You can't do that!' Big Lon advanced. 'An' no point waving that pistol either, because we both know it's only got one shot.' He gave the sergeant a smug grin. 'Nor could you have got that musket loaded, soldier boy, not since we heard her ladyship yelling down at the cove.'

'I have another pistol,' said Hen calmly. 'And as you can see, I always keep them loaded.'

Big Lon glanced uncertainly at her dangling reticule, which bulged sufficiently with a bottle of laudanum, scissors and other items needed in an emergency to look as if it might contain another pistol, though in fact its companions were under her pillow in her bedroom, one pistol being quite sufficient to take to church. Sergeant Drivers moved closer to Hen, making it obvious that he would protect her.

Big Lon glared at him. 'Still two to one,' he challenged. 'Want to try it, cully?'

'Three to two,' said Hen as the girl swung a wooden stool at the back of Big Lon's head. He fell, dazed. Luke still clutched his privates.

Hen held her hand out to the girl, now standing by the bed. The girl paused, then took it.

'Go load the musket and get a second one. Give them half an hour to recover and gather their possessions, then take them back to the convict barracks,' Hen ordered the sergeant, holding the girl's hand in hers: a strong hand, despite her slender body, and not trembling, even after her ordeal.

Hen stared at her two ex-employees, Lon still shaking his head on the floor, Luke curled up against a wall in pain. 'If they resist, inform the guards they attacked me and a female guest.'

'That's a hanging offence, Miss Hen,' said Sergeant Drivers quietly. 'Do you want them on the gallows?' Lon gave a harsh cry that might be fear, or anger.

Hen ignored him. 'I do not wanted them hanged, nor given the lash. I would prefer they simply accompanied you to the barracks. If they go quietly, merely say I have no more use for them.'

The sergeant hesitated. 'I don't want to leave you alone with them.'

Hen cast her gaze around the cottage and grabbed an axe by the doorway. She handed it to the girl, who seemed to know how to hold it, then took the knife from the hearth. 'Go,' she ordered.

Neither Lon nor Luke attempted to rise. Nor did they look at her. They seemed to have accepted their return to the barracks was inevitable. Their only face saver now was to ignore her.

But she kept the knife when the sergeant returned with the muskets, slipping out the door as he aimed the first musket at Lon and Luke. The girl took her hand from Hen's as they left the cottage. She began to run towards the trees, dropping the axe by the cornfield. Hen ran after her and lightly touched her arm. The girl stopped as Hen pointed to the house.

'Do you speak English?'

The girl looked at the ground. Her hair was extraordinarily dark, and curled about her face; her skin was quite perfect.

'Please come with me,' said Hen quietly, hoping her tone would be understood, even if her words weren't. 'I want to see if you are hurt.' She could already see a bruise forming around one eye and now that she was closer she could see blood matting the hair on the back of the girl's head. There could be far worse damage, unseen.

'I will take you home, I promise,' Hen said softly. 'But we need to keep you safe till the men in there have gone.'

She had no idea how much the girl understood. But this time, as Hen walked towards the house, picking up the axe, then beckoning, the girl followed her. Hen unlocked the gate, then shut it after them, locking it again. Sergeant Drivers and Mrs Cook were the only others who had keys.

The small kitchen was hot, the fire banked down for Mrs Cook's return. The girl sat on a chair, which answered one question. She had used furniture before.

Hen moved slowly, taking a glass, filling it from the unglazed jar of lemon barley water that Mrs Cook made fresh each morning, leaving it on the window ledge for the evaporation from the pottery to keep it cool.

The girl took the glass and examined its transparency, before sipping cautiously, then taking a longer drink.

Hen wet a cloth, then gestured to her own hair, then to the girl. 'May I?'

The girl looked at the floor. Hen approached, and cautiously touched the girl's head near the wound. The girl flinched, but did not move away.

A small cut only, Hen saw with relief as she sponged the blood away — even small head wounds bled copiously. And the girl did not seem dazed. On the contrary — she held herself in readiness to run.

Voices outside — Luke yelling obscenities about Hen, her ancestors, and Sergeant Drivers's possible antics with cows and sheep. Hen waited till the voices faded and the men had presumably gone down to the cove for the sergeant to row them back.

Which left at least six men still unaccounted for, one of whom was probably too drunk to even feel curious. Six men who must have heard the screams and the shot, and not even come to investigate. They had not helped this girl or Hen. On the other hand, they hadn't helped Big Lon and Luke.

The bread in the bin was yesterday's, but good. Hen cut two doorstop slices, buttered them, spread them thickly with honey and handed one to the girl, then took a bite of the other.

The girl began to eat, her face still cast downwards, though her eyes darted up now and then to Hen.

Hen sat and pressed her hand to her chest. 'My name is Auntie Love.' Hen was too familiar, and Mrs Bartley still felt dishonest, the name she hid behind.

The girl didn't speak. Hen cut them both another slice, then sat on the chair next to the girl again.

'Do you understand me?'

'Yes.' The word was almost a whisper.

'Where do you live?' Her lack of clothes suggested the girl was a wild native, and had been caught near the Peninsula, but she might also have been brought over from the colony or even delivered by a pimp.

Hen realised in sudden horror that she had no idea of what might have happened there in her other absences. Worse — what had Sergeant Drivers known, or guessed, but never told her? Men were supposed to need women, which was why even the Iron Duke had allowed doxies in camp. But the camp women Hen had met when they came to her mother for medical help had been willing and well paid. Hen realised she had come to trust the sergeant; to rely on his judgement, too. Had she been gullible again?

'Men in black,' the girl muttered.

'What men in black?' The convicts' clothes were dun coloured.

'Men in black take to Native Institution. Run away.'

Hen stared at her. The girl evidently referred to the men the governor had appointed to round up native children, to teach them civilised farming and housewifery. Mrs Macquarie had spoken of the Native Institution in glowing terms. Twenty students were presently enrolled, and two had already married natives who farmed their land, showing that the Indians could be civilised and were intelligent enough to learn.

This girl seemed both bright and capable. It had taken at least two men to tie her down. Had more of the workmen been part of this before she arrived? Hen thrust that thought away for later.

'Did the men hurt you?' Hen gestured to the top of the girl's legs.

The girl looked at the floor again. 'My name is Jessica. I am fourteen years old. Today is Monday.' The words were clearly recited, with perfect mimicry of an educated English accent.

'Jessica?' That was not the name the girl's family would call her, but was the name to use with a colonist, like herself. 'Would you like more bread, Jessica?' Hen kept the words clear and distinct.

'Yes, please. I would like more bread.'

How many phrases had the girl memorised? But she clearly knew their meaning, if not the days of the week. Hen prepared yet another slice of bread and honey. The walls breathed the heat of both sun and kitchen fire.

Should she take the girl out to the verandah, so they could check that Sergeant Drivers was rowing the men back to the colony?

No. It was more important to get Jessica somewhere safe. Hen did not know where Young Lon was. He lived in the cottage with his father. Perhaps he had left after his part in the rape had finished. Others of her men might have, as well. The girl must leave, and quickly, in case any other of her men realised she might identify them as abusers, and try to track her down.

Which presumably was exactly what the girl had been doing, heading back into the trees, till Hen led her here. Hen stood, opened the door, then said slowly, 'I am coming with you.'

Past the cabbages, wilting despite the previous day's watering, through the orchard, each young tree guarded by a circle of manure, according to William's advice, through the last gate, but even there she and Jessica could be seen from the men's quarters, for the trees had been felled, their branches stripped for kindling, piled to dry, the logs waiting for the saw or adze. She would need to appoint another foreman now ...

At last they were among the trees, the camel humps of rocks, a small snake, dark as a shadow, pretended it was a fallen branch. The girl strode forwards now, no longer keeping close to Hen. Hen had to lift her skirts to keep up. These were the wrong shoes for walking. The soft blue leather was already torn. When would Sergeant Drivers be back?

She glanced behind, saw a last glimpse of the sea as the girl hurried inland. Hen limped behind her. The trees grew thicker now, away from the salt air and wind. The soil looked better, too. Was this still her property? She had only walked the boundaries once, to check the surveyor's axe marks on the trees.

Downhill now. Hen realised she should have looked behind more often, so she would recognise the way back. What if she were lost there? If darkness fell she must keep still and wait for the sergeant to find her. But why should he imagine she would head into the trees, instead of hailing a passing boat to take her to safety at the McDougals'?

A pile of boulders, both flat and rounded, looking like a giant's turds. A thin trickle of water, which the girl followed, and they were there.

At first glance there was almost nothing: a spectre of fire, heat not smoke shimmering above it; the scent of grilled fish; sheets of bark propped up against each other; thin-limbed women, most as naked as the girl, dark as the snake. Down the hill children laughed on a beach even smaller than her own.

Nothing. And then she looked again, with the eyes of a woman who had known many camps, and knew what worked and what did not.

The scrap of fire was enough. More would waste wood, and make the camp hotter and more obvious. The sheets of bark were enough, too, and better than a tent, their bark thicker than canvas, and angled to catch the eastern breeze, but miss the wind that blew up from the south.

No armchairs, sofas or dining tables, but once you were used to it the ground was more comfortable than sitting politely upright, your back never touching the chair, your hands in your lap or resting well mannered on the table. The children she could glimpse down on the beach were well fed and healthy, far more bonny than those of the colony, who had drunk rum with their mother's milk and still craved it, leaving their bodies wizened compared to these. And these children laughed. How long had it been since Hen had seen a street child laugh? Had she ever seen it?

The women wore no clothes except for a string around their waists, like Jessica's, with woven bags suspended from them and more string dangling in front, like a short apron. But suddenly Hen felt it was her dress that was out of place, the muslin stuck to her sweaty skin. The women wore no shoes, but her slippers were almost rags after the walk on unpaved ground. She wished she did not need them. Nor did the women wear bonnets. Hen took hers off automatically, to let her hot scalp feel the breeze.

A woman stood. Her hair was streaked with grey. Hen had been wrong. This woman wore a dress, though the front buttons were undone. She held her arms out to the girl. Jessica ran straight to them like an arrow, was clasped, hugged, gently checked while she and the older woman talked in a language too fast and strange for Hen to even make out where each word ended or began.

The girl began to cry. The woman hugged her again, staring at Hen. 'Who are you?' she demanded.

Chapter 24

A Lemon Barley Water

Lemons, four, sliced thin
Barley, one cup
Water, four pints
Sugar, one cup

Soak the Barley overnight then boil all for the Time it takes to say a Prayer. Strain and drink within two Days. The Barley may be saved for Soup.

From the Notebooks of Henrietta Bartley

'I am Auntie Love.' For some reason it still seemed right to give the name she had acquired here, not the one she'd brought from England.

'God is love. Love is good. Reverend Johnson taught me that. He was a good man and loved. His wife was good and loved. My name is Birrung.' A pause between each statement.

'Reverend Johnson was the clergyman before Reverend Marsden?'

'Reverend Johnson came on the first big ships.' The words seemed dragged from the woman's memory. 'The big ships brought sickness. We died, or fled. I was sick. Mrs Johnson saved me, then I saved her when she gave birth. She called her baby Milbah. I am Birrung. Me.'

'You lived with the Johnsons? They taught you English?'

No reply. Hen's eyes moved to another woman she had not noticed before, a little younger than Birrung, wearing what had been a skirt. She had placed dried fungi on the coals of the fire. The second woman led Jessica to it. Jessica leaned over, breathing in the smoke, then seemed to open her whole body to it, although she scarcely moved. The woman crouched too, tugging Jessica's hands till she sat, closer to the smoke.

Hen turned back to Birrung. 'Jessica?' She could smell the smoke now herself, slightly sweet, almost like incense. She breathed it in deeply, felt herself relax. Suddenly she could hear birds she had not noticed before, the scuttle of a lizard in the bark.

Birrung looked at Hen expressionlessly. 'The men in black shot our men. They took two girls. We broke the fence one night. Jessica ran with us but Araboo had died.'

Hen tried to match the story with Mrs Macquarie's conversation. The men who had been shot must have been rebel natives. Then the girls were rescued to be educated at the orphanage. The women and children had moved here to …

No, the two stories did not match. Hen had met many cultures in her first fifteen years; she had known more happiness around her in a camp of tents than in her father's borrowed Chelsea mansion; she had owned almost as few possessions as these women. Or not nearly as many …

Her eyes told her what her mind was slower to accept. String bags dangling from the trees, filled with roots that were not potatoes, grain that was not wheat, purple berries that were not plums, nor anything she had ever seen. A grindstone, almost identical to the ones she had known in Portugal. A hearth stone next to the fire, just like the one Mama used to make flat bread if there had been no time to unpack the skillet.

The bags hanging from the string about each waist. Bags that bulged like her reticules with tools or medicines, for Hen had caught another whiff of the smoking fungus and felt calmness spread across her like a tide that would not ebb. She who had been born in battle, who had lost her love in battle, who had nightmares where the dead faces of Waterloo loomed. Who had tried to escape battle and come here.

This day would change her forever.

'Who are you?' repeated Birrung.

'I am you,' said Hen.

Chapter 25

A Flat Bread, Most Excellent, Quick & Nutritious

Take grain, one cup, and grind it smooth. It may be wheat, rye, barley, the seeds of native grass or portulaca. The Best in the Colony for this comes from the Native Grass that cuts your Fingers. The Natives shake it loose with Sticks. Add Water or Oil as needed and press flat, but the 'sharp grass' will need no Oil nor Water. Bake on a hot Hearth Stone quickly on both Sides.

From the Notebooks of Henrietta Bartley

It was the smoke. It was memory — of who she had been before those years in Chelsea chained her to politeness and the pretence that she could be a lady. Hen was not a lady. She was a camp brat, skilled in every aspect of survival, and she had met no equals until now.

The black skin did not matter. The nudity did not shock her, because she had always known the bodies under clothes, bodies that needed healing or laying out.

She watched Jessica fetch a basket, grind and knead and bake upon the rock, use her fingers to spread something from a bark container and hand her ...

... bread and honey.

Suddenly all of them were laughing, even her. The bread was almost black and oily, the honey a faint green, and both were some of the best she had ever eaten.

And, yes, the smoke helped, but these women were made to laugh, despite the tragedy they'd seen, just as Mama laughed because you had to laugh to make life good.

Boys and girls, unclothed, their hair tangled, some adorned with feathers, scrambled up the slope, bringing string bags of mussels to bake by the fire with leaves tossed on that smelled of spice and lemon, while Hen spread out the contents of her reticule and explained each item.

'Scissors.'

A woman grinned and held out a dark red stone with one edge sharper than her scissors and another round for grinding. Even Hen's reticule did not carry a grindstone.

Hen put out her needle, thread, oil of wintergreen ...

Birrung laid out her own needle, made of a thin hard bone, and strong string. Hen suspected Birrung's tools, like hers, could be used to mend bodies as well as sew together the possum furs that the oldest woman draped around her drooping breasts as the wind from the south began to blow.

Hen looked for the sun, dazed, but it had vanished behind the mountains. The wind seemed to thicken the air as it became dark.

'I ... I must go home.' Sergeant Drivers would be worried about her. Mrs Cook probably as well by now. Hen found she was not sure in what direction to walk. Had those stones been to her right or left?

Jessica took her hand.

'No!' said Hen. The girl should not risk going near the farm again.

Jessica took no notice. Nor would Hen have done, seven years earlier. The oldest woman — they had not progressed to names: they had shared a lot, but not names yet, except for Birrung, Jessica and Auntie Love — handed Hen a piece of the fungus. It was hard, a creamy yellow striped with brown.

'Burn it tonight and tomorrow,' ordered Birrung.

'Yes,' said Hen. This medicine was needed for shock, because Hen's world had just changed more deeply even than when she had learned Max was alive. Max had always been a might be, or might have been. This was now and real, and Hen would need the calmness of the smoke to deal with a tomorrow that held a bed and linen in a whitewashed room, a ceiling that was unchanging and so limited, unlike the sky, her view restricted to a window — and she herself had built her prison.

She felt helpless, for she had nothing to give the women in return. They did not need the scissors, for they had politely placed them back inside her reticule, and all eyes had been averted from her pistol. The women knew too well exactly what it was. Hen would not bring a pistol here again.

She was not these women, as she had first thought, though she had found more in common with them than with any person she had met. But she was still going home to the house that had been built where they must have gathered shellfish, drunk the water from the pool.

'May I come again?' She waited, breathless, for their decision.

'We are here,' said Birrung, shrugging, smiling, laughing. Because of course Hen could come again and she would bring ... Hen was not sure yet what to bring to women who had everything except their men, except wherever they had fled from, and Hen could not recover those for them.

Suddenly she laughed too. She pulled her dress over her head, then shimmied out of her petticoat. For a moment she wished she didn't have to put the dress back on. It smelled of sweat and gunpowder. But arriving back at the house naked except for a bonnet and ragged slippers would invite anything from assault to confinement in whatever ward Surgeon Bowman used to confine the mad.

She slid the dress back on and handed the petticoat to Birrung, who handed it to Jessica, who put it on and laughed, then tore off the dusty frill at the hem and draped it from a branch to be used as ... something, not a frill.

And then Jessica walked, and Hen followed her, leaving reality behind.

It was hard to accept that the kitchen was not real. It was in fact extremely real and so was Mrs Cook, still in her best Sunday grey, tearing into her as if she were five years old. Sal and Millie had been commanded to their rooms. 'Heading off into the bush like that, all by yourself. I have a mind to spank you, but men paid five shillings just for that and you don't deserve I do you for free. What were you thinking, girl?'

Hen had not known that Mrs Cook even liked her, until now. Or that Sergeant Drivers loved her — not till she saw the expression on his face as she walked safely through the gate after he had returned to find her gone. Hen realised with a sudden shock that in the past few months of quiet routine here on the Peninsula she had grown to love them too. The three of them had become a strange kind of family, forging not just lives together, but affection.

'Well?' demanded Mrs Cook. 'You could have been taken by a whaling ship for all we knew, or bitten by a snake and we'd never even have known where to look for you! The two of us 'ave been waitin' here ...'

Hen glanced at the sergeant. But he simply sat at the table and let Mrs Cook finish her invective. Hen decided it was best to do the same.

Jessica had left her as soon as Hen could see the fallen trees that marked the beginning of her paddocks. The petticoat was pale yellow, but it disappeared into the shadows just like the girl.

Hen should have asked Jessica how the men had caught her. She should have asked how many had attacked her. There were so many questions that needed answers, including the extremely good ones Mrs Cook was asking her now.

'So what have you been doing, so long away, and why the hell, my girl, did you go away into the bush at all?'

'Sergeant Drivers told you a native girl was taken prisoner? I took her home.'

'Home? Where is a native's home here?'

The answer, possibly, was anywhere, though Hen suspected that the true answer was 'the best place for a campsite' with many criteria that must be met. Instead she stayed silent.

'They might have killed you,' said Sergeant Drivers shortly, carefully not meeting her eyes. 'You've seen what those spears can do.'

She had. She had also seen no spears and no men. But she had only seen the smallest crumb of the women's lives. Yet she had also seen no babies — the youngest child was perhaps three years old. Had their men been killed? Or had the women taken the children further from the settlement for their safety, while the men had stayed behind?

'They didn't hurt me,' she said wearily. Suddenly she needed sleep, but here and now ... which was getting realer every moment ... she had other duties too. 'You took Lon and Luke to the barracks?'

'Yes. They went like lambs. I told them I'd give evidence against them if I heard they'd been bad-mouthing you or ever came near you again.'

'Thank you,' said Hen. She met his eyes, saw nothing in them except truth. 'Have you seen Young Lon?'

'Met him at the dock. He was in a shanty down at The Rocks. There's a girl he likes there. I took him to the barracks to see his father then rowed him back here.'

'Young Lon didn't know what his father was doing?'

'No.' The sergeant paused then added, 'He saw nothing wrong in it, just thought the old man was foolish, to risk a soft life for an hour with a native girl. I told him his pa can't come back here. Young Lon accepted it. Argued, but he accepted it. He knows as much about farming as his father, I reckon.'

A problem solved. But there was a question she had to ask. 'Did you know about this, Sergeant?'

Sergeant Drivers hesitated before he answered, but she heard truth in his words. 'I knew the men had women out here on Sundays now and then: willing ones. I knew some of the men were trying to get native women, too. They'd beckon them to come ashore in their canoes, pretending to trade fish for whatever they held up in exchange. There'd been ... trouble ... when we first came out here. I put a stop to it and didn't think I need bother you with what had happened after that. They must have waited till I was away today.'

Which possibly explained the spear injury she had treated months back. Retribution, which probably had nothing to do with the group of women she had met today.

'Is the girl badly hurt?' the sergeant asked quietly.

'They hadn't had time to hurt her.'

'Thank God for that.' His prayer seemed sincere.

'Pity you didn't keep 'em here till I got back,' said Mrs Cook with low-voiced savagery. 'I'd 'ave made sure that Big Lon never forced a woman again. Nor managed with a willin' one, neither. How did they get hold of her?'

'Big Lon said he found the girl stealing corn,' said Sergeant Drivers. 'She might have come in one of the fishing canoes.'

Relief washed through Hen like the tide. The men had no idea there was a camp of women close. She also knew now what gift she could take her new acquaintances.

She bit her lip. Should she trust the sergeant with the knowledge that there was a camp of women nearby? But if he didn't know, he couldn't help protect them. She trusted him with her life now, but Jessica's?

She met his eyes, and knew the answer.

'She didn't come in a fishing boat, but please let the men think she did. I don't want any of them to guess there are women near here. But from tomorrow no man is to go beyond the sheep paddocks.'

'Young Lon will want to check his traps. There's fresh meat out there and furs.'

'Tell Young Lon that he may set his traps and hunt for two hundred yards past the paddocks, no more. If he goes beyond that he will be returned to the barracks. There are enough animals after our corn and greens to give us all the meat we need.'

The sergeant nodded. 'I'll tell him that. He'll obey, too, seein' what happened to his pa.'

'If we need more fresh meat and I cannot purchase it, then you may go into the woods to hunt.' The animals had stopped coming to the waterhole now that so many people used it, though wallabies and possums still made nightly raids on the fruits and vegetables.

The sergeant looked embarrassed. 'Miss Hen, a wooden leg ain't good for hunting.'

'Then I will do the hunting, and call you if I need anything carried back.'

He raised an eyebrow. 'How long has it been since you hunted anything? Ten years?'

'Not quite three. An acquaintance of my father's asked us for a week's shoot. Though I disgraced myself.'

Mrs Cook grinned. 'How?'

'I shot a bird on the ground, before the beaters had a chance to make them fly. Well, how was I to know? I'd only seen animals shot for food before.' Nor had she realised that a woman's role was to watch and admire, not to outshoot most of the men in the party. She'd had to make do with conversation with the governess after dinner, nor had she and her father been invited again.

Mrs Cook gave a shout of laughter. 'I'd like to 'ave seen it. That's the gentry for you, sending birds up to be shot, instead o' quietly wringing their necks. They do get up to some tricks to fill in their days. I knew one cove used to dress up like Princess Caroline ...' She broke off. 'Well, enough o' that. I'll enjoy the looks on the men's faces when you bring them back one o' them hoppers, or a brace of duck. Here, get this into you.'

Mrs Cook ladled out a bowl of stew from the pot on the hob, and placed it in front of Hen — a bowl that smelled extremely good: fish and oysters in a white wine sauce, with the garlic Hen had grown fond of in the Peninsula. 'Eat it up, every bit of it. And it's more than you deserve.'

'I'm sorry I worried you.'

'Yes. Well.' Mrs Cook seemed to be remembering that Hen was only ten or so years younger than her and the sergeant, and her employer as well. But formality of that relationship had gone forever, if it had ever been properly there at all. Love deserved love, and who else did Mrs Cook and the sergeant have to love? Who else did Hen have, now?

'I met the girl's people,' said Hen, spooning up more soup. 'I'm going to visit them again. This soup is wonderful, Mrs Cook.'

'You ain't going nowhere without the sergeant.'

'I may not have worked in an ... an establishment,' said Hen firmly, 'but I can take care of myself. Jessica's people are all women. Her mother, grandmother, aunts ...' which Hen thought was also probably accurate. 'I think their men may have been killed.'

'Well, thank the Lord for that,' said Mrs Cook, with no trace of sympathy for strangers. 'The last thing we needs is rampagin' natives.'

'Yes. We have our own rampaging brutes. Sergeant, are there any other men I should dismiss? I have been far too sentimental. I don't want any here who might attack a woman, nor any who will steal from the natives.'

He hesitated. 'Probably should get rid of another two then. Maybe three who might do something if they were Sunday drunk. I'll think on it.'

'But Young Lon stays? And Samuel?' She didn't want to lose Lon's skills, and she liked young Samuel.

'I'd keep 'em both.'

'Good.' She tasted an oyster in the stew. 'Aren't either of you eating?'

'I've et,' said Mrs Cook, just as the sergeant replied, 'At the table with you?'

'Why not? I remember when we had a chicken dinner together. You had no objection then.'

'Well, I could eat again,' said Mrs Cook. She ladled out two more bowls of stew.

Hen thought of the fungus in her reticule. She had planned to inhale some of its comforting smoke in the night, but it no longer seemed a good idea. For this was real life too and, despite all she had felt back at the camp, she was longing for her bed with cool sheets, the feather pillow, for Sal to fill her bath with water so she could wash off dust and sweat, and for Mrs Cook to serve her fresh bread in the morning.

The woman who was Auntie Miss Hen Not Henrietta Love Gilbert Bartlett Bartley had experienced many different lives. This afternoon's meeting had merely given her back the girl she had forgotten.

'Crow-sants tomorrow morning,' said Mrs Cook, savouring her stew. 'Just the way you like 'em, duckie.'

Croissants, and they *would* be exactly how Hen liked them, hot and buttery, with peach jam. But she must make sure Mrs Cook did not call her duckie in front of visitors.

On second thoughts, Mrs Cook would be as aware of that as she was.

Auntie Miss Hen Not Henrietta Love Duckie spooned up her stew with great enjoyment.

Chapter 26

Young Maize to be Baked Upon the Fire

Maize in the Colony is most oft boiled in the Cauldron. To bake on the coal soak it unpeeled in Water then insert Knobs of Salt Butter within the Husk. Turn with Tongs on the Fire till the Husk is Black & the Young Maize within Extremely Healthful. Old Maize is Dry & must be Parched and ground for Flour, or fed to your Stock.

From the Notebooks of Henrietta Bartley

APRIL 1821

Dear Mrs Macquarie,
How kind of You and His Excellency the Governor to invite me to Dine on Tuesday. I accept with Pleasure.
Yours most respectfully,
Mrs H Bartley

The pot of boiled corn had been lifted from the fire. Both the metal pot and the corn had been most acceptable as gifts. Gulls skimmed the ocean, fishing. This new camp faced yet another beach, and one protected from the increasing cold of the south winds. Somehow the women had known when Hen headed to their old camp. Jessica had waylaid her, only halfway there, and brought her here.

She had visited the women almost every day in the weeks since Jessica's rescue. Only Mrs Cook and the sergeant knew that she came here. The rest of her staff accepted her daily walk as the kind of constitutional ladies took to provide the exercise others had from work.

Hen held up an oval berry. 'So this is poisonous when it's green, but when it is deep orange I can eat it, and dry it too?'

Birrung looked at her speculatively. 'Only if you don't want to have children,' she said, using gestures to help Hen understand the native tongue that Hen was beginning to speak, though with mispronunciations that caused hilarity.

Hen nodded, hoping she had understood the advice correctly. The plant grew in large amounts on her own property, springing up in the ploughed ground from bird-dropped fruits. She could think of several of her patients in the colony who would be glad of a tisane made from these, though she would need more advice before she could estimate the dose and how frequently it must be taken to be both safe and effective. She would also need to consider whether supplying women with the tisane would bring down the wrath of Surgeon Bowman.

'And this one is for aching joints?' she asked, this time in English, pointing to a collection in the basket of brown specks that had been yellow flowers in spring, interspersed with bark from the same tree.

Birrung answered in the same tongue. 'Yes. You drink, or wash. When drink must be same colour as bark. Stops other pain as well.'

Any pain relief beyond willow bark or the fruit of the poppy was extremely welcome.

'Rub this on the chest for gail galla, cough and sweat disease,' instructed Birrung.

Consumption? Influenza? It was difficult to compare remedies when neither party knew the other's words for the condition or disease. Only experience would teach her enough, seeing how the women actually used the plants, learning from them as she had from her mother. It was all very well to know a plant might ease pain, but what dose would help, and what dose would kill?

The past weeks had been an exchange of skills. Hen had sewn up a small boy's foot, cut on an oyster shell, then she and Birrung had compared remedies to keep the wound from festering. The art of sewing up a wound seemed to be unknown to them — old Booroo tried to tie up the cut foot with a strip of wet leather, string and a poultice made from crushed grubs, till Hen brought out her needle.

This had led to a comparison of remedies to keep a patient still. A most insignificant bush yielded a paste that made the skin entirely numb. Its drawback was that the leaves had to be chewed to make the paste, which left the mouth numb for hours too, and it must be newly made each time, or it might ferment and lose its usefulness. It would be useful if she had only one patient but if she had more wounds to treat the preparation would make her unable to talk or eat for most of the day.

Luckily most other remedies seemed to be made merely by grinding up a leaf, a root, a flower or bark, liberally mixed with spit to draw the remedial properties out. Others, like the fungus, could be burned and the smoke inhaled. The grub paste, too, was easy to prepare, though Hen was not quite sure exactly which one was the medicinal grub she had been shown, as several kinds were eaten, and all looked similar to her eyes.

Hen had already used a tea from a plant that grew in the moister gullies to cure Samuel's ringworm, as well as giving it to Sal to gargle for her sore throat. But that was one of the few remedies she felt confident enough to use.

She had also learned how to catch and cook a fruit bat. The flesh was surprisingly sweet and tender, but Hen doubted Mrs Cook would want to deal with one, nor roast an echidna in the ashes, and certainly not dannugannawa, the wood grub, with its creamy nutty flesh, or balluda, the snake. The snake tasted a little like roasted eel, but there were parts that must be cut out and it needed to be well cooked, and, like many of the medicines, Hen knew she was not yet competent enough to try it unaided, especially as her fields now held sheep for mutton.

But Jessica had shown her how to catch mullet in nets, and yurungi, wild duck, and mirral, pigeon, too, scattering food on the ground and waiting in high branches, feeling like a little girl again, climbing trees barefooted. At a quiet hooted signal the carriers dropped their nets at once, then shinned down the trees to gather in the haul of birds. Jessica seemed to think it amusing that Hen knew none of these indispensable skills, and was even more amused in teaching her.

Twice Hen had brought back wild duck or pigeons for Mrs Cook, who carefully did not ask how a mistress who had merely gone on constitutional with nothing more than her reticule and pelisse could bring home dinner, and with no lead shot in it to remove before cooking, either. The fat native pigeons, grey with a white streak, like a shawl, had been especially delicious.

'Auntie Love! Auntie Love!' Five children, ranging perhaps from two years old to ten, chanted her name as if it were the funniest rhyme in the world. 'Auntie Love!' They tugged at her hands, the chant was becoming a question. 'Come and swim?'

Hen hesitated. She could swim a little — there had been camps where the only way to wash had been in a river, with its welcome coolness too, while the other women took turns to watch to make sure no man approached. Today day was cool for the colony, but now at midday warm by European standards.

She felt eyes upon her and looked around. Birrung looked amused. Jessica laughed. 'Can you swim, Auntie Love?'

Hen nodded, glad she had that skill, at least. She slipped off her bonnet, her sturdy half boots, pulled down her garters, then her stockings. The children circled her, entranced.

This was why the children had asked her to swim, she realised. They remembered her taking off her dress and the petticoat underneath. She lifted up her dress, slipped off her petticoat, then her chemise. The children scampered in delight, possibly at so many layers, or maybe at finding she was even whiter underneath them all, then splashed back through the tiny waves, ducking into the mud to pull up mussels.

Hen shut her eyes. She felt the sun on skin that had never been exposed outdoors before. The breeze almost tickled. The sand breathed sunlight on her feet as she walked towards the rippling harbour. The water prickled on her ankles, knees and thighs. At last she let it take her and began to swim, paddling furiously to stay afloat.

A child dived down and swam below her, making a wave that sucked her in. She struggled for control for a moment, then her feet found the mud, and her face discovered air again. But her hair had come loose and straggled wetly down her back.

The children laughed, and Hen laughed with them. Henrietta Gilbert Bartlett or Bartley had vanished, and her responsibilities with her. This was sunlight and cool water, the taste of salt on her lips, the scent of possum roasting. Jessica waded towards her, grinning. 'I will teach you swimming too, Auntie Love.'

This was happiness.

She arrived home to find the sergeant waiting for her, sitting on a large smooth rock about fifty yards into the trees from her newly cleared fields, his musket and a covered basket on the rock beside him. His hands were at rest, neither whittling nor holding a pipe, as most men might do to occupy their time, but watching dolphins dive near the shore. It must be their feeding time, she realised, to bring them in so close. The sergeant's face showed nothing but peace, and pleasure in the animals' movements.

'Hunting, Sergeant Drivers?'

'Waiting for you, Miss Hen. You have a visitor, Surgeon Wentworth. Mrs Cook thought you might like these.' He handed the basket to her.

Hen opened the lid. A hairbrush, ribbon, a freshly pressed muslin dress, fresh stockings, slippers instead of the half boots she wore now, a small and decorative bonnet. She automatically touched her hair. The short front curls had frizzed around her face. The rest was still damp from swimming.

'I'll wait by the cabbages,' said the sergeant tactfully.

She changed quickly, shoving her stained and wrinkled clothes into the basket, pulling her hair back into a quick knot, trying to change shoes without getting twigs and dirt on her feet. She hurried out into the gardens. 'How do I look?'

'Apart from the leaf in your hair?' He reached over and removed it. 'Beautiful. You were always the prettiest girl in camp, Miss Hen.'

She flushed, uncomfortable with the compliment, and saw that he realised it. 'I meant, am I respectable enough to see visitors?'

'Well, you *look* respectable.'

'But a respectable woman doesn't ...' She broke off, unwilling to admit to a man she had been swimming, and naked at that.

'Go walking without a maid or groom in attendance?' he suggested, amused, as they rounded the carrots and trellises for the peas.

'Thank you, Sergeant.' She smiled at him, handed him the basket, and went in to her visitor.

She found Surgeon Wentworth in the drawing room, examining the notebook she had left on the desk previous night. He looked up as she entered, and bowed. She curtseyed politely.

'Excuse me looking at your private papers, Mrs Bartley. I was caught by the sketch of the snake and its eggs, and found I could not stop reading. Fascinating observations.'

'Why, thank you, sir.' A tray with claret and Mrs Cook's excellent oatcakes already sat on the table. 'I'm sorry I wasn't here to greet you. I often take a walk at this time.'

'And use your walks to great purpose, I see.' He gestured at the notebook. 'Forgive my coming unannounced. I had an order to give McDougal, and he offered me his skiff and a man to row me over.' He gave her what was still a young man's grin in a wrinkled face. 'A treat for an old man, to see such feminine loveliness.'

'I hear you do not lack for feminine company,' Hen said dryly.

He laughed. 'You shouldn't listen to gossip, Mrs Bartley, especially if it is true. But the snake you have sketched here ...'

'And poorly, I am afraid.'

'It may be no work of art, but it is sufficient. So the snakes here may either reproduce from eggs, or bear their young alive?'

'Yes, sir.' She did not add that some of the eggs were edible, and even tasty if eaten at an early stage of their development, but the unborn snakes were venomous, and should not be eaten except when prepared by expert hands.

'How did you discover it?' he asked curiously.

She hesitated. Poisonous snakes were not to be impulsively investigated. 'I have made the acquaintance of some native women,' she admitted cautiously.

'Ah, that would explain it.' To her relief he did not seem shocked. 'My son William Charles had close friendships with the native lads as a boy. He learned a lot from them, including the route across the Blue Mountains.'

The credit for that had been given purely to William Charles, and his colonial companions Lawson and Blaxland. But of course the natives must know routes across the mountains. 'I am glad you don't think my friendship unsuitable, sir.'

He sobered. 'I did not say that, Mrs Bartley. There are many, if not most of good society in the colony who would be shocked at a woman calling a native a friend. I would suggest discretion.' Another smile. 'A skill I have yet to acquire.'

'I will do my best to be discreet, sir.'

'Good.' He glanced at the notebooks again. 'Have you thought of writing a paper on your discoveries?'

'No sir,' said Hen, startled. 'I didn't think any scientific journal would accept an article by a woman.'

'You might try the London Zoological Social Society. I have friends among its members. I will write you a note of recommendation.'

'Thank you, sir. I would enjoy the scientific correspondence.'

'I would give you rubies, Mrs Bartley, or sapphires to match your eyes. But I am glad a gift of possible publication pleases you more.'

She laughed. 'You are an abominable flirt, sir.' But he had indeed given her a gift beyond rubies.

Should she tell Birrung she was writing up the knowledge to send overseas, she wondered the next afternoon, as the mussels the children had gathered steamed in seaweed by the small fire that gave exactly the correct amount of heat but no smoke at all. But she did not have the native words to explain what a scientific paper was, nor a zoological society, nor even paper and ink, though Jessica could probably explain the last two.

Down on the tiny beach two of the boys stood motionless with their spears, waiting for fish. Hen had noticed that none of these women fished from canoes. She had no doubt that they refrained to help keep their presence secret. Suddenly one moved in a flash of arms and body, then held up his spear in triumph, a large fish, still wriggling, on the end of it.

Birrung laughed, as the boys made their way up to the fire to cook their prize. She stood, and began to climb down to the beach. Hen followed her.

Birrung untied the basket about her waist, then emptied out its contents behind a rock. She grabbed a length of driftwood, then to Hen's surprise strode out into the water till it was waist deep. She threaded the loop of the basket around the stick, then drove it hard into the water. Both stick and basket vanished. Birrung waded back to shore.

'Wait,' she said to Hen.

The mussels were delicious, as were the roots from a vine with orange berries — only one tuber from each vine, Hen noted, so that the vines would keep growing. The roots were also so fibrous despite their sweetness that Hen was still picking fibres from between her teeth when Birrung pointed down to the beach. The tide was out, the flats that were muddy sand exposed. And

there was the driftwood stick, still holding the basket in place —
a basket that seemed to be flapping about, though even as Hen
watched the movement stopped.

Birrung said something to the children. Three girls clambered
down the slope, presumably to retrieve the fish from Birrung's
basket. Birrung began to speak again, but so quickly, and with
so many new words that Hen held up her hand to show she
didn't understand.

Birrung laughed. 'Men catch fish take this long,' she said in
English, stretching out both arms. 'Women catch fish only long
as this.' She showed an inch between her fingers.

Hen glanced at the boys, carefully not noticing the two smaller
fish the girls were carrying up the slope. She caught Birrung's
eye, then laughed with her.

'I will make you an o'possum cloak for next winter,' said
Birrung, half in English, half in her own language. 'No spears
needed, just quick hands. A woman's way. The meat is good,
too.'

Hen imagined herself sitting on the verandah in a possum-
skin cloak, like the one Birrung had in her small shelter. She
could even get a colony seamstress to line it with silk, and make
a fashionable collar for it, and a muff to match.

But she would not, for friendship was warmer than any cloak.

Night: the gentle flicker of candlelight on her desk; Millie and
Sal quietly chatting next door in Hen's bedroom as Millie was
making up the fire, and Sal was mending the skirt Hen had
torn that afternoon, a lack of household discipline unthinkable
back in England. Frogs croaked down by the pool. It would rain
tomorrow.

Hen took up her pen, and dipped it in the ink, but not to write
in the notebooks she had kept since she was a child. Finally she
knew the words she had to send to Max, and at last she was sure
she wanted to send them. The sergeant could carry the letter to
William tomorrow, so that it could be sent on the next delivery of

supplies to Gilbert's Creek, well before the Waterloo anniversary might tempt Max to come to the colony again.

The Peninsula
Sydney
New South Wales
Dear Max,

I pray this will not be hard for You to hear. Due to the well-meaning Interference of your Brother-in-Law, both You and I believed the other dead after Waterloo. I only discovered the truth when I visited your Mother after my Father's death. I came to find You, but discovered You had married, and were happy, as I am happy too.

I have stayed in the Colony and am comfortably situated, with Friends and a life I enjoy. I now call myself 'Mrs Bartley' so that no one might guess the Connection between us.

If you have no objection, I would like us to apply to Governor Macquarie to have our marriage quietly annulled. His Excellency has been kind to me, and I feel he would also act discreetly for any man who served at Waterloo.

A letter will reach me at this address, or care of McDougal's Stores. Please be assured that I wish only for your Happiness and that of your new Family, and will do all I can to ensure it.

Yours, with sweet memories of the short time we had together,
Hen Bartley.

Chapter 27

A Useful Infusion for Boils and Infection

Take of the native Bugle a Handful, and seethe in Water an
Hour. Use fresh made. A poultice of the Bugle, chopped,
and mixed with One Part crushed oats warmed, may also be
Efficacious.

From the Notebooks of Henrietta Bartley

The note came at breakfast, which was usually served on the
verandah — a kedgeree of rice and fresh fish and chopped
hard-boiled egg today, all lightly spiced, which it seemed had
been a favourite of those clients at the 'house of extremely good
repute'. Hen also found it delicious, which was convenient, as
it was one of Mrs Cook's favourite meals, both to cook and
to eat. Hen suspected if she had disliked it it would have been
served a little less often until she had acquired the taste. It
was also a much appreciated change from over a year of daily
morning porridge.

Hen took the note from the messenger, a middle-aged man
in convict drab, barefoot, with the calluses that meant he had
gone without boots for many years. She did not recognise him
from either Laura's or the McDougal households, nor was he in
the livery of Government House. 'Thank you. If you follow the
path you will find the kitchen, where I am sure Mrs Cook will
give you breakfast. I will send for you when I have the reply
ready.'

She broke the seal as the man strode towards the kitchen with an eagerness that implied he had either a large appetite or little chance to eat the superior food of a well-run household.

Dear Mrs Bartley,

Mr D'Arcy Wentworth having been so good as to put your name forwards as a possible nurse during the colony's current influenza outbreak, His Excellency Governor Macquarie has requested I ask for your attendance. The hospital has too few experienced staff for this crisis. I would be grateful for your nursing assistance.

Cordially yours,

Surgeon Bowman Esq.

Hen read the note through again, imagining the surgeon's chagrin at being commanded by the governor to ask for her help, then realising with concern that she'd had no idea there had been an outbreak of influenza.

Her visits to the colony during the past two months had been limited to Sunday church services, with dinner afterwards either with the McDougals or the Salisburys. None of them had mentioned influenza, which meant there had been no cases in either household. But influenza could spread quickly, especially in the cold and smoke of convict dwellings by the docks. The hospital must indeed be overstretched for Mr Wentworth and the governor to call for her services. Hen suspected that it was only Surgeon Bowman who added the word *nurse*.

But of course she must go. And, thankfully, no surgery would be required for influenza, even if it descended to the lungs, only good nursing, tisanes and broths. She hurried to her writing desk for pen, ink and paper, and hastily wrote a note to assure Surgeon Bowman that she would be there by early afternoon, then added two more notes to Mrs McDougal and Laura to warn them to keep the infection from their households, and for Mrs McDougal senior to temporarily suspend her school till the contagion eased, for the young and elderly were both most susceptible.

Mrs Cook must be put to making bone broth, and flasks of strong combined feverfew, marshmallow, elderberry, honey and mint tisane as well, to be doled out by the spoonful or added to a mug of hot water if possible, for it was unlikely the hospital would have either bone broth or tisanes. Hen was about to ring for Sal to fetch Sergeant Drivers, to tell him to get the boat ready to take her across the harbour, when she paused.

Influenza, and any of the other new diseases the colony had brought, were especially virulent among the natives, whose bodily systems had never encountered them before. The women's camp seemed isolated enough to be safe, but what if other natives joined them, bringing the contagion from elsewhere? And was the contagion truly influenza, or something worse? The early symptoms of Yellow Fever could be taken for it. Too many ships flew the Yellow Jack flag for that suspicion not to linger.

She changed quickly from her muslin housedress to one of tough flannel that could be boiled, and swapped her slippers for half boots. A few minutes was sufficient to give the notes and threepence to the messenger, instructions to Mrs Cook and the sergeant, who had taken to breakfasting in the kitchen. It seemed he also enjoyed kedgeree, as well as toast well slathered with strawberry jam.

'Could you ask Sal to pack a bag for me, please, Mrs Cook? I may need to stay a week or more, probably at the schoolhouse.' It was within walking distance of the hospital and more convenient than the new mansion, and Mrs Grathholme, the widowed teacher in residence, would be glad of company in the upstairs rooms. 'I will be back in about an hour and we can leave then.'

'You're not heading off to them natives now, are you?' demanded Mrs Cook. 'Not content with going into that hospital and catching who knows what …?' Hen saw the little woman was seriously concerned.

'Dear Mrs Cook, please don't worry. I've never caught more than a sniffle in my entire life, despite all the hospitals I have been in. But how did you know where I intended to go?'

Mrs Cook cast her eyes at the sergeant. He shrugged. He'd watched her leave each day, possibly even followed her part of the way, watching for the gleam of cloth through the trees. Somehow there always seemed to be a job to do at the end of her property so he could check she had come back safely.

'I will be an hour, no more,' Hen repeated. She fastened her bonnet and strode down the path through the orchard, seriously concerned.

The native remedies were excellent, but from talk in the colony, the previous year's influenza had killed many of the natives, while sparing almost all in the colony. This outbreak might be worse. If there was more illness than the women could cope with, the women needed to know they and their children would be welcomed and helped in her home.

Sergeant Drivers would keep the men under control. Mrs Cook must keep the spare bedrooms in readiness, and whatever opinions she held of natives to herself. Nor could Hen come to the native camp again till the epidemic was over, in case she brought the infection with her. They must not go to the colony till the illness was spent, either.

But it would only be for a month or so. Influenza vanished with the warm weather. She scrambled down the slope to their camp.

The Rum Hospital was indeed overstretched. Men lay on rough pallets of straw between the beds, even along the corridors. The women's ward, too, was overfull, though the wing kept for the military was tolerable. But no one who could afford nursing at home would come to the hospital. Each ward stank of the same mould, mice droppings and urine, the air filled with a chorus of a multitude of coughs.

At least a short survey showed her that the illness was indeed influenza. There was no black vomit or other symptom of an even greater virulence.

The nursing seemed to be done by elderly female convicts, as tipsy as when she had first encountered them. Their duties seemed to consist of nothing but removing chamberpots and bringing water, leaving the patients to cook their own rations in the meagre wardrooms' fires, eat them raw, or starve. There was no sign of Surgeon Bowman. It seemed the emergency was not sufficient to require his presence.

Hen requested pen and ink to scribble a quick note to William — pillows were needed to help the afflicted breathe and she would pay the cost.

The day sped by: she marshalled the nurses to dispense one tablespoon and no more of her syrup to each patient in a mug of boiled water and to make sure they drank it, too; she organised soup to be heated in the kitchens, to the anger of the two orderlies who assumed that room was their quarters, and for them alone; she sent a note to His Excellency's secretary, asking for more assistance — whoever he sent would be untrained, but emptying chamberpots or helping weak men to use them needed no training.

There was in fact little she or anyone could do for influenza, except give the syrup to ease the cough and fever, and make sure enough healthy fluids went in, and the resulting other fluids were hygienically collected and disposed of.

By dusk there was still no sign of Surgeon Bowman. Hen enquired about his whereabouts from one of the more sober convict attendants and found he was at his estates, though a messenger could be sent if a case required a surgeon's services. Hen was relieved rather than annoyed — she did not want to have to endure his frowns and, to give him justice, his skills as a surgeon were unnecessary. Only organisation of the nursing was needed, and as he was incapable of providing that, it was best that he be away.

Nurses and orderlies might grumble behind her back, but they did her bidding. She had discovered at a young age that anyone who gave orders was presumed to have the authority to give them. She marshalled the new convicts assigned to the hospital into two twelve-hour shifts, with instructions to let the men sleep during the night, but offer them syrup if their cough kept them awake.

The few cases that had progressed to congestion of the lungs she had shifted to another ward, then had them dressed in fever jackets, found in a cupboard and probably not used since Mr Wentworth's time at the hospital. Each patient was to be given inhalations of the hot water topped with eucalyptus oil (several bottles of which were found in yet another dusty cupboard). Surgeon White, the colony's first healer and interested, like her, in native remedies, had found this to be excellent for anyone congested in the nose or chest, just as the kino, or eucalypt sap, was most excellent for cleansing the bowels and thus the body of virulent humours.

It was only when Hen proceeded to the females' ward a third time that she found another nurse, sober, and undoubtedly not a convict: a woman dressed in black bombazine with a white apron over it like her own, spooning soup into a toothless woman in between her coughs.

'Mrs Bartlett!' What was she doing here? Or in the colony at all? Had Max decided to act on her letter immediately?

The other woman looked up at her. Her face was thinner than Hen remembered, her eyes sunk with weariness. 'I'm sorry. Have we met? I can't remember ...'

'I'm Mrs Bartley.' The other woman showed no recognition of the name. So Max either had not seen the letter yet, or had not told her of its contents. 'I appeared at your house at breakfast not quite a year ago,' Hen added. 'You have been called to assist here too?'

'No. I offered to help.' The last of the soup drunk, Mrs Bartlett carefully wiped the patient's wrinkled mouth, then stood, so unsteadily that even a passing mouse might knock her down.

Hen took her arm. Mrs Bartlett followed her, possibly too tired to wonder where she was being led. Hen made her way to Surgeon Bowman's office, then pulled the bell. 'Tea and buttered toast,' she ordered the startled servant. 'At least six slices with honey or jam, then toast another six.'

'Don't have no butter, miss.' He seemed to assume Hen had been given permission to use the office.

'Then toast without butter. And bring a bottle of brandy, too. Now. Mrs Bartlett, sit down, do. What are you doing here? Is ... is your husband with you?' Hen was suddenly afraid that Max might be a patient. But of course if he were ill he would be tended at home.

'Leo is back at Gilbert's Creek. I ... I have to tell him ...' Her voice choked.

Hen took the chair next to her and held the work-rough hand. 'Tell him what?'

Mrs Bartlett closed her eyes. 'Henrietta caught the influenza three weeks ago. It ... it was so quick. She seemed hot the night before, but I thought that it would pass. The next morning she seemed to burn and could not breathe. I brought her here — it seemed faster than sending a note for a surgeon. But ... but she died.'

It was like a sword thrust. Max's daughter, the child of this good woman here. 'I ... I am so deeply sorry. More sorry than I can say.'

Mrs Bartlett rubbed her eyes. 'I cannot make myself believe that she is dead, and in a coffin and buried too. It was too long a journey to try to take her home.'

'And Juana and Andrew?' Hen asked urgently.

'That is why I came to Sydney,' the other woman said simply. 'They are on a ship for England under the care of Mr and Mrs McGregor. There has been ... trouble at Gilbert's Creek. Some of the wild natives killed two of our shepherds. I brought a note to the governor, asking him to send soldiers, but it seemed best to bring the children away with me. Juana and Andrew's grandparents — their father's family — have been asking that the children visit England. This seemed to be a good time to send them, to accompany the McGregors. Andrew will inherit the estate one day, and Juana needs a chance to see a wider society. They both do, though I hope they might return ...' Her voice faded.

Hen sat silent. Her own experience led her to believe that any shepherds killed by the natives might have been treated so in retaliation for crimes the shepherds had first committed.

But this was not a time to discuss that. Neither Andrew nor Juana would know of the loss of their sister. Max would not know his child was dead. Possibly he had not even seen the letter yet. And this poor woman …

'I am so afraid,' whispered Mrs Bartlett. 'Could Juana and Andrew have caught the influenza before they left?'

'How long ago did they leave? Were they in Sydney long?'

'They sailed the day after we arrived. That was eight weeks ago. No, seven.'

'I am sure they are safe,' said Hen gently. 'The infection seems to have come on a ship only a month ago. It has spread rapidly. There wouldn't have been time for them to be infected, and I doubt anyone on board is likely to have caught it, either.'

'But Henrietta did.' Mrs Bartlett closed her eyes in anguish. 'I should not have stayed in Sydney, no matter what Leo said. It is my fault, all my fault.'

'It is no one's fault. How could you possibly have known influenza would strike so quickly? Who is with you at your town house?' She must send them a note. Mrs Bartlett needed sleep, and proper care.

But the other woman shook her head. 'There are no servants, just two men who come each week to see to the gardens or make repairs. I thought I could easily care for the child and myself while I ordered the supplies we need. But … but I could not care for Henrietta. I let her die.'

'You didn't,' said Hen quietly. 'There is little that can be done for influenza.' Apart from recognising it early, she thought, so that the child might be given extra fluids to help control the fever, and stimulants to help her heart. If only Mr Redfern had seen her in time, or Mr Wentworth. But she would not tell the child's mother that.

'You should not be alone there,' she said instead.

'I stayed here to help, to nurse. I cannot go back … I tried to enter the door and found myself running back to the hospital, as if I'd find Henrietta here. I should not have left her, not in the cold earth and all alone.' Mrs Bartlett buried her face in her hands and sobbed.

Hen let her cry. Grief could not be bound. Like flesh within a corset, you could confine it for a while, but it would still be there. Her mother had told her that every grief has its own ration of tears.

Hen wondered where the other woman had slept. On a pallet on the floor of the wards? Had she eaten at all? For the first time she felt fury at Surgeon Bowman. Someone should have noticed a gentlewoman stunned by grief, and found her refuge, or at least made sure she'd slept and eaten properly.

Tea arrived, with a flask of brandy, and wedges, blackened at one corner, that presumably were toast, with surprisingly fine china cups and a sugar basin. Hen poured out a cup of tea, added brandy and sugar, then pressed it into Mrs Bartlett's hands. 'Drink this, and dip some of the toast in the tea. Then you are coming home with me.' If Mrs Bartlett had been nursing here for three weeks and had not caught the infection, then hopefully like Hen she was one of those who never sickened with it. She held the other woman's wrist a moment as she took the tea. Her pulse was steady. Her skin did not seem fever hot, nor her eyes fever bright. Surely she would already have caught the contagion if she was going to sicken, and Hen would make sure the clothes she wore now were boiled.

Mrs Bartlett sipped obediently. She seemed steadier after her tears. 'I couldn't impose on you, but thank you.'

'It is no imposition and there will be no argument. You will stay at my home tomorrow, too, and keep to your bed all day, and let my staff look after you. I must be back here tomorrow, and I hope you are still asleep when I leave.' The laudanum would make quite sure of that. 'But I will see you tomorrow night.'

'I … I don't even remember your name.'

'It's Mrs Bartley,' Hen repeated. She handed her a handkerchief, one of the dozen kept in her apron pocket.

Mrs Bartlett blew her nose. 'Ah, of course. I ... I think I would like to sleep. But I cannot go back to our house.'

'You do not have to,' said Hen quietly. 'And I promise, you will sleep.'

Chapter 28

Botany Bay Kino, or the Sap of two Species of Eucalyptus Kino, may be Obtained by tapping small Holes in the Trees. Mix the Sap with an equal Part Water; Filter it then dry to a thick Syrup or Powder in a cool Oven or in the Sunn. Efficacious for Dysentery, Compacted Bowels, Diarrhoea, and Putrid Sore Throat, or when thorough Cleansing of the Body may be indicated. One Teaspoon for each Pint may be added to Preserve Wine or Syrups.

From the Notebooks of Henrietta Bartley

By the next morning no new cases of influenza had been brought to the hospital. Nine patients could be discharged; four had died overnight, two with pre-existing ailments, and the other two frail and elderly.

Hen wondered wearily how many children or old people had died or needed help but hadn't been cared for in the hospital. But she still lived by her father's advice: she would not let concern for those she could not help interrupt her work for those in her care.

By mid-afternoon she had the hospital organised according to the principles of Surgeon Gilbert: rosters of orderlies and nurses, the kitchens supplied from her own purse with sufficient supplies to provide good bone broths with vegetables and barley and bread or biscuit to soak in it, to be served three times a day, with tisanes to be served on constant rotation. She would send the tisanes made from herbs and flowers from her own garden and storeroom. Colonel Salisbury had provided two sergeants he trusted to oversee the kitchen work, to make sure all was provided to the patients rather than sold at market.

Hen's duty now was at home.

She found Mrs Bartlett sipping tea on the verandah, still dressed in one of Hen's own nightdresses, slightly too short, with a loose morning robe over it and a cap for her hair. Hen curtseyed, then added, 'Please don't get up.'

'I feel as if my legs don't belong to me,' the other woman confessed.

'You've been through far too much.' Though the unsteadiness might also be due to the laudanum with which Hen had dosed her hot milk the night before, and which Mrs Cook had put in her morning tea. But there would be no more laudanum now. Mrs Bartlett had needed sleep. Now she needed to mourn.

'How do matters stand at the hospital?'

'Much better. There are good people in charge now.' Hen did not mention she had been the one to put them in charge. 'I have also sent a messenger to leave a note at your house to say you have come to stay here.'

'Thank you. I ... I do not anticipate that Leo will come to Sydney. He will be busy with the insurrection there, and will not want to bring the troopers back to Sydney until he is sure there will be no more trouble; nor will he expect me home yet. I can't tell him about Henrietta in a letter.'

'She seemed a lovely child,' said Hen tentatively.

'Oh, she is! Was. She was already beginning to talk. She could say Mama and Papa and Juana and Andrew. Well, it was really Juju and Du ...' Hen wondered if Mrs Bartlett knew she was crying. 'She loved animals so much. We have a verandah very like this one. Henrietta would sit safe in her leading strings there for hours, just watching the wumbut or the kangaruhs or the birds in the trees. Her whole face would light up and she would point at the animals, so we could have the happiness of seeing them too. I ... I so wish she could be buried there.'

Hen was about to suggest they might rebury the child at her home in a few years, then stopped. She had known it done many times for loved ones who had died on service in other countries, but their coffins would have been sturdier than the colonial ones. It would be an added tragedy to expect a coffin and find instead just small bones.

'You love Gilbert's Creek?'

Mrs Bartlett nodded. 'I love its beauty. It's been like a paradise these last two years, the wild animals, the lambs, the river to fish in. The children ran wild, just a little. I think it's good for children to have a little wildness in their lives.'

Hen smiled. 'I agree.'

'I know they must go to England for their education, and to know the estate Andrew will inherit, but I hope both will wish to return. I would not have sent them so soon if it had not been for Mr and Mrs McGregor returning just as the violence broke out. His Excellency has sent twenty troopers down there to help us. I hope —'

'Twenty troopers!' interrupted Hen, startled. 'I apologise, but surely there is no need for so many.'

'His Excellency says it is best to strike hard at the beginning, rather than let more trouble brew. Steven ... my first husband ... used to say the same. I am glad Leo will be so well supported.'

Hen nodded politely. Somehow it was easier to think of a husband called Leo as quite a different person from Max. Especially one who had twenty troopers to punish what might well be crimes of retribution.

'I feel guilty sitting here drinking tea when there is so much that needs doing.' Mrs Bartlett gave the beginnings of a smile. 'But your housekeeper refuses to give me my dress again. She said it must be washed after being at the hospital.'

'She is quite right.' Hen did not think it was the time to give a lecture on the relative theories of infection. 'There is nothing that others can't do now at the hospital. You need rest before your journey home.'

Somehow she was able to say that without pain, possibly because she liked this woman, as well as feeling sympathy towards her. A woman who had automatically chosen to help others to survive her grief rather than have hysterics and who, even now, felt she should be of use. A woman who loved the beauty of the colony, instead of scrabbling for its wealth. Hen resisted a sudden temptation to ask more about Max, how they had met, or what their life together was like. She had truly relinquished him at last, she realised. All she needed was to know he was happy.

Which he would not be, now, with his shepherds killed, and soldiers, and with the news of the death of his child to come. But Hen knew with only a slight twist of her heart that the time would come when Max would be happy again. There would be more children, and days and nights spent with this intelligent and kind woman. A lifetime of happiness.

She stood. 'I need to pick herbs to make more syrups for the hospital. You should probably rest again.'

The other nodded. 'I think perhaps you are right.'

'I'll bring you dinner on a tray. You need to eat, even if you don't feel hungry.'

'Yes, Nanny.' It was definitely a smile now.

Hen smiled back. 'I apologise for ordering you about. It's habit, I'm afraid, Mrs Bartlett.'

'It's what I needed,' said Mrs Bartlett quietly. 'I had lost myself for a while, I think. You have brought me back again. Please, do call me Elizabeth.'

'Thank you, Elizabeth.' Hen was grateful to drop the name Bartlett and its memories. 'My name is Hen. I know it sounds odd — it's a nickname my father gave me.'

She waited for the other woman to make any connection between Hen and Henrietta, but she didn't. Nor was there any chance of hiding her name, with the sergeant referring to her as Miss Hen. Mrs Bartlett rose shakily and accepted Hen's arm to help her inside.

Chapter 29

A Tisane for Influenza

This must be taken at the Beginning of the Infection. A
Tisane with Honey and Marshmallow should also be given
when the Cough develops. Laudanum will ease a Cough but
do not administer it if there are Difficulties in Breathing.

    Elderberries, three Cups; Peppermint leaves, half Cup;
Yarrow leaves, one Handful; Water, one Pint. Bring to the
Boil & leave to Cool. Strain. The Liquid may be kept one
Week, or longer if boiled with equal Honey. Dilute with one
part boiling Water. Feverfew may be added at Discretion.

From the Notebooks of Henrietta Bartley

'Mrs B?' Hen opened her eyes to find Mrs Cook at her bedroom
door at the Peninsula. She had decided to sleep at home, not just
to keep her guest company, but because there was little need for
her services now at the hospital, with the nursing re-organised
— at least for a while.

'Yes, Mrs Cook?' Dawn shone silver between the curtains.
Sal had not lit her fire yet and the room was cold.

'It's that Mrs Bartlett. I heard her muttering and peered in.
She ain't looking good.'

Hen swung her legs out of bed. 'What is it? Influenza?'

'Maybe. Mrs B ...' Mrs Cook hesitated. 'I don't feel none too
good neither. Like snow one minute, like a boiling kettle the
next.'

Hen felt Mrs Cook's forehead. She should not have risked bringing Elizabeth here, she realised. Her sympathy for the other woman — and the sudden reminder of Max — had unsettled her judgement. 'To bed with you. Now. I'll bring you a tisane too.'

'I can't leave you to …'

'You can and will. I am quite capable of cooking.' Hen grabbed her wrap. 'I'll see you to bed.' Mrs Cook was likely to ignore her order and continue to make breakfast for the household.

Hen helped her into her nightdress, a voluminous calico in which the skinny body was entirely wrapped, then brought in a spadeful of the coals from the kitchen fire to build a fire in the bedroom fireplace. Sal peered in from the next bedroom.

'Don't come in,' said Hen quickly. 'We don't want you or Millie catching the influenza either. You don't feel ill?'

'No, ma'am.'

'Excellent. Could you please ask Sergeant Drivers for two roosters plucked? I want to make more soup. Then make the bread and then breakfast for the household.'

Sal stared. 'Mrs Cook says I've a lead hand with bread.'

'She has indeed,' said a voice from the nightdress.

'We will sop it in soup and no one will notice. But you and Millie are not to come into this room, nor Mrs Bartlett's, and tell me at once if anyone else is ill.'

Hopefully only Mrs Bartlett — Elizabeth — had brought the infection and it could be contained.

Hen took time to dress and put on an overall apron before entering the guest room. She found her guest feverish. Her face was greeny white, and she was difficult to rouse.

'Millie!' she called.

'Yes, ma'am?'

'Coffee, strong and sweet, and bring the syrup in the green flask from my medicine shelf, and a spoon. Quick, girl.'

Hen piled the pillows up behind the sick woman, raising her to make it easier for her to breathe, but even that did not seem to wake her. Hen took the coffee, syrup and spoon from Millie at the door, then sat on the bed next to the unresponsive woman.

'Elizabeth? It's time to wake now.' Hen gently opened Elizabeth's jaw and spooned in the smallest possible amount of coffee. To her relief, Elizabeth swallowed. Hen spooned in more till it was gone.

Suddenly Elizabeth blinked. 'Henrietta,' she muttered. 'I have to see to her ...' She struggled briefly, then lay back as Hen put a comforting hand on her shoulder.

'Shh. Henrietta is safe. You need to drink this.' Hen poured out a large spoonful of the syrup. Elizabeth made a face, but swallowed.

'I'll be back soon. Sleep now.' She hurried out and fetched a bowl of yesterday's soup for Mrs Cook, with a slice of yesterday's bread, too. Sal would need to make the chicken soup to Hen's directions, for she could not nurse both women and cook too. Thankfully Mrs Cook seemed only slightly feverish.

'A good cup of tea and I'll be right as rain, Mrs B.'

'You'll stay in that bed till I allow you up. And you'll use the chamberpot, too.'

Mrs Cook looked scandalised. 'And have you emptying my chamberpot? I will not.'

'You need to drink as much as you can to keep the fever down,' said Hen wearily. 'I'll bring in a jug of barley water and see you drink it all. I need to see the colour of your urine, your water I mean — if it's dark you'll need more fluids. But Mrs Bartlett is not well at all. I need to spoon fluid into her, so if you ...'

'If I do as I'm told it'll be easier for you.' Mrs Cook looked at Hen darkly. 'Put you in black leather and you'd make a guinea an hour back in London.'

To her obvious horror Hen grinned. 'Two guineas at least, thank you.' She bent and kissed an even more shocked Mrs Cook on the cheek. 'Get well, my friend. I need you.' She left to go back to Elizabeth Bartlett.

The day stretched on. Mrs Cook obediently drank two jugs of barley water and two bowls of soup, virtuously filled two chamberpots, then slept, flushed and feverish, but not, Hen thought, in any danger. Sergeant Drivers delivered the roosters, plucked and gutted, with a look of concern for her safety he could not quite hide. Sal and Millie chopped vegetables and simmered soup. Hen sat by Elizabeth Bartlett's side and spooned broth and syrups into her. Elizabeth did not fully wake but swallowed.

About two o'clock, by the chiming clock in the hallway that Sergeant Drivers wound each night, her eyes opened. 'Hen,' she murmured.

Hen put the bowl of broth and spoon down. 'Elizabeth! Do you know where you are?'

'In bed.' The green eyes looked amused. 'And in your house.' Her voice was weak, but clear.

Hen shut her eyes in a brief prayer of thanks. 'You have the influenza. A bad bout, but you are recovering.'

'I'm glad. Leo has known too much loss. He should not have to lose two wives.' Elizabeth smiled at Hen. 'This is the first time I have seen you without your bonnet on. Your hair is just like Leo's first wife's.'

'My hair is a dashed nuisance,' said Hen, wishing she had thought to wear her cap. 'I apologise for my language,' she added. 'I spent too long in military camps as a child.'

'As did his first wife.' Elizabeth's eyes were thoughtful now. 'She was a military surgeon's daughter. That is how they met.' She paused, breathed a moment, then added, 'His arm was shattered, and it looked like he would lose it, but she sewed it up and then they married, there on the battlefield.'

'It sounds most ... romantic.'

'You took charge at the hospital,' said Elizabeth quietly. 'You have cared for me here. Hen with golden hair.'

Hen carefully concealed her horror. Not now, she thought, please, not now. Do not add this grief to all that this woman has suffered. She managed to smile back. 'There were many women with blonde hair following the drum. You, too, were nursing, just as I was. As a widow I have no family in my care, so could help there, that's all.'

'Hen Bartley,' said Elizabeth softly, her eyes closing again. 'Steven told me he glimpsed a girl on the field at the Battle of Waterloo, and who they said came to the battlefield for days afterwards, who tended the injured better than any surgeon. They called her the angel, and said that any man she helped would live. Steven said she was beautiful, even in her apron in the mud. But Leo says his wife died the day of the battle, so his wife could not have been the angel.'

Hen laughed shakily. 'Nor I. I am not an angel, as anyone can testify, including my housekeeper this morning when I ordered her to fill her chamberpot for me. She has the influenza too, but not as badly as you. I had better check and see if she has filled it again. Will you sleep now?'

'Yes, I will sleep. Hen, do you think we are united with those we love after we have died?'

'I don't think we are ever truly parted from any love,' said Hen quietly.

'I think you might be right.' Elizabeth Bartlett closed her eyes again.

Hen checked the fire: strong enough to keep the air warm, but not too hot for fever, and the chimney drawing well with no smoke to irritate the lungs. She realised that Elizabeth did not have the influenza cough yet. That would come tomorrow perhaps, and linger too. She would need careful nursing to make sure the infection did not become inflammation of the lungs.

She moved to the bed, felt Elizabeth's forehead — hot, but not desperately so. Her pulse was weaker than Hen would have liked, but steady, and she was also too pale. The days she had neglected herself after her daughter's death had taken their rent of her body.

Hen felt uneasy. Elizabeth had not asked to use the chamberpot, despite the liquid Hen had spooned into her all day.

She would briefly check on Mrs Cook and then return. More coffee, she thought.

Mrs Cook was slightly more feverish, but Hen had expected that as evening drew closer. She was also surprisingly docile, accepting the spoonfuls of syrup, the new jug of barley water, even Hen sponging her face, neck and arms with cool lavender water. 'It does feel good,' the woman muttered.

Hen suddenly wondered when anyone had last tended to Mrs Cook, she whose job was caring for others. Had Mrs Cook ever had a mother who cosseted her? Or had she been like so many London children, put carelessly to the breast while her mother drank gin and lifted her skirts for a few minutes for any man who'd pay for it. Her thin frame, despite the plenitude of the kitchens she had worked in, made the latter scenario more likely.

Hen could hear Sal and Millie in the bigger kitchen down the walkway. But the coals still glowed in the small kitchen fireplace. She poured hot water onto the coffee grounds, then quickly ate a slice of heavy bread with cheese while it brewed, and tried to think.

She had hoped Elizabeth had forgotten any possible connection between herself and Max's first wife. There was, after all, the presumed proof that his first wife had died on the battlefield. The similarity of Bartlett and Bartley, Hen and Henrietta, however, would be harder to believe a coincidence once Elizabeth was strong enough to think clearly once again, as would the military background, especially if Elizabeth remembered their conversation on her early morning visit, almost a year back.

A strange year, after so many months when her one encompassing vision had been to be with Max, then more months, of envisaging herself at a smaller version of the hospital that her father had superintended, but this one for the children of the colony.

And now? Hen carefully poured the coffee through the filter — two cups, one for herself, the other well sweetened for Elizabeth. Now she was content, even happy. A new world of medicine and friendship had opened up for her with Birrung and Jessica. If Elizabeth proved well enough she would visit the camp tomorrow to make sure none there had caught the illness. Though it would be more prudent perhaps to wait, to make sure she had not contracted it herself. Then she must ...

Hen stopped, cups in hand, as the question she had kept at bay with other thoughts echoed down the hall as clearly as if she had spoken it herself.

Did she still want Max Bartlett? Because what had been impossible a year ago might be possible now. There was no child left illegitimate, nor two children left abandoned. On the contrary, it might be many years before Andrew and Juana returned to the colony, if they ever did. Elizabeth was more likely to visit her children in England, even, perhaps, to stay in England in the comfort of her in-laws' home, despite her love of the beautiful but remote Gilbert's Creek. Her marriage to Max might even have been forgotten in England, except by a few close relatives or friends. No scandal would blight her life if Elizabeth went back to live there, with an income, perhaps, to give her independence.

And if Elizabeth made the connection between Henrietta Bartlett and Hen Bartley? If Elizabeth realised her marriage was not legal, that Max's first wife lived? She was a woman of courage and integrity. What if Elizabeth offered to vanish to England?

Hen sat and stared at the brass coffee pot sitting on the table, as if it could give her clarity. It was possible. It was also impossible. She liked Elizabeth Bartlett. Elizabeth had forged a good life with Max, one to which she clearly wished to return, despite the tragedy of Henrietta, or the temptations of a prosperous estate in England.

No. Henrietta Bartlett had died in a cannon blast at Waterloo, and if necessary Hen would find witnesses to prove it. Would Sergeant Drivers lie for her? Perhaps. Almost certainly, if the sergeant thought it was to free Hen from a husband she didn't want.

And yet I love him. The words lingered like a song in the warm kitchen air, as sweet as baking bread. I love Max Bartlett and he would love me, if we were to meet again.

So they must not meet. She had accepted a life without him, but she was not sure of her resolve if she spent time with him. The annulment could surely take place with separate testimony from them both.

Hen picked up the coffee and trod down the corridor to the guest room. Elizabeth was asleep, resting on her piled pillows, a slight smile on her face, as if her dreams were sweet.

Hen put the coffee down and reached over to feel her temperature. It was only then that she realised Elizabeth was dead.

Chapter 30

To Bake Bread with No Yeast

This is most common in the Colony and is called 'Damper',
for the Fire must be damped by scraping away the Coals
before it is cooked or it will Burn. For each loaf take no
more than 3 cups wheat Flour, a half cup water that has
been poured through fine Wood Ash to make the Flour
rise, and 2½ cups water or buttermilk. A Scots Friend
adds a little Treacle. Mix quickly with a Knife, for Over
Mixing makes a Heavy Loaf. Place in a greased Pot and
replace the lid, then put on the Fireplace and cover with
hot Coals, or in a hot Oven. In a cold Oven it will be heavy.
An Experienced Hand may cook half this Amount on the
Hearth by a Fire. Cook perhaps 45 Minutes by the Clock
but a Good Cook will know their Oven and its Timing.
Some cook their Damper in the ash and hope to dust it with
a Bullock's Tail but this is Ineffectual and a sad Waste of
good Provision.

From the Notebooks of Henrietta Bartley

Hen sent a note to Mr Wentworth to ask him what needed to be
done about a death in the colony. To her surprise and enormous
comfort he had himself rowed across the harbour to her, using a
stick now to help him up the path to her house. Sal ushered him
into the drawing room, where Hen sat at her writing table trying
to compose a letter from 'Mrs Bartley' to Max.

'Mr Wentworth!' She stood and curtseyed as he bowed. 'You should not have troubled to come all this way.'

'I would cross the ocean for one of Mrs Bartley's smiles.' The flirtatiousness left his face as he added, 'A bad business, this influenza, though the contagion is receding now. It was kind of you to take in a stranger.'

'We met at the hospital. Mrs Bartlett had volunteered to nurse.' Hen felt it easier to let him think there had been no other connection between them. 'Please, sir, do sit. Millie, will you bring tea, or would you prefer claret and a biscuit, sir?'

'The claret, thank you. My dear, funerals are a man's business, not a woman's. I know Mr Bartlett slightly. I will send a note to his property, advising him of what has occurred. My man will supervise ... what is needed here ... this afternoon.'

Mr Wentworth was treating her as if she had never seen death before. But indeed the end of life was different when it was someone you had cared for, a woman so much like herself. Hen grieved not just for her loss, but for the friendship that could not have been, and never would be now.

'Thank you. I am most truly grateful. But there is another blow for Mr Bartlett. His baby daughter died of the influenza a few weeks ago — that was why Mrs Bartlett was at the hospital. She stayed on to help with the nursing after her child died. The babe had not yet reached her second year.'

'As so many babes in the colony do not, though we are better here than London.' Mr Wentworth looked at Hen with concern. 'You are quite well yourself, my dear? You look tired and pale.'

'I am tired,' she admitted. 'My housekeeper has the influenza, and I have been nursing her and Mrs Bartlett and directing the cooking. But I am quite well.' It was her mind that was in turmoil.

Millie brought the claret decanter, the glass and a plate of biscuits on the silver tray Hen had brought from England. Mr Wentworth took half a glass quickly, declined a biscuit and stood. 'I must not keep you further, Mrs Bartley. But if I can be of assistance, or any of my household can, pray do not hesitate to call upon our services.'

'I will not, sir. You have been so very kind.'

'I will call on you again after the funeral service.'

'Thank you,' she said again. Women did not go to funerals. Strange that they should have the job of washing the body and laying it out, all of which she had done for Elizabeth, dressing her again in her newly washed clothes, ironed by Sal. But funerals themselves were judged as being too emotional for fragile womanhood to stand.

Mr Wentworth bowed, kissing her hand.

Mrs Cook was unchanged — not dangerously ill, but still feverish. In Hen's experience this might continue for another week, but with good nursing would not progress to inflammation of the lungs. The little woman was too ill to move from her bed, but well enough to be bored, until Hen had the idea of reading to her from her chest of books from England when she wasn't cooking or picking the herbs — with only one patient to nurse she was able to rescue the household from Sal's and Millie's attempts.

Most were medical or herbal texts, but Hen had purchased Mrs Shelley's recently published *Frankenstein* just before the *Ivy* sailed. She had assumed that despite it being a work of fiction, there would be interesting medical details but, beyond the possible reanimation of tissue with electricity that was still far from proven, although there was no doubt an electric charge affected tissue, alive or dead, the plot was ludicrous from a scientific point of view.

Had Mrs Shelley no concept of how quickly dead tissue changed, or that tissue from one person could not be sewn onto another? If it could have been there would be no man without an arm or leg in England!

But the story itself was fascinating, and Mrs Cook was soon engrossed. 'Imagine if we had one of them machines. Why, I could attach it to a dead rooster ...'

'Or a rat,' said Sal, who had come to the door with another jug of lemon barley water, and stayed to listen. Millie had crept after her.

'Or I could sew chicken legs onto the lamb roast, and have it march itself to the oven ...'

Hen could only be glad that the electrical device was fiction.

She did not return to the hospital. Mr Wentworth called to give her details of the church and graveyard service conducted by the Reverend Marsden. He had even arranged for a two-man boat to sail down the coast and up the river to Gilbert's Creek to inform Elizabeth's husband of her death, and the loss of his child.

The hospital, he told her firmly, was all in good order. The orderlies were now following her directions, with no new influenza cases turning up. Hen was not quite sure that was the truth — the hospital was in such chaos with the lack of leadership that she doubted even the men William had sent to see her orders carried out could have made a lasting impression. But she did accede to Mr Wentworth's firm request that she not go back there.

Nor did she want to. Her household had lost one person to the influenza. Mrs Cook might overtire herself in Hen's absence and still needed good nursing. Sal and Millie had soon forgotten her order to keep out of the sickroom, and someone must make food for the staff, and neither Sal nor Millie could even slice bread neatly nor toast it evenly. Boiled salt beef with potatoes and carrots was the limit of their culinary skills. And they, too, might still go down with the fever.

Hen had no wish to go back to the hospital, or the colony. She might so easily meet Max there, if he came to Sydney to visit the graves of his wife and daughter or to take their remains back to Gilbert's Creek.

She could only hope a man grieving for his wife and daughter did not care that the wife had legally not been his at all and the child illegitimate in the eyes of the law and the church. Love was love, and now the law had no say in the love Max felt for his family.

Instead she pushed her body with hard work, hoping to ease her mind. She assuaged her guilt at failing to attend the hospital by making cough and fever syrups for use there, labelling them clearly, though possibly few if any of the attendants could read, or even make out her diagram showing a spoon next to a sun and a moon, for a dose both night and day. But both syrups were innocuous if given in the wrong amounts, or one instead of the other.

Young Lon killed one of the sheep and hung it in the meat house adjoining the dairy. The household ate roast mutton and Mrs Cook had more rich bone broth. Bread to bake, butter to churn — at least Sal and Millie knew how to milk cows and churn butter now. Her household was still forbidden to go to the township, in case of contagion.

Samuel managed to pierce his foot with a garden fork while planting potatoes. Hen had him soak it in rum and eucalyptus oil — she had found that the addition of the oil was the only way to stop the men stealing her supply of medicinal spirits — then when the blood was flowing clean, sewed it and bound it with a pad of rose and lavender oil, and then oilcloth, to keep it dry and clean.

'Bring it to me to dress again each morning and night,' she informed him, as he drank a cup of sweetened tea, his face white with the shock and pain. Deep wounds could often become infected, though enough blood had flowed for her to believe it would be safe. 'Why weren't you wearing your boots?'

'Keeping them for best, Mrs B,' said Samuel solemnly. 'Wouldn't want to muddy them.'

'But I provided them for you to work in, to prevent exactly such injuries as these. When they are worn we will find a cobbler to repair them, and buy you new boots as well to wear to visit the township.'

Samuel stared at her. 'I'd have two pairs of boots?'

Hen nodded.

'Well, I never. Two pairs of boots!' The thought clearly consoled him for the wound to his foot. And at least he will now wear his boots when he is able to work again, she thought, for the sooner they wear down the quicker he will have his two pairs.

She went back inside to make custard and apples baked with sugar and cinnamon, as well as a coddled egg to tempt Mrs Cook's appetite, and to demonstrate to her that Hen could indeed prepare an excellent meal.

Chapter 31

A Syrup for the Cough

Take Onions, peeled & sliced thin. Cover with Honey &
leave Overnight. Strain off the Juice thus made & give one
teaspoonful as needed.

From the Notebooks of Henrietta Bartley

The Sydney winter climate might be warmer than England's
summer, but Hen's thyme and mint plants still refused to replace
the leaves she'd picked, nor were there more feverfew or lavender
flowers, and the large quantities of syrups made in the last two
weeks had sorely tried her reserves of dried herbs.

She put on her gardening apron, took a wicker basket and her
bonnet — Mrs McDougal inspected her each time they met for
traces of too much sun upon her complexion — and her scissors,
and went to see what the herb garden might provide. Auntie Love
might swim with nothing on, she thought with grim amusement,
but Mrs Bartley wore a bonnet even for a half-hour harvest.

She wandered along the beds that grew alongside the house,
sheltered from the sea winds with rock walls. There was still
plenty of rosemary, of course, and motherwort too, which would
help ease a cough but could be dangerous for a pregnant woman,
so must not be put in the hands of the unwary.

There were also onions in abundance in her stores. Perhaps a
syrup of honey and onions would suffice. If Surgeon Bowman
had returned he might insist on cupping those with fever,

so a medicine to soothe a fever might further debilitate the unfortunate who'd had a pint of their blood removed.

But there was enough thyme to pick for Mrs Cook's syrup, as well as for that lady to use for her excellent stuffed shoulder of mutton and chicken pies once she had recovered. She would not be pleased to find her cooking herbs depleted when she regained her kitchen.

Hen had half filled her basket when she saw the sailboat. At first she thought it was headed for the sea, but then it turned, the red-coated men handling the sails with ease, skilfully bringing it to shore without the need to row. She stepped over to a rock overlooking the cove as four barefoot troopers, their trousers rolled up, jumped out to pull the boat further up the sand. The fifth man wore hessians and a well-cut jacket, but the cabbage tree hat of a farmer. He waited till the craft was beached before stepping out himself, his well-polished boots still dry.

She had known him as soon as the boat had turned her way. Max. He waited while his soldier crew put their boots back on, retrieved their gun pouches and their muskets, and handed Max his. For a moment Hen wondered why he had brought armed men to her peninsula. But the boat might well belong to the troopers who had sailed to Gilbert's Creek, and who had offered to bring him here, and no one, soldier or civilian, would leave muskets, shot and gunpowder — nor anything else of value — unattended in a colony of thieves.

Max strode out of sight, towards the stairs up the slope. The troopers followed him.

She could not move. She could not even think what she might say.

Suddenly Sergeant Drivers stood next to her. She had not heard his wooden leg on the rock. 'Should I call the men and see them armed, Miss Hen?'

She shook her head. 'That is Mrs Bartlett's husband. I ... I glimpsed him when I first met her. She told me they had a party of troopers down there to deal with ... rebel natives.'

'If you would like to go into the house, Miss Hen ...' The sergeant's tone was urgent. She glanced at him. Sergeant Drivers's hair was prematurely greying, and several teeth had fallen out during his long imprisonment and at sea. And yet she all at once wished no other company than his.

She suddenly wished she had confided her marital position to him, and to Mrs Cook too.

There was still time to retreat to the house, and have the sergeant inform Max that she was not at home. She could even run into the bush. But she could not do that to a man whose wife and child had died.

Whatever Max wanted — to hear about his wife's last days, to discuss the annulment she had asked for, to ask for comfort — she had to stay to hear it.

'I ... I would prefer to meet Mr Bartlett out here.' She managed a smile. 'No tactical retreat necessary.'

'I'll get my musket,' stated Sergeant Drivers. He limped quickly back towards the storeroom where the arms were kept without waiting for a reply.

Six years, she thought. What do I say first?

But Max spoke before she could, hailing her as he came up the path. 'I'm looking for your mistress, Mrs Bartley. I gather my wife is staying here? A Mrs Bartlett?'

Hen turned to stone. It had never occurred to her that Max might see her, even glimpse her, and not recognise her. But she had been fifteen on the battlefield, her head bare. He was more familiar with the portrait of the angel in battle than the person it had been based on. To him she was long dead. And it was no wonder he took her for a servant, in her apron and gardening bonnet.

Nor did he know Elizabeth was dead, to hail her so cheerfully. It was also obvious he had not read her letter.

She forced herself to move, to speak. Time, she thought. I need time to think! But there was no time now.

Perhaps ... just possibly ... she might avoid a confrontation now, she thought dazedly, and let him grieve before he faced the knots of their relationship.

On impulse she gave her voice a hint of Mrs McDougal's Scots. 'I'm Mrs Bartley, sir. I'm that sorry, but Mrs Bartlett died of the influenza three days ago. Mr Marsden himself took the funeral service.' Her words tumbled into each other at the look on his face. 'Surgeon Wentworth sent you a letter but your ships must have passed on the voyage.'

'What? Impossible.' Max stood stricken. Once more she was shocked at his tallness, the tan of his skin, his strength, so different from the man she had married on the battlefield. And yet, in some deep way, he was the same.

She could not go to him. She could not touch him. She could not even look directly at him, but must keep her bonnet shading her face. 'Sir, I cannot tell you how much this grieves me, but your daughter died as well, a week before your wife. It was the influenza, too.'

The troopers stood, muskets in their hands, mouths agape. 'Perhaps your men would like a drink in the back kitchen, sir. Tell Millie that I sent you there.' Hen gestured to the building. The men set off, obviously unwilling to share their master's grief and probably hopeful there'd be rum. They'd get none in her house, but there was still a keg of Mrs Cook's ale untapped.

She hesitated. If she and Max went inside she must take off her bonnet and he would see her hair, as untidy as at Waterloo and as golden. But she could not leave a stricken man standing here on the path.

'Will ye come to the verandah, sir? I'd ask ye into the house but we have illness, here, the influenza: 'tis the reason your puir wife came here. She and I nursed the sick at the hospital together — it's bad in the colony now ...' She led him through the gate and around the path to the verandah, keeping carefully ahead of him so he could not see her face.

'Andrew and Juana?' Max asked. She could hear his fear. She had known a laughing adventurer, ignoring his agony. This was a grieving husband and father, and one she pitied deeply.

'Fine and healthy I imagine, sir, for they were safe on the ship long before the illness took hold in the colony. Mrs Bartlett was tired, working at the hospital after your puir daughter's loss, and rather than leave her alone at your house I invited her here, hoping with rest and good food she would recover. But she must have taken the infection at the hospital, for she was ill the second day that she was here. Will ye take a seat, sir?' She took one just slightly behind his, so that the bonnet still shaded her face.

'Will you tell me what happened? Tell me everything. I ... I can't seem to take it in. Henrietta too ... I can't ... And Elizabeth was so full of life and love. Are you sure of all this, Mrs Bartley?'

'Certain sure, sir, for Mrs Bartlett told me herself of your daughter's death, puir lady, and I attended her in her own illness. I am so sorry.'

'What will I tell the children?' It was almost a cry, echoing for the seagulls to hear. 'How can I tell them this?'

It would be almost a year before they heard the news. Hen hoped Andrew and Juana would have settled with their grandparents by then, felt loved and secure with them, able to accept their comfort. And this man, their stepfather, this man who led soldiers with muskets pursuing men who were fighting for their land — would Elizabeth's children ever return to the colony now to be with him? Or would Max go to England to be with them?

'Mrs Bartlett and I nursed at the hospital together, as you know. She had been there working for weeks before I came, caring for the unfortunates.'

He shook his head, as if all words had flown on the south wind.

'We nursed her well, sir.' Hen tried to fill the silence. 'Usually the influenza strikes the old and young, but this took the strong and healthy. And it was quick. One night and a day only, though we did all we could.'

'You had a doctor to her?'

Hen could not say it had never occurred to her to call one. 'All are busy, sir, and it would not have helped her to carry her across the water to the hospital. It was so quick — she seemed to be improving.'

'They said at the hospital you were a kind of doctor yourself. One man called you Auntie Love.'

Hen stilled, wishing she could fade into the air. 'I've heard they do that, sir,' she said cautiously.

'He said you removed a boy's leg, and that boy is walking with a peg leg now, and training to be a clerk. But you could not save my wife?'

'No, sir.'

He sat silently. She wondered if he was crying, if she could slip inside to leave him to his grief. She made a slight movement.

He turned to face her fully. 'You remind me of someone.'

'Many people have said that, sir. It seems I have one of those familiar faces.' She suddenly realised she still wore his signet ring, had worn it ever since that day on the battlefield. She slid her fingers between the folds of her skirt.

'I haven't seen your face, but I wonder why you attempt a Scots accent. Please take off your bonnet, Mrs Bartley.'

'Sir, I am well aware of your grief, but I have another ill person I must attend to. I will call your men.'

'You will take off your bonnet.' It was an order.

She undid the ribbon, lifted it and looked at him.

He said nothing. Did nothing. She had thought, despite the years, even with his second marriage, that if he ever saw her he would cry for joy. He had named his property for her, named a river and his daughter for her, kept her portrait on his wall.

The silence lengthened. She heard the seagulls call, the waves lash on the rocks below. She could not read his thoughts.

'How long have you been in the colony, Henrietta?' he asked at last. Each word stabbed like an icicle.

Hen managed to keep her voice calm. 'I have been here for about a year. I discovered you had recently married the day after

I arrived. I saw you and Elizabeth together, and you were happy. I thought it best you should not know.'

'*You* thought it best? How could you take that on yourself? You let me be a bigamist! To take the best woman who ever lived into a sham marriage.'

'You had already married her! Was I to break your home?'

'You should have given me the right to choose, to at least know how things stood!'

'I wrote to you over a month ago, suggesting our marriage be quietly annulled. I didn't want to write until I was established here.'

He gave a snort of derision. 'We have had two ships dock at Gilbert's Creek in the past month, with supplies for the troopers, and mail as well. There has been no letter. I suppose you will tell me now it must have been lost.'

'It must have been.'

'Easy to claim. And why come sneaking up on me after all these years? Why let me think you were dead? The family paid you off, is that it, and you needed more? I am sure it was, just as they paid off the doxy who had her claws into my brother up at Oxford. To think I mourned you as an angel all these years. I even named my daughter for you. My poor, darling little Henrietta.'

'Max, you are letting grief unhinge you. *I* thought *you* were dead! Your brother-in-law told me so when I recovered consciousness in Brussels. He faked a casualty list with your name on it. He told you I was dead as well, rather than pollute the Bartlett household with my presence. I took your name and I wore black, and I mourned you, too. I had no need to be paid off. My father was named Superintendent of Hospitals by the Duke of Wellington himself. I am wealthier than you, sir, and my father would have had a knighthood if he had lived.'

He gazed at her. Grief and shock had twisted their strength to anger. 'How did a mere army surgeon come by a fortune?'

She was not going to detail her father's investments, nor divulge the teeth of dead men warehoused in England. 'Look around you,' Hen said coldly. 'Does this look like the dwelling of a woman who would sell the man she loved? I dine at His Excellency the Governor's table, and call his wife my friend. I changed my name slightly so we could not be connected, and purely to save your marriage.'

'So when did you find out I was alive?' He had let anger swallow his grief, as that was easier to cope with. Hen could see it simmering, looking for an outlet. She could almost feel its tendrils.

She shut her eyes. 'My father died.' She tried to keep her voice matter of fact. 'I had kept house for him, the house that went with his position. When I inherited his fortune I thought perhaps your family might be in need. I had no knowledge of how wealthy they were, nor their position in society. My father's man of business located them for me. I visited and met your mother.'

'My mother knows?' he demanded incredulously.

'Your mother will vouch for all of this. She told me you had named a river for me, that you had grieved for me, were possibly still grieving. She encouraged me to find you, for your letter announcing your marriage didn't reach her till after I had sailed.'

'You have been writing to her?'

Hen hesitated. 'Yes.'

'Even though you had put off my name and any claim on me?'

'Yes. I like your mother and she has been kind enough to like me too.'

'A daughter-in-law, writing to her husband's mother?'

'At first perhaps ...' She did not know what made him so furious his hands shook. This was not transmuted grief alone. Yes, there had been pretence and she could accept that he was angry he had not been given the choice ...

'So you waited here, with your potions and your surgeon's knife, knowing my mother had accepted you as my wife. You befriended the woman who had taken your place and lured her here ...'

She surged to her feet. 'Good God, are you accusing me of murder?'

'Why not? A battlefield brat, that was what my brother-in-law called you.' He gestured at the house, its grounds. 'How much did all this cost you? Your entire so-called fortune? No respectable woman would choose to live like this, alone. But you did not intend to be alone for long, did you?'

'You are insane! I liked your wife, deeply. I met her again purely by accident, and invited her to stay because she was exhausted and grieving, and should not have been alone. She liked me too.'

'That was convenient.'

'You are ridiculous. Let us draw a line under this. You do not know what you are saying.'

'I know exactly what I am saying, and what I will say to the governor too, and what I will say when they string you up for murder.'

'I loved you!' she shouted. 'I would never have hurt you nor anyone you loved. I could have claimed you a year ago and I did not. I would not have claimed you now.'

'So you say, but —'

'Who did you marry, back on the battlefield?' she demanded. 'The woman you named your daughter for, or a hussy who gave you up for money, and would kill a good woman for a fortune she does not need? I cannot be both.'

He stared at her, blinking, as if seeing the past again, perhaps finally seeing her clearly again, as he had once in that small eddy of safety at Waterloo. But just now she did not care.

'Surgeon Wentworth will attest to my sorrow at Elizabeth's death. I can show you my account at the Bank of New South Wales, and you may write to my man of business. The governor's wife can assure you of my good character. Will that satisfy you? I have been called many things in my life — unwomanly, or impudent — but no one has ever accused me of using my medical skills to harm.'

She found she was panting in her fury. He had wounded her where she was most vulnerable. She was the rescuer, not the villain. He sat, heavily, on one of the verandah chairs, and covered his face in his hands. 'Hen ... I should not have said that.'

'Not called me a murderer? You are the one whose hands are washed in blood!'

Max lifted his head. 'What?' He stopped as a volley of shots rang out, and scrambled out of his chair. Hen followed him. She reached the garden in time to see the troopers finish reloading and fire in unison again at dark figures dragging or carrying others back towards the trees.

Two of the figures dropped. One small figure already lay still. Another stumbled to her feet and tried to limp towards her friends, holding her hand against the wound to her hip ...

'No!' Hen screamed. She ran towards the troopers.

'Hen! Stop! It's dangerous!' Max ran after her, grabbing her arm. She pulled away from him and kept on running. She was vaguely aware of him running next to her, of the sound of Sergeant Drivers's peg leg thudding on the path as he tried to keep up. Of course the sergeant would be with her ...

The troopers were reloading with the efficiency of men who had done it a thousand times, powder, shot, almost in unison. Hen forced her body faster. She grabbed a musket just as it's owner raised it to his shoulder again. Its shot hit the ground.

'Out of the way!' The trooper pushed her away so heavily she fell. But she had distracted him, and the other two as well. Hen gazed with relief as the last of the dark figures vanished in the shade of the trees.

'Miss Hen!' The sergeant stood above her, musket raised. 'Are you all right?'

'Yes,' she panted, struggling to her feet.

The trooper who had pushed her looked at Max. 'Saw them advancing from the trees, lieutenant. We got seven of them. Four down, the others may not get far. Should we pursue?'

'Stand where you are! They are my friends!' cried Hen, scrambling to her feet. 'They were coming here for help!'

She grabbed her skirts and ran to the bodies on the ground. Bodies ... many bodies, fifty thousand bodies around the village of Waterloo, bodies piled and crows pecking ... she blinked, and was in the colony once more, with the sergeant beside her, and Max behind her, ordering, 'Stand down.'

Hen kneeled by the first body. He was a boy she had laughed with, swum with. He had been the first to offer her the wriggling white grubs from a grass tree. She had eaten them purely because he so obviously felt he was offering her a treat. His face had been blown half away.

There was no time to mourn now.

'Miss Hen! This woman is still alive.'

'Birrung!' Hen ran to her and pressed her hands to the blood pulsing from Birrung's abdomen above her tattered skirt. The sergeant stood over them both, musket pointed at Max and the troopers. But none of them approached, though the troopers held their muskets raised.

Birrung stared at her, trying to say something. 'It will be all right,' said Hen meaninglessly. 'It will be all right.'

'Miss Hen?' Hen glanced up at Sal's anxious face. She, too, carried a musket she'd seized from the storeroom. Hen could see her workmen clustered at the barracks, where Sal and Millie must have been serving their breakfast. The workmen stared at Hen, the bodies, but made no move to come closer.

'Leave me the musket and bring my bag!' she ordered Sal. 'Hurry!'

'Yes, Miss Hen.' Sal ran back into the house. Hen kept pressure on the wound. The sergeant crouched awkwardly beside her, musket still pointed at Max Bartlett and his men. 'Looks bad,' he said quietly. 'The old woman over there is dead, too, but I saw the girl near the trees move. I can keep pressure on the wound if you want to see to her.'

'Jessica,' said Birrung clearly. Her hands fluttered, then lay still, her eyes fixed on the sky she no longer saw. Hen lifted her bloodstained hands. 'Over there,' said the sergeant, standing up awkwardly using his musket as a crutch, then raising it to his shoulder again.

Hen grabbed the second musket. She stared around wildly, then she saw the crumple of petticoats half hidden by the trees. She ran. 'Jessica!'

The sergeant limped after her, half turned to keep his musket trained on the troopers. But Max stood in front of them now, and the troopers had lowered their firearms.

'Jessica? Jessica darling ...' The girl was trying to drag herself into the bush, blood welling from her shoulder. She did not seem to see Hen until she crouched next to her. 'It's all right, Jessica. They will not shoot you now.' Could not shoot her, for Hen's body shielded her. The sergeant stood guard again as Hen shrugged off her pelisse to make a pad to staunch the bleeding.

'Hen.' Max began to walk towards them, his men at his side.

'Back!' shouted Sergeant Drivers, aiming his musket.

'Stand down, man,' Max ordered him.

'Mrs Bartley commands here. One more step and I shoot.'

'Take your men away, Max Bartlett. Now!' Hen called. 'You are frightening her.' She turned back to the girl. 'Jessica, you will be safe now.'

The girl's eyes drooped shut, her breathing fast and shallow.

'Here, Mrs B.' Sal dropped to her knees next to her, bag in her hands. Vaguely Hen was aware of Max saying something to her as she hauled out what she needed. But at least his men retreated. He started towards her again.

'I said stand back!' Sergeant Drivers aimed his musket once more.

'Surely you do not think I would harm her.'

'You stood at Miss Hen's own door and shouted at her, and now blood has been spilled on her land and a girl she knows is dying. So take your men and leave.'

Hen poured rum over Jessica's wound. The girl screamed, writhing at the pain. Her eyes opened, unseeing. She struggled to crawl away again, her hands weakly scrabbling at the dirt.

'Jessica, it's me ...'

'Auntie Love?' Jessica turned her head, tried to focus.

'Yes. I'm here. You're safe. I will always keep you safe. Now swallow this.' Miraculously the girl obeyed. Her eyes closed again, this time from the laudanum.

Hen cautiously removed the blood-soaked pelisse. It looked as if the projectile had hit the girl side on, tearing her flesh from shoulder to mid-chest, but had not penetrated. 'Sal, press this pack against the wound. I need to stitch it quickly to stop the bleeding, but you must press against the rest of the wound as I go. Can you do that?'

'Yes, Mrs Bartley.'

'You don't faint at the sight of blood?'

'Not bloody likely.' Sal almost seemed amused. Hen realised vaguely she had no idea what crime the girl had been convicted of, then let the thought go as she focused on her stitches. The wound was wide. Hen had to stretch the skin to close it. It would not heal evenly, and her breasts might possibly look misshapen, but she could not pause to make the stitching neater.

She made six stitches across the length of the wound. Blood oozed between them. She began to add more stitches. Finally, endlessly, she was done. She reached for the lavender oil, the rose oil, the basilicum powder, hesitated, then smeared on a compound of garlic first. Garlic impeded healing, but it seemed to halt infection, too. She would wipe it clean tonight ...

A linen pad across the wound, bandages to bind it. Jessica moaned. Hen shut her eyes in a brief prayer of gratitude — laudanum affected people differently. She had been afraid she might have given too much.

'Good work, Sal. Could you go and make the bedroom next to mine ready?'

Sal stared at her, the suggestion shocking her as the sight of bodies on the ground had not. 'A bedroom, Mrs Bartley? But she's a native.'

'She is my friend,' said Hen wearily. Where did Sal think Jessica should have been taken? The barracks or the storeroom? She realised that quite possibly that was exactly where Sal, and most in the colony, would think a native belonged.

But Sal merely said, 'Yes, Mrs Bartley,' and left, lifting her skirts as she ran.

Hen looked around for the first time since she had begun stitching. There was no sign of Max Bartlett or his men, but Samuel and Lon were carrying a door they must have hastily pulled off its hinges. Hen stood unsteadily, musket in her hands, then found Sergeant Drivers's arm supporting her.

'Leave it to us, Miss Hen. We'll see you back at the house.'

'No. I have to stay with her.' If Jessica woke on the way to the house she would need Hen's hand holding hers. Nor did she want the sergeant to face three armed troopers by himself if Max and his men returned.

But Max did not reappear and Jessica did not wake. Hen accompanied her inside where Sal — the excellent girl — had laid towels over the bed linen. The two men transferred Jessica gently, the sergeant issuing quiet orders for the best way for it to be done. He hesitated. 'I'm going back to check there are no more wounded. I'll lock the gate behind me, but I'll be within call, Miss Hen.'

'Thank you, Sergeant. Sal, warm water and cloths.'

'Got them ready.' The girl had seen wounds before.

Hen gently washed the blood away from Jessica's chest and arms and stomach, then washed her legs, the knees scratched and filthy from the ground as she'd tried to crawl away, as were the hands that had tried to pull her weak body to safety. None of the other wounds were deep, but Hen applied the garlic to them anyway.

'That does stink, ma'am,' said Sal.

'It should prevent infection. Help me pull the towels away.'

'Shouldn't we put her in a nightdress first?'

'It would disturb the wound.' And Jessica might feel trapped within the clothes when she woke, as she had been trapped back at the Parramatta Institution. Hen pulled the sheet and quilt over the girl.

'Broth, ma'am?'

'Yes, please. Add honey to it, one spoonful to the bowl. You are a tower of strength, Sal.'

'I'm a bit small for a tower, ma'am.' But Sal looked pleased. She was back with the broth within minutes, and the medicine bag too.

Hen measured a few drops of laudanum into the broth, then slid the spoon between Jessica's lips. She had to replace the blood Jessica had lost, and quickly. But could she swallow?

She did.

She was young, strong, healthy. Hen believed she would recover.

But what then?

'Miss Hen?' Sergeant Drivers stood at the door. 'There are no more injured people that I can see. We covered the bodies. I didn't like to move them in case their people come for them.'

'Thank you, Sergeant.'

Hen doubted the bodies would be retrieved, not after the sudden attack, and with illness in the camp. Possibly, even probably, the women were leaving the area already. She had betrayed them, not deliberately, but by inviting them to a place that in her arrogance she believed she could keep safe. 'I will ask Jessica when she wakes what we should do, if the bodies are still there tonight.'

'How is she, Miss Hen?'

'I've given her laudanum. She should sleep for a few hours.' She stood. 'I must see Mrs Cook. She will have been worried by the noise.'

'Sal has told her what happened. Millie stopped her coming out to help you.'

'How?'

The smallest of smiles. 'She sat on her.'

Millie was an elephant and Mrs Cook a bunch of twigs in a calico nightdress. 'An excellent improvisation, Sergeant.'

'I agree. Miss Hen, Mr Bartlett is waiting to see you.'

Hen looked at him in sudden alarm. Were his men even now pursuing the people who had escaped?

'His men are waiting by the boat,' the sergeant added quickly. 'I took Mr Bartlett to the verandah. The gate is locked again. Samuel and Ned are in the kitchen.'

'Thank you, Sergeant.' After their shouting match her whole household by now would probably know that she and Max Bartlett had been married. Were married.

Hen flushed. The sergeant's life was bound to hers, as was Mrs Cook's. They were also her friends. She should have told them of her situation, should not have so blithely assumed Max would not suddenly enter her life again.

The sergeant's eyes were filled only with concern. 'Would you like me with you, Miss Hen?'

'There is no need, Sergeant. But thank you.'

'Would you have any objection if I remained nearby?'

He would hear whatever she and Max had to say to each other. 'No Sergeant, no objection. Thank you again.'

She heard his peg leg clunk down the corridor, presumably to the drawing room, where he could hear what was said on the verandah, where Max wouldn't see him. Hen pressed a kiss to Jessica's forehead, then walked through the drawing room, nodded to the sergeant, then out its door to the verandah. Max stood, gazing out over the harbour. He turned as she approached.

'Well, Mr Bartlett, which of us do you think will hang for murder first?'

He stared at her. 'I don't understand.'

'You accused me of murdering your wife earlier. Now your men have murdered an innocent woman and friend of mine, killed a child, and killed and wounded several others, presumably at your orders. I think you would have a hard time proving I showed any ill intent for your wife, but I will very easily demonstrate the harmless intent of and my prior invitation to those women and children you've had slain here today.'

Except, Hen realised, that she had called no doctor to bleed Elizabeth, had dosed her with potions of her own, had not let any other hands tend her. A case could be made, if Max Bartlett chose to do it.

But he ignored the reference to his own accusations. 'Killing natives isn't murder,' he said quietly. 'Governor Macquarie declared martial law here years ago. Any native may be shot on sight if they come near a house or settlement, unless they have a government pass.'

'Governor Macquarie did that?'

'With good reason. You do not seem to realise the ferocity the natives are capable of. Those Indians today were naked and approaching a dwelling. There must have been at least twenty of them. My men acted reasonably in the circumstances. They merely tried to protect you.'

'Protect me! They were all women and children. They carried no weapons. And they were not naked,' said Hen, suddenly deeply weary. 'Two women wore petticoats. The other women had their baskets on their belts. There may be passes in them.' Did Jessica have a pass? Almost certainly at some stage, though she might no longer have it. Hen would have to apply ...

'They were still advancing on this house —'

'They were my friends,' she repeated. 'I'd told them to bring any here who caught the influenza. That is what they were doing. Are your men unable to see the difference between spear-carrying attackers and women helping the sick to shelter?' Who will die now, she thought in anguish. Even those who weren't shot might die, because not only could they not be nursed here, but they must be carried to a place of safety, if one could be found. How many more might die with proper care so delayed?

'The law of the colony may say you and your men are not murderers,' she said coldly. 'The law of God and of humanity says that you are. Please leave my property, and do not return here.'

'Hen, I need to —'

'I have no interest in what you need. Leave.'

Sergeant Drivers stepped out of the drawing room onto the verandah, musket at the ready. Sal followed him. To Hen's surprise her maid carried a musket again, pressed expertly to her shoulder, ready to aim if necessary. 'I'll accompany you down to the cove, sir,' said Sergeant Drivers politely.

'I'll wave you goodbye from the top of the path.' Sal had not curtseyed, nor was her tone polite.

Hen did not curtsey either. She turned and walked back into the house.

Chapter 32

A Cure For Grief

Grief may kill, even if the Death takes other Forms. Grief must be treated with Kindness, Quiet &, above all, Time. Chamomile or Linden Tea may help the Mind & Body relax. Food must be Good, Simple and Warming. Walking quietly in gardens or Woods may be Efficacious.

From the Notebooks of Henrietta Bartley

JUNE 1821

And yet when the sergeant and Sal had gone inside again Hen walked back onto the verandah and watched Max Bartlett and his men sail the boat back to the colony. The waves dappled the sand, the clouds shivered across blue sky, unaffected by the human drama between sea and sky.

She should be inside, tending to her patients, but she needed this, the last time she would ever see him, not because she loved him — she had no idea what she felt, impossible to know, because she did not know the Max Bartlett of today. She did know she hated not just what his men had done, but the ignorance and lack of compassion he had shown.

And she needed to see him gone, from her life and from her property.

The small boat surged through the water, green today under the hovering clouds. It rounded the next peninsula, and then was gone.

She stayed, unable to move. Once she moved it would be into a future that contained little that she valued, and evil she could not change.

The women would not return. They would not blame her — they must have seen her try to stop the slaughter. But their camp had been too close to the colony, had always been too close, and they had trusted she would protect them. She couldn't. They knew it now, and so did she.

'Miss Hen?' Sergeant Drivers stepped out.

'Yes, Sergeant? I ... I need to thank you.'

'There's no need of thanks. I came to see how you were.'

'Quite well,' she said vaguely. She had no idea how she was, or even what would happen now. Would Max pursue the charge that she had killed Elizabeth? She didn't think so — it had been uttered in shock, and grief. But she would not be easy until she knew for sure.

And their marriage? Would he ask Governor Macquarie for an annulment? Or simply vanish, perhaps, to England, where the marriage might be annulled but she would have no say in the proceedings, might not even be informed.

Would Max do that? Who was the man that she had married? She simply did not know. 'Sergeant, please, if you can, don't tell anyone of this.'

'Which part of it?'

'All of it. But especially,' she stumbled over the next bit, 'that my husband is still living. That his marriage was bigamous.' That he and his soldiers had murdered innocent people, that she was praying for night to come, bringing the oblivion of sleep, and that her sleep would never end. 'I will inform Mrs Cook. I ... I should have told you both about my ... my situation. I am so sorry I did not. I owe honesty to both of you, and much more.'

'It woudn't have been easy, Miss Hen,' he said gently. 'I won't speak of it. If anyone else overheard what they shouldn't have, I'll make sure they don't speak either.' He almost managed to keep the pain from his voice.

She glanced at him, but once more his face was expressionless.

But she knew what lay behind that now. She had been pretending to herself that his love for her was brotherly, or even avuncular, because that family kind of love was all that she could offer, while tied to Max. The sergeant would never have spoken of love, she knew. The distance between Mrs H Bartley and Sergeant Drivers, felon, was too great. But he had assumed she was free; bereft of a partner, like himself, choosing to be alone, having lost a love. But she had not lost a love, merely mislaid it. Or had love drifted from her like the clouds?

The sergeant lingered, even though she didn't speak, standing quietly as she looked out at the shimmering waves, the spires of smoke rising across the harbour from the colony. Wood smoke, not the sulphurous smoke from the troopers' firearms, the stench of Waterloo. At last he said, 'Miss Hen, you told me once that life would get better, if I let it. It will for you too.'

'Thank you.' She managed a small smile, then turned back to watch the water. Of course the days to come would be better than today. That was the trouble. This day, and yesterday, could be tucked away with the Battle of Waterloo, the rats and crows among the piled bodies in the aftermath.

But she did not want to leave today behind. She must remember it. She and Max Bartlett, like so many of the soldiers, guards and convicts, had brought Waterloo to a new land. They had been bred in England's decades of almost continuous warfare, of battlegrounds where Waterloo was only the largest, not the worst, and which had accustomed them to slaughter.

Kill the enemy, take the battlefield, move on. They had no concept of coexistence, something even she had not entirely managed, she who had a foreign mother, who had been brought up with other cultures, and had not necessarily seen British ways as irrevocably the best.

The colony's path was set. Auntie Love could not change it, nor Mrs H Bartley. And Hen? What life did she have now?

'Mrs Cook has been asking for you,' said the sergeant quietly. 'She wants to get back to her kitchen but Sal won't let her have her clothes until you say she may.'

'Thank you, Sergeant. I'll go and see her.'

Life, unasked for, began to trickle back.

'Tomorrow,' Hen compromised, 'and only until midday. You still have a bad cough.'

'Half the colony coughs, and they ain't got the 'fluenza.'

Which was true. Consumption and inflammation of the lungs were rampant in the colony, with its putrid odours, damp walls and leaking roofs. 'But you have had the influenza. Sal and I can manage the kitchen.'

'I were in charge of a kitchen when you weren't yet a gleam in your pa's eye.'

'Then you must have been the youngest cook the world has seen. You may get up tomorrow, and only for a while.' Hen handed her a glass of lemon barley water.

'Who made this? There's not near enough sugar.'

'I made it.' She bent and kissed Mrs Cook's forehead. 'I'll help you dress tomorrow. You'll be wobbly as a jelly after the time in bed.'

'And whose fault is that?' muttered Mrs Cook. Then, 'At least you know a good jelly's supposed to wobble. You could have used the calf's foot that girl made as a house brick. Thank you, duckie.'

Hen carefully didn't notice the word of affection that should not, possibly, be offered to an employer, even one who had just kissed your forehead. Mrs Cook gave a polite cough, as if to erase it. 'Mrs Bartley, Sal says the native girl is in the room next to yours.'

'Her name is Jessica. I hope she will remain with us when she recovers. She has nowhere else to go. Do you object to a native, Mrs Cook?

Mrs Cook looked startled. 'Me? Tiger Rose back in the house was black as coal. Best friend I ever had, exceptin' you. Used to dress in a tiger skin and charged more'n all the other girls put together. It was Tiger Rose who brought me extra feedin' when I were in prison. Wouldn't have survived if it weren't for her.'

A friend. Of course a servant could be a friend. She had been blind.

'Mrs Bartley.' Mrs Cook seemed to be using the name now to show that a kiss and the words 'friend' and 'duckie' or not, she still knew Hen was her employer. 'I heard when you and that man were yelling.'

'You understood?'

'That you and he were married once.'

'I'm sorry. I should have told you.'

'Don't bother me none, duckie. I bin married three times now. I ain't told you about any o' them, 'cause none o' them stuck. But I were young then. I'll choose a better man if I dip me toe into marriage again.'

Hen blinked. Hadn't Mrs Cook claimed she didn't have the 'attributes' for marriage? And three times? But probably the three 'marriages' were in name only, not law. According to Mrs Macquarie all too few of the convicts had ever been legally married and, despite the governor and Mr Marsden's efforts, most still saw no reason why they should be.

Mrs Cook regarded her thoughtfully. 'You thought what you'll do when he comes back?'

'He won't be back.' Not after their mutual accusations.

'I'll warrant he will be. You're rich, duckie.'

'He doesn't need money. He married me thinking I was penniless.'

'An' now he knows you ain't. No man o' sense throws away a fortune.'

Hen sat, suddenly stricken. Legally, a married woman's fortune belonged to her husband, unless it had been tied up on her behalf in the marriage settlement or the will that left it to her. Her father undoubtedly would have done just that, had she married again.

All this, her home, her acres — even the teeth in England — belonged to Max Bartlett.

Mrs Cook patted her hand with her monkey paw. 'I knows what you're thinkin', duckie. But there's two ways to get rid of a husband you don't want. The first is a carving knife under the ribs and up, but that's messy. An' don't look like that, 'cause I ain't ever done it. Never had no need. The second is what they calls a nullyment.'

'An annulment?'

'That's it. Say you're a virgin an' your marriage vows ain't worth a fig. An' it's easy to be a virgin as often as you like. Lady Liz back at the establishment were a virgin every month for a year, an' I can show you easy. Just need some vinegar, an' a bit o' chicken skin with chicken blood mixed with water. You —'

Fascinating as this was, Hen had to stop her. 'I really am a virgin.'

Mrs Cook stared. 'What, you? With your attributes?'

Hen nodded. 'I already wrote to Mr Bartlett suggesting our marriage be dissolved, but it seems he did not get my letter.'

'Well, he's a dillydabber an' no mistake to let a prize like you escape. But you're all squared then.' She winked. 'An' if he tries anythin' from now on, you just tell him you'll get a nullyment 'cause he weren't able to do the job, and will tell the world about it. That'll send him flying with his tail between his legs.'

'He won't be back,' Hen repeated wearily. Grief suddenly washed through her like a tide. She remembered Birrung's laughter the first time Hen had eaten snake, the firmness of Birrung's hands as she showed Hen how to use the tiny grindstone the women carried in their waist baskets, the taste of the oily flat bread, baked on rocks and made from seeds the children had collected down at the cove further along the harbour.

The children, she thought with anguish. What will happen to them now? She would try to find them, but she already knew that she would fail. They had gone with the days of laughter and friendship and the opening of a world she had not even had the chance to understand.

Instead she was left with the knowledge that even this peninsula was not far enough away from Waterloo. The loss of Max, more surely even than in Brussels, for the man today was not the one she'd married. Or perhaps he was, and she had merely lost the husband of her imagination, and that was a small thing, compared to the tragedy of the remnant family who had trusted her.

Mrs Cook patted her hand again. 'You've had a right time of it, and no mistake. You tell Millie to bring you water for a warm bath. An' ask that girl Sal to bring you some of that broth you've been shoving at me and a plate of toast, even if it is heavy as a brick, and get yourself to bed.'

'I need to tend to Jessica.'

'Millie can sit with her and call you when she wakes. You have that bath, duckie.'

Mrs Cook had not bathed in all the time Hen had known her, though she did take a bucket of hot water into her room each morning for the usual 'Wash up as far as possible, and down as far as possible, and make sure possible is washed well too.'

Hen automatically lifted her hands to her hair. It felt matted. She realised it was probably blood splattered, and possibly her face was too. She had washed her hands and arms, but that was all. Her dress …

She would not think about her dress, except to give it to Sal to wash and then to keep for herself, or sell.

'I'll bathe, Mrs Cook. And I'll rest. Thank you.'

'We made a good life here, Mrs B. You remember that.'

'I will remember,' said Hen.

Yes, I will remember, she thought as she made her way across the breezeway to the main kitchen. She would remember Birrung, remember all she had taught her, remember there had been an infinity of knowledge Birrung had not had time to give.

She would remember swimming naked with people who were far closer to her than Max Bartlett had ever been. But memory was all she would have. She doubted any natives would return to this peninsula again.

But she still had life, and memory. Birrung's life should have stretched before her, rich in grandchildren, laughter and knowledge shared with the young. What of the wounded, the sick, among Birrung's people. What of Jessica, who had no one, except, perhaps, Hen.

Do not cry about what you cannot help, but save your energy for what you can. Her father's philosophy was good. But Birrung's family had lost more than in any battle, for when a battle ended even the survivors of the losing side might go home. Hen would live in comfort here, while they fled to who knows where.

She would bear the grief; she must bear the guilt too; nor would she ever forget it.

Hen found 'that girl' Sal straining what should be calf's foot jelly but was instead made with chicken bones in the main kitchen. A vast pot of stew simmered. Loaves of bread from the outdoor oven cooled on the benches. Normal life began to seep into the turmoil of the past few hours. Hen smelled the fragrance of the kitchen, and found it good.

'Thank you, Sal. You were magnificent.'

Sal grinned. 'A bit like the old days, ma'am.'

'What were you transported for, Sal?' It was a question most people carefully refrained from asking in the colony.

'Seven years for possession of stolen property, ma'am.' The grin grew wider. 'What I weren't transported for was being a highwayman's moll. Lost count o' the times I had to dig lead pellets out of him.'

'Where is he now?'

Sal lost her grin. 'Hanged in Newgate.'

'I'm sorry,' said Hen quietly.

'Well, I was too, ma'am. Didn't think I'd ever smile again. But I have since I came here.'

'I'm glad. Would you mind asking Millie to bring me a bath? I think I need one.'

'I think you do too,' said Sal frankly. 'Want me to attend you, ma'am?'

'I don't think I need a maid,' said Hen. She saw Sal's sudden watchfulness. Did Sal think that after all this Hen would dismiss her? 'I do need someone who'll stand with a musket for me though, and help me stop a girl bleeding to death. That person has a position with me for life, and all I can do to help her if she ever decides to leave my employ.'

'Thank you, ma'am,' said Sal, suddenly intent again on straining the jelly.

Now to bathe quickly, to remove the blood before she saw Jessica again. And then for the hardest task of Hen's life.

Jessica lay sleeping, her hair dark against the white pillow. Hen sat, felt her forehead, then her pulse, then looked at the colour of her fingernails. Jessica's pulse was steady, the flesh behind her fingernails pink, not white. She was warm but not hot. She would need nursing for a week and no exertion for a much longer time.

Jessica needed a future, too. Hen prayed it would be possible. She could not bear that this girl's life might be saved only for more assault, hunger and fear.

Hen sat on the chair by the bed and watched her.

The light faded from the window. An owl boomed beyond the house. Another answered. A year ago Hen thought owls only hooted, did not even know that o'possums slept all day, that goanna meat was sweet and tender but must be cooked well, and was excellent for Disorders of the Stomach.

The girl woke so slowly Hen did not realise she was the observed as well as the observer. 'Auntie Love, why are you crying?'

Hen had not realised she was. She held a glass of lemon barley water to Jessica's lips, waited till she had drunk, then quietly she told the girl what had happened: that Birrung had died, and the boy, whose name she did not know, and others had died, or were hurt, or not, but had vanished.

The girl listened, looking at the blue silk quilt cover, not at Hen. Her bare arms looked very dark against its shine, her bandages white against her skin. She did not speak, nor show emotion.

'Do you understand?' asked Hen at last. Perhaps the combination of shock and laudanum had left her confused.

'Yes.'

'Jessica, it was my fault. I allowed the men to bring their muskets onto my land.' And I knew they had just come from killing natives, she thought. I should have known troopers would be likely to see anyone with dark skin as an enemy. Her focus had been entirely on Max Bartlett and herself, and because of that, people had died.

'No. Auntie Love, I have known white people all my life. At the Native Institution we were taught that all us mullabu yura, all wirreengga, should be killed if we do not become the good natives who do what the palm skins want. One day muskets come for all.'

Hen looked at her hands, indeed the pale colour of a native's palms. 'It should not have been today,' she said quietly.

'Do not carry this, Warruya Love. You are ngalaiya.' The word meant more than friend. It meant someone who would stand by you in battle. This had not been a battle, but simply slaughter. Nor had Hen faced those muskets with the women she loved.

Did Jessica understand forgiveness? It seemed Jessica saw nothing in Hen's behaviour to forgive. But Hen would never forgive herself.

She shut her eyes briefly. The next question was too much to place on the girl, but she had to ask. 'Jessica, I don't know what to do with the bodies.' They should not be left there for the goannas and the crows.

Jessica lay quietly, thinking. 'I don't know who they all are,' she said at last.

'I don't think you should try to see them. Does who they are matter?' But of course it mattered, Hen realised. Her father had a military funeral, her mother's had been in a church she'd loved, even though it had meant a two-day journey. 'I … I don't think you should see them. You need rest.'

More silence, but not an uncomfortable one. Hen felt herself relax for the first time in a week. They shared this problem.

At last Jessica said, 'There are things that should be done that I don't think you can do.'

'Can you?'

'No.'

'I … I hope no one of your ngurunggamila will come back for the bodies. This land is safe now,' Hen assured her quickly. 'But I … I cannot say it will always be safe. I think your family will leave the area. They may be gone already. I will go to the ngurunggamila at first light tomorrow.'

She should have followed the women and children into the trees that afternoon, leaving Sal to care for Jessica, taking her surgery kit with her, urging the injured and the ill to come back to the house. She had not gone because …

Because she had been too shocked to think. Because she had pale skin, not dark. Because this was her house, and her first priority must be to the people in it. Because despite her kinship with the native women, in a time of crisis she had instinctively taken the wounded Jessica behind house walls, instead of seeking safety in the bush. Even, perhaps, because of Max Bartlett, the faint thread of who they had once been that still bound them.

Hen touched the signet ring she still wore. A married woman must wear a wedding ring, as should a widow. But she would replace it. Today, for the first time, she knew she was not Max Bartlett's wife; nor had she ever been. She had found one gleam of joy in the square of safety at Waterloo that had been quickly extinguished.

And Waterloo had followed her here, the world-view of the battlefield: fight and do not count the dead. Gain ground, one foot, one yard, one mile after another, shooting, slashing all who got in your way. And, just as Waterloo had destroyed the wheat crop, turning it to blood and mud, Sydney Town had turned the beauty of the harbour into the rotting squalor of The Rocks, its cobbled streets strewn with filth, its water undrinkable unless it was strained and boiled.

If only it were possible to take the best of England, the best of France, too, and Portugal, the Indian verandahs and wide breezy streets, the Chinese tea and carpets, the Moorish understanding of anatomy and mathematics, and weave them into a new whole. But everyone, it seemed, was wedded to just one identity, except for her and Jessica. Even Mrs Cook seemed to have known exactly who she was, though her name was hidden.

One day, Hen thought, I will know who I am. So far she had found only what she was not. Not a wife, nor a widow. Not entirely an English lady. Not entirely a surgeon, for without the conversation and experience with other surgeons that was and would always be denied her, she would never have more skill and techniques than she had now. Medicine would move on, but her knowledge of it would not, except, perhaps, from books and journals, and neither replaced the hands-on learning that a surgeon needed.

She was not a native of this country either, though sometimes she might dream of taking off her dress again, feeling the air upon her skin, the tickle of the waves, of striding through the trees with everything and nothing ...

'The women have gone now.' Jessica's soft voice interrupted her thoughts.

'How do you know?'

Jessica did not answer.

'I ... I must decide what to do with the bodies — with Birrung and the little boy.'

'Bury them, as the bodies were put into the soil at the Institution. It would not be ... correct. But it would not be not correct. I do not have the right English words.'

'May I have prayers said for them?'

'Of course.'

'Even English ones?'

Jessica made another weary gesture. Hen's heart bled for her. She poured more lemon barley water from the jug on the bedside table, then held it to Jessica's lips. This time the girl made no move to hold the glass, but let Hen feed her. The news she had just absorbed had weakened her.

'Will they have left a message so you can find them?'

'I know where they are going.' Jessica added a word Hen did not understand.

'That is a place?' It might just have meant 'far away and safe'.

'Yes.'

'You can get there?'

'Yes. They will travel many ...' Jessica frowned '... days ... weeks to get there. It is the wrong season to be there, but it is safe.'

Was it? Did Jessica and her people know the colony was sending tentacles not just along the coast, but over the Blue Mountains now, rowing up rivers to places like Gilbert's Creek? Probably, Hen thought. 'Not the right season' sounded like the mountains, perhaps: country too hard for horses and men with muskets to access easily.

'I can help you get there.'

'No.'

Did Jessica fear they might be followed, or that Hen might reveal where they were? She had so arrogantly thought she could offer them safety ...

'May I stay with you?' asked Jessica.

More tears. Hen did not bother to wipe them. She had so hoped Jessica would ask. 'Are you sure?'

'I would like to live with you.' Jessica looked at the floor again. 'I would like to live with the ngurunggamila and have your house to visit. But now no ngurunggamila is safe. I will wear dresses. I will learn what they taught at the Native Institution. That way I can live. My children will be safe.'

At least my home is better than the Native Institution, thought Hen bitterly.

'I love you, Warruya,' said Jessica softly. 'You gave me food even though I did not ask.' Hen felt she did not just mean the bread and honey. 'I do not live with you just to wear dresses and be safe. I would like to be with you always, to still be my Warruya if I marry. Always, always, always.'

'I love you, too. I … I want more than I have words for you to live with me.' She took Jessica's hand. 'We will hunt possum, we will still swim.' Till more of the land around here is settled, she thought.

'This is good,' said Jessica reverting to the chanted phrases taught to her in her imprisonment.

'I will formally adopt you.' Hen saw the word adopt was unfamiliar. 'Be your Auntie under English laws.' Though English laws only allowed for a mother or father kind of adoption. Laws made for inheritances, not for love.

'Yes,' said Jessica.

Neither girl nor woman smiled. This was commitment, not a celebration. Hen was glad Governor Macquarie's successor had not yet arrived, one who might have an even more violent view of natives. Governor Macquarie would sign whatever needed to be documented to give Jessica legal standing in the colony as Hen's ward, even the ability to own property. The governor would see Jessica's adoption as a way to help civilise the natives, instead of Hen's thwarted desire to be more like them.

Jessica would be safe as long as she wore frilled muslin and neat shoes, a bonnet and plaited hair, or as safe as any woman could be. Hen wondered if Jessica could bring herself to use a pistol …

… but of course she would. This daughter only six years younger than herself had been hunted, imprisoned, escaped, captured, had fought off rapists, had now chosen a life completely different from her family's.

I am her family, thought Hen, and she is mine. Why had she ever thought she would never have a family?

What should an aunt or mother do now? Hen stood. 'I'll go and bring some stew. I'll eat it here with you.'

Her daughter nodded.

Chapter 33

To Remove Stitches

Boil Instruments in Rosemary Tea, then bathe the wound
with the tea before removing with scissors & pointed tweezers.
Dress with Rose Oil after each Stitch has been removed.

From the Notebooks of Henrietta Bartley

Dear Surgeon Bowman,

May I offer my sincere Apologies for my Absence at the Hospital.
Illness in my own Household prevented Me from returning.

Please accept my Admiration for the Work you do for the
Colony.

Your humble Servant,

Mrs H Bartley

She could not face the colony, and not just because Max might
still be there.

Surgeon Bowman probably had not even returned from his
estates to notice she was not at the hospital, but Samuel took
letters to the McDougals and Salisburys explaining Hen's
absence from the Sunday church services and dinners for a few
weeks, and assuring them that if illness struck their families she
would immediately attend. Laura's and Mrs McDougal's notes
in return confirmed that their households remained free of the
influenza, with news of family members, colony gossip and the
summary of three Sunday sermons from Mrs McDougal.

Two graves had been dug on the inland boundary of her farm, an almost inaccessible side of the peninsula that Jessica had chosen. Hen expected the men to object to the work of digging the thin shaley soil. None did. To Hen's surprise all attended the funeral.

No clergy were present — the Reverend Marsden would have laughed at a request to preside over a native burial. The men held their hats at their hearts as Hen said the prayers. The blanket-wrapped bodies were lowered into the soil.

Jessica did not attend, nor any of the household women, as was customary.

There was no funeral feast. Only Jessica and Hen had known Birrung, and neither felt like feasting; nor were there relatives who had travelled from far away who needed to be fed. Jessica appeared one morning with new wounds to her face, self-inflicted. Hen had seen similar scars on other native women, and warned Millie and Mrs Cook with a quick look not to comment.

Mrs Cook had risen from her sick bed to preside over each morning's bread making and breakfast, then slowly stayed up for more of the day as the week progressed. Sal worked in the kitchen or dairy, except when Hen asked her to wash or iron or mend a dress. Like so many convicts, Sal found working with the colony's abundance of food irresistible.

A cow gave birth to a bull calf — a disappointment to Hen, as she would have liked to keep a heifer for the butter and cream that was unobtainable from goat's milk. She suspected the men rejoiced, imagining roast beef for Christmas once the steer had some months of fattening on him, for she had no need of another bull.

Hen showed Jessica how to milk, and the basics of dairying. The native girl shared the tasks with Sal, each with their stool and bucket on either side of the cow, taking turns to churn the butter and to paddle it, black hands and white. Hen now had fresh butter again instead of salt and buttermilk for her complexion. Most nights a pot of milk stood at the edge of the enclosed stove so they could skim off the thick yellow clotted cream the next morning.

The two girls laughed together. Hen did not think she could laugh again. But at other times Jessica sat listlessly, as if remembering the past or wondering about the future. Hen wished she had more surety to offer. Convict women might take a place in colonial society, but Hen did not know of any native woman who had achieved acceptance. Could Jessica be the first? Or was it too much to ask, to expect Jessica to suffer the insults of the ignorant to attempt this?

Guilt nibbled night and morning. She had not just lured the natives there — she had done nothing to avenge their deaths. Even her letter to Governor Macquarie, outlining the events, in case at some later date the graves might be seen and remarked upon, spoke only of how the natives had been shot *by Soldiers who chanced to Land Here* and *by Mistake, thinking the Natives were attacking, instead of seeking Succour for their Illness.*

It was even true.

One day crawled into another, broken only by nightmares of fifty thousand men lying with their eyes picked out, but this time they wore no uniforms and their skins were dark, or by the mopoke cry of the binnit bird that perched in the bay tree slowly growing outside Hen's bedroom.

The waraburra bloomed, the flower the colonists called Botany Bay tea. Hen and Jessica harvested the flowers and dried them to add to the China tea leaves. Jessica approved of them for their health-giving powers and all enjoyed the taste, even Mrs Cook going so far as to drink a pot in the mid-afternoon instead of a mug of ale. Hen chattered dutifully, smiled dutifully, even laughed dutifully, even though she still felt nothing except a grief that would not fade. She did not want those she loved to worry about her.

But they did worry, even if they said nothing. Mrs Cook made Hen drink a posset each evening. Jessica drew her out into the sunlight to sit on the stone ledge overlooking the harbour, as if the sea wind might blow happiness through her as it tussled with the leaves of the trees.

And Sergeant Drivers was there. Always, when Hen sat on the verandah, breakfasting with Jessica, when they sat on the rock or harvested herbs in the garden, he guarded the path from the cove, musket in hand.

The garada returned — Hen did not know the English nor Latin name for them, or even if they had one. The birds' glossy feathers shone as black as ever, screaming and yelling in the tree tops as they inspected what Hen's men had done to the land since they'd rested there before. They stayed to shred the wattle bark and the straggly she-oaks by the cove, then flew in a black wave across the harbour.

Invitations came from Laura, to dine and to a whist party. Hen declined. Mrs McDougal sent notes that were both stern and kind, as Hen missed more Sunday services, and the family dinners afterwards. Hen pleaded tiredness, and reminded Mrs McDougal of the nagging cough that lingered after influenza, without actually saying that she suffered from it. Days passed and she hardly noticed they had gone.

One day I will show you how to call whales, Auntie Love, Birrung had promised. We will make our feet sing in the sand and the whales will answer. Every time I see the sand now, I will remember, thought Hen.

She remembered the women's laughter as she tried to explain why she wore shoes, women's shoes that were supposed to protect the feet but so soon wore out. Birrung had pointed out that if she went without shoes, her feet would grow tough enough not to need them.

Birrung had promised her an o'possum skin cloak for the next winter. Would there be o'possums where the women and children had gone now? Please, she prayed, let them be safe, and warm, with all they need around them to be well fed.

And slowly numbness faded. Finally Hen realised she was waiting.

He came in the early morning, rowing a small boat she recognised as one of William's. She had not forgotten they knew each other slightly: one of her reasons for removing herself from the McDougal household so soon had been the chance that they might meet if he visited the warehouse.

He wore no gentleman's coat, no cravat, no starched shirt points to his chin. Moleskin trousers, a flat hat like any farmer wore … She watched him pull the boat up onto the sand, pull on his boots again, knew he had seen her sitting there on the verandah, writing today's addition to the notebooks she had kept since she was a child. Colonel Salisbury was correct. A verandah was an exceedingly useful addition to a house.

'Miss Hen?'

'It's all right, Sergeant. I will see him.'

'I won't be far away.'

'I know,' said Hen.

The sergeant moved away, presumably out of sight. Drifts of mares' tails streaked the sky, promising a guwara, a high wind, by tonight, but the harbour was so calm she could have seen a penny splash.

She knew now exactly when she would see Max's hat appear as he came up the path. He lifted it to her politely and proceeded around the side to the gate. For the first time Hen realised the eccentricity of the house she had designed. This house had no front door — nor had she even thought to add one, nor noticed its lack before. No carriage would ever pull up there in front of its portico for a guest to knock and ask admittance when a butler, maid or footman opened it. All must enter here either by the side gate, and then knock on the door to the small kitchen, or walk along the house then step up onto the verandah to reach the door that led to the hall, the drawing room and dining room.

She had built a woman's house, one where no master could formally entertain.

She waited for the knock on the back door. It didn't come. She listened to his footsteps on the path, stood and curtseyed.

Max removed his hat and bowed. He wore a black armband, but no other sign of mourning.

'Mr Bartlett. Please sit down. Will I call for tea or have you come to warn me there is a warrant out for my arrest?'

She waited to see what name he'd call her by. Instead he simply placed his hat on one of the wooden hooks placed on the wall for that purpose, said, 'No tea. Thank you,' and sat in a cane chair.

Once she had saved a dress in tissue paper to wear to meet him, washed her hair and brushed it till it shone. Today she hadn't even taken off her apron. She simply looked at him.

He wore two pistols at his belt, but then she carried two in the reticule that dangled from the back of her chair. This was the colony, after all. He seemed thinner and less tanned, but his face was smooth from recent shaving, just as it had been last time, when he thought he would meet his wife.

Did he think of her as a wife now? 'Are you mangi, married?' Birrung had once asked. Hen still did not know the answer to that one either.

At last he said, 'Hen, I'm sorry.'

'For which crime exactly?' she asked dryly. 'Bigamy, desertion, murder or slander?'

'For all of it. Every bitter untrue word I spoke. Nor can I tell you how ashamed I am, how sorry, about the death of your friends at the hands of my men. Killing women and children is the worst of crimes. I knew it then and am ashamed I did not admit it. How is the girl you rescued?'

'Her name is Jessica. She has recovered, though the scar will be with her always.'

'I'm sorry,' he said again. 'I was in shock, disbelief and grief. I know that is no excuse, but it is the reason. I found the letter you sent,' he added. 'It had been sent to the Sydney house, presumably because Elizabeth'—he hesitated slightly over her name—'was in residence there. But as it was addressed to me she hadn't opened it.'

Hen was glad. At least Elizabeth had been spared the knowledge of bigamy in the last weeks of her life.

'I have been speaking to William McDougal too. It seems you are a close friend of the family. Colonel Salisbury also mentioned you ...'

'So you know I am no fortune-hunting adventurer?' she replied dryly.

'I'm sorry,' he repeated. 'Sorry for everything. We could add the seven deadly sins if you like, too,' he offered. 'Vanity, avarice, lust ... perhaps not sloth. I've never been accused of sloth.'

She managed a smile at that. 'I think you are a good man at heart.' She had not been mistaken, that day of battle. She had thought then, and now knew again, that they had seen each other truly. But who they had been then was only part of who they were now. 'You were simply swallowed up by Waterloo.'

She saw by his expression Max did not understand. 'I mean the whole mindset that led to it, those long years of war with France. The colony is built on a world that sees nothing odd in killing thirty thousand soldiers in a day, leaving ten thousand orphan children starving and countless eyeless beggars craving for a crust. It's the right of any gentleman to take whatever he can win.'

Max frowned. 'I have never thought in those terms.'

'Nor had I, till this year, when I met people who think differently.'

'You mean the natives?' he asked incredulously.

'Yes. But these people are the ones being killed. I imagine the way they view the world will die with them. It's a good view, even if I do not want to live their way, or not entirely. Do you know even their battles — and they have them — must begin by mid-afternoon and end at twilight, so the carnage must be limited?'

'That's good to know,' Max said slowly. 'It's true, I've never known an attack to occur in the morning. That means the natives would be unprepared if we attacked their camps at dawn.'

'Guninbada,' she swore. It was the ultimate insult — an eater of human faeces. She stood and paced the verandah. She was vaguely aware of Sergeant Drivers casually inspecting the herb gardens, his musket under his arm in case the chamomile rebelled, close enough to come to her aid if needed. 'I am trying to tell you about a view far more civilised than ours, about people I admire, and all you can do is take that knowledge to make it easier to destroy them?'

'More civilised?' Max stared. 'Have you seen the native gunyas? They do not even know how to read! I can understand you feel protective —'

She walked again, unable to keep still. 'Of course they can read, you fool, though they write on rocks or read the trees, not books. Every native learns to read in childhood. Their gunyas are cleaner, healthier and more comfortable than the rat-infested hovels most colonists and Englishmen live in.'

'Hen —'

She turned on him in rage. 'No native goes hungry unless all do. Their laws make it impossible for them to conceive of a Battle of Waterloo. Can you even imagine a society like that, you with your war-horses and sabres? Perhaps that is why the natives have been so powerless. They too cannot conceive of people so different from themselves, people who assume that they have a right to all the land and money they can possibly acquire, and do not count the cost in lives and misery.'

She waited for an angry retort. It didn't come. At last he said, 'It is not easy to see the world differently.'

'On the contrary, sir, it is extremely simple. At Waterloo the world changed about us in seconds. We who were on that battlefield changed with it, or we died.'

'I would have died without you.'

'I know. It's strange, but until this last month it never occurred to me to imagine what you'd done that day before your wound. You had been killing people. How many men had you killed the day you married me? You were cavalry, so possibly there were many.'

'I didn't count,' Max said shortly. A silence, then he admitted, 'Forty-two.'

'You did count?'

'Yes. I see their faces, too.' He looked out at the harbour, the clear blue water, then added, 'I see them at night sometimes. I can describe almost all of them, if you wish me to.'

'I have enough faces staring at me in my sleep. I do not need yours, as well.'

Yet perhaps then there was hope, for him, and for the girl so used to war she did not think what happened to her patients after she sewed them up.

Suddenly he began to cry, wracking sobs that shook his body. She moved to comfort him, then she wept too, his arms around her, hers on him.

She wept for Birrung, for the loss of the richest friendship she had known, wept for her father, the barren years of unnecessary widowhood, for Jessica and the bitter choice she'd had to make, for Sergeant Drivers, Mrs Cook and Sal, for the whole colony trying to map their lives on the worst qualities of England: power and privilege, squalor and ignorance.

Finally, as if governed by the tide and not themselves, both stopped.

Hen stepped back, found her handkerchief, wiped her cheeks, her chin, then dabbed her eyes, while he did the same to his. She glanced into the drawing room but could see no one. The whole household must have heard. The only explanation for their absence must be Mrs Cook, guarding the door from the back kitchen. Even Sergeant Drivers had vanished.

She sagged back into her chair and, finally, so did he. 'I loved her, Hen.'

'I know. Elizabeth was very easy to love.'

'I would have torn the sky apart for her.'

He'd begun to tear a land apart, but she didn't mention that. Nor did she ask, 'Did you love her more than me?' because of course he had. Hen was the love of an afternoon, and Elizabeth the partner of two years, a woman he may have admired deeply ever since he'd travelled to the colony. Love began and then it built, like friendship, or a garden, or skill with surgery.

They sat silently, letting the sound of the breeze in leaves soak into them. 'Are you happy here, Hen?' he asked at last.

'I don't know,' she answered honestly. 'I love Australia. I cannot love the colony.' Nor even most of her patients there, for hers was the only compassion most of them had ever been offered, nor would they offer it to others. Sydney was not a town that valued kindness, but success, measured in terms of land and riches acquired, or at best the numbers of souls saved in the manner a church prescribed, or a legacy of grand buildings and fenced fields.

'Would you prefer to live at Gilbert's Creek?'

What exactly was he asking? 'To fight a war with you?' she temporised.

'The rebel natives have been dealt with.'

'Killed?'

'Yes.' Max met her eyes. 'But they killed my shepherds first.'

Anger began to grow again. 'Perhaps they were justified, or saw no other solution. Colonists, not just the convicts, assume they have the right to rape native women, to evict families from land that is their home. Did you ever once think the natives might have had reason to attack the shepherds?'

'No,' he said honestly. 'Until a week ago I thought of the rebel natives only as enemies.'

Had he understood what she'd been saying? Could he understand?

At last he added, 'I hope there might be peace with the natives now.'

'You did not kill them all?'

He seemed genuinely startled. 'Of course not. We caught and executed two of the young men. That was enough to subdue the rest.'

She looked at him, unbelieving. Four of his troopers had shot seven women and children there within minutes of their arrival, killing at least two of them, simply because natives appeared from the trees. Those men had not understood restraint. Her men — even under her own supervision — had attacked and captured at least one native girl. Could Max possibly be ignorant of what his men did around him, as indeed she had been ignorant as well?

And Hen had lived with battles most of her life. Max Bartlett had seen but a single season of war. He had absorbed the ethos of Waterloo, kill or be killed, stand firm and defend your post. He had not had time, perhaps, to understand the soldiers under his command, to see which ones enjoyed killing, and which ones merely endured it as their duty. Assuming he was telling the truth now, of course. But she did not think Max would lie. Perhaps it was her lies that had hurt him most.

'Why do you want me to go to Gilbert's Creek?' Did he still feel bound to her in marriage? Surely they had both seen how far they had journeyed from that afternoon on the battlefield.

'Because I need to leave the colony for at least a year, or longer, and the men there — and five thousand sheep — need someone capable in charge. I must go to England. The children should hear of their mother's death, and their sister's, from me, not in a letter. They need to know I am still their father, and always will be, though my life will be in the colony, not England, should they choose not to return. Both William McDougal and Colonel Salisbury speak of your organisation here with admiration.'

In every dream she'd had of meeting Max Bartlett once again, it had never occurred to her that he would offer this. 'I'm not a farm manager.'

'You don't call this a farm?'

She hadn't thought of it as such, only as a home that needed a degree of self-sufficiency. But with some preparation — and the support of Sergeant Drivers, Mrs Cook and Jessica, and whoever else of her household would go with her, she thought it probable she could manage Gilbert's Creek. She suddenly realised that if there were indeed native families still living there, Gilbert's Creek might be a far happier place for Jessica than the colony. They would be strangers, and not her people, but they would be likely to befriend and accept her, as Jessica's people had accepted Hen.

'You and your father established a square of safety in the battle and held it. You have done the same here.' Max gestured at the house, the gardens, the men digging the new land for potatoes, then reddened, apparently remembering his men's actions. 'Or you tried to. And, to be honest, I know no one else who would be capable and who is free to go so far from the colony, and who I would trust. I can't stay there just now, but nor do I want all I have built to be lost.'

She sat and looked at him thoughtfully. All this man had ever seen was the surgeon's daughter and the colonial lady in her comfortable establishment. He had not seen Auntie Love, her bare body in the wind.

'I am adopting the native girl your men injured — as my daughter, not my servant. Her name is Jessica. She's fourteen.' She said it as a challenge.

He absorbed that, nodded. 'She can translate the native speech for you.'

How could a man live in a land so long and be so ignorant? 'She will not be able to speak their language, just as a Spaniard cannot necessarily speak French. Distance means different nations here, just as it does in Europe.'

There were only so many times you could imply a man was a fool without his anger. She waited for it. It did not come. At last she added, 'I will not have soldiers on any property on which I live. There will be self-defence, if necessary, but no attacks.'

Max considered that. 'I leave it to your judgement. You might feel differently when you are there, so far from the barracks here in Sydney Town.'

She had never once thought of obtaining assistance from the barracks. 'Nor will I sail to your home. The Duke of Wellington said that you must ride territory to know it. I would go overland.'

That did startle him. 'That will take weeks. Months.'

'There is a road over the mountains now.'

'Little more than a track, despite the governor's claims, and Gilbert's Creek is three times as far again, with no tracks at all for two hundred miles. It takes only two days by sea and river, if the wind is kind. Hen, the affairs there will not wait three months.'

He was correct. Even now the shepherds he had left might have reverted to not just the crimes they had committed to be transported, but others they had learned. 'Very well,' she assented. 'The first time, at least, I will travel there by boat.'

His face relaxed in relief. 'Then you will go?'

'I have nothing to keep me here.' Only friends, and her home. But as he said, it was only a two- or three-day journey, and she could visit them, as well as check on her property. But there was much that must be said first.

'Max ...' It had been six years since she had used his name. 'You do not have to be bound to me nor I to you. The marriage can still be annulled.' She flushed. 'Any doctor can examine me and find me to be a virgin. The governor could arrange things quietly, now there is no stigma of bigamy.'

'I'm not asking you to be my wife, Hen.' He met her eyes. 'Perhaps I never will.'

'I must tell you that I am no longer sure I wish our marriage to be fact, either.'

He nodded. 'I think we saw each other truly at Waterloo, but we have both changed since then. I need time to grieve, Hen. I had a wife, a family, a family home. I have lost them all. I need to see Juana and Andrew happy, and ensure they have what they need in the years to come, before I can make any decisions about the life I will lead from now on.'

'What if you find another more suitable wife while you are in England?'

'I doubt it. But if you find a husband you prefer, I will help arrange your freedom. I loved you that first afternoon,' he said seriously. 'I think, when we have time to learn about each other, we might still wish for the same things. You said you wanted peace, but adventure too. Gilbert's Creek may give you that.'

It might. It would offer challenge, at least. She needed that as much as Mrs McDougal needed purpose.

She also had far less power than he did to legally end their marriage. While both might apply to the governor here, or the courts in England, until the marriage was annulled he could legally direct her to live wherever he so ordered. He could take control of her property, every aspect of her life. Thankfully, this seemed not to have occurred to him. But managing his farm was something she might possibly find benefitted her, too.

Jessica was not the only one who needed healing. Suddenly Hen longed for time away from the Peninsula, for the scenes of the past months to be less vivid in memory and dreams.

'My friends may be native women.' Hen met his eyes. 'If I find they are friends they will be welcome in the house at Gilbert's Creek.'

'Some were Elizabeth's friends too. They will grieve for her.'

She stared. Her view of Max and Gilbert's Creek ripped then mended in a different shape. Elizabeth had not told her she had native women friends. Why should she? Hen had not shared her private friendships either, in a colony where so many would not understand them.

'You accepted that?'

'Hen, the natives helped me build my first stringy-bark hut. They warned me days before a flood so I had time to get my sheep uphill. I had nothing but goodwill for them, until they attacked.'

'But did your men?' demanded Hen. 'How did your shepherds tending those flocks behave beyond the sight of your house?'

He sat, silent. 'I don't know,' he said at last. 'I never thought to question it. I assumed they were like the tenants back at home.'

'Your tenants weren't convicts.'

'Hen, I can't give you all the answers you want. I truly have never considered the things you talk about.'

'But you didn't object to your wife's friendships with the women?'

'Of course not.' He gave her a wry smile. 'There were no other white women at Gilbert's Creek for real friendship.'

He did not understand. Could he ever? But nor had he instantly rejected her views. Perhaps he could learn ...

'There is no one else I can ask, Hen. Will you look after Gilbert's Creek while I am away? I must go soon.'

A place far from the colony, where Jessica would be safe, where Hen might do the good that had proved impossible here. 'Yes. But on my own terms.'

'Which are?'

'I have the right to hire and fire all employees.'

'Of course.'

'And make all business decisions, though, where possible, I will ask your advice first.'

'I will be at least six months away, and my answer at least six months more. The decisions must be yours.'

'Good. And if you do not return in four years — or are not on your return journey by then — I will have the right to buy the property from you.'

'Yes. But you forget we are legally married. A wife's property is her husband's.'

She gazed at him in horror. So he knew!

'I didn't make the law,' Max said quietly. 'I will never hold you to it.'

'If you choose not to return in four years, you will have our marriage annulled?'

'If that is what you wish in four years' time, then yes.'

Did she trust him? It suddenly occurred to her that while he could deny they were married — she had only that slip of paper and the entry in Père Flambeaux's church to prove it — she would find it much harder to deny if he wished to claim her. She had taken his name for five years, exchanged letters with his mother for nearly two years, letters that had undoubtedly been kept, and which spoke of her marriage to Max.

Yet she trusted him. But was she a fool to do so?

She raised her voice. 'Mrs Cook? Sergeant? Would you mind coming out to the verandah?'

The door from the drawing room opened at once. Mrs Cook emerged, with Sal and Jessica as well. Sal curtseyed. Mrs Cook and Jessica did not. Sergeant Drivers limped around the corner of the house and up the stairs, musket under his arm.

Hen stood and looked at Max. 'Would you mind leaving us, so we can discuss this?'

He looked at her incredulously. 'With your servants? Hen, these are private matters.'

'Not so private, since you yelled them for all to hear three weeks ago.'

Max looked at the small group, who stared back at him, except for Jessica, who looked at the floor. Mrs Cook seemed amused and Sal wary. Millie peered from the doorway. Sergeant Drivers showed no expression at all. Max looked at Hen again, shrugged, and then strode down the stairs from the verandah. He vanished around the side of the house.

'Well?' asked Hen. She sat, suddenly finding herself trembling. 'Should I go? And will you come with me?'

'Yes,' said Mrs Cook and Jessica, just as Sal said, 'No.' Sergeant Drivers said nothing.

'I don't mean you shouldn't go, ma'am,' said Sal hurriedly. 'Just that I'd druther stay here.'

'Be a challenge goin' somewhere new,' said Mrs Cook thoughtfully. She eyed Hen. 'You stay here too long and you're going to be getting yourself footmen and stuff. The colony ain't what it used to be.'

'Jessica? It's a long way away, long past the mountains. Birrung told me the languages change the further away you go.'

Jessica shrugged, still looking down at the boards of the verandah. It was impossible for Hen to read her emotion. 'Someone will understand me. Languages are easy.'

Hen looked at her speculatively. She, too, found languages easy to learn, though she doubted her French was as good as Jessica's English. But Jessica would surely be safer at Gilbert's Creek than at the Peninsula.

She suddenly realised she wanted to go to Gilbert's Creek, had always wanted to. It was what she had dreamed of on the voyage: a vast farm in a wild land, not a small holding on a peninsula, where the rules, both legal and conventional, hemmed her in. But going to Gilbert's Creek also meant keeping Max Bartlett in her life.

She did not want to be married to him, but nor did she want to be irrevocably *not* married to him, or not yet. Her journey from Waterloo had been far longer than his. Despite his actions, some connection remained. Perhaps, eventually, they might even once again stand on the same ground.

'Sergeant Drivers?'

'I don't think he'll come back,' said the sergeant slowly.

The sergeant had always been better at assessing men than she. If Max chose not to return, the decision about her marriage would be made for her. Or did the sergeant let his hope that Max Bartlett might vanish cloud his judgement?

What did she want? She wasn't even sure how she felt. She shut her eyes for a moment.

'Well, duckie?' demanded Mrs Cook.

Hen opened her eyes, to find the sergeant gazing at her. 'You'll come as foreman?' she asked him.

'Of course. Wherever you need me.' His voice and face did not quite hide his emotion.

'Then we will go,' said Hen.

Chapter 34

To Keep Eggs

Eggs will keep for a Year or more if gently covered with clarified Butter or Bees' Wax, melted. Wrap & store in a dark Larder.

From the Notebooks of Henrietta Bartley

Gilbert's Creek
New South Wales
Australia
March 1825
Dear Max,
I hope this finds You and your Family as well as it leaves my Household. It is a little sad for one who loves this Country to know that Andrew and Juana have no wish to return here, but this Land must hold hard Memories for them.

The small brown Frogs with multi-patterned backs are making their sawing wood noises as I write this. I wish that You could hear them, or smell the Eucalyptus from the Logs in the Fireplace, and that it might make you Homesick for Australia. The Frogs saw at their Logs the Day before it rains, but I am assured by Gari, who as I have mentioned before is the most knowledgeable of the native Women, that we need not fear a Flood this year, for the Cuckoos are laying Eggs in nests on lower Shrubs and Branches, instead of high in the trees for a Flood Year.

A Vast Mob of Emu passed below the House Yesterday. At first I thought it an Earthquake, seeing the Earth quiver brown, but the Ground did not shudder. I asked Gari where they were headed but, though she told me, I am none the wiser, alas, for the Native Name meant nothing to me. She also pointed to the south-west, but that was no help either, as it was most Obvious which direction the Birds were heading. My Men snared over a dozen Emu, which is more Meat than we can eat, but I will have the rest rendered down and bottle the Oil, for it is most Efficacious for Liniments.

The last Letter I had from You was dated a year ago. I hope others from You have not been lost with the Ships that carry them, for Mr McDougal says that several have sunk this Year rounding the Cape. That Letter made no mention of you returning to the Colony. Possibly You have made a decision on this Matter and the Letter is Lost. If You have Decided to Return I am happy to continue to manage Gilbert's Creek. But if you have decided to remain in England, I would like to buy the Land and Stock from You, as we agreed I might after four years.

It is necessary to add that His Excellency Governor Brisbane has recently granted me four thousand acres adjoining this Property, extending West along the River. His Excellency does not follow Governor Macquarie's Liberality in his Land Grants but, as You know from my Letters, is a Veteran of the Peninsular Wars as well as Waterloo and His Excellency holds my late Father in high Regard and His Excellency and Mrs Brisbane have also shown me great Kindness.

His Excellency's Policy now is to only Grant Tickets of Occupancy to those who have Proof of Industry and have also already Stock for the Land and can Provide for one Convict for each hundred acres, all of which I have done to his Satisfaction. I already have the Certificate of Occupancy, and the Surveyor and his Team are due next Month to formally Mark the Boundaries, as well as another four thousand Acres which I will have the Option to Acquire.

If you decide to have our Marriage annulled but still wish to return to the Colony, I will build my own House further up

the River. I hope you do not object to me as a neighbour. I have
Friendships and a Life in this District that I do not want to lose,
and Ones I do not believe could be replaced. For the first Time
in my Life I feel I have done with my Life's Travelling, and wish
to Journey no more except in Knowledge and Understanding. I
will keep my Sydney property, for Mr Lon remains an excellent
manager with Mr McDougal's oversight, but the Memory of the
Tragedy there is too strong for me to ever see it as my Home again.

I hope you will excuse what seems a Precipitate Acquisition of
nearby Land, but Rumour, that strong Songstress in the Colony,
sings that Governor Brisbane may soon be Recalled. Mrs Brisbane
also warned me that His Excellency plans to shortly begin selling
Crown Land at five Shillings an Acre instead of the present system
of Grants, in order to help Fund the Colony. Laws Change so
quickly in our Colony, dependent as it is on one Man's Rule,
that I would be Remiss not to act on my Foreknowledge from
Mrs Brisbane.

His Excellency and Mrs Brisbane have included me in the
invitations to the Waterloo Dinners each year as well as other
Entertainments. I attended with pleasure the three Waterloo
Dinners and Balls after the War in England, but now find myself
unwilling to attend again or dance in Celebration. Waterloo was
indeed a splendid Victory, but it now feels wrong to Celebrate what
was Won while forgetting what was Lost, as well as Those who
still must bear the Scars and Poverty of its Aftermath.

Your Mother told me, on that single Day we spent together
when I was looking for You, that You had flung Yourself as far
across the Globe as You could to escape the memories of Waterloo.
I felt the same as I sailed into Sydney Harbour, its Beauty and
Peace so far at variance with the Noise and Slaughter of that
Battle. But with every year I spend in the Colony I see Battle
spreading further and, with it, the Conviction that those who win a
Battle have the Right to take the Land. We fought the monstrous
Invader Napoleon at Waterloo. Here we are the Invaders though
none in the Colony appear to think so, despite the Letters to His

Excellency from the Home Office that Mrs Brisbane showed me, that urge some Restraint in the Dispossession of the Natives. Mrs Brisbane dismissed the Letters angrily, stating that we bring Civilisation. I believe however that Most come to this Colony either as Miscreants or for Profit above all.

I have only just heard that last winter three whaling Ships anchored at the Bay at the head of this River and slaughtered six Men, two old Women and three Children in an Attack on their Camp to capture Women for their Ships. None were taken, and the Natives escaped back to their summer Campgrounds here, but I fear for their Safety if they return to the Coast this Winter, as it seems they will.

As for Myself, I feel even more deeply than when we last met that the best Future for Australia would be a mingling of the Native and English ways and that Both may occupy the Land for the Benefit of All. We British may have the trappings of what we think of as Civilisation, the clothes, the comfortable Cottages, and the Muskets, but the Natives' respect for the land and other People greatly exceeds ours, as does their knowledge of this country. The success of Gilbert's Creek could not have been achieved without that knowledge. I seem however to be the only Person in the Colony who believes this, unless there are Others as Remote as I who also do not make their Feelings widely known on the Subject.

Ten years ago I would have followed wherever my Husband led. I hope I am not turned into a Shrew, nor an Antidote (though I fear my Skin shows the effects of so much Sun). I would not expect my Husband to be led by my Petticoats, but to Respect my Choice to live Here, and in the way I choose, and with those I choose as my friends, irrespective of their colour or social background.

Please excuse my Indelicacy of speaking to You in this Way, but the Oceans between Us, and the Peculiarity of our Situation make it Necessary.

I enclose a separate financial Accounting.

With all Wishes for Your continued good Health and future
Happiness.

I remain,

Henrietta Bartley

Post Script. It may Amuse you to know that Magistrate Bell
of the Hawkesbury has a Novel Way of granting Divorce. If
the Couple can both Immediately proclaim The Lord's Prayer
Backwards he will Allow it. So far None has managed this Feat.
I do not recommend that either of us try!

Blue sky, the shadows under the branches twisting like small
snakes as the breeze blew the kurrajong leaves. Hen sat cross-
legged by the tiny campfire, dressed in her habitual skirt of
stout calico, her fingers automatically plaiting the stringy-bark
strands, while Gari ran the finished plaits through the flame tip,
her hair the same colour as wood ash.

The bark's sap sizzled, making the string waterproof, strong
enough to make a bull-pen or a hammock for a man or a
fishing net. Gilbert's Creek was a mere stream, despite its deep
waterholes carved into the granite rock, and its few fish were
small, but the river that it joined ran deep, its curves edged with
lagoons thick with waterlilies, their stems like a tender celery,
and the thick pollen that made excellent flat cakes cooked on hot
rocks or made into dumplings in Mrs Cook's stew.

Max had chosen good land: vast river flats with lagoons so
thick with duck that Sergeant Drivers claimed he only needed to
fire upwards and four ducks would fall at his feet, rich in turtles
and fish so large they needed every inch of the outdoor oven to
bake them. The country was naturally lightly timbered, and now
that sharp teeth of grazing sheep had removed most of the small
shrubs, the grass grew even more thickly. The sheep had also
nibbled the minyan daisies, with their sweet fat roots, to such an
extent that they had vanished from the land, as great a loss to
the natives as potatoes to the Irish. Yet none of the native women
had told Hen this, but had waited till she could see herself.

It distressed Hen that her own sheep — or sheep she managed — had so thoroughly devastated one of the chief native food stuffs, as well as many of the native grasses that gave them seeds to make their breads.

But, after all, she told herself, the land which had once fed perhaps fifty natives now had crops of potato and corn and other vegetables, enough for the natives and her household too, with surplus vegetables sent four times a year to sell in Sydney, as well as the annual wool clip.

The house that Hen could see through the trees looked strangely like the one she had designed at the Peninsula, though the local rock was granite, not convict-hewed blocks of sandstone. Like hers, it had a single storey with a wide Indian verandah and a walkway to the kitchen, which Hen suspected had been Max's original dwelling, with extensive vegetable gardens and an orchard. Both houses had been built with the same purpose: to gaze out, one at the harbour, one at the river.

The house also bore heartbreaking evidence of the short time Elizabeth and her children had inhabited it — rosebushes out the front, a roughly built rocking horse, cushions stitched with love and filled with native duck down, feather mattresses and quilts. One of Hen's first orders back to the colony had been for Elizabeth's and Henrietta's bodies to be brought back here, to be buried by the rose garden. It was right that they should rest here, for this was a good house, and a loved one.

Max's workforce, however, had not been good: wizened convicts who, without his oversight, brewed poteen out of the potatoes and lay drunk in their shepherds' huts while the dingoes and native cats ate the lambs and who, just as she had suspected, regarded any native woman or native spear or bag of nuts as theirs to take.

Within a month Hen had replaced all but two of them, with Sergeant Drivers as overseer. He knew men. He also knew far more about sheep than Hen had suspected with the few she'd kept back at the Peninsula. Samuel, too, was proving an excellent worker under his direction, and so was young Wurumu, who had not just learned how to erect fences under the sergeant's direction in the past three years, but to ride a horse, and shear, herd and dag sheep.

Nearly a quarter of her stockmen were young native men, wearing trousers and shirts, all of them taught their skills by the ever-patient sergeant, as good at keeping young men in order as he had been in the Peninsular campaign. Wurumu even lived in a cottage, as did the three native women married to Irish political prisoners who had once fought to free their own distant country from the English. Now they seemed to want nothing but their ticket of leave and to learn enough about this country for the farms they'd have in the future to prosper.

The Irish convicts had changed as quickly as Jessica had changed, as Hen had changed, and the land, too, was changing.

But some things should not be changed. Like making the best string in the world.

Hen picked up another strand of bark to weave into the rest. The best string was made from uneven pieces, to leave no weak spots, like a square in battle where the loss of any part would mean the whole failed.

She found Gari watching her. 'What is wrong, Auntie Love?'

The old woman spoke the native tongue, except for Hen's name. Many at Gilbert's Creek spoke both their own language and English now, as well as the native languages of other groups further away. Gari refused to speak English except for words that had no equivalent; nor would she sleep in a wattle and daub cottage, or Wurumu's new stone one. She had laughed and simply said, 'The sky is too low.' Most of her people still felt the same. A cottage could not be moved to welcome a cool wind, or exclude a cold one, to follow the seasons to catch young eels or winter fish, or the early summer blooming of the lilies, rich in pollen, or the orchids with their fragrant sweet tubers beneath the soil.

'What should be wrong?' temporised Hen.

'You are unhappy.'

344

Hen had hoped it wasn't obvious, but Gari saw everything. Hen had no idea how old she was, or even if the natives measured years in numbers, but she was almost certainly far older than the colony. Hen tried to find the words for her feelings. It was hard, even in English. 'Jessica wants to marry.'

Gari laughed. 'Jessica is already married.'

'She still lives in my house.'

Gari shrugged one shoulder. Yes, thought Hen, Jessica stays only because I would be unhappy if she left. A marriage was still a marriage even if the couple did not live together.

'You do not like Wurumu? He lives in a cottage.' Gari used the English word for that. 'He rides your horses.' Horse too was an English word, her voice disapproving.

Gari believed you must feel the earth under you as you slept, and smell its air, to be part of it and to understand it. Hen almost agreed with her. She preferred to feel the land beneath her feet, and had found herself cramped and confined in both body and spirit in the years she had spent in the house in Chelsea, or visiting other houses in England.

But a bed was more comfortable than a possum-skin cloak on the ground, and a roof welcome when the summer sun drank the earth's green and left it crackling gold, or the sky turned into water, for this country seemed to either have torrents or blazing blue sky, never the gentle grey rain of her childhood.

Did she like Wurumu? Hen tried to find a true answer. 'He seems a good man,' she said at last.

Actually Hen had rarely spoken to him. It seemed that the gap between a woman's world and a man's work was as strong among the natives as in English society. But Wurumu was polite to her and spoke English well, though she suspected his English vocabulary was limited to the words he needed for work for the sergeant too used some of the native words these days. 'Do you like him?' she added.

Gari carefully stared at the string as it moved through the flame, not at Hen. She did not answer. Was it because Gari didn't think it any of her business? Or because she disapproved of the cabbage tree hat, shirt and trousers Wurumu wore, and the cottage he had helped build, presumably for Jessica?

Hen sat, trying to untangle her emotions, as complex as the string. Was she unhappy because Wurumu was dark skinned? She now had more close friends with dark skin than palm-coloured.

Yes, of course, she thought. Land, money and position meant security in the world beyond Gilbert's Creek, and for that Jessica needed a husband with skin the colour of a native's outstretched palm, not the back of his hand.

'She's too young,' Hen temporised.

Another amused glance from Gari. The local young women usually married long before they were eighteen, as Hen herself had done. 'She needs to see more of life' would also have no meaning there, where the comprehensive learning of this one ever-changing landscape was essential for survival of not one, but all.

Hen shut her eyes, leaned back and let the tree trunk take her. Old woman trees, the kurrajongs. They would care for you and show you the way. At times she felt again like the girl on the battlefield, keeping a small place safe while wolf teeth shredded men and howled.

'Sometimes I feel helpless,' Hen admitted.

Gari smiled at that.

They finished the string as the children came running: a dark-skinned mob, but some lighter than others. The dogs trotted behind them, with the usual native dog expression that seemed to say, 'We just happen to be going in the same direction as the humans.'

'Auntie Love, we have fish!' Their English was perfect, the accent her own, except for one who had a touch of his father's Irish lilt. The dogs took up their positions on the rocks above the camp. A native dog always had to command the highest spot. Their noses coincidentally pointed to the campfire, where there might just happen to be food.

Hen smiled. 'It is a magnificent fish!' The natives did not eat meat during the hot season they called burran, though she didn't understand why. But they ate fish at other times, too.

A small girl looked up at her. 'Magnificent?'

'It means very, very good. It's almost as big as you are.'

The girl grinned. 'It's for you, Auntie Love. The men bring many, many fish.'

'Thank you.'

A boy elbowed her away. 'We have turtle for Mrs Cook.'

The girl pushed him back, then subsided as Gari made a small noise to show that she was watching. 'Mrs Cook will make turtle soup,' the girl said, showing off her English.

The boy clutched at his throat, as if being forced to drink something terrible. Everyone except Hen and Mrs Cook, who had discovered soup in the kitchens of the wealthy, thought soup was a sad waste of ingredients. The English and Irish poor ate meat three times a day when they could get it. The natives also liked food you could get your teeth into, except for the very old. But even those who could only manage lily bread or cakes or soft fat grubs would not drink soup — good water and good food ruined by combining them.

Hen laughed with the others and put the turtle in her basket. The fish on the other hand …

'I carry the fish,' declared a small boy, with pigeon feathers in his tangled hair.

'No. I carry the fish. My uncle caught it!' An even smaller boy tried to pull it away.

'You will all carry the fish,' said Gari in the native tongue, proving what Hen had long suspected: the old woman understood English as well as anyone on the property, even if she would not speak it.

Nor would she stay at Gilbert's Creek this winter, despite Hen's urging. When the lilli-pillies ripened — sour, but most excellent for jams and jellies once sugar had been added — Gari and all those who did not live in cottages would mend their possum-skin cloaks, then travel down the river to warmer coastal areas by the sea for the winter. Each time they left Hen wondered if her friend would still be among them when the white climber's blossoms covered the trees and her people returned, the young women first, to harvest the stringy-bark and gather food, then the younger hunters and, finally, the older people, arriving when the camp was set, the fires lit and food waiting for them ...

Hen had heard from Jessica that several of the whalers had also been killed in the most recent attack. She did not ask for details, but worried privately that if the whaling captain reported that rebel natives had attacked his crew, a contingent of soldiers might be sent to deal with the trouble-makers.

Every time she went back to Sydney more whaling ships were anchored in the harbour, and the black smoke from the fires as they boiled down blubber wafted from their camp at Manly as well as on her journey up the coast. The whaling station down at Twofold Bay was a permanent settlement now, with vast fires to boil down the blubber. Sometimes when the wind came from the south on the voyage up the coast Hen could see the black belch of their smoke against the blue. If it hadn't been for the sandbar near the estuary that kept larger ships from entering the river and sailing up to its fresh water, Hen feared there might already have been a settlement far nearer to Gilbert's Creek than she would like.

Hen still did not understand why it was so important to make the winter journey to the coast. Four years of long, almost daily conversations with Gari, learning how to use fig sap to snare young birds for baking, or which leaves should be steamed in a pit of hot rocks for skin complaints or even to remove the lice her new convict workers invariably arrived with, and she was only just beginning to understand how much she did not know, not just about native medicine but how they saw the land and each other. Or perhaps she still did not understand at all. There was food enough for all now, even in the winter. Why not stay?

The children chatted and laughed in their own language, six of them taking turns to carry the fish. Hen remembered the days when she had found nudity a wonder. Sometimes as she gazed at the pools in the creek she dreamed of swimming in them by moonlight. But if any of the men saw her lantern and followed her, the gossip would soon get to Sydney. Even the natives did not swim by moonlight. Gari had told her of the bunyip that dragged down swimmers at night though Hen was not sure if this was real or legend, or a story to stop children — and her — from swimming at night when logs or lily stems under the water might snare the unwary.

The children bounded ahead of her along the river flats, leaping over logs left by the last flood, pointing at the platypus that ducked down to its nest as soon as it heard them, at the hole where Caroline the wumbut lived, named for the Brussels landlady who was as strong-minded as this animal that invariably found its way through or under any fence to her vegetables, then up towards the house on the hilltop where Mrs Cook would give them bread and honey or, even better, strawberry tarts or the Welsh cakes rich in home-grown currants that Mrs Cook made for Hen, and which Hen ate in memory of the father who had loved them.

Hen lingered at the garden gate.

She could see all of Gilbert's Creek from there: the river flats where the cattle grazed, the hills of sheep, each mob with its own shepherd to herd the animals together at night so they didn't stray and to keep them safe from wild dogs. Only half a dozen of the shepherds' huts were visible, scattered through the trees, wattle and daub with stringy-bark roofs.

There was the storeroom, stoutly built from stone, with barred windows and a locked door that only she, Mrs Cook and Sergeant Drivers had keys to; the geese, who slept each night on an island in a pool that had once been a river bend till a flood had straightened the flow again, leaving a refuge for the geese from native cats. The hens were in their own fenced run — the only way to keep them safe.

'Good evening, Mrs Bartley.' Wurumu sat on the grey stallion that none of her other men could manage, nor Hen, who rode only if necessary. The big horse snorted and stamped at her, then quietened as Wurumu patted his neck. Wurumu raised his hat, exactly as a gentleman should. His accent was a perfect mimicry of hers.

'Good evening,' Hen replied stiffly. She would have liked to ask if Wurumu had been visiting Jessica, but a woman of either culture did not question the doings of a man she respected.

The horse trotted on. Hen could hear children's laughter in the kitchen, and Mrs Cook's indignant tones.

'Two tarts apiece and no more! Out of it, you little varmints, or you'll feel the wooden spoon on your backsides. Well, maybe three tarts ...'

Mrs Cook seemed to enjoy Gilbert's Creek, with no footmen or butler to challenge her dominance of the house. She dealt with a brown snake in her kitchen by bashing its head with a soup ladle, and an importunate suitor had been served lamb's testicles in batter.

Hen walked around to the side door, then down the hall to her bedroom, panelled with the local red cedar, its wide curtainless window looking out onto the gardens and river, the rosebushes Elizabeth had planted now well grown and in autumn bloom.

But Elizabeth Bartlett had obviously not had time for curtains, with two children and a baby to care for, nor, it seemed, had she enjoyed reading, for the books in the study were Max's or her own. It was strange — Hen felt the influence of the house's dead mistress often, but could not imagine Max there, perhaps because his letters seemed to anchor him in England. But he was not anchored, she reminded herself. In that last letter he had still written as though he would eventually return.

Would his views have changed if he did? With every letter she wrote she tried to show him the people and their land, to make him see what she did as she walked across his acres. He even sent his regards to Gari and to Jessica now, though she did not know if this was from genuine respect or a wish to please the woman managing his estate.

Hen removed her bonnet then changed into a muslin dress, with slippers instead of boots. A proper English lady again, she proceeded to the drawing room to find Jessica, pen in hand, writing an entry in the notebooks of useful receipts Hen had been keeping since she was a girl.

'What are you adding?'

Jessica wiped the pen nib neatly, then pushed it into the potato Hen kept on the desk for that purpose. She too wore a muslin housedress, pale pink against her dark skin, her hair, like Hen's, now cut short at the back and left to naturally curl at the front, a fashion Laura had assured them was the latest kick in London, or had been the previous year when her fashion journal had been shipped. The cuts Jessica had made after the loss of her family had healed to almost imperceptible scars.

'I have added how to use the nose bone of the kangaruh, for ...' Jessica hesitated, miming digging at her arm.

'Digging out splinters or removing pus from a wound?'

'Splinters, that is the word.' Jessica took up her pen again.

'Jessica, I must talk to you.' Hen smiled at the puzzlement on her daughter's face, for of course Hen was already talking to her. One only realised how odd one's own language was when explaining it to others. 'It's about your marriage.'

'Yes, Auntie Love.' Jessica put the pen down, and looked at the floor.

Hen took a deep breath. 'I would like to give you the Sydney house and land as a marriage portion.'

Jessica shook her head without looking up. 'I do not think Wurumu will live there.'

'I know.' Hen had expected some sign of surprise, or gratitude. Jessica seemed to regard the house and its land as no more than a gift of an apple. 'But if you owned the house, there are many men in Sydney you might choose for a husband.'

She waited for a protestation of love for Wurumu. It didn't come. Instead Jessica looked up and smiled. She moved to the sofa and took Hen's hand. 'They would not, Auntie Love. They would take the house and cast me out.'

'But ...' Hen stopped. 'How do you know?'

'I listen and I watch, Auntie Love,' said Jessica gently. 'Here and when we go to Sydney. When I came to live with you, I thought I must learn to dress as colonial women do and speak their English to be safe. But I still would not be safe in town. I am safe here.'

'I'm sorry,' said Hen helplessly. 'I thought ...' That giving Jessica land and money might make her socially acceptable. But Jessica was right. There was even less chance of her being accepted into colonial society now than there had been four years earlier.

Governor Brisbane was a good and able man, a scientist who had almost certainly accepted the post for the chance to study the southern constellations he now had little time for. But he had even less interest in — and respect for — the natives of the country than his predecessor, who had hoped to civilise them even if he had never glimpsed the civilisation already there.

Jessica gazed at her watchfully. 'Auntie Love, I will not move to Wurumu's cottage if you will be lonely.'

Hen managed a smile. 'You will only be just down the hill. We must sort some linen for you to take, and other necessities. Perhaps we should begin tomorrow.'

Jessica hugged her enthusiastically. 'We will call our first child after you. We will —'

A cough interrupted her. Mrs Cook stood in the doorway, as monkey boned as she had been when Hen first met her. Out in the kitchen Hen and Mrs Cook would sit together, chatting over a cup of tea and the housekeeper's impeccable buttered scones. Here in the drawing room Mrs Cook still observed the proprieties. 'Begging your pardon, Mrs B, but the boat's headin' up river. About time the sergeant were comin' home.'

Hen ran for her bonnet and boots again. It was impossible to predict the boat's return, as the necessary stores might take days or even a month to find and purchase. There would be sacks of sugar wrapped in oilcloth, four dozen axes and twelve mattocks and much else, including letters, not just from the colonies but possibly from England too, left waiting for her at McDougal's stores ...

Chapter 35

An Excellent Liniment for Itching and The Whites

Take Native or English Nettles, one Cupful, one Cupful
tender native Bracken Buds, bruised to expel the Sap. Seethe
in a Cupful boiled Milk. Strain and use that Day.

From the Notebooks of Henrietta Bartley

Gilbert's Creek now had a rough wharf down on the river bend,
repaired after each flood. The boat was already moored as Hen
strode down the hill, with Sergeant Drivers supervising the
unloading. He had filled out in the last four years, a small square
man in his middle thirties, whose moleskin trousers almost hid
his peg leg.

He took off his hat to Hen as she approached. 'Everything
you ordered, Miss Hen, except the nails. McDougal says he
can't get them for love nor money, not till the next ship from
England at any rate.' He grinned. 'I didn't forget Mrs Cook's
new skillets this time either, so she won't be after me with her
rolling pin.'

Hen still remembered the first time she had seen the sergeant
grin again. It had been the first New Year's in Gilbert's Creek,
when an emu had crept up behind the feast trestle table under
the trees and made off with Mrs Cook's detailed gingerbread
model of the house.

'She says to tell you there's saddle of mutton with herb stuffing
in the oven. I saw jam tarts cooling on the window sill too.'

'Ah, she's a wonderful woman, especially after two days at sea and Sal's cooking back in Sydney. Sal don't get any better with practice. And here's your mail,' he added, suddenly sober.

Hen took the bundle eagerly. A seed catalogue, a magazine, a parcel that must contain the books she had ordered, and even greater treasure: letters from Laura, Gwendolyn and Mrs McDougal, two others with a Government House crest, invitations probably for events long past and, yes, three from England, two from Mrs Bartlett and one from Max ...

She forced her gaze up from them. 'Thank you, Sergeant.'

She clutched the letters to her, keeping them to read alone. She would need to rewrite hers to Max, no doubt. A hundred of the small green birds flew chattering into the trees in front of her. She smiled. Surely Max could not exchange this for the fogs of England. She had been foolish to even imagine he would. Thank goodness she had not sent the letter, doubting he'd return. A man did not write to a woman for four years if he did not intend to have her in his life, just as a woman did not manage his property without feeling a commitment to him, too.

The fury and tensions of their last two meetings had slowly faded in Hen's years at Gilbert's Creek. The man she saw in memory now was the one she had married, or the happy man she'd glimpsed on her second day in Sydney, not the man of grief and anger. Surely he would see her judgement had been proved correct when he returned: the native men so capable as stockmen, their whole camp helping to roof the cottages or harvest potatoes, everyone joining the vast feast of corn boiling in vats, with butter to spread on the cobs, and sheep on the spit.

Jessica had left the sitting room, knowing Hen would want solitude to read her mail. Mrs Cook would be tending her roast mutton and the fish, probably now stuffed with lemon slices with the help of Bridget and Sarah, the native wives of two of her Irish former rebels. The women had adopted European names to please their husbands, though Hen wondered if the attack down at the coast had also been a factor in their decision to live permanently in their husbands' cottages across the river from the main house.

She managed to sit before she opened Max's envelope, sea-stained and a little mildewed at one corner. It was dated nine months earlier, on 18 June, the anniversary of Waterloo and their marriage. Had Max written it, perhaps, after a Waterloo dinner, or did he too find them uncomfortable, the desperate men she had seen that day now transformed into heroes, the real heroes now all too often desperate and forgotten …

The letter might have arrived the day after her boat had left the last time and so been waiting for her at the McDougal warehouse for three months.

My dear Hen,

She smiled. He had not called her 'My dear' in his letters before.

I write this in haste, before giving it to Lieutenant Pilgrim, who will sail on the St Geraint in two days' time. Forgive me if it is garbled. I will write more fully as soon as I am able, but felt you must be apprised of my decision as soon as possible. I regret it was not made sooner.

I will not be returning to New South Wales.

The room swam like the midsummer air on the newly cleared hills. She looked again, in case she had misread it, but although ink blotted the hand was clear.

Tonight for the first time I realised I have misled myself, and you, thinking I might still return. I need to begin again, in a land with no hard memories. Harry Smith, who has been acting Mayor of Cambray in Picardy during the Occupation, is talking of South Africa, a colony of enormous opportunity, yet not as hazardous or as long a voyage from England and my family here.

I beg you will forgive me for what you must inevitably see as cowardice and lack of resolution. Lieutenant Pilgrim also carries a letter from me to Governor Brisbane, requesting that Gilbert's Creek be transferred to your name, that is, to Mrs Henrietta Bartley. Lieutenant Pilgrim has already purchased my property in Sydney. I have also consulted a solicitor about the annulment of our marriage. He has informed me that as we have always lived apart, and are domiciled at different ends of the world now, there should be no difficulty. It may even have been achieved by the time you read this. I will of course write to you as soon as the matter has been settled.

Please do not think I have not loved you. You are worthy of a far better man than I, and I hope that you will find him, or perhaps even have.

You should know that I will always think of you with love, even if we do not meet again,

Maxwelton Bartlett

Her hand shook as she placed the sheet of paper on the table. She must have known this, in her heart, when she wrote that morning's letter, offering to buy the land.

Nothing had changed. Life would go on.

Everything had changed. And it would still go on.

Harry Smith. She had not thought of him for years, nor Juana. Harry would have sent her his regards if he had known Max was writing to her. But of course Max would not have told him about her. A wife at the other end of the world, known by another name, was easily discarded.

Max had promised her nothing he had not given her, she reminded herself, except on that one day when the world was mad. And yes, he had begun the annulment of their marriage — 'the matter' that needed settling — without consulting her, except for the agreement of four years before, but she had changed her name without telling him he had a wife still living, and both decisions made for the eventual good of the other.

She owned Gilbert's Creek now, or would soon, as well as all that had been in doubt before. And she would be free, as soon as official word arrived from England. And yet she felt no different; even, perhaps, bereft of what she had not even been sure she wanted.

She automatically opened the other mail. Mrs McDougal's first, containing summaries of the last twelve sermons, with a grudging admiration for the new church, where at least the hymns could be heard, and the news that baby Henrietta had cut her first tooth, Rab had ridden his first pony, and little Jean had learned to recite her first poem by Robbie Burns. Gwendolyn's letter also contained details of that momentous event. Laura's three pages gave her details of the last dinner at Government House, noteworthy because it was the first time Laura had been invited there since Governor Macquarie, with his kind views on emancipated convicts, had left the colony.

Governor Brisbane showed no such indulgence, but at last both Colonel and Mrs Salisbury were on the Government House invitation list again. Laura had worn silver lace over a dusty blue silk, and the sapphires her husband had given her after Henry's birth. (There had been rubies for the birth of Oliver.) The convict girl was now every inch a colonel's lady.

Hen lifted Max's letter once more.

'Miss Hen?' Sergeant Drivers stood at the door.

'Yes, Sergeant?'

The sergeant looked at her face, then the letter, then examined Hen's face again.

She flushed.

'News from England, Miss Hen?' he asked quietly.

The sergeant must have seen the letter, and known who it was from. She managed to keep her voice steady. 'Yes. You were right all along, Sergeant. Mr Bartlett has decided not to return to Australia.' She managed a smile, too. 'It seems I am now the owner, as well as the mistress here.'

Sergeant Drivers nodded slowly. 'Good to know, Miss Hen.'

'Did … did you want something, Sergeant Drivers?'

He hesitated. 'There's matters I didn't want to talk about before the men. I heard talk when I was in Sydney. There's been a hunt.'

'Don't tell me fox hunting has finally come to the colony?'

'They hunted natives,' he said bluntly. 'Not far from here, either.'

Hen gripped the sofa edge. 'Again! Where? How many?'

'Down south of here, in that bay the whalers use. Don't know how many were killed. Dozens, maybe, much worse than the attack down river last winter. The sailors were boasting in the shanties they'd got them all. Killed all the men, that is, and carried off the women for their doxies. It's getting bad, Miss Hen. Bad indeed.'

'The governor did nothing?'

'What could he do? There was no one to witness it, except the men who did it.'

'The women on the ships?'

'Will either stay quiet if they know what's good for them, or will have been left on one of the islands, like the whalers did back in Macquarie's time.'

Hen closed her eyes. It had taken Governor Macquarie two military expeditions to prevent Kanguruh Island from being used as the headquarters for the slave trade in captured native women, as well as native boys who could be trained as crew. Governor Macquarie had eventually succeeded, but there were so many islands …

This afternoon — no tomorrow, for it would be dark soon — she must convince Gari, convince them all, that the coastal land was no longer safe. She opened her eyes again. 'Thank you for telling me, Sergeant.'

'There's another matter,' he continued tentatively.

'Yes?'

'Mrs Cook has asked me to marry her.'

Hen blinked. 'It is usually the man who does the proposing.'

He smiled, but she could see the tension behind it. 'Well, you know Mrs Cook.'

She did. Mrs Cook and Sergeant Drivers were the best friends she had in this world, for she would always be slightly a stranger to the natives, just as she would always be slightly strange to them. But Sergeant Drivers was the one person in this colony who knew the long voyage of Hen's life.

She had seen the growing closeness between the two since they had come with her to Gilbert's Creek. She had also known that given the least encouragement, which she had been extremely careful not to give, Sergeant Drivers might have declared his love for her instead.

Mrs Cook would be aware of that, as well.

And Hen might have loved him, if she had felt free to love — loved him as a husband, not just as a friend. The social inequality that would make their union impossible in England mattered little at Gilbert's Creek. She could love him now ...

The sergeant would become Mr Driver, owner of a vast estate. He had steadily been copying the accent and manners of the gentry ever since he was assigned to her. Most in the colony were careful not to enquire too deeply about the backgrounds of others, in case their own pasts were examined as well. Those few who knew his true background, like the McDougals and Salisburys, liked and respected him. They would accept him at their dinner tables, even if they had wished for Hen a more advantageous marriage.

And now she was free. The sergeant knew she was, as well.

Did Sergeant Drivers, too, have nightmares of a wheat field turned to mud and blood, of eyes staring from a wall of bodies?

The sergeant looked at her, his expression impossible to read. 'It's a good life here,' he said simply. 'Better than I ever dreamed. You were right, Hen.'

It was the first time he had not called her 'Miss'.

He waited. For a smile, for her to reach out her hand? She did neither. Could do neither. How could she explain that when you had spent five years believing you were married, you could not suddenly feel unmarried?

Instead she asked, 'What did you answer Mrs Cook?'

'I haven't given her an answer yet,' he said slowly. 'I need to ask your permission.'

She had not expected that. 'Why?'

'Mrs Cook's served out her seven-year sentence. I was sentenced to fourteen years. I've still got five of them to go.' Which was not what he wanted to say, and they both knew it. For a moment she was tempted to ask him to wait — for days, or weeks, or even months — while she absorbed the news from England.

But that would not be fair to Mrs Cook, nor to the sergeant. It would be tantamount to saying 'I might marry you, or I might not. And if I don't, Mrs Cook, then you can have him.' She could not do that. Yet she loved him, and because she loved him, she had been careful not to let that love become that of a woman for a husband, to thrust away any thoughts of what his touch might be like, or even his companionship in the drawing room, after the lamps had been lit ...

The silence had lengthened. The sergeant filled it.

'Mrs Cook wants a proper wedding, in that new church, the banns read and everything witnessed.' He still showed no expression. She knew now that Sergeant Drivers felt most when he showed nothing at all.

'That sounds very splendid,' said Hen cautiously.

None of the other marriages at Gilbert's Creek had been official — even now, few colonial marriages were, or not until the couple found themselves near a church or preacher, by which time they might have had several children.

And she still did not know if her marriage had been annulled or when she might be free to marry. She might not know for years, especially if the ship carrying the letter was sunk, or simply changed its route to another destination on the voyage. Nor could she hurt Mrs Cook, who'd had so little in life, including love, when Hen enjoyed so much. She was sure, too, that their marriage would be happy, for their companionship had grown close over the years. Yet the words seemed torn from her as Hen said, 'Of course you have my permission, Sergeant, and my congratulations too. Mrs Cook will be a splendid Mrs Drivers.'

He simply nodded. 'If it's all the same to you, Miss Hen, I think I'll be Mr Cook.'

And the convict Drivers would be gone forever, Hen realised, just as there was no record of a Mrs Cook on the convict transports. Mr and Mrs Cook would only legally exist as soon as their marriage was recorded, with her and another witness who would not mention the change of name as they signed the register. No wonder Mrs Cook wanted the marriage recorded properly in the new church. Their children and grandchildren need never know there had ever been two convict ancestors.

'It's a good plan,' said Hen slowly.

'Knew you'd understand,' said Sergeant Drivers.

'I do. I wish you every happiness, Sergeant.' And, now that she had agreed, it seemed she could see nothing but the strength of him, his quiet certainty, the hands that could shift a barrel of nails but gentle a horse.

'Thank you, Miss Hen.' Ah, the Miss was back again. But he still stood in the doorway.

She didn't move.

Then the sergeant left, his wooden leg thumping down the hall. She could almost feel his absence. Hen stood and stepped over to the window. Dusk thickened the upper sky to grey, and lit it flaming pink on the horizon, but the sky to the east was cloud black. The rain the frogs predicted would come soon. The last swallow flew up to its nest under the eaves as the first owl hooted down by the orchard, hoping perhaps to catch a mouse or bandicoot before the storm.

Hen stared out at the shadowed land. She had just dismissed a good man, a man she trusted, loved as a friend, a man she knew now she desired, a man who would make an excellent husband.

Why? Did she even want a husband? The scents of hot earth, sheep, the river floated up to her, with the faint perfume of roses.

She had known England, Portugal, Spain, France and Belgium. None of them tempted her to return. This was not the peaceful paradise she had thought, but it was a land to love.

Just now she only knew one fact for certain.

Max Bartlett was a fool.

Chapter 36

The Native Preparations for Childbirth

A Hole is dug and laid with Sand heated over a Fire and lined with Leaves of Several Species. Hot Water is Poured on, creating Steam and in the Final Stage of Childbirth the Mother is supported squatting over the steam. The Babe is caught by the Midwife, the Cord tied, then cut and rubbed with a Mix of Ash not from the General Fire but burned for the Purpose then cleaned with the warmed Ash. Meanwhile the Mother lies in a Bed of warm ash while the Women rub her Stomach to help expel the Afterbirth. The mother then squats over another Steam Hole, edged with paperbark so no Steam escapes. She then lies in more warm Ash for three Hours. The baby is rubbed with Goanna Oil and Ochre to repel Insects then laid in Sand next to her to Suckle and will be Laid in Sand when Not Strapped to her back for many Months, Gravity and Sand taking the Place of Napkins. Dried Moss may be used to capture any Effusions.

These Methods are most Efficacious, and the new Mother is oft striding about the Camp after Three Hours. Such is my Trust in them that I would Choose a Native Midwife over one from the Colony should It be Needed.

From the Notebooks of Henrietta Bartley

The bride wore purple velvet with a low neckline that would have revealed a bosom if she'd had one, a new pearl necklace, and a hat with emu feathers. The groom wore pale hessian trousers, a cream waistcoat, a dark brown gentleman's coat and a starched collar reaching to his chin.

The reception was held at the McDougal School for Deserving Students, Mrs Cook reclaiming the kitchen once again for roast goose, roast beef, a dozen cold pork pies, and not a hint of the elderly mutton or wild duck or turtle, kanguruh or emu so often on the Gilbert's Creek tables. Mrs McDougal, Gwendolyn and William attended, and not just as the bride's former employers. William and the sergeant had forged a close working relationship in the years that the new 'Mr Alexander Cook' had been Hen's foreman.

'Och, he's a fine-looking man,' said Mrs McDougal, looking approvingly at the groom. Hen wondered if Mrs McDougal realised the punch she was drinking so freely contained brandy as well as cold tea, cloves and orange juice. 'Ye'd easily take him for a gentleman.'

'Very easily,' agreed Hen.

'You could have *made* a gentleman o' him too, if ye had wanted to.' Mrs McDougal waited to see Hen's reaction.

'He's happy as he is,' said Hen quietly. 'He is my friend, and so is his wife.'

Mrs McDougal inspected her. 'Your complexion is standing up well. Ye've been wearing your bonnet and using the cucumber lotion I sent you?'

'Yes,' said Hen, quite truthfully, for she did wear her bonnet — sometimes. And she had used the cucumber lotion twice before it grew a coat of mould. She had not bothered to make more: if her complexion had survived her years outdoors, it was probably due to her Spanish mother's olive skin.

'Ye'll no' find a husband on that forsaken farm o' yours,' said Mrs McDougal bluntly.

The whole colony — or its upper echelons — already seemed to know that Leowine Maxwelton Bartlett was not returning to the colony, and that Mrs H Bartley, a wealthy widow and with a fine estate, was thus available for courtship, though they presumed she had waited as his fiancée, not his wife. Laura and Gwendolyn had already produced dinner companions for her — a lieutenant, a major, a sea captain minded to retire to a farm, especially one so well set up, and a 'landed gentleman', who seemed not particularly attached to any of his many properties. Hen had enjoyed their company for an evening, and even accepted a morning's ride with Major Henderson.

She liked the major even more after the ride. He had served in the Americas, and then the Lowlands after the French war, but had not shared in the carnage of Waterloo. He'd pointed out various birds to her with enthusiasm and asked if she had seen any of the strange creatures that Mr Flinders had brought back, including the wumbut. He had laughed as she told him of Caroline's successful raids upon her vegetable gardens. Yet Hen had pleaded the need to help with the wedding plans as an excuse not to ride with Major Henderson today.

I am a fool to think that love will come like a waterfall, she told herself. Surely that only happened at fifteen. And yet …

'You've not remarried either,' Hen pointed out.

Mrs McDougal looked carefully at her glass of punch. 'There hae been offers, I will admit, and nae all just wanting a handy housekeeper. But I remember my Angus. Love's rose has only bloomed once for me. I have my William, and my grandchildren, and more to come, perhaps.' Her gaze was suddenly shrewd as she looked at Hen. 'Ye'll not have bairns nor grandbairns without a husband. You're all alone here.'

Hen smiled. 'I have a daughter, almost fifty employees, and friends.'

Mrs McDougal most carefully said nothing. She had never accepted that a native girl could be Hen's daughter, adoption papers or not. Nor had Hen ever tried to explain to her, or Laura, her friendship with an elderly, dark-skinned woman who wore only a string belt all year and a possum cloak in winter.

Hen did not try once again to change her old friend's mind. At least Sergeant … Mr Cook's … latest warning had meant that Gari and her people had at last not gone to the coast for winter. Hen had not anticipated their grief at abandoning their winter living ground, but Gari wore new scars on her cheeks and forehead. The wounds had healed under a balm of Hen's making, which Gari had accepted, even though her own was good. Hen hoped this was to show that she was not blamed for the actions of others with her skin colour.

Nor had Jessica come to Sydney. Hen suspected the young woman never would again. What was there for her in town? Jessica's new cottage boasted stone walls, and four rooms that could be added to as her family grew. Her husband — though no colonial record would show their marriage — had added the name Alexander to his own.

Hen had not known until today that Alexander was the former Sergeant Drivers's Christian name. Wurumu must admire his foreman enormously to have taken it for himself. The baby, who would be called Love if she was a girl, and have the surname Alexander, was due in December.

'You could stay here a month at least,' said Mrs McDougal temptingly. 'No need to be sailing south tomorrow.'

She could. A longer stay in Sydney would give the newlywed Mr and Mrs Cook time in the Gilbert's Creek main house alone together. She and Laura could go through the fashion magazines and choose fabrics for Laura's dressmaker to sew for her. Curtains for the house at last, too, and some of the Chinese silk carpets that William imported. The house was truly hers now she no longer need fear Max would return and accuse her of having claimed it from Elizabeth …

She would give a dinner party at the Peninsula, she decided, the first she had ever given since her days as hostess for her father. She would invite Major Henderson, too.

She glanced at the man she would forever think of as Sergeant Drivers, tapping his peg leg in time to the music, as couples and even single men — for there were never enough women in the colony — got up to dance. Perhaps she could choose to love someone else instead.

'Ye'll find a lot to occupy yourself in Sydney,' urged Mrs McDougal. 'The school is doing verra well, even if the lads and lassies don't study Greek and Latin like they teach at Parramatta. I've trained over fifty lassies now in how to make a proper cock-a-leekie. There's nae a one employed in our household or the warehouse who can't read, add figures, write a good hand and recite the poetry o' Rabbie Burns.'

Hen smiled at her, the oldest friend she had, in every sense, sipping yet another cup of the not-so-innocent punch, her cheeks flushed, her fingers showing none of the arthritic stiffness that had plagued her when they first met. 'I'm glad they know their Burns.'

'There is nothing like a good poem for expressing the feelings,' agreed Mrs McDougal. She put down her punch, and stood up. 'I will now recite a poem for the happy couple,' she declaimed.

The table grew silent. William looked slightly uneasy — he had evidently realised his mother had been inadvertently imbibing. But the words of the poem she recited were clear.

'O my Luve is like a red, red rose,
That's newly sprung in June;
O my Luve is like the melody
That's sweetly played in tune.

'So fair art thou, my bonnie lass,
So deep in luve am I;
And I will luve thee still, my dear,
Till a' the seas gang dry.

'Till a' the seas gang dry, my dear,
And the rocks melt wi' the sun;
I will love thee still, my dear,
While the sands o' life shall run.

'And fare thee weel, my only luve!
And fare thee weel awhile!
And I will come again, my luve,
Though it were ten thousand mile.'

The new Mr Cook smiled, and leaned to kiss his bride again. Mrs McDougal bowed her head in acknowledgement as the guests clapped, then sat, to find her punch had been replaced by a cup of tea. She sipped it, then helped herself to the sugared almonds Mrs Cook had prepared. Mrs Cook had reminded Hen to make sure every guest ate several of them, for the lowest number of almonds eaten by a guest would be the number of children in their marriage.

Children, thought Hen. Mrs Cook was still young enough to have several children, but Hen had never guessed she wanted them.

To have a child of her own ...

My arms are empty, thought Hen. Max's love had not been strong enough to last ten thousand miles, but if there was one commodity the colony did not lack, it was men. Perhaps love still waited for her, someone who loved the bush and her, and would still do so till all the seas gang dry.

She looked back at Mrs McDougal, sipping her tea. 'Would Gwendolyn lend me her cook for a couple of days? I would like to give a dinner while I'm in Sydney.'

Mrs McDougal smiled.

Chapter 37

A Ginger beer

Take two Lemons, sliced; Sugar, two cups; Water, sixteen
Cups; add to this a tablespoon grated Ginger. Boil till the
Lemons be soft, & cool till the same Heat as your Wrist &
add a pinch of yeast to the Whole. Cover and leave for a
night and a day. It is then ready to strain & drink. Do NOT
seal in Bottles or the Bottles may explode. It may be Casked
in wood, but should be drunk within four Dayes.

From the Notebooks of Henrietta Bartley

Hen sat at ease on her verandah at the Peninsula, watching as the
boat which was to have taken her home sailed without her, carrying
the newlywed couple, twelve barrels of nails (at last), three rolls of
calico, six Dutch ovens, as well as the saucepans, cutlery, bed linen
and other furnishings Hen wanted Jessica to have in her cottage.

The wind blew from the nor' west, bringing a tang of smoke
from a bushfire up in the Blue Mountains that William Charles
Wentworth, Mr Wentworth's son, had been the first white
man to cross, with two companions, four servants and five
dogs. William Wentworth had recently returned from England,
where he had qualified as a barrister but decided not to pursue
the law. It would be interesting to meet him, thought Hen. She
always visited his father on her visits to Sydney, borrowing one
of Colonel Salisbury's horses to ride down to Mr Wentworth's
'Home in the Bush'.

Hen poured herself another cup of tea from the pot. Sal had kept the house well polished, though Millie had left to marry. Young Lon had married too. The gardens, orchards and cow paddocks had flourished under his management. Even the view was much the same, for she could not see the bustling wharves from her peninsula. Sunlight glinted on the water, except for the sweep of grey dapples as a cloud passed over. A ship slowly came into view, flying the navy flag.

It could almost have been four years earlier except for the absence of native canoes, those tiny vessels that seemed always in imminent danger of sinking or catching alight from the smouldering fires used to cook the fish as they were caught, but which never seemed to suffer either disaster.

Hen realised it had been years since she had seen groups of natives casually observing the antics of the colony from the hills behind the houses. She had heard there were places where they congregated or camped, but had not witnessed any, and the only natives she had encountered had worn trousers or a skirt at least. And there was still no way she could think of to find out where Birrung's family had gone, or even if they still survived.

She forced her mind back to her dinner party ...

It was a challenge to be a hostess once again. Her dining table would seat twelve in comfort. The furniture might be shiny but the silverware was tarnished. Sal and Young Lon's wife could polish it, but she must borrow footmen from Laura to serve — she had already borrowed Gwendolyn's cook who, thanks to Mrs McDougal, could read well enough to follow Hen's receipts, for Hen did not want to serve the McDougals the dishes their cook usually produced.

Two courses, she decided: saddle of mutton with Eglantine sauce and wood pigeon pie the centrepieces of the first course, with wild duck if it could be procured for the second course, and fish baked in the French manner, served with sorrel sauce. It was time to investigate the vegetable gardens and orchards, as well as the storeroom, to see what her land could provide. Asparagus?

She left the teapot and cup and saucer on the table, took her bonnet from its perch on the back of the chair and headed down the path to the gardens. All seemed in perfect order, the paths neatly gravelled, carrots in neat rows (Carrots Nancy, with parsley and honey?), leeks, cabbages (one never served cabbage at a dinner party, she had discovered in her first year at Chelsea, and leeks only at a family meal).

Ah, asparagus, perfect, and well manured too, half of it allowed to go to fern but enough new sprouts above the soil to ensure enough for all her guests. Asparagus with hollandaise sauce, and perhaps chicken Marengo, Napoleon's favourite dish, a gentle irony only those who had served in the Peninsular Wars might understand. Potatoes souffle? She looked around, but no potato plants were visible. Where had Young Lon planted potatoes? He must have moved them to one of the new plots ...

'You!' she called to a man wheeling a barrowload of cow droppings up from the lower paddock. 'Would you mind showing me where the potatoes are?'

The man didn't turn. Was he deaf? 'Excuse me! Where are the potato plants?'

He wheeled the barrow faster. She was sure he'd heard. She strode after him and grabbed his shoulder. 'Please answer me when I call —' She stopped, as the familiar face stared at her. Big Lon.

'I sent you back to the convict barracks,' she said flatly.

The man stared her full in the face. His own was fatter and redder than she remembered it, the veins purple on his nose. 'The guards sent me back here.'

'I am well aware of how the convict system operates, Mr Lon. I select my men. I do not have them imposed upon me.' Hen wondered how long Big Lon had been living there. Ever since she had gone down to Gilbert's Creek, perhaps, carefully hidden away by his son on her or the sergeant's brief visits back to Sydney. Hen had not told the house staff she would be staying until that morning. None of the farm workers would have known it yet.

'I'm a good worker,' Big Lon stated. 'You wouldn't have that sparrow grass you was peerin' at if not for me. Nor the potatoes you was after neither, not in this soil.'

'You were dismissed for assaulting a woman.' Hen found she was shaking with fury. To have this going on behind her back and for all these years.

'That was long ago, missus. I'm assigned to me son now that he's got his ticket of leave, not to you.' He turned his back on her and began to wheel the barrow again.

'Stand still while I am talking to you!' Her voice could have been that of any of the officers of her childhood.

Big Lon froze, then turned.

'Your son is employed by me. He has my permission to have convicts assigned here as needed. He did not have my permission for you to return.'

'Take it up with him then. Mebbee you should leave men's business to them as understands it.' Big Lon turned and began to spade the manure onto the asparagus.

Hen found Young Lon in his cottage, still breakfasting. Every other morning she had been there she had seen him working. It seemed his industry was kept for her rare appearances.

'Mrs Bartley!' He stood up, almost upsetting his tankard of ale. He had grown taller and broader in his years in Australia, tanned and well muscled. His wife nursed their baby across the table while a toddler gnawed a crust at her feet. Hen glanced around the kitchen: the flag floor well swept, a fire in the hearth with a pot suspended over it, shelves of crockery, saucepans and skillet, ladles and spoons hanging from the mantelpiece above the hearth. The table held a bowl of late season's apples, wrinkled but still good, a loaf of fresh-made damper, a crock of butter, a jar of jam, and a hunk of what looked like the same cheese Hen had eaten for her breakfast: all produce of this property.

'I thought you were leaving with the tide this morning, Mrs Bartley. You should have told me you were staying. I would have —'

'I have seen your father,' she interrupted him.

She had expected excuses. He gave none. He had evidently believed that his duty to his father — even, possibly his duty to her acres, for his father worked hard and well — outweighed whatever wrong the man had once done. But he must also have known she would object, otherwise his father's presence would not have been hidden from her.

'What do you intend?' he asked quietly.

'I don't know. I can no longer trust you.'

'Without my work, and my father's, you would not have this place as it is today.'

'I am aware of that. But I cannot have anyone in my employ who I can't trust.'

'You're not turning us out!' Mrs Lon clutched her baby.

Hen shut her eyes briefly. She could imagine, all too well, what would happen to this family if she sent them back to the main colony. In time, even within a year, Lon would — probably — be given a similar position. He had his ticket of leave now, no longer condemned to the barracks or roadwork in chains. But that employ might be far from Sydney. There would be no cottage, almost certainly no garden, his family condemned to the squalor of The Rocks, living in a skillion, buying the foul Tank Stream water from the carts that plied the streets, cooking on a meagre fire in an alleyway, the Sydney slums so pitifully like London's, where more than half the children died of typhoid or dysentery before they were four years old.

She could not do that to Young Lon's family. But neither could she ignore this.

'I don't know,' she said again. 'I intend staying in Sydney for a while. We ... we will talk of this again.'

It took two weeks to organise a dinner party, reminding Hen why she had not done so before. So much work for four hours' conversation, restricted to Major Henderson's on her right and young Mr William Charles Wentworth's on her left. He was almost as rugged and handsome as his father, though far more untidy. Hen had already read his *A Statistical, Historical, and Political Description of the Colony of New South Wales and Its Dependent Settlements in Van Diemen's Land, With a Particular Enumeration of the Advantages Which These Colonies Offer for Emigration and their Superiority in Many Respects Over Those Possessed by the United States of America.*

Sadly Mr Wentworth spoke with all the verbosity of his book. Hen was quite ready to agree that the colony needed its own government, but he gave her no chance.

'We must bring Australia from the abject state of poverty, slavery and degradation to which she is so fast sinking, and to present her with a constitution, which may gradually conduct her to freedom, prosperity and happiness, Mrs Bartley,' he assured her. 'I will hold no situation under such a government as this.'

Hen suspected that no position would ever be offered to him by Governor Brisbane, and that an elected government would be of much the same calibre as the men sent by His Majesty as governor, or worse. A colonial governor only governed with the reasonable agreement of the gentlemen he governed, as poor Governor Bligh had discovered when he went too far against the officers' will.

William Charles Wentworth obviously intended to impress her. Sadly the impression was probably not the one he intended to make. She was glad when the plates were changed and she could talk to Major Henderson instead.

A successful evening, enjoyed by all her guests, ending with a lamplit convoy back across the harbour, the lights reflected in the water.

Her dinner would have conveyed to Major Henderson that she would indeed be a most effective wife. It was only as Hen let herself be undressed that night — Sal resuming her old position of lady's maid, for an evening gown of figured silk with lace overlay must be fastened up the back and her hair dressed in a far more complicated style than Hen could manage by herself — that she admitted to herself she would rather have spent the evening in the Gilbert's Creek kitchen with the sergeant and Mrs Cook.

'The man is advocating a nation of freebooters and pirates!' declared Major Henderson. He had called in two mornings later to give her a first edition copy of Mr Wentworth's newspaper, *The Australian*. 'He did not even ask the governor's permission to publish!'

'Does Governor Brisbane object?' asked Hen.

'His Excellency says it is expedient to try the experiment of full latitude of freedom of the press.' The major shook his head. A quite handsome head, and all of him in good proportion. But Hen still had to hold back a yawn as he read out, '*Independent, yet consistent — free, yet not licentious — equally unmoved by favours and by fear — we shall pursue our labours without either a sycophantic approval of, or a systematic opposition to, acts of authority, merely because they emanate from government*. Who does the man think he is? A convict's son, and his father not much better.'

'His father is a friend of mine,' said Hen gently. 'One whom I admire very much.'

'Ah, so that is why you invited the son to dine. No offence intended, I am sure! An admirable old man. But his son ...'

Hen smiled. 'His son loves to hear his own voice, and this newspaper will give him every opportunity to do so. Will you take tea, Major? William McDougal has had a new shipment of Darjeeling.'

The major did take tea, with scones quickly made by Hen herself, having no cook now Gwendolyn's had been returned. Luckily the oven was hot, and the major so deep in reading *The Australian* he did not notice Hen's absence as she made them.

She reflected that she owed Mr William Wentworth a debt of gratitude. If it had not been for his publication it might have taken her far longer to realise that the major, too, bored her witless.

Not quite to her surprise Mr William Wentworth called on her the next day to provide her with her own copy of *The Australian*. She was pleased to tell him she had already read it, but she declined a visit to his property on the Nepean. She suspected both he and his father hoped she would consent to be a suitable wife for a man aiming for colonial aristocracy, now his hopes of marrying young Elizabeth Macarthur had been dashed. Her father had decreed there could be no possible alliance with the son of a convict woman and a father tried for highway robbery, even if he had been released for lack of evidence, and born out of wedlock at that.

William Charles Wentworth was already wealthy; his father was perhaps the richest man in the colony, even wealthier than William's chief competitors, the merchant Campbells. Mr Wentworth senior was loved and admired. But his son would need a wife of pedigree if he were to be accepted by the landed gentry, even the minor gentry of the colony.

The days passed: breakfast gazing at the harbour again; days over in the colony, and evenings, too, sometimes. Hen had been two months in Sydney now: long enough to have bought upholstered sofas for Gilbert's Creek, a pair of large Chinese ornamental vases to stand by her front door, curtains for every room; six Persian carpets, one intended as a wedding present for Mrs Cook; and enough newly imported books to keep her reading for several months.

She had enjoyed a picnic with the Salisburys, and temporarily eased the colonel's gout by persuading him, yet again, to take fish instead of red meat and reduce his consumption of port and burgundy as well as consume a glass of sour cherry juice twice a day (she was well aware he would relapse as soon as she left

Sydney, despite the agony in his feet). She had succeeded in getting Mrs McDougal to remove her woollen stockings long enough to massage a mix of laudanum and soft soap into her arthritic knees morning and night; and she cured William's persistent nose bleeds with an application of warm ash and opium, a more permanent cure than old Mr Wentworth's recommendation of a cold object held to the scrotum.

Within three weeks the news that 'Auntie Love' was back in the colony had spread across the shanties of 'the docks and Rocks', possibly by her first patient, Jem, now walking steadily on his wooden foot and earning an excellent wage as a clerk in William's business.

Most of her new patients were children, and the majority of those suffered from consumption, which could only be treated by good food, good air and rest, none of which she could give them unless their parents took up her invitation to work for her at Gilbert's Creek. But none would accept the isolation there nor what they rightly suspected would be a life of hard work and no rum. The most Hen had been able to achieve was isolating a small girl with the measles so the infection did not spread; successfully treating a putrid throat and lancing a leg ulcer; and stitching and setting the crushed fingers of one of William's men.

There was still no hospital for children in the colony unless they were from convict or military households. There was not even a dedicated ward in the Rum Hospital for children and although the Asylum for Orphaned Children had improved so much that a child might even survive a stay there, most orphaned children did their best to stay away.

But Hen no longer had any faith that she could establish a safe harbour for sick children. The politics of the colony were too volatile. She presently enjoyed the patronage of Governor Brisbane to the extent of dining with him and his wife twice, during which meals he mourned the lack of time to not simply watch the heavens at night or shoot parrots by day, or any other activity than work, sleep and meals.

Her Waterloo reputation had enabled her endeavours so far. But there was no guarantee Governor Brisbane's successor — and he hoped for one soon — would be equally well disposed to her, or to any enterprise run by a woman.

It was time to go home. It was also time to admit that Gilbert's Creek *was* her home and that she had no wish for a husband who might either expect her to leave it or concede its management to him. And even if she found the most amiable man in the world, willing to be henpecked, or Hen prodded, she could not marry any man she would not love till all the seas gang dry.

It was time to give Young Lon her decision too.

It had, in fact, been surprisingly easy to make. Young Lon had worked hard and well for her. This was his family's home, and no longer hers.

No, she did not entirely trust him, but she did trust him to keep the property maintained. And if he wished for his father, too, to have the security and comfort of her property, she had no choice but to accept that. This was a colony where past crimes must be carefully forgotten.

She knocked on the cottage door, then opened it when no one answered.

The cottage was empty. No kitchen table, nor chairs, no coals in the fireplace, no crockery on the shelves — crockery and furniture Hen had paid for. She did not bother to see if the beds and linen had been taken too. She did check the storehouse where the tools and muskets for hunting were kept. The muskets were gone, and the tools, apart from a shovel with a broken handle, and a useless bucket with two slats missing. The Lons had taken everything.

She walked slowly back to the house. Sal was in the kitchen stirring the stew Hen had begun.

'Mr Lon has left,' Hen informed her.

Sal looked at her in surprise. 'I thought you knew, Mrs Bartley. Mr Lon said you told him they must clear out.'

Hen shook her head. They must have taken the cottage furnishings away at night, or when she was dining with Laura or the McDougals. 'I didn't. But they must have supposed I would. Did Mr Lon say if he had found a position?'

'He didn't say nothin' about that. Didn't say nothin' about nothin',' said Sal, a little too quickly. The Lons had obviously poured out their grievances to her.

Should she hunt for them? Tell them that they might return, or offer the money she would have given if she had ordered them to leave? Even tell them she would not have them put on a charge for stealing her belongings?

But the colony had grown too large for her to find the family again easily. They might even have crossed the mountains, or settled on land along the Hawkesbury. Nor did she actually want to find them. She was indeed glad they were gone.

'I will ask Mr McDougal to find a new caretaker and gardener,' she said slowly. 'But I would like you to agree with his choice, as you'll be much in their company.'

Sal blinked at the radical idea of one servant being part of the interview for another. 'Thank you, ma'am.'

'You are happy here, Sal? Minding the house?'

Sal stared. 'O' course.'

'You don't want to marry?'

Sal laughed, showing gaps in her teeth that had not been there four years earlier. 'Go to live in some man's hut instead of living here? No, thank you, Mrs Bartley.'

'A man you wished to marry would be welcome here.'

Sal flushed. Hen suddenly realised that Sal, too, might have a far different life there when Hen was at Gilbert's Creek and she had sole possession of the house. She might have followers who stayed the night or even a week — but on her terms.

'I'm glad you're here, Sal,' she said gently.

She was glad, too, that she was going home.

Chapter 38

A Pumpkin Currie:
a most Delicious & Useful Receipt
from a Friend's Service in India

Take a large hard-skinned Pumpkin of the Colony. With a sharp Axe, break it into pieces the size of half a Tea Cup, then peel each one, & remove the Seeds.

Take one teaspoonful: cumin, coriander, turmeric, garam masala, chopped chillies to taste (I use one but my Friend commands his cook to add six), two onions, chopped, twelve cloves of garlic, chopped, & seethe all in three tablespoons lard or cooking oil on the lowest Heat until the onions are soft, stirring so the Spices do not burn. Add two cups Tamatas peeled & chopped, two cups of the chopped Pumpkin & Water enough to simmer till the Pumpkin is soft, the time it takes to sing a long Psalm six times.

Any Cooked Meat may be added to heat with the Pumpkin, but not Emu.

From the Notebooks of Henrietta Bartley

Dear Major Henderson,
I hope this finds you in good Health. Thank you for your kind Note. I so enjoyed our Rides and our interesting Conversations on the Verandah.

Hen stared at the large sign now adorning her front gate.
Sergeant Cook (he had regained his rank, it seemed) looked at
her impassively. 'Mrs Cook made it herself, to thank you for all
your kindness.'

'It ... it is a most thoughtful gift. And so large, too.'

'Mrs Cook says that all grand homes have their names out
front.' His voice was still toneless.

'Indeed. It is quite time the property name was displayed.'

It was certainly displayed, in letters three feet high,
proclaiming to all who climbed the path from the river that they
were on the property of Gibbers Creke.

'Mrs Cook never did have much schooling,' said the sergeant.
'Not writing and such. Just what Mrs McDougal pressed upon
her.'

'She has more than enough knowledge in other areas.'

'Indeed she has,' said Sergeant Cook.

Hen caught his eye. Laughter suddenly bubbled, and then his
laughter too.

It was wonderful to be home.

'And what is all the commotion about, I'd like to know?'
demanded Mrs Cook, arms akimbo at the kitchen door. Hen
blinked at the sight of her. A bright blue dress instead of her
invariable black, and what had once been mouse hair was now
most gloriously red.

Mrs Alexander Cook had no need to stay in the background
now. 'Welcome home, Mrs B,' she added. 'We wondered when
you was to be back.'

'I'm just admiring your sign. Thank you! I adore it,' said Hen
truthfully.

'Well, now,' said Mrs Cook, pleased. 'It's little enough to thank you. It just so happens them natives brought up a brace of ducks for your supper, and there's fresh peas and new potatoes as well, and two cows in milk so there'll be a syllabub to follow.'

'Roast duck with peas and new potatoes.' Hen thought fleetingly of Big Lon again. 'Couldn't be better,' she added.

'With good English sage stuffing, and orange sauce in the Spanish way you showed me.'

'Thank you! You look beautiful, too. Marriage must suit you.'

Mrs Cook cast an appreciative eye at her husband, standing with Hen's bags. 'Yes, well, he's had his knees under my table for the last five years, so he knew what he was getting. But it's good to be married. It was a slap-up do, weren't it? Don't be dawdling there all day,' she added to the sergeant, 'get these bags inside. I've got a pot of tea brewing, and scones I made soon as I saw the sail on the river.'

Mrs Cook strode back into her kitchen.

Hen gave the sergeant a grin. 'Under petticoat rule?'

He grinned back, a smile of total happiness, perhaps the first she had ever seen him give since that first night they had eaten stolen chicken on the Peninsula. 'Better than any officer in the army.' He followed his wife indoors, his wooden leg tapping on the paving stones, Hen's bags under each arm.

Hen took one more look at her new place name, and another at the fields behind her, the sheep like rocks grazing among the trees and on the river flats, then followed him.

The gum trees had red tips on their leaves from new growth after summer rains. A new koala had moved into a tree near the house, its shrieks so bloodthirsty that one of the garden boys came crying to the kitchen one night, sure it was the bunyip come to eat them all, till Mrs Cook gave him a clip around the ear, a mug of hot milk and a currant bun, and the sergeant promised to show him the 'monster' the next morning.

The fires the natives lit had worried her the first year, till Gari explained they were as important as keeping the rock pools clear in the creeks above the river. The small, well-tended patches burned the land so lightly you could walk through the flames with bare feet — or, in Hen's case, boots. They were arranged to contain the areas lightning struck in summer storms and to bring new grass for kangaruhs and now her sheep. Apparently many of the orchids used for food, for medicine and which were important in other ways Hen could not quite understand, needed fire in certain patterns ...

One day, perhaps she'd understand. She had brought dresses back from Sydney for Gari and the other women, which it seemed they liked for the same reason she and Laura did — they were pretty.

The wool clip had been the best ever, and was already shipped to England via Sydney. Spring honey dripped from the comb into buckets in the storeroom. The first of the year's corn crop had been harvested, the cobs shucked and dried. The natives had done most of the work, employed by Hen or not, pushing off the papery husks, with the customary feasts each afternoon of as much buttered young corn as anyone could eat. Hen regretted she'd missed them.

Jessica bloomed in her pregnancy. She was near term now. She came to dine with Hen that first night, but without her husband. Wurumu might live in a cottage, but Hen suspected he didn't want to dine with knives and forks and the unfamiliar ceremony of a table. Or perhaps women's conversation would bore him.

Hen checked Jessica's pulse and the baby's position. Jessica accepted it patiently, though Hen knew Gari and the other women monitored the pregnancy too. Native babies almost always lived, and Hen had never known a native woman to die in childbirth, despite a quarter of the colony's wives eventually suffering that fate. She was glad her adopted daughter would have the help of skill and experience far beyond her own.

Mrs Cook brought in the duck, with the sergeant carrying the peas and potatoes behind her. 'Won't you join us?' asked Hen impulsively.

'Us eatin' in the dining room, Mrs B?' The woman who had taken in all the goings-on in the 'interesting' house in London looked scandalised at the idea of sitting at a dining table.

'Why not? I've eaten in your kitchen often enough, and the sergeant has eaten at my parents' campfire. Jessica, would you set another two places? Sergeant, will I fetch a bottle of wine from the cellar, or would you prefer ale?'

He gave her a wry grin. 'Ale.'

'Then I'll fetch that. You sit down, Mrs Cook.'

'There's the orange sauce to bring too ...' Mrs Cook hovered by a chair.

'I'll find it.' Hen would probably never have a husband to sit at the table with now, nor children of her own. But she did not have to spend her life dining alone.

Home. It was a lovely word. A forever word.

The curtains hung deep blue against the red grain of the timber that lined her rooms. Carpets now shone red and blue on polished wooden floors. Jessica's cottage also had a new chest of linen, a cradle made by a Sydney craftsman, and another chest filled with baby's and children's clothes selected by Laura. It was everything that could be cosy, from the mantelpiece above the fire to the enclosed stove, selected by Mrs Cook and paid for by Hen.

The cottage was also, Hen suspected, rarely used, except when it was cold, or raining, when a half dozen people or more might shelter there. Why sit alone in your cottage, one or even two of you, when company and laughter awaited around the fire? Just as Hen herself had been drawn to the camps' fires in her youth — far more cheery than tents or billets.

The days lengthened. Heat settled its vast hand across the land. Hen grew into a new routine: breakfast on the verandah with the

Cooks; a day of farm and homestead work, as well as research and writing up her notebooks; and a formal dinner with them in the dining room, with all three changing into fresh clothes for the meal, even if none of them wore formal evening wear.

The ceremony marked the Cooks' change to gentlefolk. Mrs Cook was now 'my friend and lady housekeeper'. The sergeant was Manager of Gibbers Creke instead of foreman.

In between those meals Hen took whatever hospitality she was offered, from a fistful of baked bunya nuts offered by a child to grilled kangaroo tail and soda bread at one of the shepherds' cottages, or potatoes baked in the ashes, eaten with vast quantities of the butter that both the Irish and the native people loved; mulberries plucked from her own trees; the first of the damsons ...

Sergeant Cook grew a moustache and waxed the ends; he was proud of its length and shine. 'Adds a bit of pepper to a kiss,' Mrs Cook proclaimed. 'Just as long as he don't grow it any longer and tickle me back in bed.'

And Hen laughed, rejoicing in their happiness, able to silence the whisper that said, 'That might be me' except at two in the morning, when the owl's *book* woke her, and she found herself still in her bed alone, a bed that would always be empty, because when a woman had loved two men — and one with a love that would not go dry, even if it must now stay the love of a friend, not a husband — when she had wasted the chance of married life twice, life would be unlikely to offer her a third.

Chapter 39

A Soupe of Pease

Take Pease, fresh, four Cups, Potatoes, peeled, four, Butter,
a quarter cup, the Broth of Chicken Bones, eight Cups, salt,
enough. Boil until the Potatoes soften, no more, mash, and
serve it forth. It suits Invalids, and Babies being weaned, and
suitable too if a Governor comes to Dine, especially if a little
cream or chervil, chopped, is added for completion of the
dish.

From the Notebooks of Henrietta Bartley

The boat sailed up the river three days after Christmas as Hen
climbed the path, sweating and smelling of sheep that had
become fly-blown in the heat and damp, the maggots wriggling
into their flesh. The affected wool must be cut off, the maggots
killed with neat spirit, the wounds dressed, all of which the
sergeant had instructed the men how to do, but she still liked to
check it had been done.

And there was the boat, with four men in it, two dressed as
gentlemen, one with a clergyman's collar, the other two evidently
the sailors.

She glanced down at her stained skirt, her bonnet trailing in
her hand. Her hair had not seen a brush since the morning. But
the men in the boat had seen her. She could not politely vanish
to the house now. She began to walk towards the dock, where
the sailors were already tethering the craft, then found she had

two shadows, the sergeant descending from the house, musket in hand, then Wurumu was loping up from the shearing shed.

One of the gentlemen strode up, leaving the other to supervise the unpacking. Suddenly she stopped, staring at him.

Max.

Vaguely she was aware of the sergeant gesturing to Wurumu. They melted back as Max reached her, smiling, removing his hat, smiling, smiling, smiling as if he had no doubt about his welcome. A Max who looked heartbreakingly like the man she had seen that morning five and a half years earlier with Elizabeth: a happy man coming to meet his wife.

'Hen!'

For one heart-cold moment she thought he was going to kiss her. Instead he grasped her hands, lifted one towards his lips, hesitated, then laughed. 'They're filthy!'

'Dagging sheep,' said Hen briefly.

'The place is looking wonderful. You are looking wonderful. Stained dress and all. You have no idea how good it is to be back.'

She stared at him. 'Max ... you wrote me a most decided letter saying you would never return.'

'Ah, Bartlett, is this your good lady wife?' The man was fifty perhaps, white hair drawn back in the old-fashioned style as he removed his hat and bowed to her. 'The Reverend Professor Pilgrim, Balliol College and the London Zoological Society. I enjoyed your paper on the habits of the wumbut. Bartlett here says you study the native medicines, too, a particular interest of mine. I wonder if you have come across the sugar bush they have described in Van Diemen's Land?'

The cannon had not exploded across their square at Waterloo. It was the only explanation. She was suddenly twisted into the life she and Max would have had if they had not been parted. Then Max said, 'Perhaps we could leave that till later, Professor. Hen, I know this is a surprise.'

'Indeed,' Hen managed. 'Please, both of you, come up to the house. Your men will bring your luggage. Professor Pilgrim, I would like to introduce my friend and housekeeper, Mrs Alexander Cook ...'

Mrs Cook had not only removed her apron, she must have flung off her cotton dress and replaced it with one of puce silk. She curtseyed, as a lady might to a gentleman, not as a servant. 'Welcome to Gilbert's Creek,' she said, her accent close to Hen's own. Hen noticed with amusement that Max did not seem to recognise the woman he had met almost five years before.

'Mrs Cook, this is the Reverend Professor Pilgrim and ... and Mr Max Bartlett. Professor, Max, this is my manager, Mr Alexander Cook, and my head stockman, Wurumu Alexander, who is married to my ward, Jessica.'

The palm skins bowed. So did Wurumu, so fractionally later that probably only Hen realised his was in imitation. Max glanced at the sign on the gate, blinked, then grinned at her.

Hen ignored the grin. 'I ... I must change. Mrs Cook, would you mind showing Max and the professor to their rooms? You will want your old one, Max.' She had chosen not to use his, nor Elizabeth's. 'Tea on the verandah, please?'

'Certainly, Mrs Bartley,' said the newly refined Mrs Cook, only a sideways glance giving due warning that if the gentlemen were going to be followed by footmen and a butler, Mrs Cook and Hen would be having strong words in private.

And at last Hen was alone. She repressed an urge to have hysterics, quickly stripped off her stained calico and replaced it with green silk, hauled off her boots and cotton stockings and shoved her feet into slippers — she did not have time for silk stockings and garters — washed hands and face in the wash bowl and was drying them when a knock came at the door.

She opened it. Max looked at her, not smiling now. 'May I come in?'

She stood aside as he did so, thinking he was the only man to have ever entered her bedroom except her father. But Max *was* her husband ...

'I'm sorry,' he said. 'I'd assumed you would be pleased. I realise now I should have written, but I didn't want to wait. Mrs McDougal said you had refused any attachment. I thought ...'

'Mrs McDougal?'

'We have corresponded since I left the colony,' he said quietly.

'I don't understand. Your letter was so ... decided. I assumed I was free.'

'You were free. Are free. Or will be, if you choose.' He ran his fingers through his hair. 'I am not doing this very well. I had to grieve, that first year. I could not let myself even wonder how much I loved you till I had mourned Elizabeth and Henrietta. And when I knew I wanted to be your husband, I realised I had to give you the same chance to decide as I'd had, the chance you'd never had, while I'd believed for years that I was free.'

'You truly always meant to come back to the colony?'

Max hesitated. 'Let us say I always hoped I would want to come back. I love this country deeply. I loved you, too, but both loves seemed broken and I didn't know if they would mend.'

And Mrs McDougal had told him Hen had indeed inspected potential husbands, and had wanted none of them. Mrs McDougal, the one woman in the colony who knew the entire story of her marriage, the one woman confident enough in her own moral world to interfere in it. Mrs McDougal, quoting to her softly, 'And I will love ye true, my dear, till all the seas gang dry.' Offering her a choice, but also making sure Hen would know her love was true when she finally reclaimed it.

'But you made Gilbert's Creek over to me.'

'If I am your husband, remember, it belongs to me anyway. But only if I am your husband.'

'You said you would have the marriage annulled,' she said slowly.

'I have, or almost. It merely needs your signature on the documents I brought with me. Once you sign that, and then the deed to Gilbert's Creek, you are free. It is your choice to make, Hen. Will you accept me as husband, at last?'

She gazed at him. 'You must be confident I will say yes, to have sailed halfway across the world again.'

'I am not confident at all,' he said tensely. 'If you say no, then Gilbert's Creek is yours, as I promised. It is now more yours than mine anyway. Hen, I've gone about this badly. I imagined sailing up with the professor. You would enjoy talking to him and ...'

'And after dinner someone would play the piano the house still lacks, and we would waft out to the terrace, which we do not have either, and you would propose to me with the scent of roses, which are not in bloom in this heat?'

'Something like that. I did hope bringing the professor would help my case. He has been demanding information on wumbuts and other creatures on this country all the way here.' He grinned. 'He tells me the London Zoological Society are even considering admitting women to their membership now.'

'A professor is certainly better than a mob of troopers.'

'Hen, I also have a marriage licence. I know we are legally married, but not in the eyes of the colony. The professor is empowered to marry us. He knows our true situation,' he added quickly. 'But rather than make that public, a second wedding here, discreetly, would stifle any gossip.'

She gazed at him. He had lied to her once more, and once more with the best intentions. But he offered honesty now, and deserved the same from her.

'I don't know,' she said slowly. 'I am not saying no.'

He smiled, though it was not the confident smile that had met her. 'La, sir, this is so sudden.'

'Exactly that,' she admitted.

'I will force you to nothing, Hen.'

Except he was, by the mere fact of existing. Where would he go, if she denied him Gilbert's Creek? Could they live side by side if she left this part of the property to him, and moved to her own?

'Tea,' she said, longing for a cup. Longing for certainty. Longing, she realised, for the one thing that would make this day the happiest she had known. Love.

She simply did not think she loved him.

Dinner, made bearable only by Professor Pilgrim's questions of Jessica, demanding a comparison of the saps of every native tree she knew. An amiable old gentleman, Hen thought, till she caught him glancing at Max as he carved the mutton and realised Professor Pilgrim was carefully easing the awkwardness. Max had not queried Jessica's presence, nor, thankfully, did the young woman seem to remember him from the slaughter back in Sydney. She sat, a full-blown rose of pregnancy, laughing as the professor mispronounced a word.

Wurumu had once again not come with her, although invited. Hen might never know why not, she saw, for there were matters about the interactions of men and women that Gari would not discuss, nor Jessica, or not with her.

Mrs Cook and the sergeant had not joined them at the table either. There would have been no one to serve the meal as it should be served in a gentleman's residence, and every chance Max would have remembered them halfway through the apple pancakes, seeing past the newly red hair and the sergeant's waxed moustache to the convicts he had met at her property in Sydney.

The men pleaded weariness after their journey, to Hen's relief, not even sitting with the port when she rose from the table. Nor did Max try to bid her a private good night, for which she was grateful. Jessica also left without querying her about Max. How could she have explained their relationship, when she didn't understand it herself?

She closed her bedroom door and began to unbutton her dress.

The discreet knock on the door was followed by its opening. She wrapped her arms around her dress to pull it together, then relaxed as Mrs Cook said softly, 'I waited till his nibs was safe in his room. You shut the door on him?'

Hen managed a smile. 'He didn't ask.'

'More fool him, then. No judge of men, neither. I've put his two in the old barracks, and made sure the courtyard gates is locked, and the house too. I wouldn't put it past either o' them to be dimble damblers.'

'You think I shouldn't ... Max and I shouldn't ...'

'I ain't sayin' that at all.' Mrs Cook sat on Hen's bed. 'I think you ought to take him.'

'I don't love him,' said Hen slowly. 'Everything I felt for him back then has gone.'

'Well, what did you expect?' demanded Mrs Cook. 'That all the birds would start singing and a sunbeam would light his face so you knew he was the one?'

'Something like that. It was like that the day we met.'

'When you both thought you might die and had to hurry up and love?'

'If I marry him ... agree to be married to him ... things will change.'

'You mean he won't want me and Alexander at his dinner table, nor breakfast neither? That ain't the end of the world, duckie. Things is goin' to change anyway. I'm breedin'.'

Hen tried to show neither the pang, nor the surprise. 'That's wonderful!'

'It is at that. I'm almost three months gone now. An' I reckon if I can do it once, I can do it again too. I'd like a passel o' brats. I'd like them to play with yours, too. Duckie, love can grow, like it did for me and Alexander. That Max is a good man — one thing I learned back at the establishment is how to judge a man. He's clean —'

'Well, yes,' said Hen.

'You'd be surprised who ain't. He'll let you tell him what's what, too, an' there ain't many men who's strong enough to accept a woman like you, or me.'

'Do you think he loves me?'

'I think he loves the idea of bein' in love with you. Havin' you and this place an' brats running round yer ankles. An' that's what you want too. Me and Alexander,' she added casually, 'might build a house of our own. Even get a grant of land for it, next to yours. I'd train up someone to take me place here, and Alexander would be around if needed.'

And not getting in Max's way, as he resumed the reins of the property. Removing the echoes of what might have been between Hen and the sergeant. A house of her own for Mrs Cook, who had never had one, who never would have one if Hen stayed unmarried, for the sergeant would never leave her here alone.

'Love can grow, duckie.' Mrs Cook winked. 'An' I picked up a few tips at the establishment, which I'll kindly share with you, if it wants manuring, so to speak.' She stood, stepped over to Hen, still standing unbuttoned, kissed her cheek, and slipped out the door.

Hen undressed slowly. Unwillingly she faced the truth of all Mrs Cook had said. If she accepted Max all of them might be better off, including herself. And yes, love for Max probably would grow, even without Mrs Cook's helpful offer of manure. If she had met Max the previous winter she might be in love with him now.

They might even build the paradise she had dreamed of, her family and the Cooks', Jessica's and Wurumu's, a community of friendship and understanding. She pulled on her nightdress, trying to see what might be gained instead of lost. Children. Friendship — for she had no doubt Max would be beguiling company. His invitation to the professor had been the best gift he could have brought her. A land of peace and happiness.

She woke to the scream of geese, protesting at strangers; a musket shot; the blaze of a lantern in front of her all mixed with the pain of a hand grabbing her hair, pulling her up and awake.

A face leered at her. 'It's me, Mrs B,' said Big Lon, and grinned his rum-soaked fumes at her.

Chapter 40

To Waterproof Boots

Take Candlewax, one part, Oil of the Olive, Almond or Mutton fat, two parts. Melt both together. Apply with a Rag weekly, and Polish well.

From the Notebooks of Henrietta Bartley

He had lost his front teeth in the past months, from brawling or even scurvy perhaps, away from the vegetables of her gardens.

Instinctively she kicked. He laughed, expecting it, holding her at arm's length. He did not expect her teeth as she twisted, biting so hard into his wrist that she felt bone. He screamed, dropped her, pressed his other hand to the welling blood. She scrabbled across the floor, trying to get to the pistols under her pillow. His boot met her ribs.

'Oh no you don't, my lady.'

'Help!' she managed, but knew it was futile even as she drew breath. Fires leaped out the window: the nearby shepherds' cottages. Were the men and their wives being burned in their beds? Another musket barked, and what sounded like a pistol shot.

Men — strangers — laughed down the corridor. She managed to stagger to her feet, tried to duck past him to the door. The old man grabbed her hair again, the blood seeping from his wrist not stopping him from hauling up her nightdress.

Another pistol shot. Big Lon stared at her, puzzled, then dropped at her feet, the back of his head spilling blood and brains.

Mrs Cook panted at the window, her nightdress white against the night. 'Come on,' she hissed. 'They've taken the storerooms and house.'

Hen staggered to the window, felt Mrs Cook's wiry hands on hers, and she clambered out the window and prepared to jump.

'Hen?'

Max appeared at the door, a pistol in each hand.

'You get out here too!' growled Mrs Cook, as Hen landed beside her. Max took a hurried look down the hallway, shut the door, hauled the dressing table against it, then ran across the room, nimbly sliding out the window as if he had done it a thousand times. 'What's happening?' he demanded shortly.

'Cove what worked for Mrs B got 'er 'ouse keys copied,' said Mrs Cook shortly, the accent she'd used that afternoon vanishing as she peered into the darkness. 'You've brought a boatload of villains down on us, that's what you've done,' said Mrs Cook shortly. 'They followed you down here, and yer two unlocked the gates for them, and lit the lanterns to show them the way up here.'

'How did they get the keys?' panted Hen, then guessed before she heard the answer.

'The Lons had yer keys copied afore they left, as Young Lon was kind enough to tell me when he dragged me from my bed.'

'They didn't —?'

'Use me? That weren't the attributes 'e wanted from me. Took me to the kitchen at pistol point, and Alexander too, hoppin' without his leg.'

'Where is he —?' Hen began desperately, just as the sergeant limped quickly up from the roses, his wooden leg attached and under trousers once again, making his way by moonlight and the flickering shadows from the fires.

'Got to get away,' he said briefly. 'Get down to the boat before they find us, sail up to Sydney and bring back troopers.'

'Run from them?' demanded Max. 'We can rally your workmen here! Surely they have muskets?'

'One musket apiece, and that's assuming they will all fight for us.' The sergeant stared into the moonlight, assessing.

'You aren't even sure of your own men?'

'I'm sure of six of them, but the cottages on this side of the river are burning, and the men inside them likely already dead. The rest of them? I don't think any would fight against us, but they might well decide they won't fight for us, either, and stay safe across the river.'

'Then we will order them to fight,' said Max grimly.

'With one musket apiece? The house is well nigh impregnable once the gates are locked and the shutters up, and now the invaders have the muskets from the storeroom. We can do nowt except bring this to the governor. Hush!' They moved back into the shadows of the rosebushes by the wall, as two men appeared about thirty yards away. They gazed around, then seeing no movement, vanished again.

Hen moved closer to Mrs Cook. 'How did you get away?' she whispered.

'He wanted me to unlock the larder for 'im, so I did, an' clobbered 'im wiv a cheese,' said Mrs Cook, as another figure loomed in the black and red light.

'I heard the sound of the sacred geese warning the Romans!' whispered the professor, looking more excited than scared. He too had paused to pull on trousers. 'I armed myself. I stood like Horatius holding the bridge in the hall. But alas, I had but two pistols and no sword, and had to retreat out the window.'

'They'll be after us,' said the sergeant grimly. 'They can't afford to have witnesses. To the boat, now.'

This time Max didn't argue.

'Ladies, dapple mud on your nightdresses. That's it. Now keep in single file,' the sergeant whispered. 'Try to move from shadow to shadow. Look down — you're easiest to see when they can see your eyes. I'll go in front. Follow my feet.' The sergeant was already limping downhill, weaving in and out of the shrubbery.

Hen suspected a rib was cracked, but she could breathe, and she could run, and that was all she needed now.

Night air on her skin. Grass, bark under her feet. She glanced back. Jessica's cottage stood black against the stars. Lons' men had not been able to burn its stone. Was Jessica there, and Wurumu? Please, Hen prayed, let her be safe up at the camp tonight. Let them all be safe there, too.

Through the orchard, and then a yell from up at the house. 'Over there!'

A musket shot. Mrs Cook crumpled.

Such a small body, a child's almost, even her pregnancy hardly showing. Blood welled from her side through her nightdress.

And Hen had nothing, not her reticule, pistols, even her nightdress was filthy. She kneeled down, pressing her hands to the wound. 'Give me your shirt,' she demanded, not caring which man took her order.

'Hen, we have to move —' began Max, even as another shot whirled past them. The air of Gilbert's Creek smelled of gunpowder, of sulphur, the air of war ...

Mrs Cook looked past her, at her husband. 'You'll look after her, lovey,' she breathed.

For a second Hen thought she referred to the baby — the baby that could never be born now — then realised Mrs Cook meant her.

'Yes,' said the sergeant, as Mrs Cook's eyes opened even wider, staring unseeing at the stars, her mouth gaping. The sergeant gripped Hen's arm. 'Run,' he said.

They ran, the sergeant falling behind. Two more shots. Hen glanced back, to make sure he had not been hit ...

... and saw nothing. Only smoke, a wall of it behind them on the hill, and tiny teeth of flame, hiding them from the pursuers from the house. A woman's voice called, 'Run, Auntie Love. Run!'

Jessica! But even to call her would help their pursuers find them. Hen ran. Her boat bobbed at its mooring, next to Max's, and a larger one the invaders must have come in. Max jumped in, held out his hand for her as the boat rocked beneath his feet, and then helped the sergeant, unsteady on his wooden leg. The professor scrambled in, surprisingly able, and began to shove the oars into the rowlocks.

Something moved on the larger vessel. Someone. A man stood, holding a musket, another looming behind him. And yet they did not fire.

The professor held one oar, Max the other. Hen huddled in the prow, the sergeant next to her, shielding her from shots from the other boat. She tried to see through the smoke and darkness on shore. Figures moved. Shadows, impossible to tell if they were the invaders or her men from the more scattered shepherds' huts. But if so, they could so easily be picked off by the men who held the house. Max had built a fort, and she had maintained it. Those who held it now could keep it, even against a much larger force.

Their boat surged forwards up the river. Still the men on the other boat did not fire. Suddenly their own boat slowed.

'What is it?' she hissed.

Their boat lurched. Hen felt water nibble her bare toes, her ankles. Laughter echoed from the other boat.

'They stove her in just above the water line,' said the sergeant grimly.

So this boat would float, but only until it held the weight of someone, anyone, trying to escape. Brilliantly planned, thought Hen. Not only stopping escape, but killing those who tried, drowning them mid river.

Unless they could swim. She had never seen the sergeant swim, but then he would not have with her watching. Could he swim? Could Max and the professor?

The professor snatched one of Max's pistols from his belt as if in answer to her question, placed it between his teeth, carefully removed his boots, then slid into the water, striking out for the shore furthest from the house. The ship shuddered as the water slipped up to Hen's waist, cool, caressing, deadly. They had seconds perhaps till the boat sucked them down.

Hen pulled her nightdress over her head just as Max yelled, 'Jump!'

Hen stood. The boat shivered at the movement, but the water was only knee deep now. She leaped. She heard, glimpsed, felt, the two men jump either side of her, found her bare body still knew what to do in the new element, arms, legs obeying Jessica's instructions from years earlier, found herself listening for the sound of the children laughing as they swam around her.

Instead she heard panting, a muffled cry. She turned, treading water, to see Max and the sergeant struggling, sinking, perhaps three yards apart.

They could not swim.

She did not choose. Years afterwards, she still told herself she did not choose, even though she admitted that had she chosen she would still have done the same. Vaguely she hoped the professor would see the problem, would swim back, would help the other man.

Arm over arm to get to him. He had half sunk. She had to dive, like the children had dived for mussels, had to grab his arm, and use all the strength she had to haul him upwards. Her lungs screamed, her ribs. She pulled upwards to the air, gasped, managed to push his head into the air too.

He breathed. She breathed. No one else breathed beside them.

Max was gone.

Chapter 41

To make a Kedgeree

Take Cooked rice, one Cupful for each Person; Fish, fresh
or smoked; Turmeric, Cardamom, Cumin to Taste, as Spices
lose Flavour with time, and Butter, sufficient. Fry the Spices;
add fresh Butter and as it melts add the Rice and Fish. Peas
may be added to advantage, and chopped Eschallotts, or
Chilli for those who do not feel a Meal Compleat without
Perspiration enough to drown a dog.

From the Notebooks of Henrietta Bartley

'Don't struggle,' she managed to say. But the sergeant didn't
struggle. He allowed her to tug him as she swam, focusing on
gulping air in the moments when his head was not submerged as
she towed him clumsily, minute upon minute, hour upon hour,
dark air and darker water, his body growing heavier and heavier,
the river bank receding all the time.

She could not reach it. Would never reach it. Nor would she
ever let the sergeant go. She pushed her body onwards, trying to
swim with two legs, one arm. Then suddenly she felt the sergeant
pull away from her.

'No,' she gasped. But it was Professor Pilgrim, back in the
water, taking the sergeant's weight. She aimed for the shore
again. Three strokes later her arm met soil. Her feet flailed for a
purchase, found it. She scrambled up, then leaned down to help
haul the sergeant from the water.

And heard the shot, as she was silhouetted against the stars. Felt the shot. Felt the pain but did not realise that blood flowed, because she was already wet. But blood was warm and river water cool and she was falling once again.

'Max! Where are you!' yelled Professor Pilgrim, as Hen crumpled. She heard a shout, another musket bark.

Time stopped.

'Hen,' said Max.

Hen opened her eyes. Max smiled at her from the ground, blood on his captain's uniform. Père Flambeaux smiled wearily, her father smiled, his face shadowed. Death flowed around them, but Hen bent to Max's lips.

The kiss was colder than it should have been. But we are dead, thought Hen. Of course our lips are cold.

This time, an eternity of time, as they drew apart, no cannon roared at them. No cannon could part them now.

'I love you,' said Max, so seriously she could not look away. 'I loved you from my first glimpse of you. I did not change, I could not change, even when I lashed out in grief and anger, fury at myself for what I had done but aiming it at you.'

'You always loved me?'

'We still have not danced together,' said Max softly. 'I promised we would dance. Yes, I will always love you. You were my angel then. You are my angel now, my angel of Waterloo.'

'But I am not an angel,' protested Hen, but Max still smiled, as if he didn't hear her.

'My angel, angel, angel,' he whispered.

'Auntie Love, Auntie Love, Auntie Love.' The whisper changed.

She moved, but did not fly, because she was not an angel, no matter what Max said, and had no wings. She moved like a woman being carried on what felt like a leather cloak. She could not see who carried her, for every time she opened her eyes all she saw were shadows, and pain too, pain peering down at her:

she had always known pain was an enemy but now he had a form too. But if she shut her eyes she could see light, and pain could not keep up with her.

If she kept her eyes shut perhaps she would find wings, could fly to Max again, because she had not told him that she loved him. She must tell Max because he should not die without being told that he was loved.

But when she opened her eyes the light had lost its gold, and become yellow, the smoke of Waterloo.

Men died around her, ten men, fifteen thousand men, fifty thousand; bodies left for rats to chew and crows to peck the eyes. Grass that would grow greener after its crop of blood.

And yet the world was still and quiet around her, despite the muskets' thunder and the men slashing with their sabres so close by. All that mattered was this tiny square of peace, miraculously safe from all the carnage beyond. Somewhere in this square her father worked, cutting, stitching, saving men. Max lay propped against the wall of dead, smiling at her. She could almost feel his hand, warm while she was cold.

'Auntie Love!'

The cannon snarled, and she was gone.

Chapter 42

A Native Hen Broth: a recipe for when all else has failed

Take four native Hens, plucked & gutted, one bunch parsley, seven carrots, peeled & topped, six onions, peeled & topped, or whatever Vegetables you find. Add a river Stone, washed.

Cover all with Water & simmer till the Stone is soft. Throw away the Hens and eat the Stone. Otherwise strain the liquid for a reviving broth.

From the Notebooks of Henrietta Bartley

'Auntie Love. Auntie Love.'

The trees sang to her and the wind. She tried to open her eyes to see them, but her eyelids were weighted with brick. Why try to open them when the song was sweet? When slipping back to sleep relieved the pain, which grew to a small sun and then somehow retreated …

'Auntie Love.' She lay on possum skins, not on a bed. She tasted milk, and found she suckled like a babe. Perhaps she was, and her life a vision of things to come. The pain crept in, then seeped away.

She heard a woman give one short, sharp scream. Jessica! Hen opened her eyes. She saw the kurrajong leaves above her, then heard a baby's cry.

'It is a girl,' said Gari's voice, and Hen relaxed, for Jessica was cared for, and when Hen slept she did not have to think of pain, or Mrs Cook, her blood redder than the new carpet in the hall …

She woke being carried again, on a cloak she now knew was possum skin. She smiled at the sky, for a baby had been born and nothing mattered. She felt a bed below her, a bed with linen sheets, just like her own. She was not a baby then, but herself and this was home.

Sleep drifted round her, and she let herself float upon its tide.

Chapter 43

A Most Efficacious Fungi

The Fungi is found only on the old Trees, and it is said, only found when Needed. It is a dull cream, with orange Striations, and must only be used once it has been colonised by Insects and is quite Brittle. When burned the Smoke procures a Euphoria or Pain Relief. It may be used directly on a Wound and is an effective Styptic. When steeped in Alcohol, one Pint to one large Fungi, the Effect is magnified: one tablespoon six times a Day. The Fungi can be Steeped two Times or Three but loses some Effectiveness each Time.

From the Notebooks of Henrietta Bartley

She woke and it was afternoon. She lay in her own bed, her shoulder bandaged. She felt it carefully. Kangaruh hide placed over a fungi poultice, the wet leather shrunk to tighten as it dried around her wound. She felt ... odd, which she suspected was not blood loss nor infection, but a native remedy to make her sleep, to take the pain.

'Ah, so you are awake. Excellent.' The voice was a man's, English, aristocratic. She blinked, and found Professor Pilgrim sitting in the armchair by her dressing table, white haired, neatly shaven, in clean and correct breeches, shirt and jacket but no cravat. He held up a decanter of whisky in salutation.

'Did it happen?' she managed.

Miraculously, he understood. 'Yes,' he said gently. 'It

happened. But it is past now. Agamemnon, Hannibal, Napoleon and your poor convict invaders, all dead and gone. The natives waited till daylight, till the invaders thought themselves masters of the field, and emerged to find that spears can be thrown faster than muskets can be reloaded.'

'How many of the Lons' men are left?'

'None,' said the professor, still smiling at her gently. 'We killed them all, as Henry killed the prisoners at Agincourt. We want no witnesses. I believe the governor and others might misunderstand that the natives were defending you, seizing back what had been taken. When I return to Sydney I will explain how convict renegades attacked, but Max and your men defeated them.'

'Max?' she asked, the thinnest thread of hope.

'I'm sorry.'

She did not ask if Max had struggled from the river, and had been shot, or if he'd drowned. She did not want to know she had killed him, or rather, how she had, for if she had never misjudged the Lons, Max would be alive. The war he'd found here was of her making.

'Who else is lost?'

'Five of your men, including your native head stockman. We found him here, in the house, in the corridor outside your room.'

Wurumu had never entered her house before, but he had stormed it as a warrior to defend her, as the son-in-law she had never quite admitted that he was.

'He never saw his daughter,' said the professor softly. 'His wife has called her Love.'

'Sergeant Cook?'

'Is with his wife.'

'He died too?' She could not bear it. Would have to bear it.

'No,' said the professor quickly. 'The natives carried her up to the house.'

'She is alive! I have to see her.' Hen tried to sit up. The world shivered. The professor hesitated, then went to the door and called down the corridor.

Jessica appeared. She wore a string belt from which hung a small string basket. Her breasts were milk full. Only her hair, still fashionably cut, spoke of the colony. Hen knew her daughter would never again occupy the stone cottage, nor any other English dwelling place. But she was here now, for Hen.

'You should be resting,' whispered Hen. 'Your baby ...'

'She is the most wonderful baby in the world,' said Jessica, in the language Hen had not heard her use for five years, the Sydney language, which was not quite the language here.

Jessica's face had new wounds across her cheeks and forehead. Hen reached up to touch them, but they were shallow. Not made by the attackers then: these were like the cuts the girl had made after her last people were shot.

'Mrs Cook?' asked Hen.

Jessica shook her head. 'Sleeping,' she said. 'Gari bound the wound but I ... I do not know if she will wake.'

Of course she would wake! If somehow Mrs Cook had survived till now, she could not die. 'Will you help me go to her?'

'If you drink this.' The words were still Jessica's in her own language, but the drink was lemon barley water, and freshly made. Hen drank, and found her legs would work, one arm slung over her daughter's shoulders.

She stumbled down the corridor to her friend.

Chapter 44

Instructions for a Home medicine chest,
Suitable for the Colonies

Needle, waxed Thread, Scissors, Whetstones, oiled Silk,
Tweezers, Lye Soap, medicine Glasses, Eye Dropper, Cotton
Wool, scraped Lint, Arnica, Rose Oil, Ipecacuanha, Epsom
salts, powdered Rhubarb if fresh cannot be obtained, Castor
Oil, Boric Acid, Basilicum powder, Laudanum, Alum,
Mercury, Camphorated or Eucalyptus Oil, Kino, Magnesia,
Mint oil, Lavender oil, powdered Rosemary, Camphor. It is
useful to also keep a Bottle of Vinegar, Onions, clean boiled
Lard, small Jars and bottles, Elderberry juice, bottled,
mouldy Bread kept in a jar, Spiders' Webs, Goanna and Emu
oil if it can be obtained.

From the Notebooks of Henrietta Bartley, with a Foreword by
Professor Ignatius Pilgrim, Balliol College, Oxford

Mrs Cook was awake, breathing too fast, and too shallowly, and
far too pale. Of course she was awake, thought Hen. 'You were
dead,' Hen said to her, as Jessica helped her into an armchair by
the bed the Cooks shared. The sergeant sat on the other side, his
wife's hand in his. He looked pale, unshaven, but unhurt.

Mrs Cook chuckled weakly. 'Learned that from Carrie the
Corpse, back at the establishment,' she panted. 'Two guinea for
half an hour, she charged. Fooled you, didn't I? But you'd never
have left me. Tricked Lons' men into thinking I were dead, too.'

'You're going to live,' said Hen fiercely, as Mrs Cook's breath grew shallower. 'Jessica, bring my bag. And the cordial in the brown bottle. Hurry!'

'I'm dyin', duckie. But I'm glad to say goodbye. You'll look after him proper … this time, won't you?'

Hen met the sergeant's hollow gaze, then turned back to the woman on the bed. 'Always. But you will be here too!'

'Have a dozen brats and call them after me,' muttered Mrs Cook, yawning.

'Let me see the wound.' Hen lifted the sheet that covered the small body. The mattress below was wet with blood, the leather bandage too. 'You should have called me! Jessica …'

'It can't be stitched, Auntie Love,' said Jessica softly from the doorway, bag and bottle in her hand. 'Some things can't be mended.'

Hen reached for the bandage, felt Mrs Cook's hand on hers. 'Love you, duckie,' Mrs Cook breathed. 'Waited … to … tell you that.' She glanced up at her husband. 'Love you … both … till all the seas … gang dry …'

Hen stopped, as the hand grew limp. This death was not the one learned at the establishment.

The sergeant gave a hoarse cry and buried his face in his hands. He began to sob. Jessica moved to him, put her arms around him, held him, as Hen sat there, the dead woman's hand in hers.

Time passed. Hen let it.

At last she asked to see the dead, so the sergeant could sit with his wife. Jessica hesitated at the door to the courtyard. Hen understood, or rather, did not understand, except for the realisation that Jessica could not or should not see her husband's body. 'I can manage,' she reassured her, and realised that indeed she could, if she walked slowly, and did not jar her wound.

The invaders' bodies still lay in a line outside the gate. Hen stared at their faces, trying to recognise each one, but the corpses had bloated. She could only identify the Lons. The other men wore the faded grey of convict garb. A trench waited for the bodies in one of the vegetable plots. Sensible, she thought vaguely. There should be no grave plots to mark what had happened here. Professor Pilgrim had been right ...

'Mrs Bartlett?' She hadn't realised the professor walked behind her. 'We'll be getting rid of this lot before breakfast. Your men are in coffins in the scullery. We've dug graves for them in the family plot, but were waiting for you to be strong enough to be at the service.'

She didn't say that her name wasn't Mrs Bartlett. It didn't matter now.

The bodies in coffins were unswollen, for it was cool in the scullery. Max wore fresh clothes. Wurumu was a warrior again, the bone through his nostrils, the string at his waist, a short spear laid next to him, though its barb was clean. Yet it seemed Jessica had decided he would not rest according to his people's ways, but should be buried in 'the family plot' by the roses, where Elizabeth and baby Henrietta lay.

And both Wurumu's lying out and his burial were right. Wurumu had died a warrior, but had lived as a stockman, as a husband and — sometimes — in a cottage.

She gazed at the others: Samuel, who had found sunlight and a love of growing for a few years of joy; O'Donnel, who had fought for Ireland but lost his life far away from it; Jimmy the Dabber, the best pickpocket in London, though if he had been he would not have been caught. Any horse had gentled at his touch. Johnny Three Tooth, a quiet man, who tilled her vegetables and only wanted a dog for company.

The dog, a dingo cross, lay under the trestles, its head on its paws. Someone had placed a bowl of water there, and a bone with meat on it, still untouched.

'Would you leave me a minute?' she asked the professor. 'Indeed, the fresh air has revived me,' she added, when he looked dubious. It hadn't, and he knew it, but left the scullery anyway.

Hen pulled up a chair, then took Max's cold waxy hand in hers. 'I'm glad we married. You've given me all you promised, even if we never danced. I have had peace here, for a while, and adventure. And if I have lost that peace now it was my fault, not yours. I ... I did love you then. I saw you truly. Life drifted us apart. If we'd had time we would have found the partnership you spoke of back at Waterloo. If only we'd had time.'

She waited for his answer. The world swam a little till she realised it would never come.

She smiled at him and it seemed that the man in the coffin smiled faintly too. 'You will lie here with Elizabeth, and Henrietta, and one day I will lie here too. Goodbye, dear Max.'

She stood and pressed a kiss to his cold forehead, only the second time she had kissed him, and the last. She turned to Wurumu, though she would not use that name again, if Jessica kept to native tradition. He would be buried as Alexander, the name he had chosen but never spoken, to leave his soul free. We will inscribe the name Alexander Gilbert on his headstone, she thought, and no one who saw his grave in years to come could ever guess who he had been. One day we will all lie there, our strange and savage history forgotten.

Mrs O'Donnel occupied the kitchen, wearing a black dress she must have found in one of Hen's chests, even darker than her skin. Her face too was marked for mourning. Hen was content for her to take possession of both clothes and kitchen, indeed anything she wished, for what she'd lost.

Hen could not face her bedroom again. Every night there she would see Mrs Cook at the window, or Big Lon's face above her. Jessica took her to the day bed on the verandah, where she sometimes had slept when the day's heat was trapped indoors. Jessica left briefly, then returned with the baby, as naked as she was. Love's umbilical cord was tied with string, dried with charcoal. Her plump feet batted the sky as her mother sat across from Hen and began to feed her.

It was perhaps the only healing Hen could have endured, and the best. Life continued. So did love.

Mrs O'Donnel brought out a tray with tea, and buttered toast. The toast implied bread made recently, the oven lighted, all as if Mrs Cook still ordered it. Three cups, three plates. Cherry jam, for those who wanted it. A tea cosy Mrs McDougal had knitted. A jug of lemon barley water, covered with a fly-proof cloth. 'Will that be all, Mrs Bartley?'

'Thank you. I … I don't know how to thank you.'

Mrs O'Donnel didn't curtsey. Hen was glad she hadn't been taught that.

And finally the sergeant emerged, his face washed, but still unshaven, his limp more pronounced. He sat and took the third cup as Jessica poured the tea from the silver pot Hen had brought from Chelsea. He sipped, and watched the river.

'She will expect a proper wake,' said Hen at last.

'She deserves that, and more.'

Hen sipped her tea, too. The toast was good. For a moment she wondered where Professor Pilgrim was. Possibly interrogating Gari about the local saps, not just from botanic passion, but because he was an intelligent man who knew the three on this verandah needed time to assess their wounds, their lives, alone.

Hen regarded her companions. Her daughter, who had faced kidnap, rape, the slaughter of her family, the death of her husband, who had returned to who she was, and who she'd always be.

As Hen must return to who she was, as well. The camp brat, the surgeon's daughter. Her father had held the square at Waterloo. Now his daughter must do her duty too.

She glanced at the sergeant. 'Do you know where my fortune comes from, Alexander?' It was the first time she had used his name.

He seemed puzzled. 'Your father's pension?'

'Not just his pension. My father had teeth collected from the dead at Waterloo,' she stated. 'They are being made into false teeth now, and will be for years still to come.' If she and the sergeant were to go on from here, he must know what her life had been built upon.

She waited for his look of horror. Instead she saw understanding and compassion.

'It doesn't matter, Hen,' he said quietly. 'It was you who told me that all we owe the dead is to live life well.'

Hen nodded, as Jessica bent again to her baby. This man would never say he loved her. Max had known books, poets, the world of pretty phrases, all closed to Sergeant Cook. He would never ask her to marry him, either.

She would have to be the one to do that. Not today, nor next week or month, but both knew it would happen. She would not be Mrs Bartley then, but Mrs Cook. 'Call your children after me,' her friend had asked, and so she would, generations of Cooks of Gibber's Creek.

The sergeant was the one person left who knew she hated to be called Henrietta, though suddenly she couldn't remember why she hadn't liked the name. That no longer seemed to matter either.

She felt as if she were fifteen again, lost among the rats and mud and the moans of the dying thousands, able only to do her best. Ten and a half years before she had stood in the safest square on the bloodiest battlefield the world had known. Australia had become that battlefield, despite the hopes of all who'd voyaged there to leave that world behind.

She closed her eyes, remembering how the old Iron Duke had won at Waterloo. He had kept the square around him via sheer force of will. Once one square was safe others could rally around it. If only you could keep it long enough.

Her imagination suddenly seemed tangled into visions. Dark-skinned women who kept their knowledge and their duties here, a square kept safe, even if those with palm-coloured skin and muskets believed they owned the land. Women who passed knowledge on to their children and Jessica's children, and would to Hen's children too.

Hen opened her eyes briefly, then shut them again. She was suddenly too weary even to imagine any other future than the one she had dreamed of in that extraordinary year when she had found out Max was alive, and that they could make a place of peace together here. She needed sleep. She needed ...

'You'll help me hold the square?' she murmured.

The sergeant's voice said, 'Yes.' His hand gripped hers. A strong hand, a man who would stand by her till all the seas gang dry.

'I will always help you, Auntie Love,' said Jessica.

Hen had never spoken to her daughter of Waterloo, nor of infantry and squares, though the sergeant had understood. But Jessica would be here, and her daughter Love as well.

They would hold the square together.

Acknowledgements

Over forty years ago, two elegantly dressed Belgian men on their way to a wedding stopped their sports car to pick up two Australian hitchhikers. After half an hour, the men decided the journey was likely to be much more fun than the wedding, so they took us all the way to the ferry terminal to Dover, detouring so that we could see where Waterloo had been fought, and Dunkirk, and much else.

Even then, I had decided that I could never write about Waterloo. It has fascinated too many military historians, with many conflicting accounts. But I had already accidentally heard the story of one Waterloo veteran and their land grant in Australia; had discovered that this was common; had seen a calculation of the figures of Waterloo and Peninsular veterans among the early convicts to Australia. At various times, I spoke at length about the influence of the Napoleonic Wars on the colonial attitudes in Australia, but did not write anything myself.

And then, suddenly, I found that I was doing so — even beginning at the battle — instead of writing the book I had been planning for three years, and had intended to write until half an hour before I began this one. (That book has been cannibalised into this one.)

My first thanks, then, to those two young men whose names I can't remember. The best way to see a battlefield is possibly in the back of a speeding sports car, so delight overcomes the tragedy.

To Lisa Berryman and Cristina Cappelluto, and the entire HarperCollins team, my thanks once again for accepting a book that was entirely different from the one you had contracted. This book, like every other I have written, is the work of a team, not just an author, and I still feel guilt that only my name is on the title page. Cristina has created a team that is not only filled with inspired professionals, but people who have a deep passion for the books they produce, and show kindness and care for every person they work with.

Kate O'Donnell forged her way through the book, tightening, querying and, as always, being the most wonderful editor possible. In this case, her editing included email after email of support, as this book was written and edited during months of drought, bushfires, evacuations and floods. Pam Dunne and Rachel Cramp proofread and hauled out errors. Shannon Kelly coordinated everything, keeping us in line and on time, managed to decipher my writing during its many changes, pounced on clumsy phrasing and even tracked down where each insert was supposed to go, which is a labour of deep dedication. This book truly became 'a book' under his guidance. Angela Marshall took time from the bushfire crises around us to correct my spelling, my French, my knowledge of where a highwayman was likely to be hanged, and — by not finding more mistakes — gave me the confidence to actually send in a manuscript based on such broad aspects of the past. Mark Campbell created a cover of such beauty that I still keep staring at it. It perfectly, absolutely captures the themes within the pages. The cover makes use of an extraordinary artwork by Mary Jane Ansell, which might almost have been a dream of the scenes I saw in my mind's eye as I wrote the book. I cannot thank her enough for allowing us to use her painting.

Thank you, too, to all the Twitter and Facebook followers who took part in the auctions to raise money for our local bushfire brigade and wildlife in the months while this book was being written, when daylight was red and grey, and the nights were full of embers and traumatised animals. The two Mesdames Carolines, the person and the wombat, were created thanks to their generosity and support.

My greatest thanks, as always, goes to Lisa Berryman. Each book is first sent to Lisa, and every single book has been rewritten after her assessment. I wish every writer could be blessed with a Lisa in their life — a friend, editor, never-failing support in work and life, and unerring critic. Except this time ...

We both missed it. So did Kate. But there was a faint unease that grew through the editing process. I tentatively mentioned what might be wrong, and Lisa and Kate jumped on it. Of course. Henrietta Bartley had ended up with the wrong man. The entire ending had to be changed, and much of the book, more than halfway through editing.

There are few editors who'd tolerate this, much less enthusiastically embrace the change, and add further to the insight. I wish I could round up new words to say, 'Thank you, thank you, and thank you all. You are magnificent.'

Jackie French AM is an award-winning author, historian and ecologist. She was the 2014–2015 Australian Children's Laureate and the 2015 Senior Australian of the Year. In 2016 Jackie became a Member of the Order of Australia for her significant contribution to literature and youth literacy. She is regarded as one of Australia's most popular authors with her vast body of work crossing the threshold of genre and reading age, and ranging from fiction, non-fiction, picture books, ecology, fantasy and sci-fi, to her much-beloved historical fiction.

jackiefrench.com
facebook.com/authorjackiefrench